THE
WOMAN
IN THE
WOODS

Center Point
Large Print

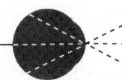

**This Large Print Book carries the
Seal of Approval of N.A.V.H.**

THE
WOMAN
IN THE
WOODS

JOHN CONNOLLY

CENTER POINT LARGE PRINT
THORNDIKE, MAINE

This Center Point Large Print edition
is published in the year 2018 by arrangement with
Atria Books, a division of Simon & Schuster, Inc.

ISBN: 978-1-68324-875-0

Library of Congress Cataloging-in-Publication Data

Names: Connolly, John, 1968- author.
Title: The woman in the woods / John Connolly.
Description: Center Point Large Print edition. | Thorndike, Maine :
    Center Point Large Print, 2018.
Identifiers: LCCN 2018018731 | ISBN 9781683248750
    (hardcover : alk. paper)
Subjects: LCSH: Parker, Charlie "Bird" (Fictitious character)— Fiction. |
    Private investigators—Fiction. | Large type books. |
    BISAC: FICTION / Thrillers. | FICTION / Mystery & Detective /
    General. | FICTION / Literary. | GSAFD: Suspense fiction. |
    Mystery fiction.
Classification: LCC PR6053.O48645 W66 2018b | DDC 823/.914—dc23
LC record available at https://lccn.loc.gov/2018018731

For Steve Fisher

1

And I will restore to you the years that the locust hath eaten . . .

—Joel 2:25

CHAPTER

I

The bar was one of the more recent additions to Portland's waterfront, although the term "recent" was relative given the rapid pace of development in the city. Parker wondered if at some point every person reached an age where he or she prayed for a pause to progress, although often it seemed to him that progress was just so much window dressing, because people tended to remain much as they had always been. Still, he wished folks would occasionally leave the windows as they were, for a while at least.

The presence of the bar was indicated solely by a sign on the sidewalk, required because the establishment was set back from the street on the first floor of an old warehouse, and would otherwise have been difficult, if not impossible, to find.

Perhaps this was why it appealed to Louis. Given the opportunity, Louis might even have dispensed with the sign entirely, and supplied details of the bar's location only to those whose company he was prepared to tolerate, which meant that maybe five people in the world would have been burdened with the responsibility of keeping it in business.

No such tactics were required on this night to offer Louis the peace he desired. Only a handful of customers were present: a young couple at a corner table, two older men eating burgers at the bar, and Parker and Louis. Parker had just been served a glass of wine. Louis was drinking a martini, very dry. It might not have been his first, but with Louis it was always difficult to tell.

"How is he?" Parker asked.

"Confused. In pain."

Days earlier, Louis's partner, Angel, had been relieved of a tumor the size of an egg in a New York hospital, along with a length of his large intestine. The procedure hadn't gone entirely well, and the recuperation period would be difficult, involving chemotherapy sessions every three weeks for the next two years, while the threat of ancillary growths remained. The call to inform Parker of Louis's presence in the city of Portland had therefore come as a surprise. Parker had intended to travel down to New York to visit Angel and offer Louis whatever support he could. Instead, Louis was sitting in a Portland bar while his partner lay in a hospital bed, medicated up to his eyeballs.

But then, Louis and Angel were unique unto themselves: criminals, lovers, killers of men, and crusaders for a cause that had no name beyond

Parker's own. They kept to their particular rhythm as they walked through life.

"And how are you?" asked Parker.

"Angry," said Louis. "Concerned and frightened, but mostly angry."

Parker said nothing, but sipped his wine and listened to a ship calling in the night.

"I didn't expect to be back here so soon," Louis continued, as though in answer to Parker's unvoiced question, "but there were some things I needed from the condo. And anyway, the New York apartment just didn't feel right without Angel next to me. It was like the walls were closing in. How can that be? How can a place seem smaller when there's one person missing from it? Portland's different. It's less his place. So I visited with him this afternoon, then took a car straight to LaGuardia. I wanted to escape."

He sipped his cocktail.

"And I can't go to the hospital every day. I hate seeing him that way." He turned to look at Parker. "So talk to me about something else."

Parker examined the world through the filter of his wineglass.

"The Fulcis are considering buying a bar," he said.

Paulie and Tony Fulci were Portland's answer to Tweedledum and Tweedledee, assuming Tweedledum and Tweedledee were heavily—if unsuccessfully—medicated for psychosis, built like armored trucks, and prone to outbreaks of targeted violence that were often, but not always, the result of severe provocation, the Fulcis' definition of which was fluid, and ranged from rudeness and poor parking to assault and attempted murder.

Louis almost spat out his drink.

"You're fucking kidding. They haven't told me anything about it."

"Maybe they were afraid you might choke—and not without justification."

"But a bar is a business. With patrons. You know, regular human beings."

"Well, they're banned from almost every drinking hole in this city, with the exception of the Bear, and that's only because Dave Evans doesn't want to hurt their feelings. Also, they help keep bad elements at bay, although Dave sometimes struggles to imagine an element worse than the Fulcis themselves. But Paulie says that they're worried about falling into a rut, and they have some money from an old bequest that they're thinking of investing."

"A bequest? What kind of bequest?"

"Probably the kind made at gunpoint. Seems they've been sitting on it for years."

"Just letting it cool down a little, huh?"

"Cool down a lot."

"They planning on fronting this place themselves, or would they actually like to attract a clientele?"

"They're looking for a stooge."

"They'll need to find someone crazier than they are."

"I believe that's proving an obstacle to progress."

"Would you front a bar run by the Fulcis?"

"At least it would be guaranteed free of trouble."

"No, it would be guaranteed free of *outside* trouble."

"If they manage to open, you'll be obliged to support them. They'll be very unhappy otherwise. You know how fond they are of you and Angel."

"Which is your fault."

"I simply facilitated an introduction."

"Like rats facilitated the introduction of the plague."

"Tut-tut."

Louis finished his drink and raised his glass for another.

"You know," he said, "that news has cheered me up some."

"I thought it might."

"You working on anything?"

"Just some paper for Moxie. Routine stuff."

Moxie Castin was one of Portland's more colorful legal figures. With his ill-fitting suits and huckster manner, Moxie appeared completely untrustworthy, but in Parker's experience only trustworthy individuals were prepared to embrace a livery that suggested the opposite. Moxie paid well and on time, which made him a *rara avis* not only in legal circles but in most other circles as well. Finally, Moxie was privy to most—although not all—of Parker's affairs, including the discreet arrangement whereby the Federal Bureau of Investigation paid a retainer into Parker's account each month in return for consultancy services. It was not a state of affairs of which Moxie unconditionally approved, although at least Parker also recognized it for the devil's bargain it was.

"You look tired for a man dealing with routine stuff," said Louis.

"I haven't been sleeping well."

"Bad dreams?"

"I'm not sure I can always tell the difference between dreams and reality. Waking sometimes seems as bad as sleeping."

Parker was already recognizing signs of the onset of a depression that had shadowed him even in adolescence, but had begun to trouble him more deeply since the gun attack that almost killed him. He knew that soon he would have to seek seclusion. He would want—even need—to be alone, because it was at those times that his dead daughter most often appeared to him.

"Angel said something to me once."

Parker waited, and it was as though Louis had

heard his thoughts, or had glimpsed the flickering whiteness of a lost child in Parker's eyes.

"He said he thought you saw Jennifer, that she spoke to you."

"Jennifer's dead."

"With respect, that's not the point."

"Like I said, I find it hard to tell what are dreams and what are not."

"You know, I don't think you find it hard at all."

Slow time passed before Louis spoke again.

"I used to dream of my father."

Parker knew that Louis's father had fallen into the hands of bigoted, violent men who hanged him from a tree before setting him alight. Many years later Louis returned for those responsible, and burned the tree on which his father had died.

"He would come to me in my sleep," said Louis, "wreathed in fire, and his mouth would move as he tried to speak, except nothing ever came out, or nothing I could understand. I used to wonder what he was trying to say. In the end, I figured he was warning me. I think he was telling me not to go looking for vengeance, because he knew what I'd become if I did.

"So I dreamed him, and I knew I was dreaming him, but when I woke I'd smell him in the room, all shit and gasoline, all smoke and charred meat. I'd tell myself I was imagining it, that these were all smells I knew from before, and the force of the dream was just tricking my mind into putting them together. But it was strong, so strong: it would be in my hair and on my skin for the rest of the day, and sometimes other folks picked up on it too. They'd comment, and I wouldn't have an answer for them, or none they'd want to hear, and maybe none I'd want to hear either.

"It would frighten me. Frightened me for most of my life. Angel knew, but no one else. He smelled it on me, smelled it after my nightmares when I woke up sweating beside him in bed, and I didn't want to lie to him, because I've never lied to him. So I told him, just like I'm telling you, and he believed me, just like I know you believe me.

"My father doesn't come to me so much anymore, but when he does I'm no longer troubled. You know why? Because of you. Because I've seen things with you, experienced things that made me understand I wasn't crazy, and I wasn't alone. More than that, there's a consolation to it, to all of this. I think that's why I came up here tonight, and why I called you. If I lose Angel, I know I'll find him again. I'll tear this world apart before I do, and maybe I'll die burning like my father burned, but that won't be the end for Angel and me. He'll wait for me on the other side, and we'll go together into whatever waits. This I know because of you. I've hurt a lot of people, some that didn't deserve what came to them and some that did, although the distinction meant nothing to me then, and doesn't mean a whole lot now. I could have questioned what I did, but I chose not to. I have blood on my hands, and I'll shed more before I'm done with this life, but I'll shed it because I'm following a different path, *your* path, and I'll sacrifice myself because I have to, because it's my reparation. In return, I'll be allowed to stay with Angel forever. That's the deal. You tell that to your daughter next time you see her. You tell her to bring it to her god."

Parker stared hard at him.

"Just how many cocktails have you had?"

The stillness seemed to encompass the entire bar. All others vanished. It was only these two, and these two alone.

And Louis smiled.

CHAPTER

II

Over ice-locked forest, over snow-frozen fields, to the outskirts of a town in the northwest of the state, to a house by the edge of the Great North Woods, to—

To a fairy tale.

The boy's name was Daniel Weaver. He was five years old, with the kind of seriousness to his face found only in the features of the very young and the very ancient. His eyes, quite dark, were fixed on the woman before him: Holly, his mother, although had one been separated from the other, no stranger would have reunited them by sight alone. She was blond where Daniel was ebony, ruddy where he was wan, light to his shade. She loved him—had loved him from the first—but his temperament, like his coloring, was alien to hers. A changeling, some might have said, left in the cradle while her true son—less troubled than this one, gentler in his soul—was taken to dwell deep below the earth with older beings, and light up their hollows with his spirit.

Except it would not have been true. A stolen child Daniel might be, but not in such a way.

18

The tantrums came upon him with the suddenness of summer storms: ferocious tumults accompanied by shouts and tears, and a potential for violence to be visited only on inanimate objects. In his rages no toy was safe, no door unworthy of a kick or a slam; but terrible as they were, these moods remained rare and short-lived, and when they had spent themselves the boy would appear dazed in the aftermath, as though shocked by his own capacities.

If the heights of his joys never quite matched these depths, well, no matter, although Holly sometimes wished her son could be a little more at ease with the world, a little less guarded. His skin was too thin, and outside of a few familiar environments—his home, his grandfather's house, the woods—he remained forever wary.

And even behind the safety of his own walls, there would be moments like this one, instances when some strange fear overcame him so that he could not bear to be alone, and he could find solace only in his mother's presence, and in the telling of a tale.

The book in Holly Weaver's hands was an edition of *Grimm's Fairy Tales* printed in 1909 by Constable of London, with illustrations by Arthur Rackham. Some blank pages, of a different texture from the rest, had been added to the volume, although she could not have said why. It was still by far the most valuable book in the house, worth hundreds of dollars, according to the Internet. It would have been worth much more had it been signed by Rackham himself: those copies went for ten or fifteen thousand dollars, more money than Holly had ever possessed at any one time, and certainly more than she could ever imagine paying for a book.

But Holly didn't know much about book collecting, and would never have contemplated disposing of this one anyway, even had it been hers to sell. It was part of her son's legacy, a point of connection with another woman, now departed.

And it appeared that Daniel understood its importance, although it was never explained to him. Even in the worst of his tempers, he was always careful to spare his books, and this one maintained pride of place on his topmost shelf. When he was scared or fractious, she would read to him from it, and soon he would fall asleep. By now she felt she could recite most of the stories from memory, but taking the book from its shelf and opening it were elements of the ritual that could not be undone, and had to be followed precisely on each occasion.

Even now, when the tale to be told was not printed in its pages.

"Tell me the special story," Daniel said, and she knew then that this was one of those nights when he was troubled by emotions too complex to be named.

"Which story?" she replied, because this, too, was part of the ritual.

"The story of the Woman in the Woods."

Holly had given it this title. Call it a moment of weakness. Call it a veiled confession.

"Don't you want to hear one of the others?"

A shake of the head, and those oh-so-black eyes unblinking.

"No, only that one."

She did not argue, but turned to the back of the book, where a length of red thread held in place a sheaf of additional pages. She was no Rackham, but she'd always been good at art in school, and had poured her heart into creating this story for Daniel. She'd even sized and cut the paper to match the dimensions of those in the original volume, and the tale itself was handwritten with calligraphic precision.

She cleared her throat. This was her penance. If the truth were ever discovered, she would be able to say that she had tried to tell him of it, in her fashion.

"Once upon a time," she began, "there was a young girl who was spirited away by an ogre . . ."

Later, when Daniel was sleeping, and the book restored to its home, Holly lay in her own bed and stared at the ceiling, her punishment commencing.

Because this, too, was always the same.

Once upon a time there was a young girl who was spirited away by an ogre. The ogre forced the princess to marry him, and she gave birth to a boy.

Holly's eyes began to close.

The boy was not ugly like the ogre, but beautiful like his mother. The ogre was angry because he wanted a son who was just as vile as he, so he said to the princess:

The woods, five years earlier. Snow falling, slowly concealing the newly disturbed ground.

"If I cannot make a boy who is blighted on the outside, then I will make him foul on the inside. I will be cruel to him, and in doing so I will cause him to be cruel unto others."

A man walking away, a pick and shovel over his right shoulder, his long hair trailing behind him in the wind.

"I will be violent with him, and in doing so I will cause him to do violence. I will be merciless with him, and in doing so he will deny mercy."

Darkness and dirt: a grave.

"In this way, I will form him in my image, and I will make him my son . . ."

CHAPTER
III

Cadillac, Indiana, was about as far from interesting as a place could get without fading entirely to gray. It had the basic infrastructure required for a minimal level of human satisfaction—schools, bars, restaurants, gas stations, two strip malls, a couple of factories—without anything approaching a heart or soul, so it was less a town than some revenant version of the same, restored from seemingly inevitable decay to a simulacrum of life.

A sign on the northern outskirts advertised its twinning with Cadillac, Michigan, although it was whispered that this relationship might have come as an unwelcome surprise to the citizens of the latter city, like the discovery of a previously unsuspected sibling living wild and feeding on passing travelers, which perhaps explained why no similar claims of association were advertised in Michigan.

Or perhaps, Leila Patton thought, the twinning arrangement was agreed before anyone from Michigan had actually bothered to visit the Indiana kin, and only when that failure was rectified did the Michiganites realize the error of their ways, prompting Cadillac, Michigan, quietly to drop any mention of interconnection. All anyone in Cadillac, Indiana, knew for sure was that nobody from Cadillac, Michigan, had responded to a communication in many years, and it didn't seem worth sending someone to find out why, northern Michigan being a long way to go just to be given the bum's rush.

Cadillac, Michigan, Leila knew, was named after the French explorer Antoine de la Mothe, sieur de Cadillac, the founder of Detroit, but that was only since the latter part of the nineteenth century. Prior to this, Cadillac, Michigan, had been known as Clam Lake, which was a shitty name by any standard. On the other hand, no one in Cadillac, Indiana, knew how the town had come by its honorific. The best guess was that a Cadillac had once appeared on what was now Main Street, and some rube was so taken aback at this manifestation of progress that it was all he could talk about for the rest of his days. By the same token, Cadillac might just as easily have been christened Airplane, or Feminist, or Jew.

Okay, Leila conceded, maybe not the last two.

Leila Patton was twenty-four, going on fifty. If the youth of Cadillac naturally divided into two camps—those who hoped (or were resigned) to work, marry, settle, sire, and be buried in Cadillac; and those who intended to get the fuck out of town at the first opportunity—then Leila occupied the extreme wing of the second cohort. Her father had died when she was seventeen: an aneurysm on the floor of the sheet metal factory in which he'd performed shift work all his life, gone before the ambulance even managed to reach the gates. Leila's mother was less fortunate. Her dying—leukemia—was long, slow, and ongoing. There wasn't enough money to employ a home-care provider for her mother, so it was left to Leila to take on the burden herself, assisted by an assortment of friends and neighbors. Consequently, Leila had been forced to defer a scholarship admission to the Jacobs School of Music at IU Bloomington. She'd been assured that the scholarship would still be waiting for her when circumstances finally permitted her to commence her studies, but Leila was beginning to feel this possible future fading into nothingness. That was what life did: it slipped away, minute by minute, hour by hour, faster and faster, until at last it was gone. You could feel it drifting from you—that was the curse—and the harder you tried to hold on to it, the quicker it went.

Which was why Leila Patton had invisible rope burns on the palms of her hands.

The whole experience—death, disease, opportunities delayed or denied—hadn't caused Leila to become any more enamored of her hometown, especially since she continued to hold down a waitressing job at Dobey's Diner. This meant serving, on any given day, at least half the ass-holes in Cadillac, and the other half the following day. But Leila needed the money: the scholarship was generous, but not so generous that additional funds wouldn't be required if she wasn't to live solely on rice and beans. She was saving what she could, but her mother's illness sucked up money like a vacuum, and the poor died harder than the rich.

So this was how she spent her time: cleaning, cajoling, cooking, sleeping, waitressing, and practicing on the piano at home; or, thanks to the indulgence of her former high school music teacher, on the superior instrument in the school's music room. And praying: praying for a miracle; praying for her mother's pain to end; praying that Jacobs would continue to be patient; praying that someday she'd see Cadillac receding in her rearview mirror before it disappeared altogether, never to be glimpsed again.

Oh, and simmering. Leila Patton did a lot of simmering because, in case it wasn't already clear, she really fucking hated Cadillac, Indiana.

It was coming up for 9:30 p.m. on this particular Saturday night, and Dobey's was winding down. Leila was one of the last waitresses working, which was always the way on weekends. It didn't bother her much; Leila didn't have so many friends that weekends were any kind of social whirl. She also got on well with Carlos, the chef, and particularly with Dobey himself, who never took a day off and lived in one of the trailers behind the diner, where he occasionally entertained a local widow named Esther Bachmeier.

Dobey was a short, portly man in his sixties, with a full head of very fine hair that was prone, on those occasions when the weather forced the wearing of a hat, to standing on end upon the hat's removal. Dobey had been born in Elkhart, but moved to Cadillac in his early teens when his mother hooked up with a mechanic named Lennart who was part owner of what was then the town's sole garage. Dobey started out working for Lennart's brother, the proprietor of what was then one of eight restaurants in Cadillac, although now only four remained. By the time Lennart's brother decided to retire from the dining business, Dobey had long been his anointed heir.

Dobey was the only man in Cadillac to have *The New York Times* delivered to his door each morning, and he also subscribed to both *The New Republic* and the *National Review*, as well as *The New Yorker*, from which he would clip cartoons to stick on the plexiglass surrounding the register. Dobey owned, in addition to the big trailer in which he lived, three smaller trailers that housed his library and associated books,

Dobey being an accomplished seller of old and rare volumes. These trailers also contained camp beds on which, over the years, various waifs and strays had been permitted to sleep in return for performing light household duties. Some stayed only a couple of nights, others a week or two, but few remained for longer than that. Most were very young women, and all were worn down and scared. Leila had made friends with a couple of them, but it didn't pay to pry, so she rarely learned much about their lives. There were exceptions, though: the girl named Alyce, who showed Leila the burn marks on her belly and breasts where her father liked to stub out his cigarettes; Hanna, whose husband enjoyed punishing her more extreme transgressions, real or imagined, by removing one of her teeth for each offense; and then there was—

But, no: best to let that one go, for fear Leila might speak her name aloud.

Eventually the girls would move on, or older women would arrive in cars or vans to take them someplace else. There was no hint of impropriety to what Dobey did, and the people of Cadillac— in a display of humanity that Leila tried hard to ignore in order to safeguard her prejudices— either turned a blind eye, or helped where they could by ensuring Dobey retained a regular supply of suitable female clothing, toiletries, and sanitary goods.

Esther Bachmeier was also involved. She was a volunteer with Planned Parenthood over in New Albany, which made a big difference in helping some of the women. Esther was big, brash, and tolerated no nonsense from anyone. Some in Cadillac didn't appreciate Esther's manner, but they'd never seen her consoling a sixteen-year-old girl who'd contracted a venereal disease from her stepfather. Dobey loved Esther quietly in his way, and she loved him fiercely in hers.

Sometimes, usually after he'd had a beer or three, Dobey would speak wistfully to Leila about perhaps visiting New York or Washington, D.C., before he headed off to bed and forgot the lure of big cities. Dobey had once been to Chicago. He claimed to have found it an interesting experience, although he said it was expensive, and the beer tasted wrong. In response, Leila asked Dobey why he'd stayed in Cadillac for most of his life, given that he didn't seem to care much more for the town than she did.

"Oh," said Dobey, "I see folks jumping here and there, thinking they're going to be happier in Fort Wayne or South Bend—"

This, in Leila's view, said a lot about the mind-set inculcated by Cadillac: even when Dobey conjured up images of escape, they didn't extend farther than the state of Indiana itself. What she couldn't understand, and what Dobey was either unwilling or unable to explain, was how a man who provided a place of refuge for those in need, and was concerned enough about the wider world to subscribe to *The New York Times* and enough print magazines to fell a forest, could only contemplate physically venturing beyond the state line when he'd been drinking, and always decided to remain where he was once he'd sobered up.

But then, Leila Patton was still very young.

"—except they don't realize what they're trying to get away from is themselves. Me, I'm as happy here as I would be anywhere else. I got my business, and my books, and Esther. When I die, a few souls will gather to send me to my rest, and they'll say my food was good and I always gave the correct change. You, you're different. You have talent, and if you stay here it'll shrivel up and die. But remember: when you leave at last, drop your bitterness off at the town limits. You don't have to take it with you wherever you go."

Leila didn't think Dobey spoke this way with any of the other waitstaff, and certainly not with Corbie Brady, who was the other waitress closing on this particular night. Corbie smoked too much, ate junk, slept exclusively with jerks, and possessed the kind of low cunning that passed for intelligence in certain circles. She and Leila tolerated each other's company, but only barely.

Currently Corbie was engaged in monitoring one of the customers with what, for her, counted almost as fascination. This man had arrived alone, taken a booth by a window with the wall at his back, and ordered coffee and a slice of Dobey's Famous Apple Bread Pudding. He was wearing a gray tweed jacket with a faint check, over a blue velvet waistcoat, white open-necked shirt, and dark corduroy trousers. His brown brogues were freshly shined. A navy blue overcoat lay folded beside him, but he had retained his scarf, a thin affair in red silk knotted loosely at the neck, and clearly chosen more for the sake of appearance than functionality. Leila, who was among the taller girls in her age group, had still been forced to look up at him as he entered, so she figured him for a six-footer at least. He appeared to be in his late fifties, with his dyed-dark hair parted on the left to hang loosely over his forehead. His cheekbones were high, his brown eyes lodged deeply into his skull and partly concealed by the faintest of tints to his spectacles, through which he was reading what Corbie had identified, shockingly, as a volume of poetry. "Bohemian" was the word Leila felt best described him: he was sufficiently exotic that had he passed through these environs a century earlier, it was entirely possible the town might now be named after him.

Dobey, Leila thought, was also watching him closely, and gave the impression he was not entirely edified by the sight.

"Go spread the word that we'll be closing up

31

in a few minutes," he told the waitresses. Leila glanced at the clock. It was still only twenty to the hour, and Dobey was generally punctilious about such matters.

"You sure?" Leila asked.

"You running the place now?"

There was no humor to the question. Dobey rarely spoke to anyone harshly, but when he did, it was best to listen, and do whatever he asked.

Leila had two deuces in her section, both older couples known to her, and already preparing to leave, while Corbie had only the stranger. Leila watched Corbie bring the check to his table. The man's slim fingers reached for it like a spider's forelegs testing the air, hovering above the paper but not touching. Neither did he look up from his book.

"I don't mean to disturb you," said Corbie, "but we're closing early tonight."

The man raised the forefinger of his left hand, an injunction to patience and silence, until he finished the poem he was reading, marked the page with a red bookmark not dissimilar to the color and fabric of his scarf, and shut the book.

"And why is that?" he asked.

"We're pretty quiet."

He glanced around him, as though registering his surroundings for the first time.

"I'm sorry," he said. "I didn't intend to keep you."

He looked past Corbie to where Dobey stood,

counting the cash in the register. Dobey glanced over, as though sensing the other's regard, but did not hold his gaze for long.

"Oh, you're not keeping us," said Corbie. "We still have to clean up. What are you reading?"

"Robert Browning."

"I don't think I know him."

"Do you read a lot of poetry?"

"Not so much."

"Well, there you are."

He smiled—not an unpleasant smile, but Leila didn't think it held much warmth. It was like watching a refrigerator try to emote.

"I like your accent," said Corbie. "Are you British?"

"English."

"Is there a difference?"

"Character. The bread pudding really was very good."

He reached into his jacket, produced a brown leather wallet, and laid a ten and a five on top of the check.

"That's too much. The bill don't come to more than seven."

"Keep it. I enjoyed the peace and quiet. It was a welcome respite."

Corbie didn't know what "respite" meant, but surmised that it was probably something good, given the other nice words with which it was keeping company.

"Well, thank you. You staying in town tonight?"

Leila thought the question sounded more flirtatious than intended, although with Corbie one could never be sure.

"That depends. I have some business to conclude, but I think it will be brief, and a minute's success pays for the failure of years."

Corbie's own smile, which she had worn throughout this conversation, did its best to hold steady against the forces of incomprehension.

"Well, drive safely." Corbie turned away, then paused and looked back at him. An idea had suddenly struck her. "Say, are you an actor?"

"Miss, we are all actors."

Corbie thought about this.

"I'm not," she said.

"Then," said the stranger, his tone never varying from amused condescension, "you're fucked."

Corbie gaped as he stood, put on his coat, nodded good night to Leila and Dobey, and stepped out into the night. Leila couldn't help but laugh.

"Jesus, Corbie," she said.

"I know. What a shitheel."

Which just set Leila to laughing harder because Corbie, for all her flaws, hardly ever swore. She still went to First Missionary every Sunday, even if the gossip around town held that Corbie Brady was more often on her knees outside church than

34

in it, her mouth filled with more than prayers.

Leila looked around to see Dobey's reaction, but he was heading into his office following the stranger's departure.

"That's funny," said Leila.

"What is?" said Corbie.

"You told him to drive safely, but I don't hear a car."

Leila walked to the window and stared out at the front lot. It was empty, and Corbie confirmed that the only vehicles in back belonged to the staff. The diner stood right on the edge of Cadillac, with no sidewalk beyond the limits. A couple of streetlights burned on the town side, but Leila could detect no trace beneath them of the man who had just left. She went to the door and locked it just as Dobey reappeared.

"I'll take care of closing up," he said. "You girls go on home now."

This was also unusual. Saturday nights for Dobey meant a couple of beers with the staff, and maybe a plate of hamburgers cooked by Dobey himself.

He signaled to Carlos.

"Carlos, you make sure the girls get to where they're going. Follow on behind, you understand?"

Leila and Corbie both lived on the west side of town, while Carlos resided on the east. This was taking the chef out of his way for no good reason that anyone could see. Cadillac might have been many things, but dangerous wasn't one of them. Nobody had been murdered in its environs for more than a decade, while the greatest risk to life was being hit by someone driving drunk, a form of mortality with which Cadillac, like many small towns, was uncomfortably familiar.

Leila stepped close to Dobey.

"Is everything okay?" she asked quietly.

"Everything's fine. Indulge me, that's all."

"Did you know that man?"

Dobey considered the question.

"I never set eyes on him before."

"Well, you sure made up for lost time tonight. You were watching him like he was planning to steal the silverware."

"I took a dislike to him, that's all. No sense to it."

"Should we call the police?"

"And tell them what? That someone came in here and read poetry? Last I heard, that wasn't against the law. I'm just unsettled. It comes with age. Go on now, git. You're done, and I'm too poor to pay overtime."

With nothing more to be said, Leila collected her coat and bag from the staff closet, and joined Carlos and Corbie at the back door.

"You think he was one of them queers?" Corbie asked her.

"Who?"

"The British guy. He dressed like a queer, and you know, there was the poetry."

"God, Corbie, you're so—"

Dobey came over to lock up behind them before anything more could be said, and Leila heard the bolts being shot home once the door was closed. By the time she drove out of the lot, following the lights of Corbie's Dodge, and with Carlos driving in her rearview, Dobey's was already dark. They arrived first at Corbie's house, and Leila and Carlos waited until she was safely inside before continuing a mile farther to the Patton place. Leila stopped her car, climbed out, and headed over to Carlos.

"I'm worried about Dobey."

Carlos had been on his feet for ten hours, and was picking up the early shift next morning. He was thinking only of his bed, but he liked Leila, and he liked Dobey even more.

"You want, I go check on him."

"Thank you."

Leila returned to her car, parked it, and walked to her front door. Only when the door closed behind her did Carlos turn his truck around and return to the diner.

CHAPTER
IV

Parker and Louis left the bar together. Louis had walked downhill from his condo to the waterfront, but was in no mood to walk back uphill. They were the last customers, and the streets of the city were largely still, apart from the occasional car passing on Commercial.

"It's grown warmer," Louis noted, and it had, even in the short time they'd been inside. Parker could hear water dripping from the surrounding rooftops.

"Winter's over," he said.

"Just like that?"

"Just like that."

Parker's car stood by the curb, but one vehicle still remained in the shared lot in front of the bar. It was a new Chevy Silverado, heavily customized, with oversized wheels and a big lockbox in the bed: a fuck-you truck. There were parts of the country, indeed parts of the state—although not many—where the ownership of such a truck might have been justified by terrain and necessity, but it was clear that this particular example had not been bought as a workhorse. Its very existence was an act of braggadocio, an effort to intimidate. And lest any doubt remained about the intentions of its owner, a pair of small Confederate flags flew from its wing mirrors, with a larger version pasted to the glass of the rear window. The truck had been visible from where they were sitting, but didn't belong to any of the bar's patrons. Parker had noticed Louis's attention repeatedly drawn to it over the course of their time together, his expression unreadable. Now Louis paused in front of the truck, taking in its every detail.

"How much you think one of these things runs?" Louis asked.

"I'd say thirty grand basic, but this monster is a long way from standard. I'm guessing sixty or seventy before the customization, and five bucks for the flags."

"Hell of an outlay to advertise ignorance."

"Clearly you can do a lot with five bucks."

"South of the Line, I could understand it. Might not like it, but I could understand. My question is: What the fuck is it doing up here?"

"Stupidity knows no boundaries."

"You think that's just stupidity?"

"No, I think it belongs to someone who defines a good day by how bad he can make someone else's."

It wasn't the first rebel flag Parker had glimpsed up here in recent times, and he knew it wouldn't be the last. He wasn't so naïve as to believe that rage and intolerance were recent arrivals to the state, but he couldn't recall them being worn so openly as badges of pride. Bigotry and hatred appeared newly empowered.

"This is the time of benighted men," said Louis.

"Perhaps, but this particular one isn't worth waiting around for."

"You know him?"

"Only his kind. Listening to them is like sticking barbed wire in your ears."

Louis took in the empty streets.

"I'll be along momentarily," he said.

"Should I start the car?"

"I believe that might be advisable."

Parker began walking. His Mustang had been waiting out winter under a cover, so he was driving a silver '09 Taurus, one of two nondescript cars he used on those occasions when discretion was required for a job. He hated the Taurus, and had already decided to trade it for something marginally less functional come spring, but he was suddenly very glad to have it on this night. He sometimes struggled to remember the car himself, so it was highly unlikely that anyone else would recall it either. He got behind the wheel, hit the ignition, and waited. Two minutes later, Louis opened the passenger door and climbed in. He was twirling a small Confederate flag in his right hand.

"What the fuck is this?" he asked, gesturing at the car.

"It's a Taurus," said Parker as he pulled away from the curb. He resisted putting his foot down for fear of landing them in a bank of filthy ice, but he was dearly wishing that the Taurus had a little more fire in its belly.

"You driving it for a bet? I'd have been better off on foot."

"Should I ask what you just did?"

But there was no need for Louis to answer, because seconds later Parker heard the unmistakable sound of a truck exploding. He kept driving, keeping an eye out for any Portland PD black-and-whites, but saw none. It wouldn't take them long to start arriving. He just hoped that the area around the bar was as empty as it appeared.

"Bet he wishes he'd gone with diesel now," Parker said.

"He can consider it a lesson learned."

Parker indicated the flag. "You keeping that as a souvenir?"

"I made a note of his license plate number. I may find out where he lives and return it to him."

"By mail?"

Louis examined the flag thoughtfully.

"If he's lucky."

CHAPTER
V

Carlos returned to the diner to find all the lights out, even the one in the back office. He drove to the staff lot and detected a warm glow from inside Dobey's double-wide trailer, followed by the sight of Dobey himself in the doorway.

"What are you doing back here?" Dobey asked.

"Miss Leila ask me," said Carlos. "*Inquieta.* She worry for you."

"They both get home safely?"

"*Sí.*"

"Then you should be home, too."

Carlos lingered, shifting uncertainly from foot to foot. He had cooked at Dobey's for more than a decade, and owed the older man a lot. Dobey paid him well, and had offered to provide collateral when Carlos wanted to buy a place of his own for his family. Dobey was perhaps the best man Carlos had ever met, and they had spent so long working together that he was now able to second-guess Dobey's wishes to an almost telepathic degree, and gauge his moods in a manner even Esther Bachmeier could not match. Right now, Carlos wouldn't have said Dobey was frightened, exactly; yes, there was fear in him, but it was edged with fury.

"Carlos, I swear, if I don't see you and your truck heading into the night in the next thirty seconds, I'll set you to scrubbing so many pans for the next week that you'll be wiping your ass with a stump by the end of it, you hear?"

"*Entiendo*."

"And Carlos, no foolishness. There's nothing to be concerned about."

"*Entiendo*," Carlos repeated. He didn't want any police trouble. He and his immediate family had their green cards, but two cousins living with them did not. He told himself that Dobey knew what he was doing, because Dobey always knew what he was doing, even as the lie seemed to take physical form and fill Carlos's tongue and throat so that he could no longer speak, not even to say goodbye.

Dobey waited until he was certain Carlos was gone before pulling the door closed behind him. He turned to face the man seated in Dobey's favorite armchair, flicking idly through a copy of Marcus Aurelius he had taken from a shelf, his navy overcoat once again folded carefully beside him, his brogues reflecting the lamplight. Behind Dobey another figure moved, this one shorter than the other, almost petite, yet with the sour-milk smell of old spilled sperm on her.

"Very good," said the man in the chair. "Now, if you'll take a seat, we can begin."

CHAPTER
VI

Parker dropped Louis off at the latter's apartment on Portland's Eastern Promenade, although he took the scenic route to it via South Portland, and his stomach tightened every time they passed a patrol car. He approached his own house in Scarborough with similar caution, anticipating the presence of police, but it seemed that nobody had witnessed what was, by any measure, a quite spectacular act of criminal damage.

He was due to meet Moxie Castin for breakfast the following morning. Parker wasn't hurting for money, but he was bored. Recent weeks had been quiet, and he'd resorted to process serving and employee background checks to pass the time. He was worried that if some more engrossing pursuits did not show up soon, he might be forced to make a habit of driving Louis around so he could set stuff on fire.

Parker was concerned for Louis. For as long as Parker had known him, Louis had been with Angel, and each man rarely left the other's side. They might have bickered, sometimes even fought, but their love and loyalty were never in doubt. Louis gave strength to Angel, and Angel tempered Louis's hardness, but Parker had always secretly believed that while Angel could survive without Louis—not undamaged, and not unburdened by great sorrow, but survival nonetheless—Louis would not live long without Angel. Louis was a man of extremes, and it was Angel who gently tethered him to normality and domesticity, albeit in a form largely unrecognizable to most other human beings.

Were Louis to lose Angel, Parker believed that Louis would in turn lose himself, and die visiting his pain on the world. Parker felt this because, although he was closer to Angel than to Louis, he had as much in common with the latter as the former. Parker knew all about pain, and the price to be paid for indulging it.

So he said a prayer for these two men, sending it forth to a God whose existence—if not the benignity of His nature—he no longer doubted. He prayed, too, for his living daughter and the one who had predeceased her, the child who still haunted the marshes, who moved between worlds.

He checked the weather before going to sleep. The temperature was definitely on the rise for the coming week. The state was done with winter. Good, Parker thought. Although he was a northern creature, more comfortable with dark and cold than light and heat, he had long since passed the annual point of weariness with the elements, and yearned to see expanses of earth and grass unsullied by patches of grim ice.

He slept, blessed by an absence of dreams.

CHAPTER
VII

Dobey sat on the edge of his bed, his knees almost touching those of the man opposite. They were so close that Dobey could inhale his scent. It was subtle, clean, and expensive, even to Dobey's unpracticed nose. It reminded him of pipe tobacco, and the High Church services of childhood.

Dobey figured that he, on the other hand, smelled only of grease and sweat. He had ceased to notice the diner's particular aroma on his clothes and skin, but he suddenly found himself ashamed of it, as though, despite being the victim of intrusion, even invasion, he was guilty of some failure of manners and hygiene.

If the visitor felt uncomfortable at their enforced intimacy, he gave no sign of it. Instead, despite his earlier indication of a desire to commence, he continued to turn the pages of the *Commentaries* with concentration. Finally, he raised the book in triumph.

"It is remarkable," he began, "how much we are haunted by faint recall. It has been many years since I opened a copy of Aurelius, but the echo of his wisdom has lingered. Let me share this with you, in part because its relevance is inescapable under the present circumstances."

He took a breath, and began to read.

" 'If you are distressed by anything external, the pain is not due to the thing itself, but to your own estimate of it; and this you have the power to revoke at any time.' Isn't that wonderful? From it we may infer that we amplify pain by our responses to it. Rather than obsessing over the nature of the suffering, and blaming oneself or others for it, it is better to establish the cause and then work to eliminate it. Does that raise any questions in your mind?"

"What do you want?" Dobey asked.

"I meant questions about Aurelius. Incidentally, this is a very fine copy: London, Parker, 1747. My, my." He ran his fingers over the binding. "Calfskin?"

Dobey nodded.

"Beautiful. For someone who spends his days serving slop to hicks, you appear to possess remarkably cultured literary tastes. Unfortunately, they're partly responsible for bringing us to your door."

"You still haven't told me your name," said Dobey, "or why you're here."

"Oh, the 'why' you can probably guess. We're here to establish the current whereabouts of one of the many mongrel bitches to have passed through here over the years, but we'll come to her in a moment. As for who I am, I go by the name of Quayle. I am a lawyer—or I was, once."

"And her?"

The woman had not moved from her station by the window. Although she was young, her hair was a platinum color that had not come from a bottle, and her porcelain skin bore the faintest of sheens. Even her eyes were gray. Dobey imagined taking a knife to her and watching it glance harmlessly off, leaving only the minutest of scratches.

"If she ever had a proper name," said Quayle, "it's lost even to her. Let's test your knowledge to establish if you're truly a scholar, or simply a salesman. Were you to be informed that one had chosen to christen her 'Pallida,' what surname might you ascribe in turn?"

Dobey stared Quayle in the face as he replied.

"Mors."

Quayle slowly clapped his hands in appreciation.

"Very impressive. Have I missed Horace on your shelves?"

"Behind your head."

Quayle turned and perused the shelves until he spotted an aged copy of the *Carmina*.

"You are," he said softly, "a most unexpected delight, but I fear that you may yet be required to concede the aptness of her nomenclature. She is death's very personification."

Dobey folded his hands in his lap.

"You talk fancy," he said. "My father told me never to trust a man who talked fancy."

"Most wise. And I admire your equanimity, or perhaps you think I'm joking about the imminence of your mortality?"

"I've seen your faces. I know what's coming. Maybe I should tell you both to go fuck yourselves. In fact, why don't I just do that? You and the tin woman over there can go fuck yourselves six ways to Sunday."

"Well," said Quayle, "allow me to explain why that's not going to happen. You're not the only one to have seen my face this evening. You're one of four, counting your staff but excluding your hayseed customers, and it'll be five if you also force me to pay a visit to Ms. Bachmeier, the lady whom I believe shares both your vocation and your bed. If you tell me what I want to know, none of them will ever be troubled by us. If you don't, then later tonight my colleague will gut your friend Carlos and bury the widow Bachmeier alive. And I liked the waitress—not the one who served me, but the other. I saw the way she looked at you. She's fond of you, and you of her. Not in any improper way, of course, but I could discern the bond between you. Leila: that was her name. I saw it on her badge. I've never had a predilection for rape, but in her case I'll make an exception. When I'm done with her, I'll let Mors start cutting."

Dobey closed his eyes.

"How do I know you're not going to kill them anyway?"

"If we were going to do that, we'd have started with Carlos while he was standing on your doorstep."

"Aren't you afraid of being identified?"

"Mr. Dobey, I've been doing this for a very long time, longer than you can imagine. A great many people have seen me, some of them under similar circumstances to your hired help, yet I have endured, and so I remain unconcerned. My colleague's face, on the other hand, tends to be the last that anyone sees."

Quayle placed a hand on Dobey's knee and gripped it gently, a gesture that was equal parts reassurance and threat.

"The name of the girl we seek—the woman, if you prefer—is Karis Lamb."

CHAPTER VIII

Far to the northeast, a warm, hard rain began to fall, working at compacted snow and stubborn ice. As the water did its work, the white seas parted in fissures to reveal the greens and browns beneath. Ground grown hard slowly softened, and the sound of the rain called to bud and branch, seed and root.

It called to buried things.

CHAPTER
IX

Outside of exceptional circumstances, Dobey rarely asked how the waifs came by his number, or by what means they knew where to find him. It wasn't as though he advertised, leaving his card tucked in the masonry at street corners, or slotted behind restroom mirrors. But as the years went by, he came to understand that those whom he helped find their way to somewhere better often considered it part of their duty to assist others in turn (*"There's this guy in Indiana . . ."*), while friends and associates of Esther also filed away his number and location, to be passed on when required.

What made him special—no, Dobey would correct himself (because vanity, preying on a weak mind, produces every sort of mischief), what made his position special—was that he wasn't part of the regular web of charities and shelters. He stood at one remove from them, and so provided a particular place of refuge for those who, for whatever reason, were not yet ready to be absorbed into the system.

But he was aware of how it had all begun.

• • •

The girl was sitting on the bench outside the CVS on Cadillac's Main Street, her backpack at her feet, her hands buried deep in her coat pockets against the cold. A faded sign attached to the streetlight beside her proclaimed this to be the location of a bus stop, but no bus had passed through Cadillac in two years, not since funding cuts did away with the route. The girl, unfamiliar to Dobey, was probably in her late teens, but her face wasn't developing at the same pace as the rest of her, and so was still that of a child. She was pretty, going on beautiful, but hers was a fragile grace, easily broken. Perhaps that was why Dobey stopped. Had she been harder-looking, he might have kept on driving, and his life would have taken a different direction.

By then Dobey was in his early fifties, and knew that he would never be a father. He'd come close to marriage a couple of times, but the final step proved difficult in each case, once because of him and once because of the other party. He had no regrets about this; better the doubts and difficulties manifest themselves before rather than after the ceremony. Had they been surmountable, he might, once again, have found himself on another journey. But now the widow Bachmeier was circling, and a chaste dance that had commenced during her husband's final illness was about to become a more intimate engagement.

Even allowing for the girl's delicacy, Dobey was still tempted to continue on his way and let someone else take care of her, a person better equipped to deal with a teenage girl. He was also aware that the last thing a young woman in trouble wanted was for some overweight, middle-aged guy in a truck to pull up and offer help. At the very least she'd have the right to be cautious, and if she had any sense, she'd start shouting to high heaven until the cops came.

Yet if everyone took that view, the pathways of the world would be littered with the remains of even more of the poor and the lost than they already were, and Dobey didn't want to be responsible for adding another casualty to the list; not that day, and not any day. So he turned back, stopped a little ahead of the girl, and got out of his truck. Now that the decision had been made, he wasn't sure of the correct distance to maintain, or what to do with his hands, and he wondered if her proximity and prettiness had somehow caused him to regress to adolescence.

The girl flicked a sideways glance in Dobey's direction, like an animal sensing the approach of a possible threat, signaling awareness as a prelude to possible flight.

"Did someone tell you this was a bus stop?" Dobey asked.

The girl's shoulders sagged, and her eyes briefly closed. She already knew, without being told more, that she'd been fed a crock of shit. It was just a matter of waiting to see if an attempt would soon be made to offer her a second helping.

"You saying it's not?"

"The bus company says it's not. I don't have much influence either way."

"Then why is the sign still up there?"

"That," said Dobey, "is a very good question. The answer, I guess, is that either nobody cared enough to take it down, or somebody cared too much."

The girl hid her mouth inside the collar of her coat and stared north. During the course of their brief conversation, she had yet to look directly at Dobey.

"Where are you trying to get to?" he asked.

"Chicago."

"You have family there?"

"A friend."

"Where you coming from?"

"Carolina."

"Jesus. North or South?"

"South."

"Double Jesus."

Although he couldn't see her mouth, the girl's eyes crinkled enough for him to know she'd smiled.

"So how come," Dobey asked, "you're sitting on a bench out here, where—officially—the buses don't run?"

The girl's eyes met his at last.

"Because another guy in a truck picked me up about twenty miles south of here, told me he'd give me ten bucks for a hand job, then dumped me when I wouldn't put out."

Dobey patted his own vehicle.

"Then I guess you'll be avoiding trucks for a while," he said, because he couldn't think of anything else to say. "Sorry" didn't seem worth the waste of oxygen.

"I guess so," said the girl.

Dobey stared north. Out of the corner of his eye, he saw the girl's head turn again in the same direction.

"If you squint up the road a ways," he said, "you'll see a sign for a diner called Dobey's. That's my place: I'm Dobey. Assuming you can tear yourself from your bench, I might be able to offer you a plate of food, a cup of coffee, and maybe a slice of pie to follow. And while you're getting outside of all that, I can make some calls and see if someone trustworthy, and preferably female, might not be heading into Indianapolis, or at least somewhere with a bus route, which would set you on your way to where you want to be. How does that sound?"

The girl gave the question some thought.

"It sounds good."

"You want me to take your bag, save you the trouble of hauling it up there yourself?"

"No, I'll keep it." Then: "Thanks."

"Very sensible of you, and don't mention it," said Dobey. "You got a name for the reservation?"

Another crinkle.

"Mae."

"Like the month?"

"No, Mae with an 'e.'"

"Well, Mae with an 'e,' I look forward to seeing you again very soon."

Dobey got back in his truck and drove on, and fifteen minutes later Mae with an "e" opened the door of the diner, took a stool at the counter, and ate enough to put Dobey's business briefly in the red while he called Esther Bachmeier. Esther came over and sat with the girl for an hour in a corner booth, and when she returned to Dobey, Mae with an "e" was crying, and Esther wasn't far from crying either.

Mae with an "e" didn't go on to Chicago, or Indianapolis, or anywhere else that day—or the next, or even the day after that. In fact, Mae with an "e" stayed in Dobey's second trailer, the one he'd bought for his already expanding book collection, for three weeks, the longest any of the women would ever remain. When she did eventually depart, it was for a shelter in Chicago, and Dobey missed her like a lost limb. In time, Mae with an "e" left the shelter for an apartment so small she had to step outside to change her mind, but it was safe, and warm, and her own space. She now lived in a larger apartment in St. Paul, Minnesota, with a baby boy and a guy who didn't drive a truck and wasn't a prick. She sent Dobey a card each Christmas, and called him every couple of months, and she'd come down to stay in that same trailer a few Novembers back to help celebrate Dobey's sixtieth birthday.

So Mae with an "e" was the first, and the others followed. Dobey remembered them all, every one, even those who stayed only a night, but Karis Lamb he recalled more easily than most, because Karis Lamb had been very, very scared.

And very, very pregnant.

CHAPTER X

Warm rain now falling in earnest on the woods of Maine, warm rain falling on field and marsh; the song of spring.

What is there to differentiate one copse from another: a particular arrangement of trees, an unusual combination of shrubs? In this case, an incision on the bark of a black spruce, like a timeworn wound on aged skin, long healed but still visible, if one knew where to look. Call it a star, cut behind creeping ivy, as though the one who made it wished to leave some sign of remembrance without attracting the attention of the curious.

A mark, a grave.

The voice of the rain intoning a name.

It was the season of awakenings.

Sleeper, awake.

CHAPTER
XI

Quayle was observing Dobey's features as one might watch a film projected on a screen, anticipating the revelations—or the fictions—to come. Dobey had never claimed to possess a poker face, but he felt certain that even had he been so gifted, Quayle would have been able to see through it with ease. Dobey thought Quayle's eyes revealed much about the man— an undeniable perspicacity, even a certain cruel humor—yet remained entirely untroubled by humanity. Sitting before him was like finding oneself under the scrutiny of a minor god.

"Let us assume," said Quayle, "that you've already tried to deny knowledge of Karis, and in reply I have opined that I don't believe you, and given you some warnings you would be unwise to ignore. It will save us both a lot of trouble."

"I don't know where she went," said Dobey.

"We're getting ahead of ourselves. When did she arrive here, and how long did she stay?"

Dobey had decided that his best, even only, hope was to answer every question as fully as possible while giving away as little as he could, and in that manner buy himself time. He was praying that Carlos had gone with his gut and called the police, so that even now Chief Dwight Hillick might be gathering his troops. He supposed he could have attempted to give Carlos some sign that all was not well, a little wink or gesture, but from her place of concealment the woman had whispered to Dobey exactly what to say, and made sure his face and hands were in full view as he spoke. Her voice had been surprisingly soft, but her breath stank worse than her body, as though she spent her downtime giving blow jobs to diseased truckers at flyblown rest stops without even pausing to wash out her mouth in between.

Quayle clicked his fingers before Dobey.

"Back with me," he said. "I hope you're just taking a moment in order to ensure a precise recall, and not because you're procrastinating, or composing a lie."

"She stayed for a few days."

"When?"

"About five years ago, maybe more. I don't remember the exact date, but it was around this time of year. Still cold."

"Why didn't she stay longer?"

"Some do and some don't. We get girls who need time to rest and figure out how to turn their lives around, to find work and earn a little money. I can always give them a few hours here or there.

Then there are others who are too scared to stay. They want to keep running because they're afraid that whatever is pursuing them might catch up if they stop."

"Such as?"

"Bad memories, bad people."

"Which do you think I represent?"

"Possibly both."

"You know, you're wasted in the food service industry. You should have gone to college. You had a future in psychological analysis. Now you barely have a future at all. Did Karis tell you why she was running? Think hard. If I have any doubts about the veracity of your statements, I may need to cross-check your answers with Ms. Bachmeier."

"It was a man," said Dobey. "She was running from a man. What else would it be?"

"Did she give you his name?"

"I didn't ask. I rarely do."

"You're sure?"

"Yes. I let them share with me what they want, but I don't go chasing details."

"Why not?"

"Because I've heard enough, and there's only so much I can take."

"Sensitive?" said Quayle.

"Guilty," said Dobey. "What some men do to women makes me ashamed of my sex."

The sentinel at the door continued to watch

the lot, a suppressed pistol hanging by her side. Dobey briefly wondered what might have made her the creature she was, at what might have been visited on her by men—because men it must have been; he'd grown adept at identifying their mark. Whatever she'd suffered, it had forged her into something awful, but it wouldn't stop Dobey from hurting her in his turn if he had to. He didn't think he could get to her before she had a chance to fire her gun, but he could probably tackle Quayle. The small nightstand beside the bed contained a lot of useless shit—old coins, plugs for cell phones that weren't even manufactured any longer, broken pencils, expired painkillers—but it also held a fixed-blade KA-BAR and a Sidewinder revolver in .22 Magnum. If he could take down Quayle, use him momentarily as a shield, and get his hand inside the nightstand—

"No," said Quayle.

"I don't understand."

Quayle dipped a hand into one of his trouser pockets, produced a coin, and flipped it to Dobey, who caught it instinctively.

"Take a look," said Quayle.

Dobey did. It was a 2005 Kansas state quarter, slightly battered and scratched, bearing the words "In God We rust" because a grease mark had prevented a clean pressing. Mint, it was probably worth a hundred dollars, but less so in its current state. Dobey recognized this particular example because it was one of the coins he stored in his nightstand, plucked from the register and added to the other rarities kept there with the intention of someday selling them on.

"My colleague appropriated the gun and the knife, but her areas of expertise don't extend to numismatics," said Quayle. "Tell me, Mr. Dobey, do you know the tale of the Comte de Chalais?"

It took Dobey a moment or two to answer. If Carlos had gone to the police, they would have been here by now. The gun and knife were forfeit. His life was forfeit.

"No, sir," he said finally, "I don't."

"Henri de Talleyrand-Périgord, the count in question, was a French nobleman, close to Louis the Thirteenth, who made the mistake of plotting against Cardinal Richelieu, a gentleman who, in the manner of many great conspirators, disliked having conspiracies aimed at himself. Richelieu ordered Henri to be executed, but his confederates bribed the executioner to absent himself in the hope that Henri's life might be spared. Instead, Richelieu entrusted the task to another prisoner, also condemned to death, but unfortunately lacking the skills required to perform a successful decapitation. It took thirty-four blows to sever Henri's head, and he was still alive until the twentieth. The lesson for you, Mr. Dobey, is that even if one is certain of death, one can die easily or one can die in great pain. So, Karis Lamb: What. Did. She. Say. To. You?"

"She said," Dobey replied, "she was running from the devil himself."

Quayle sat back.

"I'd like to be able to assure you that she wasn't speaking literally," he said, "but it would be a lie."

CHAPTER
XII

The earth is never the same after winter. The season briefly seals the landscape, holding it in suspension, but only at the cost of a greater transformation with the coming of spring.

As frozen ground thaws, the ice beneath melts, and the earth sinks to fill the spaces created. But this process is not consistent: the quantities of ice, and the speed of the melt, will vary, with the result that a previously flat surface may become pitted and uneven over the years, its weaknesses waiting to be exposed.

The spruce was among the oldest in the copse. It was only to be expected that it should someday fall, or so it would later be said, as though the imminent revelation were entirely in the natural order of things.

Not everyone would concur with this view. The tree, whispered those who knew of such matters, was not so old, and the slope upon which it stood remained relatively stable. There was subsidence, but not so much that it should have caused the spruce's hold upon the earth to be so fatally undermined, and certainly not so abruptly, with the thaw barely commenced.

But fall the tree did, and as it fell the rain eased, descending more gently now, the very heavens complicit in what was about to occur.

CHAPTER
XIII

Karis Lamb had made it as far as Seymour, Indiana, when she called the diner asking for Dobey, but he was at a warehouse in Columbus looking at broilers. Wanda Brady, Corbie's mother, had a catering background and covered for Dobey a couple of afternoons a week, and it was she who answered the phone. Wanda was prescient enough to detect the urgency in the woman's tone, and to agree, if not to give out Dobey's number, then at least to pass on a message to him.

"She says she's run away from a bad situation, and she's pregnant," Wanda told Dobey when he answered his cell. "She's sitting in a Starbucks in Seymour."

So Dobey dialed the number Wanda gave him, and a woman picked up and said her name was Karis, and she'd heard that Dobey helped people like her.

Dobey did not think of himself as a good man. He acted as he did because it had become unconscionable for him to do otherwise, but experience had taught him to exercise a modicum

69

of care. On more than one occasion, women and girls helped by him had later been tracked down by boyfriends, husbands, family, and were either forced to return by their tormentors or went back of their own volition, in some cases for reasons that Dobey didn't even wish to contemplate.

At least two of those women later did what Dobey asked every woman who passed through his care not to do, namely mention his refuge to anyone else, not unless that individual was in a similar situation to the one they themselves had fled. The result, in the first case, was an abusive telephone call. The second involved a visit from a man named Derrick Flinn—guess whose hick family couldn't even correctly spell a first fucking name, boys and girls—who arrived at the diner with a Ruger on his hip, thanks to Indiana state law's ongoing silence on open carry. Dobey was all for the Second Amendment, but even at the best of times he regarded anyone who entered a restaurant, store, or public park while flaunting a gun as a cocksucker of the highest order, and that went double for Dobey's own place of business.

So Derrick Flinn took a stool, ordered a coffee, and engaged in some general conversation with Dobey that Flinn gradually steered around to the subject of those who involved themselves in the personal lives of other men, and most particularly their relationship with their womenfolk, which is when Dobey began to recollect a thirty-five-year-old woman named Petra Flinn. Petra had come to him a couple of months earlier with so many dark bruises on her torso and thighs that Dobey might have taken her for black in the wrong light were it not for the fact that her face, her arms, and her legs below knee level had been left untouched—so she could still wear dresses in public, she said, and not embarrass her husband on social occasions.

Derrick Flinn didn't attempt to visit violence on Dobey, didn't make any threats, didn't even raise his voice, but the forty minutes Flinn spent in the diner were among the most unpleasant of Dobey's life, as Flinn squatted on the stool dressed in browns and greens, like an armed toad, while Dobey wondered if, when Flinn started shooting, he might kill Dobey alone and spare the staff.

Eventually Flinn thanked Dobey for his time, paid for the coffee, and left. He drove home and, since he was on a roll, beat his newly returned wife so badly that he stopped her heart, and was now serving life in the state prison up in Michigan City. So men like Derrick Flinn were among the reasons Dobey was very careful when any woman asked if he could come get her rather than have her travel to him.

"Who gave you my name?" Dobey asked.

"A girl who works in a coffee shop down in

Covington, Kentucky," said Karis. "Her name is Doreen: Doreen Peach Pie. She said that's how you'd remember her."

Dobey did. As far as he could tell, Doreen had subsisted solely on coffee and slices of peach pie while she stayed with him. She ought to have come in at two hundred pounds, all the sugar and fat she was absorbing, but she hardly weighed anything. Dobey could only figure that the energy generated by the vast quantities of caffeine somehow served to cancel out the rest.

"You say you're pregnant?"

"Eight months gone. Mr. Dobey, I need to put more distance between Covington and me. I've got this far on the kindness of strangers, but it's not far enough. He's probably already coming after me, and he'll find me if I don't get help. It could be he'll find me anyway, but I can't stop now. If I do, he'll take me back, and he'll kill me. He'll wait until I've had his baby, but he will kill me."

"Who is 'he'?"

"I don't even want to tell you his name. He's bad, but some of the men he associates with are worse. I don't want to share with you more than I have to. Honest, it's better this way."

And Dobey believed her. Sometimes, you just knew. He told Karis Lamb to stay in the Starbucks and he'd come get her, which he did. She was a slim, dark-haired girl, with eyes too big for her

72

face, but there was a resilience to her as well; a streak of hardness. Dobey put her in his truck and drove her to the diner. Over the days and nights that she stayed, she told Dobey and Esther a story: about a man who had at first seemed kind and different, a cultured, slightly older figure who taught literature at a private college; who was independently wealthy and collected books; who, when she finally moved in with him, made her a prisoner in his home; who, she realized, had groomed her for precisely that purpose, because he thrived on rape; who warned her that if she tried to run, he'd murder her mother and sister before cutting her open with garden shears; who claimed to consort with spirits; who—

Quayle interrupted Dobey.

"My own Scheherazade," he said, "spinning tales, in your case speckled with truth, to buy the moments till morning."

"You asked me about Karis Lamb," said Dobey. "I'm telling you."

"And you're spouting lies: not many, but enough. Karis did tell you the name of the man she was fleeing: Vernay. The girl in Covington was not called Doreen but Ava, although I can't attest to her dietary peculiarities. It was Ava who contacted you out of concern for Karis, who did indeed frequent her place of business, although it was a health-food store, not a coffee shop. Vernay believed he had worn Karis down and broken her will, which was why she was permitted some limited latitude, albeit with Vernay close by. And Ava, who had suffered abuse of her own, sensed something similar in Karis, and slowly, and very carefully, began to tease information from her, communicating with her through notes written on the backs of receipts, enough to confirm Ava's own suspicions, if not to involve the law. But Karis remained unwilling, or afraid, to run.

"And then Karis's mother and sister were killed in an automobile accident, and suddenly part of the hold that Vernay had over her ceased to exist. It was probably the spur for what was to come; that and the pregnancy. Karis remained concerned that the police would not believe her claims of rape and incarceration. It would be her word against Vernay's, and if she were unsuccessful, it would be the end of her. Even if she did manage to get away, she was afraid that Vernay or his friends would track her down. That was when Ava suggested she turn to you.

"Karis couldn't contact you directly because Vernay gave her no access to a phone, but you, Mr. Dobey, could contact Vernay. You made the first approach, using a shared passion for rare books as a point of entry into his life. Like many collectors, Vernay both bought and sold. You purchased from him, began a correspondence, and eventually you and he met. Vernay had very particular interests, mostly erotica and the occult. And you, from your trailer library, have contrived to become quite the expert in esoteric volumes, quite the bibliophile.

"It took a lot of patience and effort for all of you to achieve what you did: to get a cell phone to Karis; to track Vernay's routines for the most likely opportunity to get Karis away from him; to be available to move at a moment's notice, but Vernay was always alert. His home was secured, and he worked not five minutes' drive from it. It was Ava who came up with the idea of a medical emergency, an unexpected pain during the pregnancy, and a visit to a Planned Parenthood clinic where, thanks to Ms. Bachmeier's contacts, a rear-door escape was facilitated, with Ava waiting to drive Karis north to Seymour, from where you did indeed collect her.

"And all this you performed so successfully that it has taken me years to find the correct thread and begin to pull. I had never thought to look at Vernay's book habit, which was foolish of me, but then your friend Ava moved north and helped a woman in Terre Haute, a housewife named Petra Flinn. You may recall her husband, Derrick. He certainly remembers you. So I now had Ava, and I had you. Ava, incidentally, filled in a lot of the gaps. Regrettably, there is now a vacancy at the health-food store."

Dobey couldn't help himself. He lunged at

Quayle and managed to get his hands on his throat, but Mors, both faster and stronger than she looked, was on him in an instant. Dobey took a blow to the head that sent him sprawling on the bed, and then Quayle was behind him, holding him down, while the woman squatted on Dobey's belly like some pale sister to the demon in Fusili's *Nightmare*. She looked to Quayle for guidance, and through blurred vision Dobey saw Quayle nod.

The gun was set aside. From her jacket Mors removed a leather pouch, which opened to reveal a small set of sharp surgical instruments. She took a thin scalpel between the thumb and forefinger of her left hand, and suspended it over Dobey's face.

"I did warn you," said Quayle.

And Pallida Mors used the scalpel to puncture Dobey's right eye.

CHAPTER
XIV

The rain revealed twisted roots.
  The rain revealed stone and dark fresh soil.
  The rain revealed a skull.

CHAPTER
XV

The pain had dulled, but only compared to the intensity of the initial agony.

Dobey was once again seated on his bed, his back to the wall, a towel filled with ice pressed to what remained of his right eye, the material stained with blood and ocular fluids. In his free hand Dobey held a glass of bourbon, poured for him by Quayle. Mors had resumed her vigil by the window, while Quayle had returned to his chair.

"I'm sorry," said Quayle, "but you brought that on yourself. In a way, you brought all this on yourself. Consider it a punishment for good deeds, or for one good deed. I don't care about the others, only Karis."

Quayle ran a finger along the spines of the nearest volumes.

"I never imagined that the interior of a trailer could be so elegant," he said, taking in the oak shelves that Dobey had made and fitted himself; the items of antique furniture sourced from dealers over the years, according to the fluctuating state of Dobey's finances: the Persian rugs; the ornate lamps.

And the books: all of the books.

"We'll leave you here among your volumes," said Quayle. "I promise you. We're almost done."

He leaned forward, gazing up into Dobey's downturned face.

"Vernay is dead. I thought you might like to know that. He was, even by the lowest of standards, a wretched specimen, although perhaps Karis told you enough about him for you to be aware of this already. He thrived on rape, but a taste for rape will eventually land a man in jail, so Vernay decided to forsake the lure of fresh meat for the security of the familiar. I think Karis was perhaps the second or third woman he'd taken, although he claimed to have held her in genuine affection. It was what made her different, he said, although eventually she'd have ended up like the others, sleeping in the dirt beneath his basement floor. I believe he was considering letting her child live. I didn't bother to ask him why, for obvious reasons. As you yourself noted, there's only so much a man can bear to hear.

"Of course, it's possible that one of the others might also have become pregnant by Vernay, but didn't carry to term. Again, it wasn't a subject I cared to pursue. Clearly, though, Karis's pregnancy caused Vernay to take a new approach. Perhaps he just liked the idea of growing his own victim, because he never struck me as the paternal kind.

"But when Karis disappeared, it became important that Vernay should also vanish. If she began talking to the right people, who knew what forces might arrive at Vernay's door? Karis, Karis: what trouble you have caused us all."

Quayle checked his watch.

"We really must be going, Mr. Dobey. Think of your fine widow. Think of your young staff. Tell us the truth, and we'll be far from here before they wake to the dawn. But if I find out later that you've lied, I guarantee we'll come back and continue our investigations through them."

Dobey began to sob. He'd managed to restrain himself until now, but it was all coming to an end, and he did not want his last act on this earth to be the betrayal of Karis Lamb.

"We sent her to a safe house in Chicago," he said, "but she only stayed one night. When the volunteer went to check on her, she was already gone. But she called me about a week later. She wanted to thank me, and let me know she was okay."

"And where did she call from?"

"Portland, Maine."

"Who was the contact there?"

"There was none, or no one I can name. By then, Karis was on her own. She said she was heading to Canada."

"And that's all you know?"

"Yes, I swear."

Quayle stood.

"Then we're done."

Mors approached Dobey for the final time, still holding her surgical pouch. Dobey tried to pull away, fearing the scalpel, but Quayle restrained him while the woman produced not a blade, but a bottle and a syringe.

"It won't hurt," said Quayle. "It will be just like falling asleep."

Mors filled the syringe, tapped the needle, and reached for Dobey's left arm. And as the point pierced his skin, Dobey spoke to Quayle.

"You're dead and you don't even know it."

"I'm not sure what you mean."

Dobey felt the drug invade his veins, progressing rapidly up his arm to his shoulder, but he still retained the strength to speak. As his eyes began to close, he said, "Out there is someone who will put an end to you. You'll be torn apart, and no one will give a damn except to celebrate your passing."

Dobey's eyes began to close.

"I'm sorry," said Quayle. "The world does not work that way."

"You know," said Dobey, "you talk too much."

And thus he died.

CHAPTER
XVI

Not only a skull now: ribs, a femur, finger bones intertwined over a female pelvic cavity, here and there the yellow masses of saponification, partly shrouded in brownish gray skin and the tattered remnants of the clothing and sacking in which the woman had been interred.

Because sometimes the dead rise, and wake to a dream of life.

CHAPTER
XVII

Parker's meeting with Moxie Castin was postponed for a few days due to an indisposition on the lawyer's part, which Parker put down to Moxie's consistent ingestion of sugary carbonated beverages, but which the lawyer claimed was flu.

The delay was fortunate, because the black dog came upon Parker, a sadness that turned the world to gray. He retreated to his home, turned off his phone, and waited for Jennifer to come.

And to the north, the men and women gathered in ever-greater numbers: police and wardens; experts in bodies and experts in bone; all in the service of nameless remains.

All for the woman in the woods.

CHAPTER
XVIII

Holly Weaver stood by Daniel's bed. She hadn't read him a story that night, or the night before. When she offered, Daniel replied only that he was tired, and she could read to him another time. Holly tried to hide how grateful she was for the respite, and especially that she would not have to recite the story she had written for him. She was not certain she could have made it to the end without breaking.

Holly wondered if Daniel was already growing out of the need to have her near him before he slept, and if this was the unpicking of the first stitch, presaging a time when she would no longer have him beside her at all, when he would leave for college, or work, or a lover's bed, perhaps never to return.

But what if it happened before then? What if they took him away?

She kissed Daniel, and tried to silence the voice in her head. It had been with her since Daniel's birth, but it was speaking more insistently since the discovery of the body in the woods.

What if they find out what we did?
"Good night, Daniel. I love you."
"Good night, Mom. I love you too."
What if they come?

CHAPTER
XIX

Parker watched the sun shine low on the marshes, shedding gold upon the sea. It rose, set, and was gone. One day, then two. The house echoed to the sound of his footsteps, and his alone. He embraced the solitude. He was a man still grieving, and a grief so old could no longer be shared. It had to be endured alone.

How long now since they had been taken from him, his wife and first child? Did it even matter anymore? His years with them were slowly being stolen away, months coalescing into minutes, days into seconds. He felt himself losing memories. Susan and Jennifer, mother and daughter, were drifting into dream. This was why he had to close his door to the demands of others, even if only for a little while. In silence could he mine for recollection, and restore the beloved to remembrance.

And if he waited long enough, a different hush might descend, a listening quietude.

He sat in stillness by his window as daylight paled, anticipating the cusp, the moment when the shadows teetered on the brink of absolute absorption by descending night, until he thought he glimpsed her: movement where no movement should be, a lost girl flitting like a moth against the landscape, her ruined face blessedly hidden by hair and forest and almost-night.

Jennifer: the lost daughter.

The dead daughter.

Only then did he speak.

"Tell me."

And in speaking he caused motion to cease, all but the gentle tilt of the child's head as she heard her father's words through the barrier of walls, through the mesh of bare branches, through the mists that tried always to smother them.

tell you . . . what?

"Tell me who I am."

you are my father

"Tell me why I am here."

to die

"To what end?"

i cannot say

"I am tired of not knowing."

you mustn't be afraid

"And yet I am."

i will be with you when it comes

"And Sam?" His other daughter, the living child, to whom the dead also spoke.

she will not be there at the end

"But will she be safe?"

she is always safe

"I'm sorry I failed you."

you did not fail me

"I'm sorry I was not there to protect you."

you could not have protected me

"Had I been with you—"

then you would have died beside me, beside us

"I wanted that. I wanted the pain to end."

you mustn't be selfish, daddy

Daddy.

"You don't understand."

i do

"I cannot go on like this."

but you must

"Why?"

because they're gathering

"Who is gathering?"

because they're close

"Who is close?"

the not-gods

"The Not-God?"

no, daddy, you're not listening

not one, but many

"I don't understand."

there are gods within gods, three entities in one, mirrors of the old

"And what do the Not-Gods want?"

they want to put an end to all things

"And how am I supposed to stop this?"

by living

"Living is hard."

dying is harder

He strained to see her now. The shadows were renewing their claim on her.

and you will *die*

"Stay."

there will be pain, but i will be there to share it

"And then?"

we will go together, you and i, to the sea

The blackness became complete, and she was gone.

He closed his eyes. All these dreams, all these sorrows. No end in sight.

But it was coming.

CHAPTER
XX

Parker woke in his bed the following morning, with no memory of leaving his chair by the window. He washed, dressed, and consumed more than coffee and toast for the first time in days. The black dog had retreated.

Because Jennifer had come.

He caught up with some paperwork before booking a last-minute flight to New York. It was time to visit the patient.

The hospital room stank of suffering. Angel was still weak, and whatever he was being fed wasn't entering his system through his mouth, but he was able to speak for minutes at a time before briefly lapsing into sleep, and his grip on Parker's hand when they were about to part was firm.

"You need to look after Louis for me," he said.

Parker and Angel had already shared at least one version of this conversation prior to the operation, but Parker wasn't surprised that the other man could remember nothing of it.

"If you're planning on dying, you'd better leave him to someone else in your will," said Parker.

Angel ignored this. "Just for a while, until I'm back on my feet again."

"He's doing fine. The world hasn't stopped turning because you now weigh less."

"I'm being serious."

"I know you are."

"He's angry. Don't let him do anything stupid."

"He's already blown up a truck. Does that count?"

Angel thought about this.

"Okay, so more stupid."

"I'll do my best."

Louis was waiting outside when Parker left the room. Angel was never truly alone at the hospital, even allowing for the ministrations of the staff. When Louis was not present, a pair of unlikely but effective guardians—the Fulci brothers—maintained alternate watches over Angel's bed. Louis had acquired his share of enemies over the years, some of them through his allegiance with Parker, and it was not inconceivable that they might try to punish him through Angel.

"Well?" said Louis.

"He seems pretty lucid."

"Yeah? He was talking about religion yesterday, but that might have been the opiates. I don't want him finding Jesus."

"I wouldn't be too concerned. If Jesus thinks Angel is trying to find him, Jesus will just change his name."

This appeared to reassure Louis. Whatever Louis's conception of the next world might entail—and Parker now had a clearer idea after their conversation in Maine—it made little allowance for holy rollers in this one.

Parker left Louis with Angel, and went to have dinner with his ex-partner, Walter Cole, and Walter's wife, Lee. She was aging gently, Walter less so, but they both appeared happy and well. Thanks to their daughter, Ellen, they were grandparents, and were enjoying all the benefits of a small child's company without most of the drawbacks. Ellen had asked Parker to be godfather to the girl, Melanie. He had politely declined, but he knew Ellen understood his reasons. Years earlier, he had saved her from a predator named Caleb Kyle, and the trauma of those events still lingered for both of them. Yet he was touched that Ellen would think of him in such a way, and a bond would always exist between them, one that now extended to her child.

There were others whom Parker could have seen while he was in the city, including the rabbi Epstein and his shadow, the beautiful mute named Liat, with whom Parker had once spent a single interesting night in bed. He didn't want to turn his trip into some form of the Stations of the Cross, and so contented himself with calling by Nicola's on First Avenue to say hello and pick up some imported Italian delicacies before taking a cab to JFK for his JetBlue flight back to Portland.

Upon arrival at Portland Jetport, he bought a copy of the *Press Herald* with every intention of reading it when he got home, but tiredness got the better of him, and so he went to bed without reading of a woman's semi-preserved remains found in the Maine woods.

2.

The only ghosts, I believe, who creep into this world, are dead young mothers, returned to see how their children fare.
—J. M. Barrie, *The Little White Bird*

CHAPTER

Daniel opened his eyes. His room was dark except for the night-light shaped like a starship that burned in an outlet by the door, so he could find his way to the bathroom if he needed to go.

On the nightstand by his bed stood a glass of water, a lamp, and a toy telephone made of wood and plastic. His mother had bought it for him when he was very little because he had been fascinated by it in the store. Its buttons bore animals instead of numbers, so Daniel heard clucking if he put the receiver to his ear and pressed the chicken button, and the sheep bleated, and the cow mooed. The phone rang if the handle at the side was turned.

But Daniel hadn't used the phone in a very long time. Truth be told, the novelty of hearing animals on the other end of the line had worn off pretty fast, although he had not yet reached the stage where he was willing to discard any toy, however neglected it might have become, and so the telephone sat at the bottom of the secondary toy box in his closet. There it would probably have remained until it was time to throw out the entire contents, or take them to Goodwill.

Except two nights before, the telephone had started ringing.

Daniel turned over on his pillow to regard the toy. The base was a smiling face, and the nose glowed red when the phone rang, or an animal was making noises, but it was silent now, and the nose remained unlit.

It had taken Daniel a while to notice the sound the first time it happened. He'd been so deep in sleep that the ringing had to penetrate layers of unconsciousness to reach him, and he was confused when he woke. At first he thought the sound was coming from the smoke alarm in the hall, and he almost called for his mother, but it soon became clear that the source of the muffled jangling was somewhere inside the room. He supposed it was one of his toys malfunctioning as a battery died, but he couldn't go back to sleep while the disturbance continued. He got out of bed and went to the closet, shivering because the heater was on a timer, and the temperature felt as though it was at its lowest point. The closet light turned on automatically as the doors opened, and he had to toss aside sneakers and a couple of jackets in order to get to the box. Once done, it was a moment's work to find the phone.

The toy didn't have any batteries to remove—they were long gone—and yet somehow it was still ringing. But even with batteries it shouldn't have been making a sound, because no one was turning the handle. Yet there it was, tinkling away, the red nose flashing on and off, demanding that he pick up the receiver and listen to the voice of the zookeeper asking him to identify a cow or a lion by pressing the correct button, which was what one heard if one answered the phone, although even at a younger age Daniel had wondered what kind of zoo kept chickens and cows alongside lions.

Which was when Daniel decided, quite logically, that the only way to stop the phone ringing was to pick up the receiver.

From outside Daniel's window came the steady dripping of ice melting from the roof. Daniel didn't mind the sound the ice was making. It was comforting, like rainfall.

He wanted the phone to ring.

He didn't want the phone to ring.

He'd had no intention of putting the receiver to his ear when the phone rang that first time. He simply figured that the noise would stop if he picked up, after which he could set the toy aside and ask his mom to fix it in the morning, or just get rid of the phone—although he was concerned that this might precipitate, on his mom's part, an effort at a more organized reduction of his collection, and Daniel was reluctant to encourage such a project. He decided he might be better off detaching the receiver and leaving well enough alone.

But when he held the receiver to his ear he heard not the zookeeper but falling rain, and buried somewhere within it, like a signal fighting through static, the voice of a woman.

hello? said the woman. *hello?*

Daniel dropped the receiver and scuttled backward to his bed, but he could still hear the voice.

can you hear me?

He could have gone to his mom, but he was as much intrigued as frightened. An unexpected man on the other end of the phone would simply have been disturbing, but this—this was odd, and there was something in the voice that was almost familiar.

Daniel picked up the receiver again.

"Hello?"

The woman's voice seemed to catch, as though she were trying to keep from crying.

is that you?

"Who is this?"

what did they name you?

He wasn't sure whether to answer. Any conversation would certainly fall into the category of talking to strangers, which his mom always made clear to him was very bad, although this was a stranger on the other end of the phone, which wasn't as bad as speaking to someone in person, and a woman, which was less troublesome again.

"Daniel," he said.

The woman repeated his name, over and over, savoring it like candy.

it's lovely to be speaking to you at last

Daniel wasn't sure that he felt the same way, but he'd come this far, so . . .

"What's your name?" he asked.

my name, said the woman, *is karis*

CHAPTER
XXII

Parker met Moxie Castin at the Bayou Kitchen on Deering Avenue. Moxie was enjoying the morning sunshine at the big window table, which was usually reserved for larger parties, but since the lawyer virtually constituted a larger party all on his own, an exception had been made for him. Parker noticed that this seemed to happen a lot where Moxie was concerned: rules were discreetly bent to accommodate him, perhaps because he refused even to acknowledge, never mind obey, most of them. This meant that the only options for those involved in their creation were either to dispense with the rules entirely, which could potentially lead to anarchy; attempt to impose them on Moxie, which would definitely lead to sorrow and despair; or decide that they shouldn't apply to Moxie, which seemed the most sensible course of action. Most businesses in Portland figured it was probably better to keep Moxie Castin sweet. Everybody would need a lawyer at some point, and better to have Moxie on your side than the other guy's. And if Moxie did happen to be on the other guy's side, he might go easier on you if you hadn't crossed him in the past.

Moxie was wearing a powder-blue suit, and a necktie so vibrant it was almost a cry for help. He was drinking coffee and reading the *Press Herald*, although copies of *The Boston Globe*, *The New York Times*, and *The Washington Post* were also stacked beside him. If newspapers eventually vanished entirely, it wouldn't be Moxie's fault. He and Parker had that much in common.

"I already ordered for you," he said, as Parker took a seat across from him.

"How did you know what I wanted?"

"What does it matter? Everything's good here."

Parker had to concede that Moxie was correct, but still, a man liked to be consulted.

Moxie turned a page of his paper.

"Take a look in the bag, see what I scored at Pinecone and Chickadee," he instructed.

Pinecone + Chickadee was a gift store of more than usual eccentricity down on Free Street. One of its paper bags lay on the bench seat by Moxie. Parker examined the contents while coffee was poured for him. He tried to find the right words for what he saw, but they wouldn't come, so he settled for a simple declaration of fact.

"They're Heroes of the Torah drinking glasses," he said.

"Uh-huh."

They were four in total, each decorated in blue with a portrait of one of the heroes in question: A. Hildenseimer, Yitzchak Spector, R. Elizer Goldberg, and S. Y. Rabinovitch. Parker had no idea why these men might be considered heroic in Torah circles. All he could say for certain was that the glasses weren't necessarily improved by their visages.

"I didn't know you were Jewish," said Parker.

"It never came up, and I'm only kind of Jewish. I'm Jewish-ish. Anyway, you don't have to be Jewish to appreciate these bad boys."

He appeared to be entirely serious.

"Well," said Parker, "they're quite a find."

Swap 'em with your friends, advised a line under each portrait.

"Seems you can swap them," said Parker.

"What do you mean?"

"I guess if you have doubles, you can exchange one, like baseball cards, or go for a Torah MVP. You know, like swapping a John Wasdin for a Manny Ramirez."

"Why would anyone pick up two of the same glass?"

"Moxie, in this case I don't know why anyone would pick up *one* of the same glass."

Moxie returned his purchases to the bag in what Parker could only have described as an aggrieved manner.

"You sadden me," said Moxie.

Their breakfasts arrived. Moxie had settled on Smokin' Caterpillar omelets for both of them: three spicy eggs, hash, grilled onions, Swiss, with toast and a side of homies. The Bayou Kitchen deemed itself to have failed its customers if they could see their plates under all the food.

"Eat up," said Moxie. "You're getting thin."

Moxie, by contrast, remained a big man yet somehow contrived to run half marathons and not die. Either he was a medical miracle or God was afraid to call him in case of litigation.

Moxie filled his mouth with hash and egg, and tapped a knife on a page of the *Press Herald*. It was a short article indicating that the police still had no leads on the immolation of an expensive truck on the waterfront the previous weekend.

"You happen to hear that someone blew up Billy Ocean's truck in a parking lot off Commercial?" asked Moxie.

"Billy Ocean the singer?"

"Funny. You think the 'Caribbean Queen' guy drives around in a Chevy tricked up with the rebel flag? No, Billy Ocean, Bobby Ocean's son."

Bobby Ocean's real name was Robert Stonehurst, but everyone knew him as Bobby Ocean because he kept an office down by the Portland Ocean Terminal, and was deeply invested in various enterprises connected to boat ownership, fishing, tourism, restaurants, real estate, and any other way of turning a buck while still being able to look out his window at the sea. Bobby was smart, but his son was reputedly dumber than a stump.

"Is this a matter of concern to you?" Parker asked.

"Only because Bobby Ocean turned up at my office yesterday. Said he figured the truck business for an act of terrorism, but didn't trust the Portland PD to do anything about it. He wanted me to hire someone on his behalf to investigate the crime."

"Did he suggest a motive?"

"Bobby suspects it was an assault on his son's First Amendment rights, and on patriotism in general, owing to Billy's desire to celebrate certain aspects of his white Anglo-Saxon heritage, such as displaying the flag of the Confederacy."

"In Maine."

"That's right."

"Because where else would he choose to display it?"

"Exactly."

"And why did Bobby Ocean come to you?"

"Because we're both GOP donors. We sat at the same table at a fund-raising dinner before Christmas. He complained about the soup. Bobby Ocean gives the party a bad name."

"I may be missing something here, but since

when was flying the Confederate flag in down-town Portland an act of patriotism?"

"Don't ask me. If I could outlaw one concept, the obvious others apart, it would be fucking 'patriotism.' It's nationalism in better clothing. You know who were patriots? The Nazis, and those Japanese fucks who bombed Pearl Harbor, and the Serbs who rounded up all those men and boys and put them in holes in the ground outside Srebrenica before going back to rape their women, at least until someone tried bombing sense into them. Patriots built Auschwitz. You start believing that 'my-country-wrong-or-right' shit, and it always ends up at the same place: a pit filled with bones."

Moxie jammed another forkful of food into his mouth. To give him credit, he didn't let his feelings get in the way of his appetite.

Parker let a few moments go by before he said:

"I take it you didn't offer to help Bobby in his quest for justice."

"No, but I could have made easy money just by telling him straight-out who did it. I hear stories, some of them more believable than others, like the one about who might have been drinking in a bar on Commercial the night Billy Ocean's truck was reduced to a burned-out shell."

Parker looked at Moxie. Moxie looked back at him.

"You need me to say it aloud?" asked Moxie.

"Not really."

"I think we can agree that the gentleman in question is not the kind to smile kindly on some oversized Johnny Reb wagon parked in his line of sight."

"Possibly not."

"So: Were you with him?"

"You think I could have stopped him if I was?"

"I'll take that as a yes, then."

"I didn't know he was going to blow up the truck."

"What did you think he was going to do, write the owner a strongly worded letter? You must have realized he was going to inflict some kind of damage."

"He might just have slashed the tires."

"If I thought you really believed that, I'd be looking for a new investigator, in case someone tried to offer you some magic beans in return for a head start."

"Louis's going through a tough time. He needed to vent."

Moxie tried to compose his features into something resembling a sympathetic expression. Tried, and failed.

"A lot of folks have it tough, but they restrain themselves from committing acts of arson. God forbid I should accuse the Portland PD of even considering engaging in racial profiling, but if you think the cops haven't already asked around and come up with a description of a black man who happened to be drinking near Billy Ocean's truck shortly before it exploded, you're all out to sea. I hope he paid cash at the bar."

"He always pays cash," said Parker. "When he pays at all."

"I'm glad you can joke about this. Bobby Ocean and his idiot son can go fuck themselves as far as I'm concerned, and I don't believe the police care for either of them any more than I do, but nobody wants trucks burning on the waterfront. It sends out the wrong message, which means this isn't going to slide easily, and your friend doesn't need that kind of attention. Rein him in. Better yet, tell him to indulge his firebug impulses down in New York, or even Jersey. Someone's always burning shit in Jersey. He'll blend right in."

Parker knew Moxie was right, although he wasn't certain that Louis could be reined in, not in his current mood. At least up here Parker could potentially keep an eye on him, and there was a limit to the amount of trouble he could cause in Maine compared to New York—or indeed, Jersey.

"I'll talk to him."

"Do that."

Moxie closed the paper, and turned it so that the story above the fold on the front page was facing Parker.

"You been following this?"

Parker had caught up on the discovery of the remains of a woman in Piscataquis County. Maine wasn't immune from violent crime, and victims showed up from time to time. Perhaps it was the manner in which the body had been revealed—a thaw, a fallen tree—and its burial in a sackcloth shroud, but something about the case seemed to have captured the public imagination in the state, beyond the media's stoking of the fire because it was a quiet time for news.

"I don't know any more than what I've read in the papers," said Parker.

"I do."

Trust Moxie. No tree fell unheard in a Maine forest, not with him around.

"Homicide?"

"Suspicious death for now. No obvious signs of external injury."

That in itself was unusual. So many forms of sudden death left marks, even on semi-skeletonized remains. A bullet might bequeath a hole, a knife a scratch mark on a rib or sternum. Strangulation fractured small bones in the neck. Drugs were subtler, but even their presence was registered. Bone marrow retained toxins, and the hair and nails recorded exposure to narcotics. The body found ways to memorialize its end.

Parker knew that Moxie wouldn't have brought up the subject of the woman if he didn't have information he wanted to share.

"But?"

"The autopsy suggests she gave birth shortly before she died, and late in the final trimester. Something to do with the position of the pelvic bones, but the police also believe they may have found the placenta and umbilical cord in the same state of semi-preservation as the body."

"How long after she gave birth was she put in the ground?"

"Hard to say, but no more than a day or two. Could be even less. The presence of the cord and placenta suggests it might have been hours."

"Did your contact give you an estimate on her age?"

"Mid-twenties."

"So not a teenager."

This might have been the twenty-first century, but it was still depressing to Parker how many teenage girls felt compelled to hide their pregnancies out of shame, or fear of parental anger, until the time came to give birth, alone and unattended, with the worst potential consequences for both mother and child.

"No," said Moxie, "although adulthood is no guarantee against having a baby away from a hospital or home, either intentionally or by accident."

"Then where's the child?"

"If it died, then presumably it would have been interred with the mother. It might have survived."

"Unless it's buried somewhere nearby," said Parker.

"Why bury it away from its mother?"

"Or was taken by animals."

"Then why not feed on the mother, too?"

"You want to go into that over breakfast?" An infant body, Parker knew, would be easier to consume.

"I'm not hearing anything about animal damage to the mother's body," said Moxie.

"So the mother dies," said Parker, "either from complications arising out of childbirth or at the hands of another, and the baby is kept by whoever put the mother in the ground?"

"Or dropped off somewhere: a hospital, a charity."

Sooner or later the police would start chasing down records of abandoned infants. A more exact estimate of when the young woman had died would help, but abandonments weren't so common anymore. For the moment, though, they'd be operating on the assumption of infant remains buried in proximity to those of the mother.

Parker sat back from his food and signaled for more coffee. It came, and he waited until both their mugs were refilled before he spoke again.

"So why does this interest you?" he asked.

"The state police are keeping some details back."

It was not uncommon for the police to hold off on revealing evidence found at a scene, especially anything that might be known only to someone intimately connected with a crime, particularly the individual responsible for its commission. It was a way for the police to test for false confessions and accusations, as well as weed out time wasters and the insane.

"And you know what these details are?"

"Correct, although only one of them is relevant to me."

Parker waited.

"It's a Star of David—not carved into the fallen tree by the grave, but on another nearby, facing it."

"It doesn't mean that the star and the body are connected."

"No, but if there's one subject on which we're not short of experts in this state, it's trees. It's all still approximate, but the star was probably carved at around the same time that body went into the ground."

"And you're sure it's a Star of David?"

"It was carefully done. I don't believe there's any doubt."

"Has anyone mentioned hate crime?"

"It came up. The ME is still waiting on toxicology results. They'll take another five weeks to appear, but I don't recall hearing about many hate crime poisonings. And it's just a

Star of David: no swastika alongside it, no anti-Semitic indicators. The star looks to be a marker, even a memorial, and nothing more."

Parker glanced again at the bag by Moxie's side.

"Torah glasses," he said.

"Torah glasses," Moxie echoed, raising a hand for the check. "It may surprise you, but I tend to believe the best of people. It's because I mostly see the worst, and being an optimist is the only way I can keep getting out of bed in the morning. I think someone buried that woman but held on to her child, and I'm hoping it was for a noble reason. Whether it was or not, the person or persons responsible will be getting very worried right now. When the police find them—and my feeling is that they *will* be found, because someone who takes the time to carve a Star of David as a makeshift memorial doesn't strike me as a professional disposer of bodies—they're going to need advice and representation. Call it my service for the dead woman. Yours, too, although in your case you'll also be paid for your time."

"What do you want me to do?"

"I've exhausted my source. I've found out all I'm going to, for now."

By this Parker guessed that Moxie's contact was someone close to the ME's office rather than the state police.

"I don't have many friends in Augusta," said Parker.

"I'm a lawyer—I don't have any at all. Learn what you can. Shadow the investigation. I want to believe that child is alive."

"Against the odds."

"That's right."

"The state police may not like me riding their coattails."

"This isn't a homicide—not yet, maybe not ever. The only crime that's been committed so far is an unregistered burial."

The check came. Moxie paid in cash, and tipped generously.

"So?" he asked Parker.

"I guess I'm hired."

Moxie grinned.

"That's my boy," he said. "It's just a shame that your more unusual skill sets won't be required for this investigation. Hell, you probably won't even have to raise your voice . . ."

CHAPTER
XXIII

It had taken Holly Weaver's father two days to return to his home outside Guilford, two days during which Holly had died a thousand deaths, a hundred of them alone in the hours after the discovery of the body in the woods. Owen Weaver drove a big rig for a living, and was down in Florida when the woman was found. At forty cents a mile, that represented good money—the best he'd earned in a while, because the winter months were always slow, and her father preferred to work in New England when possible. But then, winter was bad for a lot of folks in Maine. Holly worked as a secretary and receptionist for a medical supply company in Dover-Foxcroft. She'd been lucky to hold on to all her hours in January and February—lucky to hold on to her job—while waitressing work on the weekends gave her the chance to squirrel away some cash without the IRS biting. At least Daniel was in kindergarten now, which made things a little easier. She wasn't paying as much in childcare, wasn't—

What if they found out? What if they arrived

with their flashing lights and took Daniel away?

She'd die.

Make those a thousand and one deaths.

She'd been so frightened that she hadn't even used her own phone to call her father after the body was found. They listened in to calls, didn't they: the police, the CIA, the NSA? Holly had a vision of endless white rooms filled with people, all with headphones clamped to their ears, flicking between conversations, waiting for keywords: *ISIS, explosive, murder, body, found, shallow, grave.* She knew it probably wasn't like that in reality. They had computers programmed to pick up on phrases. She'd read about it somewhere, or thought she had. Surely they could spy on pay phones too? But at least with a pay phone some prospect of anonymity existed. If you were dumb enough to talk about bad stuff on your cell, you might as well put the cuffs on your own wrists and wait for them to come by and arrest you.

So she left her cell phone by the TV before emptying the nickels and dimes from the little milkmaid money box that she kept on the mantelpiece: her "treat fund," she called it, even though she was often forced to raid it for new clothing or shoes for the boy, he was growing so fast.

A thousand and two deaths.

She put all the coins in an old sock, secured

Daniel in the child seat in case of an accident—

A thousand and three.

Enough.

—and headed to the gas station, where there was a pay phone she could use. Rain was falling, and the wipers left streaks on the windshield. They needed to be replaced, but she didn't have the money for it, not this month, and she didn't want to ask her father, because he already gave her too much. Sometimes Holly suspected that her father kept working only because of her and Daniel, although he assured her that he enjoyed being out on the road. He claimed to double-clutch down hills even while sleeping in his own bed at home, and he used a truck logbook as a diary.

Her father was part of a subspecies with its own rules, and its own language. She'd grown up listening to him talk of the "chicken chokers," who moved animals, and the "suicide jockeys," with their loads of hazardous materials. But he was also different from so many of his kind, who drifted like tumbleweeds through life: no home, or not much of one beyond a mildewed apartment; no family, or none with whom they were in contact; no money, or none beyond what they could keep in their wallets; and no future, or none beyond the next job. Owen Weaver wasn't one of the wanderers, and if he valued the freedom of the road, he treasured his daughter and grandson more. Yet he still loved that damn rig, and the solitude of his cab, and the conversations at truck stops that always began with the same question: "Whatcha driving?"

But Owen Weaver was past sixty, and his back hurt like a bitch after nearly forty years behind the wheel of various semis. Holly supposed she could have sold the house that she and her son shared, and gone to live with her father next door, but the house was all she had, and pride prevented her from parting with it—pride, and the knowledge that much as she loved her father, and much as he cherished his daughter and Daniel, he wasn't a man to share his space easily. Two wives, one of them her own mother, could have attested to that.

Holly missed her mother. She'd died too soon, at thirty-five, and her father had remarried too soon in the aftermath, perhaps out of panic at being left alone to care for a young daughter. He'd realized the error of his ways quickly enough, as did his second wife. They'd parted amicably but irrevocably, and since then only a few women had shared Owen Weaver's bed, although none lingered. Until Holly left school, her father took only local haulage jobs, mostly managing to be home in time for dinner, and often before. Holly had always known her father would do anything for her, anything at all.

Even before the "Woman in the Woods," as the

newspapers and TV reports were already calling her—which gave Holly the creeps, because it was almost as though they'd read the story she'd written for Daniel, the one she should never have committed to paper.

She dialed Owen's number, put in the total required for three minutes, and listened as the phone rang at the other end, over and over, until her father's voice came on the line requesting that she leave a message; and she almost lost it then, wanted to scream and shout, but somehow she held it together for long enough to recite the pay phone number and ask him to call her back right away. She returned to the car because the rain was still falling and the wind had picked up, but she kept the window down and the radio off for fear of missing the phone ringing, even though Daniel complained about the cold, and the boredom. She snapped at him, and he began to cry, and she didn't want him to cry, not ever, and she didn't want him to be sad, not ever. All she wanted was for him to be happy, and to know he was loved, and to call her "Mom," always.

The phone started to ring. A man emerged from the restroom, and Holly caught him looking at the phone even as she stepped from the car. She waved at him to show that the call was for her, but she wished he could have just stayed in the damn can for a few seconds longer. She didn't want anyone to remember her face, or the make and license number of her car, or the child crying in the back seat. It was why she'd held herself apart for so long; why she lived in a little house out by the woods; why she didn't mix with the other mothers at Daniel's school; why she hadn't slept with a man since before Daniel's birth; why she was alone.

So she wouldn't be noticed, so she wouldn't have to answer any questions.

She picked up the phone.

"Holly?"

"Yes, it's me."

"What's wrong? What number is this?"

"It's a pay phone. Listen, I need you to come home, just as soon as you can."

"Why? Has something happened to you, to Daniel? Are you both okay? Are you hurt?"

"No, it's nothing like that. Please take a look at the local news up here. Can you do that?"

Holly knew that her father never went far without his iPad. It kept him company on his trips. He watched movies on it, read books, everything.

"Sure. I'll pull it up right now. I'm going to put you on speaker to free up my hands."

"I'll hold on."

Holly heard the sound of movement, followed moments later by what might have been an intake of breath, and the voice of a news anchor familiar to her from Channel 6 in Portland. It was the same report she'd watched barely two hours earlier. She let her father absorb it without interruption, until the segment ended, to be replaced with silence.

"You understand?" she said, at last.

"Yes."

"I'm scared."

"Don't be."

Holly looked at her car. She could see Daniel monitoring her through the windshield. He was no longer crying. He just seemed as though he were concentrating very hard on what he was witnessing in an effort to interpret it, the way he did when they played games of animal charades.

"I'm not going to let them take him from me," she said.

"Holly—"

"I'm telling you, that's all. It's not going to happen."

"It won't. I'll start for home first thing in the morning."

"Drive carefully."

"I will. And Holly?"

"Yes."

"Everything will be all right. What we did—"

Holly hung up. She didn't want him to say it aloud.

In case they were listening.

CHAPTER
XXIV

Parker's relationship with Detective Gordon Walsh of the Maine State Police was no longer as amicable as it once had been, in large part because Walsh believed Parker to have colluded in the killing of a man in the town of Boreas almost a year earlier.

This was not entirely true: Parker would have preferred if the man in question had lived, if only so he could have faced trial for his crimes, but circumstances dictated that Parker's preferences didn't much enter into it. The soon-to-be decedent had arrived with a gun, and every intention of using it to end Parker's life. This was a course of action to which Parker, not without some justification, had certain objections. As it turned out, Louis shared these objections, and had therefore been forced to put a rifle bullet in the man's head from long range before drifting back to New York in order to avoid any awkward questions that might otherwise have been directed at him. Meanwhile, the extent to which the victim had been lured into a trap remained a matter for moral philosophers—well, moral philosophers and Detective Gordon Walsh of the MSP's Major Crimes Unit.

So it was that Parker was not entirely unsurprised to see Walsh's face cloud as the policeman emerged from Ruski's on Danforth just as Sunday afternoon was fading into evening. It hadn't been difficult to find him: Ruski's was a popular spot for cops, both local and state, and Sunday afternoons often saw the creation of an informal bullpen at the bar, mostly to talk and let off steam, but also to facilitate the discreet exchange of information. Parker generally avoided Ruski's on Sundays—it wasn't the day or place for a private investigator to arrive seeking assistance—but he knew Walsh was one of the regulars, and buttonholing him on the street would save Parker a trip. Perhaps he also hoped that a couple of beers might have mellowed Walsh a little. If so, he was destined to be disappointed.

"Go away," said Walsh, as soon as Parker drew near.

"But you don't know why I'm here."

Walsh spoke as he walked, but Parker kept pace with him, which didn't seem to bring Walsh any obvious joy.

"I do know why you're here: it's because you want something. You always want something."

"Everybody always wants something."

"Who are you now, Plato?"

"I don't think that's Platonism, just reality."

"I get reality the other six days of the week. Sundays I keep for dreaming—and not talking to you, although I'm considering extending that prohibition to the rest of the week as well."

"Individual desire is inferior to the higher ideal."

"What?"

"I think *that* may be Plato. Or it could be Socrates. I'm no expert."

Walsh stopped.

"You're ruining my day by being philosophical. And also just by being."

"You work for a law enforcement agency that quotes Voltaire on its website."

This was true. "To the living we owe respect, to the dead we owe the truth" was the ethos of the MSP's Unsolved Homicide Unit, complemented by the motto *Semper memento.*

Always remember.

"Yeah?" said Walsh. "Well, I didn't put it there."

"Walsh," said Parker, quieter now, "just give me a few minutes."

Some of the air went out of the policeman.

"I need coffee," he said.

"Arabica?"

"Okay, but the one on Commercial."

It would mean that they were farther from Ruski's, and therefore less likely to encounter any of Walsh's cop buddies looking for a caffeine pick-me-up.

"I'll meet you there," said Parker.

"I can hardly wait."

Only a handful of tables were occupied when Parker arrived. It was an hour to closing, and most people with sense had headed home to avoid the forecast rain, just as Walsh had probably intended to do until he was waylaid by Parker. It looked as though it was going to be wet on and off for the rest of the week, but at least it would put paid to the last of the city's accumulated ice.

Walsh was seated at a table to the very rear, facing the front door but concealed by the gloom. Parker went to the counter, ordered an Americano for himself and, from memory, the sweetest, most calorific coffee on the menu for Walsh. To be safe, he also picked up enough packets of sugar to cause cane shares to rise.

Walsh had divested himself of his coat and was staring at it with an air of pained disappointment, as though he had hoped that by removing its physical burden he might also relieve himself of afflictions to which he could ascribe neither name nor form. Outside, the city continued its rapid acquiescence to dusk. In the time it had taken the two men to drive down to the waterfront and seek shelter, a combination of cloud and the hour had caused near darkness to fall.

"I hate winter," said Walsh. "Thank God it's over."

He added one sugar to his coffee, followed by two more, then took an experimental sip before bringing the total to five.

Parker gestured at the empty packets.

"If it's any consolation, you're unlikely to live to see another."

"Small pleasures. We take them where we can."

A young woman drifted by, trailing the scent of soap, and Walsh's nose rose like a hound to the hunt. Parker had heard whispers that Walsh's marriage was in trouble, and he and his wife were no longer living under the same roof. The news, though unsurprising, gave Parker no pleasure: guests at weddings involving police were well advised to skip the toasters or fryers and instead club together for a deposit on the services of a pair of good divorce attorneys. But Parker liked Walsh, even if a mutuality of feeling was no longer certain, and Walsh's wife seemed like a nice woman. Perhaps they'd pull through, but only if Walsh had sense enough to ignore the tickle in his pants.

"She's too young for you," said Parker, when it began to look as though Walsh might have become fatally distracted.

"She's too everything for me."

"Long as you know."

"You the voice of my conscience now?"

"I'm not even the voice of my own."

"Long as you know."

"Touché," said Parker.

"Your boys been around town?"

Parker guessed Walsh was referring to Angel and Louis.

"I don't think Louis would care much for being called 'boy.' "

"I'm sure he wouldn't take it personally."

"I'm sure he would."

"The question still stands."

Parker knew that Walsh was keeping a watchful eye on Angel and Louis, and had been ever since they first chose to spend part of each year in Portland.

"Not so much," said Parker. "Angel is ill."

"Really? What kind of ill?"

"The tumor kind."

Walsh, who until then had been doing his utmost to maintain a tone of barely veiled hostility, now moderated it.

"I'm sorry to hear that."

"So was he. Stage-two colon cancer. They caught it before it could spread to the lymph nodes, but not before it perforated the colon wall. Still, it was close. He'll need chemotherapy once he's recovered from the surgery, although he won't lose his hair. He was more worried about sacrificing what's left of it than he was a piece of his bowel."

"Jesus. Everybody's getting cancer. I don't recall it being like this in the past."

"It was always something. I think the world just keeps finding new ways to kill us."

"How is Louis taking it?"

"About as well as you'd expect."

"That bad, huh?"

"Still waters run deep."

"Cold, too."

"If you're trying to score points, maybe you should wait until he gets back to town, so you can do it to his face."

"Maybe I will. And you haven't answered my earlier question: Has he been up here lately?"

"Can I ask why you're interested?"

"No, but let me remind you that if you're looking for information—which I presume you are, because we're sitting here—then that road runs two ways."

Parker gave up. He couldn't see any percentage in obstruction.

"He was here last weekend."

"You meet him?"

"Yes."

"Where?"

"Various places."

"Any of them on Commercial?"

"I don't recall. And this doesn't seem like an exchange of information. I think the correct word is 'interrogation.'"

Walsh arranged the sugar packets, opened and unopened, into a pattern on the table: a swastika.

"Somebody blew up Billy Ocean's truck."

"Not everyone likes R and B."

"You think you're the first person to make that joke?"

"It's not even the first time I've made it."

"Yeah? How come?"

"Billy's old man tried to hire Moxie Castin to look into anyone who might have a personal grievance against his son, or an objection to how he chooses to express his political views, on account of how you flatfoots may not be up to the task."

"What did Moxie say?"

"Moxie's Jewish. What do you think Moxie said?"

"Moxie's Jewish?"

"I know. Even I was surprised."

Walsh swiped away the sugar-packet swastika.

"It takes someone of a very particular disposition to blow up a man's truck because he doesn't like his politics."

"From what I hear," said Parker, "Billy Ocean doesn't have any politics, or none worth the name. What Billy had was a truck decked with Confederate flags."

"All of which may be true, but blowing up his truck suggests a higher than usual level of intolerance."

"And driving around the northernmost state in the Union flying the flag of the Confederacy doesn't? Give me a break. I made some calls after I spoke with Moxie. The business in Freeport and Augusta with the Klan? Word is that someone saw two men in a truck like Billy's throwing objects into Freeport yards."

In January, residents in both areas had woken to find Klan flyers, wrapped in sandwich bags and weighted with stones, lying in their driveways. The flyers were advertising a KKK neighborhood watch service, and came with an 800 number for something called the Klanline.

"And two men who might, at a stretch, fit descriptions of you and Louis were seen drinking in an adjacent bar not long before Billy's truck exploded," said Walsh.

"Is that so? And were two men fitting our descriptions seen blowing it up?"

"No."

"Well, there you go."

"You have to admit it's a hell of a coincidence."

"What, a black guy and a white guy drinking together in a bar the night a racist's truck gets torched?"

"This is Maine," said Walsh. "There are black people here who can't make black friends. You may even be the only person I know who *has* a black friend."

"You ought to expand your horizons."

"Every time I do, I live to regret it, especially when it comes to men of your acquaintance."

Walsh had briefly drifted too close to Louis during the events in Boreas, believing he could exploit Louis's knowledge to advance the course of an investigation, and got his fingers burned because of it. Parker thought the experience might have exacerbated Walsh's natural tendency to brood on old hurts.

"I wish I could help you, but I can't," said Parker.

Parker was keeping his tone level, even amused, throughout. He wasn't about to rise to Walsh's bait, and Walsh knew it. Both men drank their coffee. By now they were the last people in Arabica.

"Then I guess the whole business is destined to remain unsolved," said Walsh.

"It could be for the best."

"Could be." The troubled look returned to Walsh's face. "You know, those flyers in drive-ways were likely just the work of a couple of troublemakers. Hell, we don't have any Klan here, not since Ralph Brewster was shown the door."

Ralph Brewster was a Portland state senator who ran as the Republican nominee for governor back in 1924, when the Klan claimed a statewide membership of 40,000, largely by stoking up anti-Catholic and anti-immigrant feeling. Brewster always denied he was a Klansman, but nobody believed him, and it didn't matter much either way since he supported the organization and accepted its endorsement in turn, which helped him to win the governorship in 1924. By the 1930s the Klan in Maine was a spent force, weakened by scandal and the general reluctance of Mainers to spend too much time hating one another. That situation had largely persisted until the present day.

"But?" said Parker.

Walsh scratched at his stubble. He looked ready for bed. Parker didn't know how many beers Walsh might have drunk, but he guessed it was somewhere between "too many" and "not enough." The coffee wasn't helping. Whatever was gnawing at him ran too deep for that.

"But," said Walsh, "it's like everybody's temperature has gone up a couple of degrees recently. Klan literature and arson attacks can only send them higher, and eventually they'll boil over so that someone gets hurt. Billy Ocean is an asshole, but so is the guy who blew up his truck. If you should happen to meet him, you can tell him I said that. If he has a problem with it, I'm sure he knows where to find me."

Parker nodded. He wasn't about to pass on the message, but he knew that what Walsh had said wasn't without substance.

"That's the end of the lesson," said Walsh. "So, what do you want to know?"

CHAPTER
XXV

Quayle sat in a comfortable chair by the window of his room, its walls decorated with landscape paintings of the state of New Hampshire, its floors the original nineteenth-century boards, polished to what he felt was just the wrong degree of brightness, its furniture either corresponding to the period of the inn's construction or, as in the case of the bed, an expensive reproduction, and wished that he were elsewhere. He did not belong in this country, and perhaps not even in this time. He belonged to an older dispensation; the New World was too loud for him, its colors too intense. Most of all, he despised its desperate desire for a history, an adolescent chasing after the earned gravitas of age. A store not far from the inn professed to sell antiques, yet—as far as Quayle could tell—its entire stock amounted to no more than a random accumulation of near-modern junk. To set it ablaze would have been a kindness.

The inn sat on land sheltered from the rest of the town by a line of evergreens, the gardens barely visible through dusk and rain. Quayle's reflection stared back at him from the glass, like a cameo set against dark ceramic, and in this he found his comfort. Quayle was a creature of candles and gaslight, a liminal dweller in fog and shadow, but the animus driving him was older still, the product of a primordial murk that predated the dawn of life itself. Quayle possessed no memory of himself as an infant, or child, or even as a youth. His eyes had been opened in early adulthood, his consciousness flowering into immediate awareness of his purpose on this earth: to locate a single book, and enable it to do its work. When that task was complete, Quayle would seek oblivion. He did not wish to live to see what followed. He had witnessed too much as things stood.

But perhaps this perception of a life extended almost beyond tolerance was merely a fantasy, a disorder of the mind; that, or the manifestation of a sense of mission passed down through generations of Quayles, like a recessive gene. After all, gravestones bore the Quayle name, urns stored Quayle ashes, and the earth hosted Quayle bones.

Or someone's name, someone's ashes, someone's bones.

Beyond the open window, silent lightning lit the sky like impotent bolts of rage from a deity woken too late to prevent its own destruction. Quayle smelled burning on the air, and the fine blond hairs on his fingers rose as he extended his right hand toward the heavens, crooking a finger as though beckoning the Old God to him, inviting Him to bare His throat so that His pain might at last be brought to an end.

Then we shall both sleep, Quayle thought, *and it will be for the best.*

Tomorrow his work would begin anew. Before she went into the ground, he had obtained from Esther Bachmeier the name of the woman in Maine into whose care Karis Lamb had been entrusted: Maela Lombardi. He had an address for Lombardi in Cape Elizabeth, and already knew something of her background. Lombardi was a retired high school teacher, but—in common with the unfortunate Dobey—did not appear to work directly with any charities or women's shelters. She was a secret helper, another point of connection on a carefully maintained series of ratlines designed to lead the vulnerable to safety.

Quayle and Mors had buried Bachmeier alive, although not before inflicting such damage on her that Quayle doubted she suffered long beneath the weight of dirt and stone. He had been quite certain that Dobey was not telling the truth about Karis Lamb's call from Maine, or was, at the very least, withholding valuable information. Bachmeier was required for corroboration, and had eventually given up Lombardi.

And just as Quayle had never intended to leave Bachmeier alive, despite any promises to the contrary made to Errol Dobey, so also was

Mors dispatched to take care of the waitresses who had seen Quayle's face. Unfortunately, a concatenation of difficulties had forced Quayle and Mors to leave Cadillac with that mission unfulfilled. It was troubling, but only mildly so. Quayle had already altered his appearance through the simple expedients of a lighter hair dye, new spectacles, and the removal of his colored contact lenses. He believed he could now have passed either of those waitresses unrecognized, and the chef, too, but if time permitted he might yet send Mors after them again, if only as retribution for Dobey's lies.

Quayle wondered briefly if the killing of Dobey, and Bachmeier's disappearance, might alert others to some potential threat to themselves. He thought not: fire was the great scourge of evidence, and Bachmeier's grave would not easily be discovered. Only when he and Mors killed Lombardi—as they would almost certainly be forced to do, once they obtained the information they wanted from her—would the link between the deaths start to become apparent.

But by then Quayle would know Karis Lamb's whereabouts, and the identity under which she was hiding. His priority was to ensure that she did not have time to run before he could lay hands on her. This hunt had already gone on for too long. It was a drain on resources, and had ultimately forced Quayle to cross the water to this furious land, requiring him to abandon his London fastness. He and Mors had taken precautions: they were traveling under perfectly legal Dutch passports, but with names that bore no relation to reality; their fingerprints had been created with the aid of printed circuit boards and liquid gelatin that mimicked the thermal responses of human skin, and a variation on the same technology had been used to alter their irises. Little could be done about the photographic records of their faces now in the possession of the Department of Homeland Security, but even here preparation had paid off: the facial prosthetics were simple, easily applied, and more easily disposed of. Just as Quayle now bore little resemblance to the man who had read poetry in Dobey's Diner, he and Mors were also shadows of the two people who had passed through U.S. Customs at Washington Dulles. When the time came for them to return to England, the prosthetics could be restored in a matter of hours. Yet travel was still unpleasant for Quayle, and only the most extreme of situations could have drawn him across the Atlantic itself.

But the book required it. Until it was restored, Quayle would not be allowed to rest.

And he was so very weary.

He closed his eyes, and saw himself assemble the final scattered leaves of the volume, this creation fractured by name and fractured by nature.

This Fractured Atlas.

CHAPTER
XXVI

For once, Parker was able to be entirely open with Walsh about a client and a case. It made for a pleasant change, although Walsh appeared reluctant to accept that all might be as straight-forward as it appeared—not that Parker could blame him, given the number of half-truths and lies by omission with which Walsh had been forced to deal over the years.

Walsh was currently operating out of MCU-South in Gray, while MCU-North in Bangor was leading the investigation into the remains of the woman in the woods. Nevertheless, little went on in Maine law enforcement of which Walsh, as one of its senior investigators, was not aware.

"So Moxie is employing you to look into this out of the goodness of his heart?" said Walsh.

"Something like that."

"We don't even know for sure that the woman was Jewish."

"Moxie is under the impression that a Star of David might have been carved nearby at about the same time she went into the ground."

"Moxie knows a lot more about this case than he

should. Those details haven't been released yet."

"Moxie has his ways."

"If I find out who's been leaking to him, I'll have them trawling truck-stop washrooms for drunks and perverts."

"At least they'll have Moxie to defend them. And this isn't a murder investigation yet, is it?"

"The woman didn't bury herself."

"That's true of most dead people. When do you go public with what you have?"

"When we're dealing in facts, not speculation. You might explain the distinction to Moxie, next time he decides to throw his weight around."

Parker leaned back from the table. Lightning flashed over the ferry terminal across the street. He waited for the sound of thunder, but none came. He knew it was out there nonetheless, but too remote to hear, like a conversation in a distant room. He associated such storms with summer, not the start of spring. The strangeness of the weather was unsettling.

"Why are you so sore?" he asked.

"Because no good ever comes of you involving yourself in an investigation," said Walsh. "Because I think you were close enough to Billy Ocean's truck when it blew that your eyebrows got singed. Because I believe you colluded in drawing a man to his death on a beach in Boreas. Take your pick. You don't like any of those reasons, I got plenty more."

"This isn't about your problems with me. It's about a buried woman and a missing child."

"Don't get self-righteous. I know exactly what this is about."

"Then what harm can come from sharing information?"

"Because you don't share, you just take. You've hidden so much over the years, you should own a vault."

"I'm trying to be straight with you now."

"Straight like a snake."

"That's just hurtful."

"You're like a stone in my shoe, but no matter how hard I shake it, I can't get the damn thing out."

"Is that your way of saying you wish you knew how to quit me?"

Walsh squinted at him.

"What the fuck is that from?"

"Brokeback Mountain."

"Jesus, just when I think it can't get any worse."

One of the baristas came over to inform them that the coffee shop was closing for the evening.

"Good," said Walsh.

Parker followed Walsh to the door, and walked alongside him until they neared their respective cars, each parked within sight of the other, with Walsh's closer to Arabica. Another fork of lightning fractured the sky, so bright and sudden that Parker could see Peaks Island silhouetted against it.

And still the rain fell.

"It doesn't feel like a killing," said Parker. "What kind of killer puts a woman in the ground, then takes the time to carve a marker?"

"No kind of killer at all." Walsh got in his car and tried to close the door, but Parker's body was in the way.

"I'm good at this," Parker said. "Throw me a bone."

"Goddamn you and Moxie. I swear, the two of you could cover vacations in hell itself." Parker thought Walsh might be about to cry from frustration, and he didn't want to make a grown man cry. "Look, Moxie is right: the woman gave birth shortly before she died, the carved star may be contemporaneous, but the anthropological examiner may have picked up something the ME missed."

When buried remains were discovered, it was routine to seek advice from the anthropologists at the University of Maine in Orono. They would also be brought in to assist with the search for the infant.

"Which is?"

"The anthropologist found damage to the placenta, and was just about able to detect corresponding trauma to what was left of the uterus."

"A consequence of the birth, or an inflicted injury?"

"It's called placental abruption, but I hadn't heard of it until yesterday. It means that the placenta partially separated from Jane Doe's uterus before the birth of her child. It probably happened suddenly, and it caused heavy bleeding. In a hospital situation, she'd have been given an emergency C-section, but she wasn't in a hospital: she was probably out in the woods, and she may have bled to death because of it."

"Which makes it less likely that the child survived."

"Not impossible, but cuts the odds in its favor: if it was deprived of oxygen for long enough, it could have been stillborn. We're going to start digging, see what we can find. Meanwhile, we're running what we have on the mother through state missing persons, as well as NCIC, NamUs, and the Center for Missing and Exploited Children, just in case."

The National Crime Information Center's Missing Person File had been in existence for over forty years, and contained FBI records for individuals reported missing under a variety of categories, but generally comprising those about whose safety there were reasonable concerns. But someone had to be sufficiently worried about a potential absentee to make a report to law enforcement, which didn't always happen, and there was also no binding requirement on other agencies to forward details of missing adults to the FBI's national systems, which was why some 40,000 bodies remained unidentified in the United States. NamUs, the National Missing and Unidentified Persons System, was designed to improve access to database information on missing persons, and to address the low rate of case reporting through the NCIC. Meanwhile, DNA samples from Jane Doe and the placental remains found with her would be forwarded to the Biometrics Team at the National Center for Missing and Exploited Children. The team would ensure that the DNA was searched against reference samples in CODIS, the Combined DNA Index System, in the hope of a possible match.

Parker thanked Walsh. He had confirmed what had been offered up by Moxie's source, and he now knew more about the circumstances of the birth. He might also have convinced Walsh of his bona fides where this case was concerned.

"I hope Moxie isn't paying you for progress," said Walsh. "It's a Jane Doe in a forest grave. But if you discover anything we can't, I may find it in my heart to be impressed."

"I'll hold you to that."

"You know, I never saw *Brokeback Mountain*."

"Gay cowboys."

"So I heard. On that subject, you see Angel, you pass on my best wishes."

"And Louis?"

"Tell him to take a Xanax."

Walsh drove away. The dark was deepening, and the next flash of lightning arced like fingers of energy over land and sea, as though to pluck ships from the ocean and the living and dead alike from their rest. This time, though, Parker heard it: the rumble of thunder, the approaching storm. He raised his collar against the rain, and willed the squall to seek some more distant landing.

CHAPTER
XXVII

Quayle must have slept, because when he opened his eyes the tones of the room had altered, and the shadows were not as they had been. The Pale Child was standing on the patterned rug by the end of the bed. It was naked and sexless, its chest flat and its head entirely bald, lending it a resemblance to an overgrown, unfinished doll. The Pale Child's joints were bent backward at the knee, like the hind legs of a horse, and its elbows were bent forward, as though the three points of articulation had once been broken and deliberately reset in a state of dislocation. The nails on its fingers and toes were yellow and twisted, and neither iris nor pupil was visible in the whiteness of its eyes. Instead a hollow remained at the center of each, so that if one were offered an appropriate angle, and a sufficiency of illumination, an examination of the interior of its skull might have been possible.

Quayle did not stir from his chair. He regarded the Pale Child as one might a moth that had flitted into one's room: a presence without any intrinsic novelty in and of itself, but a distraction nonetheless. The Pale Child opened and closed its mouth, and its head bobbed in a pecking motion. Now, to Quayle, it seemed more like a featherless bird, a fledgling fallen from its nest and seeking succor from one who had none to offer.

A soft knocking came on the door connecting Quayle's room to its neighbor.

"Come in," he said.

The door opened, and Pallida Mors was revealed. Like the Pale Child, Mors was naked, although Mors's proportions were entirely those of an adult woman. Her body was extraordinarily white, its mortuary expanse broken only by the faint tracery of veins revealed by the lamplight, like distant rivers cutting through snow, and the hairs at her pubis, the mere into which these tributaries might feed. A small circular gouge mark, previously concealed by white makeup, was now visible on her right cheek. The mark was recent, and deep—a souvenir of the failed attempt to dispose of one of Dobey's waitresses—but did not appear infected.

Mors could not see the Pale Child—her nature was not like Quayle's—but she had grown adept at sensing the presence of the chthonic, the seeping of pollutants from one reality into another. She paused on the border between their rooms, as though reluctant to risk an incursion into unknown realms.

"What is it?" she asked, and Quayle was

struck by the coarseness of her voice, a detuned instrument capable only of communicating the mundane and the ugly.

"A child. Or something like a child." His eyes flicked to Mors. "But it's gone now. You must have scared it away."

If any insult was intended, Mors chose to ignore it, or perhaps failed to recognize it entirely. Even after all their years together, the workings of her mind were often alien to Quayle. One might as well have tried to understand the thoughts of a spider or a wasp: a predatory, hungry organism.

"I'll return to my room, if you'd prefer," she said.

"No, you can stay."

She walked to his bed, climbed beneath the sheets, and watched as Quayle removed his clothing. His body was without reserves of fat, an assemblage of muscle, sinew, and bone that resembled less a living being than an anatomical illustration, like some creation of Vesalius or Albinus given only the thinnest of epidermal cloaks for concealment.

He came to her then, and she shivered at his touch, for he was so very cold. When he entered her, it was as though she were being penetrated by a shard of ice; and as she held him to her, she thought that her skin must surely adhere to his, so profound was his algor; and when they separated, sections of her dermal layer would remain fixed to his, leaving her to lie with redness exposed. As he came inside her, she felt his seed spread with an anesthetic chill, proceeding beyond the chasm of her sex into her belly and her chest, her arms and her legs, until finally it found the red glow of her consciousness and dulled it to yellow, then white, then—

Quayle removed himself from her and reclined against his pillow. Mors was already breathing deeply beside him, although the stink of her exhalations went unnoticed by him; Quayle had long since lost his senses of taste and smell, and ate only for sustenance, not pleasure, just as he took little sexual gratification from any congress with Mors. It was her warmth he desired, her energy in those moments permeating the ice and permafrost of his being to connect with whatever residual heat might yet reside in the tephra of the self. Coldness was the curse for living so long, if such prolonged agony could even be termed a life.

Quayle turned his head and looked to the corner of the room nearest the window, where the shadows were deepest. From them stepped the Pale Child, which had been present for all that had transpired, sucking in the sight of congress through the recesses of its sockets. It sniffed at the air of the room, and its musky residue of sex.

"When all is done," said Quayle, "and this world is altered, you can have her. You and your kind can have them all."

CHAPTER
XXVIII

The storm swept along the coast during the night, and woke Parker by rattling the slates on his roof and testing the security of his windows and doors, like a formless entity seeking passage to new territories. When he rose the next morning, his yard was littered with broken branches, and an old bird's nest lay strangely intact on his lawn, but the day was the warmest yet, and only occasional pockets of dirty white remained in the lee of trees. Parker wiped down one of the chairs on his porch, and breakfasted on cereal and coffee with his feet on the rail, the call of birdsong for his listening pleasure.

He felt the urge to speak with Sam, his daughter, but he knew she would be preparing for school, and he did not wish to interrupt her routine. He and Rachel, Sam's mother, were now in a state of uneasy truce. Rachel had suspended legal proceedings intended to leave Parker with only supervised access to his child, a consequence of his vocation and the violent proclivities of those with whom he came in contact. The disorder of his own life had bled into his daughter's existence, to the legitimate concern of her mother, and Rachel had believed herself to be left with no choice but to seek protection for Sam from the courts.

Then, almost as suddenly as the issue had arisen, it subsided again, with Rachel unwilling to offer any excuse for her change of heart. Parker was content to let sleeping dogs lie. It was enough to enjoy time with Sam without another adult intruding, to be there for her without precondition or regulation when she needed him, even if the depths of his daughter's nature remained as mysterious to him as the remotest of ocean chasms.

He sometimes woke to Sam's voice speaking to him in the night, as clearly as though she were standing beside him in the room. On those occasions he would wonder if, in missing her daily physical presence in his life, he might be creating imaginary discourses in his sleep as recompense for her absence. But sometimes when he was awake he heard her in conversation with another child, their words carried to him as an echo from Vermont, and Parker had no doubts about the identity of the second figure, because he had heard Sam speak her name in the past.

"Jennifer."

Sam and Jennifer: the living daughter speaking to the dead.

The world could grow no more curious, Parker felt, even as he found solace in the knowledge that in time he would close his eyes in this world and open them in another, and there Jennifer would be waiting for him, and she would lead him to her god.

It was 7:30 a.m. Parker washed his cup and bowl, got in his car, and drove to St. Maximilian Kolbe, where he arrived just in time for the start of morning mass. He took a seat at the back of the church, where he always felt most comfortable. He was not a regular attendee, but his childhood Catholicism had never left him and he still derived comfort from a place of worship. On this spring morning he allowed the liturgy to wash over him, the familiarity of its calls and responses itself a form of meditation, and he prayed for his children, the living and the dead; for his wife, now gone from him; for Rachel, whom he still loved; and for the anonymous woman in the woods, and the child to whom she had given birth at the end of her life, that, alive or dead, they might both be at peace.

Daniel Weaver heard the toy phone ringing just as he was leaving the house. On an ordinary day he would already have been at preschool, but he had a dental appointment on this particular morning and so had been permitted to sleep a little later than usual. His grandfather was waiting for him by the front door, as his mother couldn't afford to take time off work.

Daniel had sensed a certain new tension between his mother and grandfather since the latter's recent return, although he was unable to ascribe any particular cause to it. This fractiousness did not trouble him greatly because his mother and grandfather often needled each other, mostly in an unserious way but occasionally in a more grievous manner that might cause them to be at odds for days on end.

"Your grandfather is a stubborn man," his mother would offer by way of explanation, which Daniel found funny because, with only two words changed, it was exactly what his grandfather said about Daniel's mother. Daniel loved them both, though a dad would have been nice. "He went away, and then he died," was all his mother would ever tell Daniel about his father.

"Did he know about me?"

"No."

"Why?"

"Because he left before anyone was even aware that you were growing inside me."

"What was he like?"

"He was like you."

"Is that why you and I look so different?"

"Yes, I guess it is."

Now here was Daniel's grandfather instead, big and strong, with his long, prematurely white hair, tattoos on his arms—pictures and words, Daniel's name among them—and a piercing in his left ear. He wore faded denim jeans, big steel-toed boots, and a black coat that hung to the middle of his thighs. Nobody else's grandfather looked like Grandpa Owen. Daniel liked that about him. Grandpa Owen was cooler than any other grandpa, cooler even than most kids' fathers.

"You ready to go, scout?" said Grandpa Owen.

"Yes."

"That tooth hurt much?"

"A bit."

"Want me to take it out for you, save you a trip to the sawbones?"

"No."

"You sure? Only requires a piece of string. I tie one end to the tooth, the other to my rig, and— *bang!*—it'll all be over before you know it, and without an injection either."

"I don't think so."

"Your choice. I'd do it for ten bucks."

"Nope."

"How about we split it? Five for you, five for me."

"Nope."

"You're no fun. Say, is that a telephone I hear?"

"It's a toy one."

"Why is it ringing?"

Daniel shrugged.

"Dunno."

"Want to answer it before we leave?"

Grandpa Owen was joking, but Daniel didn't

take it that way. No, he most certainly did not want to answer it. He wanted the telephone to stop ringing. The lady named Karis was growing more insistent with every call. She kept asking Daniel to come find her. She wished for him to join her in the woods, but he didn't want to go. Karis frightened him. Daniel didn't have the vocabulary to explain why exactly, but he thought the closest word he could come up with was "hungry." Karis was hungry: not for food, but for something else. Company, maybe.

Him.

"If it's broken, you ought to get rid of it," said Grandpa Owen. "You don't want it waking you in the night."

I want to get rid of it, Daniel thought. *I'd really like that, but I'm scared. I'm afraid that if I throw it away, Karis will come to find out why I'm not answering.*

She'll come, and I'll see her face.

She'll take me into the forest.

And no one will ever be able to find me.

CHAPTER
XXIX

Parker left the church at the final blessing, trailed by the rest of a congregation consisting mostly of those older than himself. He hadn't managed to bring the average age down by much, just enough to make a statistical difference.

He decided not to go straight home but instead headed to the parking lot at Ferry Beach, where he left his car and walked on the sand, enjoying the solitude and the sound of breaking waves. He found himself returning to something Louis had said, about how the apartment seemed smaller, not larger, with Angel in the hospital. It might have appeared counterintuitive, but Parker thought he understood what Louis meant. Loneliness could cause walls to close in—that was certainly true—but the absence of a loved one brought with it a sense of greater restriction, of possibilities denied. Parker had lost two women under very different circumstances: the first, Susan, to blood and rage; and the second, Rachel, to the disintegration of their relationship. In the aftermath of each severing, he became aware of conversations he could no longer have, of questions that were answered by ghost cadences. Some words can only be spoken to those for whom we feel passionately and deeply, just as some silences can only be shared by lovers. It was one of the elements that made the thought of starting again so hard: that which was most missed could only come with time, and he had more days behind him than ahead.

Man, he really needed to get another dog.

Parker returned to his car, mentally arranging his current caseload in order of importance. It was Jane Doe, and the whereabouts of her child, that intrigued him. He planned to travel to Piscataquis and view the area of woodland in which the body had been discovered. He could always make a call to Walsh and ask him to smooth the way, or see if he could skate by on charm alone once he arrived. After all, a man could hope. He wanted to examine the site, not because he imagined he might spot something that the police had missed, but because it was necessary for his own process of engagement with the case, a delicate balance of distance and immersion.

As he neared home, he saw a truck parked by the entrance to his property. It was a Chevy Silverado, but a few years older than the one to which Louis had put paid, and, as far as Parker could tell, apparently unadorned by flags of the Confederacy. Parker turned into his driveway, and moments later the truck followed, maintaining a respectful distance but still leaving Parker uneasy about its presence and annoyed at the trespass upon his property. He wasn't armed, finding no good reason for carrying on his way to church. And despite Louis's advice to the contrary, he rarely kept a gun in his vehicle. If the car was stolen, and the gun was stored in the glove compartment, then he would have put another gun on the streets; and if he kept it in a locked box in the trunk, it wouldn't be much use to him if he needed it in a hurry.

He checked his rearview mirror. He could see only one figure—the driver, an older man—in the cab of the truck. The bed was uncovered and empty. Parker pulled up parallel to the house and waited. The truck came to a halt while it was still some distance away. The driver got out, his hands held out from his sides to show he was unarmed. He was in his sixties, and small but stocky. He looked like a man who had known hard physical labor in his time, and probably enjoyed most of it. His hair was entirely white, and cut in a military flattop, while the face beneath was ruddy and lined, weathered by decades of exposure to summer sun and cold winters. Parker recognized him, even before he introduced himself.

"Mr. Parker? My name is Bobby Stonehurst."

"I know who you are," said Parker.

Bobby Stonehurst—or Bobby Ocean, sire to

Billy, the country's northernmost Confederate. Silently, Parker cursed Louis and his inability to turn the other cheek, but his anger was only momentary. Parker wasn't a black man forced to deal with the prejudices of others on a daily basis. Neither was he himself any particular model of restraint.

"I apologize for entering your property without invitation or prior arrangement," said Stonehurst. "It was a spur-of-the-moment decision. I was hoping you might grant me the courtesy of a short conversation."

"About what, Mr. Stonehurst?"

"Nobody calls me Mr. Stonehurst. It's Bobby, or sometimes Bobby Ocean. That particular nomenclature appears to have stuck. Doesn't bother me."

"Why don't we keep it formal?"

Aside from the issue of the truck, Parker knew enough about Bobby Ocean to want to hold him at one remove. Bobby Ocean's businesses generally employed only white men and women, but were not above contracting the messiest and most unpleasant of their service tasks to companies known to exploit immigrant workers, thereby outsourcing vindictiveness and the humiliation of the vulnerable. People of color gave his restaurants a wide berth. Service at the bar would be slow and neglectful; unoccupied tables would be mysteriously unavailable to them, reserved for patrons who might never materialize; and a vague but undeniable aura of hostility would permeate their dining experience. But Bobby Ocean also contributed generously to select charities, and supported initiatives to beautify and improve the city of Portland. He found favor with many, as long as they were Caucasian, and comfortably off. People said he wasn't a bad guy, and shouldn't be judged on his failings alone. But to Parker, Bobby Ocean's deficiencies could not be isolated from the totality of the man: they represented the core of his being, and tainted all that he did. He was poisoned meat.

"You know, I didn't take you for a churchgoing man," said Bobby Ocean.

"Have you been following me, Mr. Stonehurst?"

"I saw you pull out earlier, when I first intended to speak with you, and we happened to take the same road. I didn't wish to disturb you on your way to worship. I figured you'd be back here soon enough." He sucked at some morsel caught between his teeth, and swallowed it upon its release. "Catholic, huh?"

"That's right."

Bobby Ocean shrugged. He took in Parker, his vehicle, his home, and probably his Catholicism, too, and managed not to look obviously disappointed by any of them, but it was a close-run thing.

"You live alone out here?"

"Yes."

"It's a big place for one man."

"You offering to help with the payments?"

"From what I hear, you're not hurting for money or influence. You mind if we sit down?"

"You know, I do."

"Have I given you cause for hostility toward me? If so, I don't recall it."

"Mr. Stonehurst, you have no reason to pay me a social visit, and if this relates to a business inquiry, my number is freely available. You can phone to make an appointment."

"You don't keep an office. I find that unusual."

"If I kept an office, I'd have to sit in it. There are more productive ways to spend my time. I consult with clients at their homes or places of employment. Where that isn't possible, we find mutually agreeable venues at which to meet. My house and the surrounding land, I like to consider private."

"Is that because someone once tried to kill you here?"

"Two people tried to kill me here."

"If you'll forgive me for saying so, I'm starting to see why."

Parker looked past Bobby Ocean to the marshes glittering in the morning sunlight, at the returning birds and the sea beyond. What had started out as a good if contemplative day was rapidly taking a turn for the worse.

"Actually, I may not be inclined to forgive you," said Parker. "Why are you here?"

"Are you aware that I approached Mr. Moxie Castin about an act of violence visited upon an item of my property?"

"Mr. Castin informed me. My understanding is that the property in question belonged to your son."

"My son's name might have been on the papers, but that truck was paid for with my money. It was a gift to my boy. I choose to take personally what was done to it."

"If what I hear is true, your son elected to decorate that truck with symbols of the Confederacy. Last time I checked, the Mason-Dixon Line was still about seven hundred miles south of here."

"And last time I looked, the First Amendment continued to guarantee freedom of expression."

"You might take the view that whoever blew up your son's truck was exercising a similar right."

"Don't be facetious, Mr. Parker. It ill becomes an intelligent man. I approached Mr. Castin about the incident because I believed the Portland PD was disinclined to give it the attention it deserved."

"And Mr. Castin declined to involve himself in your affairs, just as I will, if that's where this conversation is going."

Bobby Ocean ground his heel in the dirt of

Parker's yard, like a bull preparing to charge. He even dropped his head, but when he looked up again, he was grinning. It was the response of a man who believes his opponent has made an error, one that he now fully intends to exploit.

"I didn't expect Mr. Castin to oblige me. Mr. Castin is a Semite. In my experience, they are primarily a self-interested people. Since that hardly makes them unique among the races, their cupidity arouses no particular animosity in me, nor does it occasion surprise. But I do believe it runs deeper in them than in others, and such differences in racial character should be acknowledged."

"Mr. Stonehurst," said Parker, "I really would like you to remove yourself from my vicinity."

But Bobby Ocean showed no signs of departing.

"I think that first you ought to listen to what I have to say. I'll be gone from your presence soon enough, and then, if the Lord smiles on both of us, we won't have reason to talk again. I went to Mr. Castin forearmed with suspicions about the identity of those responsible for this act of violence, and his attitude confirmed them. I've learned a lot about you, Mr. Parker. I'm told you consort with Negroes, homosexuals, and similar individuals of low moral character. Your clients have included a homeless man. You got shot chasing after the killer of a whore. You believe yourself to be defending the meek against the powerful, but you're misguided, or guilty of deliberate self-delusion. You're a weak man, and therefore you resent men without similar weakness. You form allegiances with those most like you, and use them to fan the flames of your inadequacy. You fly flags of convenience to indulge your love of violence."

Bobby Ocean spoke without spleen or viciousness. He might just as easily have been commenting on the weather.

"You know, my grandfather fought in the Second World War," said Parker.

Bobby Ocean tilted his head in puzzlement.

"Were he still alive," said Bobby Ocean, "I'd thank him for his service, but I believe he's long gone from this world."

"He is. He's buried just up the road, at Black Point Cemetery. I filled in his grave myself."

"That's something to be proud of. I mean that in all sincerity."

Parker ignored him. He was unconcerned by Bobby Ocean's opinion of him, or what passed for sincerity in this man's world. He had the measure of him now.

"He never spoke much about what he saw over in Europe," Parker continued. "I do know that he served with the Ninety-ninth Infantry, and suffered a shrapnel injury to his left leg at the Battle of the Bulge. It was only after he died that I found out how hard the Ninety-ninth

164

fought. They were outnumbered five to one, and for every casualty they suffered, they inflicted eighteen on the Germans. But my grandfather wasn't the kind to boast about his use of a gun. What he did tell me was that he was one of the first men into Wereth, Belgium, in February 1945. Do you know what he found there?"

"I do not."

"He found the bodies of eleven African-American GIs who'd been captured by the First SS Panzer Division. They were beaten and tortured before being killed. One of them was a medic who died while bandaging another man's wounds. The Germans left them where they fell."

"I have to confess that the nature of your thought processes is confusing to me, Mr. Parker. I'm struggling to see the relevance of this."

"The relevance," said Parker, "is that the men my grandfather fought spoke of the weak just the way you do. The relevance is that they, like you, displayed only contempt for those who did not share their nature, or their creed, or the color of their skin. The relevance is that I can tell where your son gets his ignorance."

Bobby Ocean inhaled deeply. The grin was long gone.

"You and a Negro were seen drinking together within sight of my son's truck on the night it was destroyed," he said. "I believe that you and he were responsible for what occurred. You're a blind man, Mr. Parker. You live by the sea, but you can't spot the changing of the tides. The time of your kind is passing, and a new order of men will take your place. Go tell that to your Negroes and your queers."

He turned away, got in his truck, and backed slowly down Parker's drive before heading west. Parker watched the road until the truck disappeared, and wondered just how much worse his day might have been had he *not* gone to church.

CHAPTER

XXX

On reflection, Parker decided that it might be counterproductive, even unwise, to head out to the burial site without some form of permission to enter. He contacted Gordon Walsh, who didn't sound overjoyed to hear from him again, but didn't sound surprised either. Walsh agreed to make some calls, and Parker drove toward Piscataquis beneath clear blue skies, accompanied by *Here & Now* on Maine Public Radio. As he grew older, he preferred to listen to sensible conversation while he drove. Music he could choose for himself, or have selected for him by one of the half-dozen Sirius channels he favored, but he always learned something from exposure to NPR. Perhaps it was just a function of realizing, as the years went by, how little he really understood about very much at all.

Parker tried to exorcise Bobby Ocean from his mind, but the man's voice, appearance, and bigotry persisted in intruding, perhaps in part because Bobby Ocean, odious though he was, had a legitimate grievance, and the burning of his son's truck would serve only to harden him in his hatreds. As for Billy, he and Parker had never enjoyed any dealings, but Parker knew enough about him to be grateful for this.

The condition of the road deteriorated as he neared Piscataquis County, and he bounced most of the way from Dexter to Dover-Foxcroft, the blacktop pitted and broken, before continuing on toward Borestone Mountain. It wasn't difficult to spot the turnoff for the burial site. A couple of news vans were parked by the side of the road, along with a pair of Piscataquis County Sheriff's Office cruisers and one MSP cruiser, which was already pulling away as Parker arrived. Troop E out of Bangor worked Piscataquis and Penobscot Counties: fewer than thirty officers for a total area of almost eight thousand square miles, including the hundred-plus miles of interstate between Newport and Sherman. Much of that land fell under the jurisdiction of local law enforcement, but when it came to serious crime, the state police held the bag.

The news crews were kicking their heels; if no infant body emerged soon, the stations would reassign their resources to other stories. A reporter named Nina Aird, whom Parker knew as a face around town as well as on TV, was smoking a cigarette and flicking idly through her phone as he pulled up. Parker caught Aird glance casually at him once before looking more closely a second time and simultaneously signaling to her cameraman to get some footage, fast. The camera was already fixed on Parker by the time he gave his name to the first of the sheriff's deputies, and he knew the reporters would be waiting for him when he reappeared. Unless something more newsworthy transpired between now and deadline, his face would be on the evening news.

The deputy waved Parker through, and he continued driving up a rutted dirt road so narrow that the branches of the evergreens at either side met above his head. About a quarter of a mile along, he saw another, much larger conglomeration of cars and trucks, a mix of police, the Maine Warden Service, and civilian vehicles.

Parker had already begun making notes of individuals with whom he might need to talk while he was up here. One of them was Ken Hubbell, the local physician in Dover-Foxcroft who served as ME for the immediate area on a voluntary basis. Hubbell would have been among the first to visit the scene, and Parker thought it might be useful to get his impression of what had been uncovered, in addition to whatever could be gleaned from the police and wardens. For the present, though, it was the latter on whom he would have to concentrate.

A dead body found in remote woodland generated a lot of activity, especially when there was the possibility of another set of remains buried somewhere nearby. While a Piscataquis County deputy had responded to the initial call about human remains, the attorney general's office maintained a protocol for homicides and suspicious deaths, so the Piscataquis County Sheriff's Office had done the prudent thing and informed the Maine State Police of the discovery, followed by the Warden Service. Ken Hubbell had quickly arrived on behalf of the ME's office, and so the accretion of personnel had begun.

The MSP now had a dozen-strong evidence response team working the scene, alongside troopers, sheriff's deputies, staff from the ME's office, and the anthropological advisors and students from Orono; but anyone with any sense deferred to the wardens, who were the ones most familiar with the terrain and were responsible for organizing the search for the infant's body. That made for anything up to seventy people on the ground in total, as well as an assortment of cadaver dogs that Parker could already hear barking in the woods as he pulled up.

A state police sergeant approached him. The badge on his uniform read ALLEN, which Parker recalled as being one of the ten most common names in Maine. Apparently "Smith" was the most prevalent, although that was probably true of most of the other forty-nine states in the Union as well.

Parker got out of the car, and he and Allen

shook hands. Allen had responsibility for all those entering and leaving the scene, and it was easy to see why. He was about Parker's age, but had fifty pounds on him, and a foot in height. It was hard to picture the trooper fitting easily into a car that wasn't specially built.

"I hear you want to view the scene," said Allen.

"If it's okay with you."

"Detective Walsh gave the all clear—although he said that if you were to fall down a deep hole, none of us should be in any hurry to rescue you."

That Walsh. What a joker.

"I'll be sure to watch where I step," said Parker. "Anything else I should be aware of?"

"It's muddy as all hell in there, but at least you're wearing good boots. Other than that, it's the usual: stay inside the marked paths, and don't pick up or drop anything. I'd appreciate it if we could hold off for a few minutes, though, just until you meet Gilmore."

Lieutenant John Gilmore was the search coordinator for the Maine Warden Service. He was as highly regarded as they came.

"Don't want to cross the wardens," said Parker.

"Sure don't. Gilmore is dispatching search groups right now, but he's expecting you. We have coffee, if you want it."

Parker accepted the offer. It was noticeably colder out here, and the ice was more persistent and prevalent than on the coast. He went back to his car, found a pair of gloves on the floor behind the passenger seat, and slipped them on. Allen retrieved a thermos from his own vehicle, and poured two paper cups of black coffee. They talked about nothing much until Gilmore appeared from the woods, trailed by a couple of civilians carrying GPS devices. He was another big man, although rangier than Allen. He said something to the civilians that sent them on their way before heading over to where Parker and Allen were waiting. Standing between the two men made Parker feel like an adopted child, his awkwardness lessened only slightly by Allen wandering off to make some calls.

"I know the face," said Gilmore. "And the reputation."

"Likewise."

"You here to stir up trouble?"

"Only if you think it might help."

"I suspect we have enough to be getting along with."

Gilmore poured himself coffee while Parker explained the reason for his presence, just in case anything had become lost in translation. In return, Gilmore brought Parker up to date on the current status of the search. A cordon had been placed around the entire area after the initial discovery, following which the wardens had conducted a general examination of the landscape and eliminated those regions unsuited to the interment of a body, no matter how small, either for reasons of inaccessibility or unsuitability; the wardens couldn't guarantee where a body would be, but they could do the next best thing, which was to say where it wouldn't be. Meanwhile MASAR, the Maine Association for Search and Rescue, had begun seeking volunteers to look for the child's remains. This whole process had taken a week to organize, but it meant that the search would be conducted in the most efficient manner possible. Now teams of between two and four volunteers, each equipped with GPS and a dog, had commenced slow walks over carefully designated zones. As each zone was cleared, the GPS coordinates would be downloaded from the devices and the cleared areas marked on a map to ensure that nothing was missed, and time and energy were not wasted in the unnecessary repetition of tasks.

"If there's another body out there," said Gilmore, "we'll find it, eventually."

"How long until you're sure?" asked Parker.

"Weather permitting, could be another week."

Allen rejoined the conversation, and Gilmore cleared up one or two further details for Parker before returning to the more immediate business of checking in with the search teams, as well as finding somewhere discreet to take a leak.

And Parker followed Allen up the well-trodden trail to the grave.

CHAPTER
XXXI

Quayle had been following the news coverage of the woman's body found in the woods. Naturally it interested him, but he had few contacts in this part of the world, and none in law enforcement. It was possible that these were the remains of Karis Lamb, but they might equally be those of another young female. Until the identity of the victim was established with certainty, Quayle would continue hunting. Even if it were Karis in the ground, he would still need to find out who had put her there.

Quayle knew that Karis Lamb had been given Maela Lombardi's name as a source of help and shelter in Maine. Since Karis had already shown herself willing to entrust her safety to Dobey and Bachmeier, with no adverse outcome, Quayle considered it highly likely that she would have taken the next step and contacted Lombardi upon her arrival in the state.

Lombardi lived on Orchard Road in Cape Elizabeth, not far from the big Pond Cove Elementary School on Scott Dyer Road, at which she had taught for many years. Orchard was tree-lined, and all of the homes were well tended. Lombardi's was one of the smaller builds: little more than a cottage, Quayle thought, and not suitable as a family home. In fact, according to the plans that Quayle found online, it was just the kind of dwelling in which one might have expected to find a retired spinster schoolteacher: single story, with a double window at either side of the central front door; two bedrooms, one barely large enough to accommodate a twin bed, the other more substantial; a living room that flowed into the kitchen area; and one bathroom. It was set back slightly from the road, and shaded by mature shrubs and hedges. It didn't have a garage, and the driveway was empty. This didn't trouble Quayle. He had no intention of approaching Lombardi by day. Orchard didn't have street lighting, so by night the only illumination would come from porch lights and the interiors of the houses themselves. Getting to Lombardi without being seen would pose no particular difficulty, and once he and Mors were inside they would have plenty of time to spend with her. They would find out what they needed to know, and Lombardi could be made to disappear. Quayle would let Mors take care of that.

So they knew where Lombardi lived, but they also knew what she looked like. The old busybody had been photographed for the local papers upon her retirement, and her name and image also cropped up regularly in bulletins from the Cape Elizabeth Historical Preservation Society, the Education Foundation, the Friends of the Thomas Memorial Library, and the League of Women Voters. Quayle wondered why Lombardi had never married or had children of her own. He thought he might ask her before she died. He hoped she wouldn't give him some sentimental claptrap about all her students being her children. He wasn't sure he could bear it.

"Where do you want to go?" asked Mors. She was driving. She always drove because Quayle had never learned, and did not care to at this stage of his existence. He was especially grateful for her presence in this land of oversized vehicles, and it made him yearn once again for their business here to be done with so he could return to London: a city in which he could walk anywhere he needed to go, or slip into the comfort of a black cab, even join the masses on the Underground, although Quayle now rarely ventured far from the river.

"Away from people," he said.

"Do you want to return to the hotel?"

They were staying as husband and wife in a motel by the Maine Mall, under names that existed only on credit cards linked to temporary accounts, supported by whatever identification they elected to present.

"No. Find somewhere I can look at the sea."

Even as a creature of the city, Quayle found comfort in the rhythms of oceans, and the ebb and flow of tides.

In this world, at least.

"You know," he said, as the road unspooled behind them, "it is believed that salt calls to salt, and we respond to the sea because we came from it, but I don't think that's true."

"No?"

Mors's eyes did not leave the road, and she betrayed no real indication of interest—but then, she so rarely did. Her body might have retained some superficial warmth, but at her core Mors was even colder than Quayle. At best, she could just about rouse herself to a state of vague indifference.

"There is a greater ocean waiting in the next life, and into it all souls must flow."

"Even yours?"

Quayle glanced at her to see if she was trying to be funny, but she was not. Still, there was no denying the presence of a certain hard wit, and perhaps a glimmer of inquisitiveness. It was unusual for her to hear Quayle speak in this way.

"No, not mine. I'm referring to the commonality."

"Why not yours?"

"Because I have been promised oblivion."

"And what of me?"

"I think you'll enter the water. I think you'll face judgment."

Mors was silent. A gull stood on the white line ahead of them, picking at roadkill. She slowed to give it time to ascend.

"Does that concern you?" Quayle asked.

She turned to him, the car now almost at a halt. Her eyes were the peculiar gray of the scum found on certain ponds, the kind that even the thirstiest of animals prefer to skirt. Mors had been marked for him as a teenager, and nurtured by a succession of carefully selected foster parents until she was ready to come to him in young adulthood, when the welfare system no longer had any cause to pay cognizance to her. She was very good, perhaps the best of all those who had joined him over the years.

"I've told you before," she said. "You can choose to believe what you want, but I think there's nothing beyond this world. In the end, we'll all face oblivion."

"But what if you're wrong? And you are wrong."

"Then the next world can't be any worse than this one."

Quayle knew all about her past, of what had been done to her before she came under his protection. Her loyalty to him was deep and unconditional, but not unrelated to what his influence had enabled her to inflict upon her

178

abusers. Quayle had regarded it as part of her conditioning, and Mors was intelligent enough to recognize that by indulging her desire for revenge, she had made herself Quayle's creature. But for her, it was a price worth paying. Whatever torments she had suffered as a child, she returned tenfold on her tormentors, and all thanks to Quayle. He had brought her a kind of peace.

You're mistaken about this world, just as you are about the next, Quayle wanted to tell her, although he kept his counsel. Who was he to argue degrees of suffering with one who had already been through her own hell?

And you are damned.

The fallen tree responsible for exposing the grave site was gone. It had not been possible to bring a crane into woodland that might conceal another body for fear of causing a further collapse, or the destruction of any evidence that might remain under the topsoil, even after all this time. Instead the tree was cut into pieces with chain saws and hauled away, leaving only the wound on the ground caused by its upheaval, now protected by a tarp that hid it entirely from view.

This was peatland, with a degree of tree cover over nutrient-poor soil. Parker had spent his youth exploring such places with his grandfather, seeking out palm warblers and yellowthroats, and the larvae of elfin butterflies among the spruces. But the ground coverage here was pitted and uneven, and marked by patches of exposed earth. It was an alopecic landscape.

Parker placed a pair of blue polyethylene covers on his boots before stepping off the main trail and following Allen to the canopy over the grave. Allen unhooked the rope securing the main flap, and pulled it aside so Parker could view the interior.

"I'd prefer if you didn't step in," said Allen. "We've taken photos and video, and searched all around, but you know . . ."

Parker understood. For now, the scene was still active. Any kind of contamination had to be kept to a minimum, and Allen was already doing him a favor by being so cooperative. In any case, Parker didn't need to proceed. He could see all he needed from where he stood.

The collapse of the tree had left a massive circular gouge, since widened in the course of the search for further remains. The interior smelled of dampness and dirt, and a faint mustiness that might just have been stale air trapped by the canopy, but was probably something more mortal.

Just slightly off-center was the grave, the position of the body unmarked by tape or rods since forensic mapping was now done electronically, using the head and groin as markers. The hole was smaller than Parker had anticipated. The restricted volume of the space occupied by her for so long seemed to accentuate the poignancy of her passing, as though in death she had huddled until such time as she might be discovered. Parker squatted and clasped his hands between his legs, almost like one in prayer. Allen didn't disturb him by speaking, but stood back in silence.

Eventually Parker said, "I was just thinking how small she was."

"She was found with her legs folded up to her chest. Less of a hole to dig. But even allowing for that, she was still just a little thing."

Parker stepped away from the canopy, and waited for Allen to reseal it.

"Are you the same Allen who faced down Gillick and Audet outside Houlton back in—what was it, ninety-eight?"

Ryan Gillick and Bertrand Audet were, respectively, a serial rapist and a mid-ranking meth dealer who escaped from custody when they were transferred to Maine General following a gas leak at the old state prison in Thomaston. They headed for the Canadian border, armed with a pair of pistols picked up from an ex-girlfriend of Gillick's, presumably one of those he hadn't raped. At Houlton, just a few miles south of the border, Gillick and Audet rear-ended a truck, an incident that attracted the attention of a passing state trooper from the Houlton barracks. Audet panicked, and shots were fired. Gillick ended up dead, and Audet was now languishing in the new state prison at Warren.

"Ninety-nine," Allen corrected. "Yeah, that was me. Sounded more dramatic on the news than it was. I couldn't recall much about it when the AG's people came for my report. I just remembered being scared."

The attorney general retained exclusive jurisdiction for the investigation of police use of deadly force. It wasn't a pleasant experience for any officer, although in more than one hundred reviews of deadly force shootings conducted over almost thirty years, the AG's office had yet to recommend that criminal charges be filed against any officer in the state of Maine.

"I heard you took a bullet," said Parker.

"Nope, took a piece of masonry from a ricochet. Hit me in the small of the back. Still hurts if I sit for too long."

"The body does take such intrusions amiss."

"Figured you'd know."

"More than I care to."

Together they walked back to the trail, and Allen showed Parker the Star of David hacked into the gray-brown bark of a black spruce on the other side. It was an older tree, approaching fifty feet in height, its branches short and upturned at the ends. Beneath the star was another indentation, but less clear. It looked as though someone might have begun carving an inscription before obliterating the marks.

"And you're sure this was made at the same time that the body was buried?" said Parker.

"Only God can be that certain, but close enough, according to the forestry people."

"What about the tree that fell?"

"Probably of a similar age to this one. Most of this thicket is black or red spruce, with some larch. It dates back to the early seventies."

Furrows appeared in Allen's massive brow. It was like watching one of the faces on Mount Rushmore frown.

"What?" said Parker.

"It's easier to show than explain. Just odd, that's all. I'll point it out to you when we go through the data."

Parker watched one of the searchers rise from a kneeling position and stretch, her hand against her lower back. Beside her, a chocolate Labrador yanked at its leash, eager for the game to continue.

"Do you have an opinion on all this?"

"If anyone was asking," said Allen, "I'd tell them that if the child died at birth, it would probably have been buried with its mother. If someone was going to take the time to put her in the ground, and carve that star as a grave marker, why not do the same for the baby?"

"And if the child died later?"

"Then I'm not sure I'd risk digging up one perfectly good grave just to add a small corpse, wouldn't matter how sentimental I was feeling. I'd bury the child someplace else. You mind if I ask how you fit into all this? You looking for whoever laid her in the dirt?"

"I'm working for a lawyer. He's Jewish. He's concerned for the infant, living or dead. So I suppose I'm looking for the child."

"Mighty Christian of him. That's a joke, by the

way. And if you're looking for the child, and it isn't buried somewhere here, then it seems to me that you *are* looking for whoever interred that woman."

Allen let his gaze drift from the dig to the trees and beyond, taking in fields, towns, cities unseen.

"And her child could be anywhere," he added.

But Parker said nothing. Like Allen, his mind was roving farther than the dig.

Why here? he thought. *Why this place?*

"You want to look at the pictures now?" said Allen, which brought Parker back—back to the hole in the ground, and the smallness of the body it had once contained, of absence and loss delineated. He thought one word, but spoke its opposite.

"Yes," he said, "let's do that."

CHAPTER
XXXIII

Daniel Weaver sat on his couch at home, watching TV and feeling sorry for himself. His mother was concerned about his two bottom teeth, which had grown wiggly, and the two top front teeth, which were also a little loose, but the dentist told Grandpa Owen that it wasn't unusual for kids of even four to start losing their primaries, and there was no reason to worry about Daniel. The dentist did find some decay in one of his molars, though, and asked if Daniel enjoyed an appetite for sugary sodas and sweet things. Grandpa Owen had to admit that Daniel would eat sugar straight from the bowl given half a chance, and the boy had yet to discover a soda he didn't like.

"He doesn't get it from me," Grandpa Owen told the dentist. "I don't dote on candy."

"What about his mother?"

"She's like me. I know she takes sweetener in her coffee, but I believe that's as far as it goes with her."

Daniel was sitting in the dentist's chair while the conversation went back and forth, the words "cavity" and "filling" still ringing in his ears, because neither sounded good.

The dentist smiled. She was younger than Daniel's mom, and smelled of strawberries.

"It's okay," she said, "I'm not trying to blame anyone. It's just that we don't like seeing decay, especially not in a boy Daniel's age. So we'll fill in this cavity for now, and keep an eye on him in case it's a sign of a larger problem, but I'm hopeful it's not. Meanwhile, let's ditch the sodas and juices, and keep candy for a treat, okay?"

This time, her words were directed as much at Daniel as Grandpa Owen. Daniel nodded miserably. He really did like soda, and Baby Ruths, and Reese's Peanut Butter Cups, and—

Well, the list just went on and on.

"Will it hurt?" Daniel asked the dentist.

"Only a little pinch at the start to make your gums numb, but nothing that will trouble a tough guy like you."

The dentist had lied. The injection really stung, and Daniel was embarrassed to feel tears squeeze from his eyes. On the way home, Grandpa Owen described it as a life lesson.

"If someone tells you something's not gonna hurt, it's gonna hurt. If they tell you it's gonna hurt a little, it's gonna hurt a lot. The only time they're not lying is if they just tell you straight out that it's gonna hurt."

None of which made Daniel feel any better about the world.

Now, with his mouth beginning to return to

normality, he reckoned he could handle a big glass of Coke without depositing half of it over his chin and clothes. Except Grandpa Owen had poured all the soda down the sink, and taken an inventory of the candy supply before jamming most of it into the pockets of his coat, leaving only a couple of bars on the highest closet shelf, the one Daniel couldn't reach even with the aid of a chair.

This, Daniel decided, was a sucky day.

Grandpa Owen was snoozing in the armchair beside him. Grandpa Owen didn't like kids' cartoons any more than Grandpa Owen liked candy, and while Daniel could usually consume both with equal gusto, the images on the TV were irritating him today.

He was just getting to his feet when the toy telephone began to ring.

CHAPTER
XXXIV

They weren't the first such images Parker had viewed, and he did not believe they would be the last, but they subsequently stayed with him in a way that others had not, and it took him a while to understand why.

Gray: a body embryonic huddled in an earthen womb sacking, a bedsheet for its amniotic membrane; the left hand drawn up to the mouth, as though to stifle some final cry; the knees to the chest, the right arm mostly concealed beneath the body except for the fingers, outstretched and visible at the hip. Hair, what remained of it: long. Some skin yet adhering to the skull. The decay would have been more pronounced had she been interred in warmer weather, but a cold-ground burial had preserved her. Still recognizably a woman, the elements of a human being discarded.

But no, not quite a discarding. This is not simply a disposal of a thing unwanted, or a repudiation of criminal evidence. The inhumation feels if not reverent, then duteous. Some care has been taken here, or perhaps his perception

189

has been influenced by the marker, a stellate testament to the presence of the dead; a sign to commemorate, but not invite discovery.

To have spent so long out here: alone, waiting.

Were you sought? Did someone fear for you? Even now is there a father, a mother, a sibling hoping for your return? If you are not to be restored alive to these others, they have a right to know of your passing, so that misplaced hope, or fears of some ongoing torment of mind or flesh, may be brought to a close.

Who put you here in this dark wood? Was it a husband, a stranger? Did you suffer? If so, I am sorry. If I could, I would have saved you from it.

Why did you die? How did you die?

Who. Are. You?

I will try to put a name to you. You have spent too long unacknowledged.

And I will find your child.

It would require darkness for Parker to start to comprehend, and sleep for him to discover an answer. In his dream he would stand over the desiccated remains of the woman, her enfolded residue, and traverse a landscape of skin and bone until he came at last to the part that was both of her and of another, a reminder that something remained lost.

The peat had preserved so much: a little more acidity to the soil, a wrapping of moisture-trapping plastic instead of porous cotton, and only bones might have been left. But nature had conspired in the safeguarding of the body, and so there was tegument, hair, and fingernails. And something more: a tendril of tissue, with a withered oval of flesh at the end.

The placenta, and the umbilical cord.

This was not alone a woman.

This was a mother.

But that was all to come. For now Parker stood with Allen, and took in the photographs and video images contained in a file on the lawman's computer. Allen had offered to call in one of the evidence technicians to go through the information, but Parker didn't want to distract them from their work, and he was also pretty sure that Allen knew as much as anyone about the investigation. He would stay in touch with Walsh for the rest.

Parker was always astonished at how fast crime-scene technology progressed. In addition to the pictures and video images, a series of 360-degree scans of the grave site and its surroundings were available to view, so that at any point an officer could place him- or herself at the center of the scene. Allen told Parker that the MSP would soon be using drones for mapping, although up here their usefulness would be determined by the thickness of the canopy.

Parker knew that little of what he was seeing would be relevant, but it was important to accept any information offered. Finally, he reached the last of the detailed images of the body. What followed were pictures of the fallen tree, and the hole left by it, both with and without the remains. Some were merely close-ups of dirt, through which Parker began scanning quickly until Allen stopped him.

"You remember earlier, when I said there might be a problem?"

"What am I missing?" Parker asked.

Allen appeared almost embarrassed.

"It's going to sound weird."

"Believe me, you're preaching to the choir."

"First of all, there's no reason why that tree should have come down. It was healthy, and the ground was stable. But once it fell, it caused the additional disturbance on the slope that uncovered the remains. Then there's the way the dirt was dispersed in the aftermath, and the extent of the body revealed after the fall." Allen began flipping back and forth between images while Parker looked on. "It may turn up in the forensic report, because I know the anthropologists were puzzled by it."

"By what, exactly?" Parker was growing impatient.

"By the fact that the body was mostly visible when it was found, but the hole made by the tree, and the direction of soil shift, should only have revealed the torso, and nothing below the waist."

Parker considered what he was hearing.

"So you're saying that someone started digging up the remains before the police were informed?"

"This land is managed by a private company called Piscataquis Root and Branch. It's a family business, and it was two of the sons who found the body. They took photos of it on their cameras after they called us, just in case of further collapses, but they say they didn't touch it, and I believe them."

"If they didn't, who did?"

"We found no footprints in the dirt, and no signs of outside interference, but there was still dirt scattered beyond the grave."

"An animal?"

"Again, no tracks—and don't forget it rained that night, so the soil was damp."

Allen displayed a few more images before closing the file and putting the laptop away.

"Then what's the explanation?" Parker asked.

"I don't have one."

"What if we were just talking, and this was just a story?" said Parker.

"You mean what if I could make stuff up?"

"I believe 'speculate' sounds more professional."

"Well, if I was 'speculating' for a story, maybe one to scare my kids when we were all sitting around a campfire, I'd tell them that the tree didn't fall but was pushed up from below the ground, and whatever did it then began digging itself out of the dirt. And when it was done, it curled right back up again and waited for someone to come along and find it. But that would just be a story, and this is real life."

Parker allowed some seconds to pass before extending his right hand.

"Thank you for your time, and your help."

He and Allen shook.

"I have four children," said Allen. "Three girls, and the youngest, a boy. His name's Jake. He came as a surprise: the last shake of the bag. He's about to turn five. The next youngest has nearly a decade on him, and the older two are both at college. We love them all, but my wife, she dotes on Jake. I guess she'd resigned herself to never having another, yet there he is."

"Five years old," said Parker.

"Five years: the same age that child would be, if it survived. Just so you understand this wasn't only a matter of professional courtesy."

Parker nodded.

"Maybe I'll see you around."

"I'll be up here for the time being," said Allen. "Not getting shot at."

CHAPTER
XXXV

Mors followed the signs to the lighthouse at Cape Elizabeth, and parked the car by a rocky outcrop created by layers of quartzite fractured to a woodlike grain, as though the beacon stood above the remains of some petrified forest. She allowed Quayle to wander off alone, and alternately dozed and listened to classical music until the day began to die. Only then did she venture out after the lawyer, her coat gathered against the sharp wind from the sea. She found Quayle seated on a rock below a shuttered restaurant, staring out at the breaking waves, as immobile as a church gargoyle, like a feature of the rock itself. He had been seated in the same position for so long that she thought she could perceive crystals of salt on his skin and clothing. Unlike her, he showed no sign of being troubled by the elements, and he seemed barely to breathe. Had she put her hand to his breast, she knew she would have struggled to detect the beating of a heart.

"It's time," she said.

CHAPTER
XXXVI

Dr. Ken Hubbell looked like the kind of physician who turned up only in nostalgic Hollywood movies and television series about angels doing good deeds. He had white hair, and a long white mustache, and his office shelves were heavy with thank-you cards, children's drawings, and photographs of the good doctor himself, some of them clearly dating back decades, mostly in the company of a variety of small dogs. He spoke with Parker while drinking herbal tea from a World's Best Grandpa mug.

"I was first on the scene after the body was found," said Hubbell. "It was a damn miserable morning, I'll tell you that. I think I'm still feeling it in my bones."

He went through the initial examination with Parker, and his contemporaneous notes from the site, even making copies of the paperwork he'd forwarded to the ME's office in Augusta.

"Anything out of the ordinary?" Parker asked.

"Beyond a young mother in a shallow grave?"

"Beyond that."

Hubbell blew on his tea.

"You were a policeman, weren't you?" he said.

"A long time ago."

"But you could still tell the difference between a body that's been dumped and one that's been laid to rest?"

"Yes."

"Well, this woman was laid to rest: I guarantee it. I'd also be surprised if the ME finds any signs of external injury."

"External?"

Hubbell squinted at Parker over the rim of his spectacles.

"You need me to test your hearing for you?"

"No, I hear just fine. What about internal injuries?"

Hubbell's eyes remained fixed on Parker.

"Such as?"

"Damage to the uterus."

"Seems like your hearing is pretty good, if you can hear all the way to Orono."

"So it's true?"

Hubbell shrugged. "It'll be out there soon enough, so no harm in me confirming what you already know: the placenta tore itself prematurely from the wall of the uterus, leading to severe hemorrhaging, and death. There's not much an amateur can do for a woman who starts bleeding out in the deep woods."

"Could the child have survived?"

"Well, someone cut that umbilical cord with a

blade, so yes, it looks like it survived the birth. Whether it lasted for long is another matter."

A blade: it had not struck Parker to ask about the cutting of the cord. He was out of practice.

"And the discovery of the body?"

"What about it?"

"I've seen the photographs." Parker paused, trying to be careful in his phrasing. "I might have expected more earth on the remains."

"There was some shelter from the roots of the tree, but she was still exposed to wind and rain. No, I wasn't particularly concerned by that."

It was an interesting choice of words, and Parker picked up on it.

"What were you concerned by?" Parker asked.

Hubbell's fingers performed a little dance on his mug, like a pianist practicing scales.

"My first impression," he said, "was that the body might have been moved."

"Why?"

"Its position didn't quite match the depression in the earth around it. The arrangement wasn't perfect."

"You didn't mention that in your report."

"Because I was probably mistaken."

"Again, why?"

"If the remains had been moved, it would have resulted in serious damage: detachment of limbs, perforation of the skin. I saw no evidence of that. The most likely explanation is some settling of the soil, combined with the action of wind and rain."

But still an iota of doubt remained, as otherwise Hubbell wouldn't have mentioned the position of the body. Parker didn't pursue the subject. He had learned enough. He thanked the physician for his time, and paused by the photographs on the shelves.

"That's a lot of dogs."

"Twenty-seven, so far, and each as different as day from night. You have a dog?"

"Not any longer."

"You have a family?"

"A daughter. She lives with her mother in Vermont."

"So you live alone?"

"Yes."

"Get a dog. Keeps you alert, keeps you active, keeps you from getting lonely."

"Funny, I was just thinking about that earlier today."

"Well," said Hubbell, "I can't call it doctor's orders, but doctor's advice. And good luck with finding the child. I'd like to think that it's out there somewhere, alive. One has to hope, you know?"

"Yes," said Parker. "I know."

CHAPTER
XXXVII

Maela Lombardi sensed intrusion to her home as soon as she closed the front door behind her, as though all her furniture had been shifted slightly in her absence, and the wattage of the bulbs reduced. A smell of pickles invaded her nostrils, and beneath it an odor that was almost male, a stink she associated with teenage boys careless in both habit and hygiene. But before she could react, a cloth had been placed over her mouth and nose, and the pickle scent overwhelmed all else.

And Maela Lombardi succumbed to the dark.

CHAPTER
XXXVIII

Parker drove back to Scarborough in a silent car. He neither wanted nor needed the distraction of the radio. He desired only to think as the light faded around him and the dig was left behind.

Someone local had put the woman in the ground. The route to the burial site was not one to be taken by persons unfamiliar with the terrain. For a start it was too arduous: trees overhung the secondary road that led to the grave, so even in daylight it would be shadowy and difficult to navigate. In addition, someone "from away" could not be certain that the road did not lead to a cabin or camp, or cleave through territory favored by hunters and hikers, or monitored by foresters. And there was the ground itself: soft, easy to break. Spruce roots didn't run deep, and a cursory search, combined with a little knowledge of woodland, would have enabled the person digging to find a relatively clear spot.

Finally, some common sense had to come into play. Even the coldest of individuals would feel concern at driving any distance with a body concealed in the trunk of a car, or hidden in the bed of a truck. The aim would be to rid oneself of the remains as quickly as possible, which meant that no one unfamiliar with the land on which the body was found would have chosen it as a dumping ground. It was not just secluded; it was too secluded. No, only a local would have adjudged it appropriate for a secret burial.

Then what of the child? Assuming it was not interred near the mother—and Parker was increasingly tending toward the belief, shared by Allen and Hubbell, that its absence from the mother's grave offered some prospect for its survival—then whoever dug the hole was either still in possession of the child or knew where it was. This wasn't necessarily a positive development: there were men—women, too, but they were rarer—whose depravity could be fed by a baby. Either way, the mystery of the lost child was likely to be solved in the region. Someone from Piscataquis or its immediate environs knew its fate.

But it was possible that some fresh information might emerge as a result of the press conference scheduled for the following day, one the local news services would be encouraged to pitch to the nationals. The infant was the hook. The body of a woman found in the woods would not be enough to draw out-of-state interest, but add a narrative in which she was not simply another Jane Doe buried in a shallow grave (and what did it say about humankind, Parker thought, that this was not considered sufficiently worthy of attention?) but a new mother, one whose child was still missing, and the media would have a mystery.

What did appear certain, though, was that the anonymous woman was not from Maine. The state currently had fewer than thirty ongoing missing-persons cases being investigated by the Major Crimes Unit of the MSP, most of which involved males. Of the cases involving women, none fit the time frame or the age profile of the recovered body.

By the time the lights of Portland appeared in the distance, Parker had put together a plan of approach, but he knew he was likely to be either one step behind or ahead of the state police in everything he did, because they would be following the same investigative processes. For once, Parker was not in competition with law enforcement, or working to protect a client whose interests might not be best served by exposure to a police investigation. Yet neither did he feel entirely comfortable about taking Moxie Castin's money for a job that the police were qualified to do equally well, if not better.

He called Moxie and gave him a rundown on what he had learned so far, which wasn't much at all. But Parker did share his belief that the person responsible for burying the woman was native to Piscataquis County, although it didn't necessarily mean that he or she—or the child, if it still lived—remained in the area, or even the state.

"Do I detect a note of unhappiness?" Moxie asked.

"Call it a pang of conscience."

"Over what?"

"I get the feeling the police are on top of this one, which means I'm uncomfortable about taking money for walking the same ground."

"You'll never make a lawyer if you start having qualms."

"I'll try to hide the pain those words have caused me. Otherwise, I think we should see what comes out of tomorrow's press conference. If all the police get is an echo, we'll talk again. If we're operating on the assumption that the child is alive, I already have some thoughts on how to proceed, but it'll be time-consuming, and unpleasant."

Parker had made a call to Walsh on the way back to Portland. According to the detective, the investigators were probably going to wait for the completion of the search, and confirmation of the presence or absence of further remains, before taking the next step, which would involve a general approach to the state's medical professionals, and pediatricians in particular, seeking information on any unexpected postnatal consultations corresponding to the time of Jane Doe's death. It was possible that this might produce some leads, but the end result would still be as Parker had suggested.

"Because nobody wants a stranger knocking on their door and asking if their child is really blood to them?" said Moxie.

"That's it exactly."

"I appreciate your honesty, even if it means you're going to die poor. I'm not only paying you to look into this, but also to shadow the police. Bill me for a few hours each day, at least for now. I'd prefer you to stay on top of it."

"There is one other thing."

"Go on."

"I had a visit from Bobby Ocean."

"He's persistent."

"He's more than that. He seems to be of the opinion that I bear some responsibility for the destruction of his son's truck. He also referred to you as a 'Semite,' and in a tone that leads me to suspect he may not have been serious about putting business your way. He came to you because of me. Oh, and he doesn't care much for blacks and homosexuals either, although he didn't express it in precisely those terms. He suggested I tell the 'Negroes and queers' of my acquaintance that a new order was rising."

"The Negroes *and* queers of your acquaintance?" said Moxie. "At least you'll only have to make one call. So the son learned at his father's knee?"

"I may have indicated something along those lines to Bobby Ocean."

"I bet he took it under advisement. Fortunately for you, he's completely mistaken about your involvement in the immolation of the truck."

Moxie never conducted any conversation over a phone line that he wouldn't be unconcerned about hearing played back to him in a court of law or in a police interview room.

"He is, but I may have struggled to disabuse him of that notion."

"Then let him live with it. Bobby Ocean's not a criminal. Any retribution he might seek would probably be through legal channels. He's a bigot, but he's not a fool."

"Unlike his son."

"Which begs the question: Why wasn't Billy knocking on your door seeking restitution?"

"I don't think Billy's father has shared with him any misguided suspicions he might have."

"Because if he did, Billy might retaliate with an act of gross stupidity."

"Which could result in Billy ending up in jail, or getting hurt—or worse."

"And," said Moxie, "the kind of person who'd blow up a truck due to its Confederate-themed décor probably wouldn't appreciate the owner getting in his face over it."

Parker considered all possible outcomes from a confrontation between Louis and Billy Ocean.

"Actually," Parker replied, "he probably would."

CHAPTER
XXXIX

Billy Ocean hated folks calling him by that name. He hadn't always hated it. To begin with, he'd enjoyed having a nickname, especially after seeing those movies with George Clooney as the con artist Danny Ocean. His pleasure had only increased when it was pointed out to him that the Oceans' movies were based on an older film, one in which Frank Sinatra played Danny Ocean, and you didn't get much cooler than Sinatra in his Rat Pack prime.

The problem was that Billy's father had been given his nickname out of a kind of respect, even a little affection. He was Bobby Ocean, King of the Wharfs. He wasn't someone you wanted to cross, but he did his best not to screw over the workingman, not as long as the workingman was white—or if Bobby did screw him over, he made sure to hide his misdeeds behind a corporate entity that could be linked to him only by conjecture.

It was natural, then, that his son should inherit the Ocean moniker, just as he was destined someday to become Prince of the Piers, the heir to the empire. Except it hadn't worked out that way, because his father didn't trust Billy enough to make him privy to the important decisions, the ones that related to multimillion-dollar building projects, the endeavors that were changing the character of the city, stamping it with the identity of a man who had started out cleaning fish guts from market floors. Bobby Ocean had encouraged his son to learn about the family's various business interests from the bottom up, to earn the respect of the men who would ultimately contribute to his wealth by laboring alongside them, but Billy didn't have time for that kind of shit. Surely that was why his old man had slaved his ass off to begin with: so his son could ascend from a more elevated position, raising his father's legacy to greater heights because he wasn't mired in scales and fish heads.

But his father didn't see it that way. His father looked at Billy and could barely conceal his disappointment. Billy resembled a bargain-basement version of his old man: soft where the sire was muscular; dull-eyed where he was watchful; and conniving where he was clever. Billy was dumb and self-centered, but he wasn't so dumb and self-centered as to be unable to perceive his father's true feelings. It was just that he couldn't comprehend the reason for them.

So instead of sitting in on meetings with developers, or managing a couple of bars and fancy restaurants with a sideline in chasing tail, Billy was scrabbling in the dirt. He knew folks around town laughed at him behind his back— and sometimes, if they'd had enough to drink, right in his face, although they always pretended after that it was all in good fun. *We didn't mean anything by it,* they'd say. *We're just joshing with you. You're a good guy, Billy.* An arm would be thrown over his shoulders. Someone would sing a semi-mocking chorus of "When the Going Gets Tough, the Tough Get Going." (This was another thorn in Billy's side: he listened to a lot of rap music, because one thing the Negroes did well was rap, although maybe not as well as Eminem, who was the best as far as Billy was concerned, and blacker than black. But Billy didn't like having a nickname associated with a Negro. It wasn't right.) So the call would go up for another round of drinks, and Billy would smile and take it because it was to this his father had reduced him: the butt of a joke, a punch for stronger men.

And then to cap it all, someone had blown up his fucking truck.

Billy loved that truck. It was everything he'd dreamed it would be, but he'd barely grown familiar with its ways before someone reduced it to a smoking shell. To make matters worse, Billy was supposed to be paying the insurance monthly, but what with one thing and another, including certain liquidity issues, he'd let the payments lapse.

Man, was his father pissed when he heard that.

Which left Billy looking for clues in the aftermath of the arson attack, only to receive shrugs in return. He knew there was no shortage of resentment toward him and his father. In a city as small as Portland, a man like Bobby Ocean couldn't rise to a position of power without leaving wreckage in his wake, and some of the resulting anger would inevitably be deflected in his son's direction. But blowing up a truck was a big step to take. Scratching it with a key, maybe, or slashing its tires: after all, Billy had done such deeds and worse to the vehicles of others. Destroying a thing of beauty like his truck, though . . .

Well, that required a debased mind.

But over the last couple of days, Billy had come to suspect his father knew more about what might have occurred than he was willing to share with his son. This inkling was the result of a conversation with Dean Harper, who had worked on the boats with his father back in the day. Now, thanks to Bobby's loyalty to those who were loyal to him, Harper served as his driver, messenger, and general man-at-arms. Dean wasn't considered bright, but he was a lot smarter than he pretended to be, and there wasn't much that went on along the waterfront to which he was not privy.

Dean Harper's weakness was alcohol, although he was hardly unique around the piers in this respect. Yet Dean was more disciplined than most in his habits. Twice a month, starting on Friday night and ending early Sunday morning, Dean went on the kind of bender that would frighten demons back into hell, which had led to him being blacklisted by all of the city's better drinking establishments, and even some of the worse ones. Admittedly Dean enjoyed a golden period for about two hours on the Friday evening, when he was still only knocking back beers and hadn't yet transformed into the hulking, brooding figure that had once, in the depths of a particularly bleak drunk, tried to ram a cruise liner with a lobster boat. It was during the most recent of these mellow patches that Dean let slip to Billy something about a "shine" being in the bar shortly before Billy's truck went "the way of the *Hindenburg*," a reference Billy didn't get, but figured involved smoke and fire.

"I can't tell you nothin' more, Billy," Dean had added. "Your old man . . ."

Whereupon Dean's mood had suddenly darkened, and he'd wandered off to bust up a pool table, leaving Billy to pay the tab and think about what he'd just heard.

A shine, the flags on his truck: it all started to make sense now. A Negro had taken offense at Billy's choice of decoration, and the end result was the immolation of Billy's pride and joy. Billy didn't know a whole lot about history, but he recalled that brave men had died for his right to freedom of expression—which Billy chose to interpret as the right to be as offensive as he chose—and those fine individuals were not going to have sacrificed themselves in vain.

Billy didn't like to think of the coloreds as shines, or—much worse—niggers. His father didn't hold with that kind of language, and had passed this on to his son. Bobby Ocean took the view that only uncouth men used racially derogatory terms, so in public they were "blacks," and otherwise "Negroes." A man, said Bobby, could demean the Negroes all he liked—Latinos, Jews, and Arabs, too—but had to learn to temper his language in both public and private. It was important to appear reasonable, to disguise prejudice with plausibility. Be moderate in your speech, his father would say, so you can be radical in your actions.

Queers were different, though. As far as Bobby Ocean was concerned, you could call them what you liked.

Bobby Ocean fucking *hated* queers.

So Billy had stoked himself with some Dutch courage and gone to confront his father with this newfound knowledge gleaned from Dean Harper. The response hadn't even been a denial on his father's part, just a quietly spoken instruction to get the fuck back to his own apartment and never again mention that fucking truck in his father's presence. Dean Harper was also given his walking papers, having crossed the line drawn in the aftermath of the cruiser/lobster boat incident, which left Billy with even fewer friends in his father's circle than before.

A Negro, Billy thought.

A fucking Negro.

CHAPTER
XL

Maela Lombardi regained consciousness in her favorite armchair. It took her a while before she could manage to keep her eyes open, and her head throbbed with a nausea-inducing headache reminiscent of the worst migraines she'd ever suffered. She heard someone moan, and was briefly confused and irritated by the sound until she realized that she was the one making it.

A man was seated before her. He was reading from a small volume in his lap, and did not so much as glance up when Lombardi exhibited signs of wakefulness. She grasped the opportunity to examine him: his build, thin but not frail; his clothing, a mix of velvets and tweeds, finished off with a pair of sensible brown brogues; his face, handsome in a cold way, the eyes intelligent and curious, but entirely without warmth. A slim, elegant finger was raised over the page he was contemplating, as though he were silently taking issue with the author's words.

Maela tried to recall how she'd ended up in the chair. She remembered being uncomfortable in her own space, and a bad smell, or combination of smells, then nothing. She was *compos mentis* enough to realize she hadn't simply fallen or taken a turn, and therefore whoever was responsible for placing her in the armchair had not done so out of any great concern for her well-being.

She tested her arms and legs. They had not been secured in any way. She could, she supposed, have tried to make a break for freedom, but she didn't imagine that she'd get very far in her current state, which probably explained the absence of restraints; that, and the fact she was a small woman in her seventies with a bum hip and a bad back, which limited her options, even under the best of circumstances.

Which these, most assuredly, were not.

The man spoke, still without tearing himself from his book.

"What are you thinking?" he said.

Maela tried to speak, but her mouth was too dry. Movement came from behind her, and a woman's hand extended a glass of water. Maela made an effort to turn her head, but even this slight exertion caused her nausea to increase exponentially, and it was all she could do not to puke on the floor. She grasped the glass with both hands to drink from it. The water was mercifully cold, and had the effect of clearing some of the fog from her mind. Her eyes appraised more closely the face of the man in the chair. She decided she didn't care for him at all.

"I was thinking," she said, once she cleared her throat, "that some of the more educated Nazis probably resembled you. Not the hoodlums like Bormann or Röhm, but those who fancied themselves sophisticates: Heydrich, perhaps, or Eichmann—those who took pride in using the correct silverware."

The man smiled. It wasn't a false smile. He appeared genuinely amused.

"That's quite a statement from a woman at the mercy of strangers."

Maela finished her water, and set the glass on the small circular table to her right, where she kept the clicker for the TV alongside a bag of sea salt caramels from Len Libby's.

"I don't believe you have any mercy in you at all," she said.

"Oh, you'd be surprised."

Only now did he give her his full attention, and Maela experienced a sensation similar to the one she sometimes felt in great art galleries, when she stared at a face in a painting by an Old Master and discerned the amplitude of centuries.

"Are you Jewish?" he asked. "I'm wondering about your earlier analogy."

"My father was a Jew," said Maela. "He married a Gentile, so according to the Torah, I'm not Jewish, and I couldn't be even if I wished it."

"And do you wish it?"

"No."

"Why not?"

"My father was the only member of his family to survive the camps. He and my mother left just in time to avoid being rounded up."

"The rest must have been unlucky. My understanding is that a great many Italian Jews survived the Holocaust."

"And more than seven thousand died, so a great many didn't."

Her interlocutor conceded the point with a regretful inclination of his head.

"That kind of history," he said, "might cause some to embrace their heritage, not reject it."

"We live in a despicable world. I don't see any reason to give repellent men an excuse to hate me further."

"Why should they hate you at all?"

"In my experience, being a woman is usually enough."

The man stared past her to the unseen figure behind.

"I suspect my colleague might concur with that position."

"Was she the one who knocked me out?"

"She was."

"Then you'll understand if I could give a fuck about her opinion. What did she use on me?"

"Chloroform."

"It's nasty stuff."

"But not terminal."

"Does that come later?"

"It depends."

"On what?"

"The outcome of our dialogue."

"What's your name? I don't favor discourse amid anonymity."

"You can call me Quayle."

"No first name?"

"Not any longer. My turn at a question: Is it true that you help women in distress?"

"I won't deny it."

"Nor should you. It's a noble vocation."

"You're a patronizing individual, but I believe its endemic to your gender."

"I'm looking for someone who might have passed your way. Her name is Karis Lamb."

Maela Lombardi did not respond, either by word or alteration in expression.

Quayle pressed her. "Is the name familiar to you?"

"I can't say that it is."

The slap to the right side of her head was so forceful and vicious that Maela felt something tear in her neck, and when she tried to straighten up, the pain made her cry out. She tasted bile in her mouth, and suddenly she was puking on herself and the carpet, and was ashamed even though she had no cause to be. She began to cry, and she didn't want to cry, not in front of these people, not in front of anyone. She had spent her life trying to protect the vulnerable from the predatory. Women and children had found their way to safety through her. If the world were fair, then protection and safety would in turn have been offered to Maela in her time of need. But the world was not fair, because men ruled it.

The woman went to the kitchen and returned with a damp towel, which she used to wipe Maela's face and clean some of the filth from her sweater and skirt.

"Do you know how I acquired this volume?" Quayle asked, once Maela had recovered a little of her composure.

Maela squinted at the cover, and caught the name in the title: Marcus Aurelius. "I found it on Errol Dobey's shelves," Quayle continued, "just before my colleague punctured one of his eyes. Dobey then began speaking more freely, but he could just as easily have done so with both eyes intact. And because I was disappointed with him for making us resort to such savagery, we burned his book collection to ashes and consigned his body to the same flames. Finally, we paid a visit to his girlfriend, Esther Bachmeier, and took her for a ride. She died more unpleasantly than Dobey, and all because he couldn't answer a straight question. Am I making myself clear?"

"Yes."

"So: Karis Lamb."

"Karis Lamb is dead."

"How do you know?"

Maela spat a fragment of old food from her mouth.

"You ought to watch more TV."

CHAPTER
XLI

History echoes, history rhymes.

Parker's grandfather, who spent most of his adult life in the uniform of a Maine state trooper, had witnessed the immediate aftermath of life's dissolution in many forms: highway collisions; assaults leading to fatality; expirations in sleep, on the street, over dinner; hunting accidents; suicide; and murder. The old man gave long consideration to the actions of mortality, and the conclusion he reached was that the moment of a man's passing was not written at the time of his birth, and Death possessed no stratagem. Death was a being of expediency; it had no need to deviate excessively from its path to find quarry. Humanity drifted in and out of striking distance, and if Death missed its mark the first time, the dupe would eventually come around again, and Death would barely have to exert itself to strike the terminal blow. Death was patient. Death was inexhaustible.

But Death also liked patterns. Death had its own cadence.

And so it was that Jasper Allen, who had

faced down Gillick and Audet as they raced for the Canadian border, and welcomed a shard of masonry into his flesh for his troubles; Jasper Allen, who bore the name of his sire, and grand-sire, and great-grandsire, back to a Jasper Allen who fought at the siege of Fort St. George in December 1723, when the Abenaki surrounded the Thomaston stockade on Christmas Day and kept it under continuous assault for thirty days thereafter, only for that Jasper Allen, the first of his line, to lose his life a few months later, when the Abenaki trapped the whaling boats of Captain Winslow and Sergeant Harvey and butchered every white man they found; Jasper Allen—father, husband—who, after the birth of three daughters, had at last been gifted a son to whom he might pass on the eponym of his forebears; Jasper Allen, state trooper, heard Death's meter, and danced unconsciously to it.

Allen was barely fifteen minutes from home when he pulled over a Honda Civic Coupe that was tearing up the blacktop on the road to Lagrange. The two young men inside were Dale Putnam and Gary Newhouse, although this would not become known until much later, just as it would not be clear why events transpired as they did until all but one of those involved were dead. Putnam had an outstanding warrant for probation violation and theft by deception. This in itself would have been enough to land him back in the county jail had he and Newhouse not also been transporting four hundred bundles of heroin in the trunk of the Honda, each bundle consisting of ten bags. They'd managed to strike a good deal on the heroin down in New York: $30 per bundle, or $12,000 for the batch, which in Maine could be sold for at least $15 per bag. So in return for their initial outlay, Putnam and Newhouse were guaranteed to turn a profit of $48,000, of which they'd have to kick back $18,000 to the guy who had fronted them the money, leaving them with $15,000 each to reinvest in heroin. This they fully intended to do, because Maine was just one big vein waiting to be fed: Newhouse personally knew three guys who were using five hundred bags a week, ten bags per shot.

So what they did not need was for some Herman Munster motherfucker dressed in blue to pull them over because they were doing maybe ten miles above the limit, especially with Putnam—who was behind the wheel—also coming down from a meth high, and thus on the verge of tweaking. All of which went some way toward explaining why, as he handed over his license, Putnam saw fit to pull a Hi-Point C9 and shoot Jasper Allen through the underside of the jaw, killing him instantly. The two men then dumped the body in the bushes, and in an effort to sabotage the dashboard cam and the hard drive in the trunk, set fire to the cruiser before driving to the outskirts of Lincoln. There they hid the Honda in the garage of a run-down property that had been on the market for long enough to suggest it would never sell, and walked to a fast-food restaurant from which they called for a ride from their money man, to whom they initially decided to say nothing about the killing of a state trooper.

Putnam had been born on the same day as the late Ryan Gillick, and Newhouse came from the same town as Bertrand Audet. But again, these coincidences would only emerge over the days and weeks that followed. The immediate effect of Allen's death—other than to leave a woman widowed, and four children without a father—was to cause the cancellation of the press conference called for the following day, and the withdrawal of most of the MSP evidence team from the dig site.

And Death, insatiable, marched on.

CHAPTER
XLII

Quayle moved his chair closer to Maela Lombardi, so near that they might have spoken in whispers and still have been intelligible to each other. As with Errol Dobey, it lent the discourse a strange intimacy, one destined to be reinforced by the act with which it must inevitably conclude: the penetration to come, the yielding of the flesh to fatal invasion, that for now remained unacknowledged by both parties.

"You appear very certain it's Karis they've found," said Quayle.

"The timing is right," Maela replied. "And how many mothers of newborns do you think are buried out in those woods?"

"I couldn't possibly say. But you might be lying."

"Why would I do that?"

"To protect her."

"I think she was already long past protection by the time she came to me. She'd given up hope for herself. It was the baby she wanted to save."

"She told you this?"

"She didn't have to."

225

Quayle looked to the woman with him. Maela caught a hint of some private exchange, a silent understanding, and realized that her interpretation of the situation was flawed. This wasn't just about Karis, or the baby. But if not, then what else could it be?

"So Dobey and Bachmeier sent her to you?"

"By way of another staging post."

"Did they inform you she was coming?"

"Esther said she might be."

"What did they share with you of her predicament?"

"Nothing, except that Karis was in trouble, and was certain someone would be coming after her, someone bad."

"The father of the child?"

"That's what Esther assumed. Are you the father of the child?"

"No, I am not."

"But here you are. Therefore Esther's assumption was wrong."

Quayle shook a finger at her in what might have been mistaken for a good-natured warning.

"I fear you're playing semantic games. Perhaps you'd like Pallida to strike you again—or, in common with the late Errol Dobey, you're curious to find out what the world looks like when seen through one eye."

Maela took a deep breath.

"I want neither."

"Then give me straight answers. What did Karis tell you?"

"She told me that the father of the baby was an occultist, and an abuser of women and children. She said that what she'd taken from him would destroy him. Those were her exact words. She didn't elaborate, and I didn't press her on it."

"Why?"

"Because that wasn't my role. I was her guardian, however briefly, not her interrogator."

"You can't have guarded her very well if she ended up in a shallow grave."

Maela winced. The barb stuck, but it didn't take her long to shake off its sting. When she had done so, her gaze seemed keener than before, and she looked on Quayle more in disappointment than disgust, as once she might have regarded a schoolchild who used an inappropriate word in her presence.

"That was unworthy, even of you," she said.

"You don't know me well enough to make that judgment, yet I concede you may be right. I withdraw the remark. In return, you might try to explain how a young woman who came to you for help now lies in a morgue after many years in the ground."

"She wouldn't stay," said Maela. Her voice trembled, but on this occasion she was not ashamed to show emotion. It was no sign of weakness: she was right to feel sorrow for Karis and her lost child, and with this came guilt at her own failings. Maela had been unable to persuade Karis to remain with her. Two nights was as long as Karis would allow herself to rest. That was how scared she was of those who might come after her. Now, gazing upon this interloper in her home, Maela appreciated that Karis had been wise to be scared.

Because Maela decided that Quayle, either by nature or inclination, was not quite human.

"But you must have passed her along to someone else, just as Dobey and Bachmeier entrusted her to you."

"I gave her some names," Maela admitted. She wiped away a tear. "She was planning to go to Canada, and I had contacts in Quebec and New Brunswick."

"But not elsewhere in Maine?"

"No. She didn't want to tarry here."

Quayle took all this in, then turned to Mors. "Well?"

"I think we should blind her," said Mors.

"I think so, too."

"No!" The word emerged as a scream from Maela's throat, more like the cry of a bird than any mortal sound. "Please, I'm telling you the truth. I drove her to the bus station, and she bought tickets for three different destinations: Bangor, Montreal, and Fredericton, New Brunswick.

She then asked me to leave, so I wouldn't know which route she'd taken."

"Didn't she trust you to keep her secrets?"

"Not if faced with someone like you."

Quayle sat back in the chair. The volume of Marcus Aurelius had remained in his left hand throughout, and now he stroked it with the fingers of his right, like a kitten curled.

"You are a formidable woman, Ms. Lombardi," he said. "I really do admire you a great deal."

"But not enough to let me live," said Maela.

She could no longer tell if she was crying for Karis or herself, for both or for all: for every frightened, bruised, and tortured woman or girl who had ever come to her seeking help and consolation. And who would take her place after she was gone? There would always be too few people in this world who cared enough to put themselves at risk for the sake of strangers, and too many who sought to inflict pain on the familiar and nameless alike.

"No," said Quayle, "not enough for that."

"Then damn you both to hell."

"I'm sorry," said Quayle, even as Mors drifted from her perch to circle and descend. "But I promise it won't hurt."

And it did not.

CHAPTER
XLIII

Parker attended the funeral of Jasper Allen. The little Methodist chapel was so full that the mourners spilled out into the spring sunshine, and the service was broadcast to the assembly via a hurriedly arranged system of loudspeakers. Representatives from police departments in New England and beyond came to pay tribute, so Parker knew a lot of the faces. He spoke with some of those in attendance, including Gordon Walsh, but otherwise kept his distance. He had nothing to offer. He had met Allen only once, and liked him. That was all there was to it.

The service was simple: some hymns, a sermon, and a eulogy from the Colonel of the Maine State Police, who had known Allen personally. They had both grown up in Millinocket, only a year apart in age. Fatalities among Maine state troopers while on duty were rare; Parker thought they might amount to double figures, but just barely, and of those Allen was only the third or fourth to be killed by gunfire. Lawmen never became inured to the deaths of their own, even in the most violent of cities, but the shock was always greater in a state like Maine, which ranked among the lowest in the Union for rates of violent crime, generally slugging it out with Vermont for the honor.

Parker listened to the colonel's words, and watched a blackbird picking at a patch of damp soil in the shadow of the chapel. It was the first blackbird he'd seen that year. Typically they didn't return to the state until later in March, closely followed by turkey vultures, then the robins and sparrows in early April. To know birds was to know seasons; another aspect of life here that Parker had learned from his grandfather. The long winter silence of the woods, fields, and marshes was being broken by avian song at last.

The service ended. Parker did not linger, nor did he head to the cemetery. He didn't want to see Allen's weeping wife again, or stare upon his shocked children. He'd witnessed grief too often to wish to carry the burden of it without necessity, or indulge in any voyeuristic partaking in the misery of others.

The car used by Allen's killers had been found burned out the night before. Parker gleaned from Walsh that a witness—a woman named Letty Ouellette—had come forward to claim that her boyfriend had picked up two men on the evening of the shooting, not far from where the car was discovered, and brought them home. Both of the new arrivals appeared nervous, and she overheard a subsequent conversation about a gun, although she didn't pick up any further details because she was exiled upstairs to watch TV and mind her own business.

The boyfriend, who went by the extravagant name of Hebron Caldicott—Heb to his associates—made a living buying and selling used vehicles, and Ouellette thought the make and model of the burned-out car sounded similar to one that had, until recently, been taking up space in the lot adjoining their property. She had also indicated, albeit reluctantly, that Heb Caldicott subsidized his income from the motor industry by distributing OxyContin, crystal meth, and cocaine, and had recently expanded into heroin.

All this Ouellette elected to share with the police because Caldicott, with whom she'd been living for the past eight months, had suggested that she might like to sleep with "Dale," and maybe "Gary," too, in order to calm them down and keep them distracted while Caldicott went out to take care of some urgent business. When Ouellette responded that she had no intention of fucking two transients just to keep them occupied—or for any other reason—good old Heb Caldicott, who seemed pretty overwrought himself to Ouellette, punched her so hard that she briefly lost consciousness. When she came to, Caldicott informed her that she'd fuck whomever he told her to fuck, and she ought to start making herself pretty for his friends, because they were going to spend time with her whether she liked it or not. He then locked Ouellette in the bedroom, at which point she decided their relationship had come to its natural conclusion, and the best thing would be to climb out a window and seek accommodation elsewhere.

She spent the night with a girlfriend, and only when she heard about the shooting of a state trooper on one of the news shows did she begin to suspect a connection between this incident and Caldicott's recent arrivals. But it still took her a further twelve hours to contact police, her reluctance to do so not unrelated to Caldicott's narcotics business, of which she might not have been entirely unaware, her personal tastes extending to a little coke, she said, but only on weekends.

Even with her suspicions, Ouellette made efforts to reach Caldicott before approaching the police. She did this, she first told detectives, because she "wanted to be sure about every-thing before she got Heb in any trouble," although she later admitted that she had been prepared to forgive Caldicott for their earlier misunderstanding involving assault and the threat of rape, because he had never hit her before and was pretty generous with the coke. Unfortunately, when she returned to their shared abode Caldicott was gone, along with his two buddies, the stash of coke, and $383 that Ouellette kept in an empty

Humpty Dumpty potato chip bag taped under her bedside table. It was this final betrayal that caused Ouellette definitively to abandon all hopes of reconciliation with Heb Caldicott, and instead hang him out to dry for whatever he might or might not have done, along with his shitweasel buddies, their families, their children born and yet unborn, and their dogs.

It hadn't taken long for the police to connect Caldicott to one Dale Putnam and his buddy, Gary Newhouse. Soon law enforcement agencies across New England, along with their Canadian colleagues over the border, would be scouring the territories for them, and their pictures would be peering out from newspapers and TV screens throughout the Northeast.

Which left only a succession of disgruntled Piscataquis County sheriff's deputies to monitor the burial site and complain about being left out of the action.

CHAPTER
XLIV

Guarding an empty hole in the ground was not, Deputy Renee Kellett had to admit, the most onerous of tasks, but it was among the dullest. Mostly she listened to music on her cell phone, and studied her coursework. Kellett had just completed her associate's degree in criminal justice, and was now progressing toward a bachelor's in public safety administration. She enjoyed working for the sheriff's department, but her ambition was to move to a federal agency, and she had no hope of achieving this without a degree.

So on one hand she was earning some much-needed overtime by sitting in her car and moving along the occasional hunter or looky-loo who strayed too close to the dig site, while also effectively being paid to study. On the other hand, the kind of manhunt currently taking place for Putnam, Newhouse, and their buddy Caldicott was rare in this state, and brought with it a buzz of purpose and excitement that was noticeably absent at this particular patch of woodland.

This was Kellett's second shift on grave patrol,

and she was hoping it might be the last; there was only so much reading and listening in solitude that a person could undertake before her mind began to wander—and in Kellett's experience, it never wandered anywhere good under such conditions as these. Maybe an artist or a writer could find inspiration in them, but she was neither, so instead of picturing great paintings, or planning prizewinning books, she fretted about how her mom was starting to misremember stuff, or forget things entirely; how, with her dad gone, she'd be left to take care of her mom unaided because her older brother wasn't worth a nickel on the dollar when it came to helping anyone other than himself; how that might impact on her plans to progress to Homeland Security or— yeah, dream on—the FBI; and why, although she was an attractive woman without any complexes or peculiarities beyond the norm, she was experiencing a dustbowl level of drought in her sex life.

Still, she performed with diligence her duties at the gravesite. At least once every hour, if only to stretch her legs, she walked the trail to make sure the canopy remained secure, because a wind had come down from the north that was strong enough to rock her car on its suspension, and if it could do that, it could also pick up a sheet of canvas and blast it toward Florida. It wasn't raining, though, which was some small consolation. This place was gloomy enough as it was, with or without a grave.

Kellett had been one of the first on the scene when the body was initially discovered. She'd never seen remains in that state before. Like all police, she'd looked on her share of the dead, but she had not previously encountered a body buried in the ground for so long yet still in a state of some preservation. The sight should have reminded her of old horror movies, creeping her out, but instead she felt only a crushing sadness that she had not yet been able to shake off entirely, although spending long hours alone by a burial pit probably wasn't helping any.

Neither was the possibility that an infant child might also be interred in the vicinity, although Kellett was beginning to believe this wasn't very likely, and she got the sense that those in command were thinking the same way. The wardens had almost concluded their search of the area, with no result. If the baby had died along with, or soon after, the mother, it stood to reason that it would have been buried with her. Kellett could have told them that to begin with.

The wind picked up, and a noise intruded on her musings: the flapping of a tarp. It sounded like the big one over the grave. She'd already been forced to deal with it once, but she'd never claimed to be an expert on knots, and it looked as though this deficiency was coming back to haunt her. At least it was still light the first time she'd tackled the rope, but dusk had descended since then, and now she'd be forced to deal with it by flashlight.

She climbed from the car, and the first drop of rain hit her on the crown of the head with the force of a thrown coin.

"Oh, for crying out loud."

It wasn't even supposed to rain. Stupid meteorologists—and how many of them were actual meteorologists anyway? Most of them were just weathermen, for Pete's sake. If they had any qualification at all, it lay in being Well Turned Out Before Breakfast.

Kellett grabbed her hat and secured it under her chin, shrugged on her raincoat, and headed into the woods. The trees offered some shelter, but the ferocity of the downpour meant that branches could only do so much. Within a minute the trail, treacherous even when dry, had turned positively lethal. Kellett tried to watch her step, but vigilance could only take a woman so far: she slipped as the tarp came in sight, and went down hard on her right knee. The fall didn't hurt, but it left her trouser leg filthy and soaked. She tested it for any tears and found none, which was a relief; it was too early in the year to begin eating into her uniform allowance.

Kellett looked to her right. Even without the aid of her flashlight, she could see the tarp waving in the wind. She didn't rush to get to it, fearful of slipping again. After all, it wasn't as though any evidence remained to be retrieved from the hole. The decision to keep it covered arose as much from a residual respect for the body it had once contained as it did from a desire to do everything by the book.

She reached the site. The knot she had tied earlier had come undone. She grabbed the guy rope, but the wind yanked it from her hand and the end lashed her cheek. Kellett rarely swore—she regarded it as a sign of poor breeding—but she came pretty close to uttering the first syllable of the f-bomb when the rope caught her.

"Give me a break, huh?" She wasn't sure whom she was addressing: God, maybe, assuming He wasn't too busy trying to separate folk intent upon beheading one another in His name. Then again, God seemed to have enough free time on His hands to help football players score touchdowns, and hillbillies win the lottery, so why not allocate a few of those spare seconds to not making her life any harder than it was? God, Kellett sometimes thought, needed to get His priorities straight.

She was just fixing her grip on the rope when she froze. She had neither seen nor heard anything untoward, yet was conscious of the rapid beating of her heart, the tensing of the muscles in her legs, and the piloerection reflex as the tiny muscles at the base of each hair follicle contracted, covering her with goose bumps.

Fear, unlike any she had ever experienced before.

Kellett released the rope and reached for her gun, crossing her right hand over her left so beam and weapon moved in unison. As she did so, she retreated to the cover of the spruce nearest the hole, conscious that the flashlight made her an easier target if she remained in the open.

"Sheriff's deputy," she shouted. "This area is restricted. You're trespassing on a crime scene."

Kellett listened but received no response, only the sound of rain falling on leaf, branch, and dirt. She drew a deep breath, and tried to determine the source of the threat. She was facing back down the trail toward her vehicle, and could see no activity in that direction. She was relying entirely on atavistic instinct by now, but her best guess was that whatever had spooked her was to the south or west of her position, because it had been behind her when she was dealing with the guy line.

She risked a look around the trunk of the tree and saw a figure clearly silhouetted between two trees, on a rise to the south of the site. Despite the bulk of its outdoor clothing, and the distance involved, Kellett was certain she was looking at a woman. Then, seconds later, the figure turned and was gone.

Kellett released a breath. Just a rubbernecker. No one worth chasing. She'd make a note of it in her log, and warn Mel Wight when he arrived to relieve her, just so he'd know to keep an eye out.

She was putting her gun back in its holster when she heard a wet, sliding sound from behind, followed by a splash as something landed in the mud and water at the base of the grave. Only then did she notice her goose bumps had not disappeared, and her heartbeat had not slowed. She drew the gun again, and quietly shifted position, stepping softly around the tree until the grave site was revealed to her.

The canvas continued to flap, and the rain fell, so her view of what lay beneath was partial and restricted. But she could detect movement in the dirt, as though some large animal were digging in an effort to conceal itself from the approach of a predator.

Flap.

And she could feel its fear, because it was so much like her own, and discern its shape, because that also resembled hers. It lay curled in the depression left by the body of the dead woman, and although the dimensions had been altered by the removal of the remains and the subsequent search for the child, still it seemed to fit the cavity with ease.

Flap.

And now it appeared to become aware of a threat

more imminent than the one from which it had fled, and as it turned its face toward Kellett she discerned the rot of it, and the hollow concavities of its eyes, and its belly, both distended yet withered, and all it was and all it might once have been. Yet it was not a thing composed entirely of bone and old skin: Kellett saw wood and ivy, twigs and small animal bones, as though it had been forced to scavenge to complete itself. It opened its mouth as a beast might in order to shriek an alarm or growl a warning.

Flap.

And then it was moving again, digging deeper into the bank, exposing a hole either recently made or previously unknown, and into this it dragged itself, its body contorting with serpentine paroxysms, until all that remained visible was the sole of a foot, a spur of bone exposed at the heel, before this, too, was gone, and the mud and dirt slid down to fill the gap behind, so it was as if it had never been, its presence in this world no more than the conjuring of an unquiet mind, even as the consciousness that had imagined it, Kellett's own, grew dim, and she fell back against the tree and let it support her as she dropped to the ground, where she sat, conscious yet unseeing, until the arrival of Mel Wight's vehicle summoned her from her stupor, and she descended to meet him, but said nothing, beyond a distant figure glimpsed, of what she had witnessed.

CHAPTER
XLV

The birth rate in Maine had been falling consistently over the previous decade, which still left Parker with almost 13,000 registered live births for the year in which the woman in the woods had died. In the quiet of his home office, he opened a map of Piscataquis in his *Maine Atlas and Gazetteer*, marked the location of the grave site, then placed the point of a compass on the dot and drew a circle with a generous radius of approximately fifteen miles. The circle did not break the borders of the county.

If he was correct in his assumption of local knowledge—and it seemed reasonable to begin with that and expand the search only if necessary—then he was now looking at just 160 registered births during the year in question. This could be narrowed still further, Parker believed, thanks to his visit to the grave: the body had been buried three feet below ground, which was a considerable depth, and suggested someone operating with little fear of being disturbed. But digging a hole of that size and draft would be difficult during the deepest winter months as the ground would just be too hard, so he could probably exclude children registered in January, and maybe even late December. He was tempted to exclude February, too, but decided to err on the side of caution: ground cold enough to preserve a body, then, yet not so cold as to be unworkable.

But in addition to births, more than two hundred legal adoptions of children were processed through the public child welfare agency in Maine for the same period, and many more using licensed private agencies. With the birth rate as a gauge, this meant registered legal adoptions in Piscataquis County probably didn't amount to more than a handful, and he could rule out any children whose age at adoption was outside his parameters.

All of which presupposed that the person responsible for burying the mother had chosen to hide his or her tracks either by registering the birth under another woman's name, or had come up with a story convincing enough to result in a formal adoption. Neither, Parker knew, would have been particularly difficult, but he decided to examine the simpler of the two options first, which was to register the birth.

Under the state's revised statutes, one of four individuals was required to prepare and file a certificate for a birth occurring outside a hospital or institution: a physician or other person in attendance at the birth; the father; the mother; or the person in charge of the premises where the live birth took place, which could be anyone from a hotel proprietor to the guy who ran the local gas station. If the mother was not married at either conception or birth, the details of the putative father could not be entered on the certificate without both his written consent and that of the mother.

In other words, there was little to stop a woman turning up with a child in her arms and filing a birth certificate with the clerk of the municipality—unless, of course, the woman was known to the clerk personally, in which case questions might be asked about the sudden appearance of an unexpected child. But Piscataquis, at more than four thousand square miles, was the second-largest county in the state, and also the most sparsely populated, with about 17,000 people residing within its borders, a lot of them existing below the poverty line. Those kinds of statistics were conducive to isolation, and places like Piscataquis, and farther north, Aroostook, tended to attract the kind of folks who preferred to be left to their own devices, by and large. This did not make Parker's task any easier.

The Division of Public Health Systems in Augusta retained most of the information he required. Parker considered taking a trip north the following day, to see what he could discover.

He also went through his Rolodex and found the name of a contact at the Maine Town and City Clerks' Association, which had more than seven hundred members across the state, one of whom might well have unwittingly registered the birth of the dead woman's child. But he'd hold off on asking for a favor until he'd scoured the vital records available to him in Augusta.

By then his back and sides ached from sitting for too long—a legacy of his gunshot wounds—and his eyes were watering. He knew that his eyesight was getting worse, but he didn't want to go back to his optometrist for a new prescription. He had somehow managed to convince himself that he required spectacles only for reading and looking at screens, and could get away with not wearing them all the time. He remembered discussing the problem with Angel, who had been noticeably unsympathetic.

"Vanity," was Angel's conclusion.

"It's not vanity. It's a matter of practicality."

"You tell yourself that. The rest of us will go for answer A: you're too vain to admit you need them. I bet you color your hair, too."

"If I was coloring my hair, I'd opt for something other than gray."

"Maybe you're being sneaky, and you're just going far enough to hide the worst of it."

"I don't know why I talk to you about anything. It's like arguing with a rubber ball."

"Buy the glasses."

"Says the man who had to be threatened before he'd see a doctor about the pains in his stomach."

"Yeah, and look where that got me."

At which point Angel had gestured to the hospital room, the bed, and the cannula in his arm. It was the night before the procedure, and the last time Parker would be permitted the pleasure of the old Angel's company. When next Parker saw him, Angel's skin would be gray, and he would be missing a length of intestine.

"I think you just holed your own argument," said Parker.

"No," Angel replied, "I was just too dumb to listen until it was too late."

Angel's voice broke. Parker reached out and held Angel's right hand.

"Late," said Parker. "But not too late."

"I'm scared."

"I know."

"Not only for myself."

"I know that, too."

"If I die—"

"You're not going to die."

"What do you know? You can't even see straight. If I die—"

"Yes?"

"I think Louis has always been looking for someone to put him out of his pain, just as you once did."

"But you stopped him. He's different now."

"No, he's not. It's still sleeping inside him, that desire for an ending. Don't ever let him use me as an excuse."

"I'll see what I can do."

"He listens to you."

"I don't think he does. You're mistaking silence for listening."

"Maybe. And you can let go of my hand now."

"Sorry."

"Don't be."

They were quiet for a time.

"If you die—" said Parker.

"Yeah?"

"I'm not going to date Louis just to make him feel better. That hand-holding, it was only me being comforting."

"Don't make me laugh. It hurts."

"I'm just saying."

"Get out of here."

Parker stood. He paused at the door.

"Angel?"

"Uh-huh?"

"No dying, you hear?"

"Yes," said Angel, "I hear."

CHAPTER
XLVI

Louis sat by Angel's bedside. Some ruddiness had returned to Angel's cheeks, or perhaps this was simply wishful thinking on the part of his partner: Angel was still pumped full of the kind of medication that left the world a blur, and made arduous all but the simplest and shortest of endeavors. Now he was sleeping while the night laid claim to the world beyond his window.

Two hours went by, during which Louis read. Reading had not previously consumed much of his time, but here in this hospital room he had begun to find in books both an escape from his cares and a source of solace when their avoidance proved impossible. Uncertain of where to start, he had sourced a number of lists of the hundred greatest novels ever written, which he combined to create his own guide. So far in the course of Angel's illness, Louis had read *The Call of the Wild*, *Lord of the Flies*, and *Invisible Man*—both the Ellison and Wells titles, due to a mix-up at the bookstore, but Louis didn't mind as both were interesting in their different ways. He was currently on *The Wind in the Willows*, the inclusion of which had initially appeared to represent some form of cataloging error, but the book had grown pleasantly strange as his exploration of it progressed.

"Why are you still here?" asked a voice from the bed.

"I'm trying to finish a chapter."

Angel sounded hoarse. Louis put down the novel and fetched the no-spill water cup with its flexible straw. He held it until Angel waved a hand to signal he was done. His eyes seemed clearer than they had been since before the operation, like those of a man who has woken after a long, undisturbed rest.

"What are you reading now?" Angel asked.

"*The Wind in the Willows.*"

"Isn't that for kids?"

"Maybe. Who cares?"

"And after that?"

Louis reached for his coat and removed a folded sheet of paper. He examined the contents of the list.

"I might try something older. You ever read Dickens?"

"Yeah, I read Dickens."

"Which one?"

"All of them."

"Seriously? I never knew that about you."

"I read a lot when I was younger, and when I was in jail. Big books. I even read *Ulysses.*"

"Nobody's read *Ulysses*, or nobody we know."

"I have."

"Did you understand it?"

"I don't think so. Finished it, though, which counts for something."

"You still read now. You always have a book by the bed."

"I don't read the way I used to. Not like that."

"You ought to start again." Louis waved his paper. "I got a list you can use."

"*The Wind in the Willows*, huh?"

"That's right."

"So read me something from it."

"You mean out loud?"

"You think I'm psychic, I'm gonna guess the words?"

Louis glanced at the half-open door. He had never read aloud to anyone in his life, nor had he been read aloud to. He could recall his mother singing to him as a child, but never reading stories, not unless they were from the Bible. He thought of Angel's bodyguards. He didn't want them to return and find him voicing rats and toads.

"You're too embarrassed to read to me?" asked Angel. "If I die, you'll be—"

"Okay!" said Louis. "Not the dying again. You want me to go back to the beginning?"

"No, just from where you're at."

With one final check of the door, Louis began.

" 'The line of the horizon was clear and hard against the sky,' " he read, " 'and in one particular quarter it showed black against a silvery climbing phosphorescence that grew and grew. At last, over the rim of the waiting earth the moon lifted with slow majesty till it swung clear of the horizon and rode off, free of moorings; and once more they began to see surfaces—meadows wide-spread, and quiet gardens, and the river itself from bank to bank, all softly disclosed, all washed clean of mystery and terror, all radiant again as by day, but with a difference that was tremendous. Their old haunts greeted them again in other raiment, as if they had slipped away and put on this pure new apparel and come quietly back, smiling as they shyly waited to see if they would be recognized again under it. . . .' "

All was still.

Angel was once again asleep. Louis stopped reading.

"That," said Tony Fulci, from his seat on the floor, "was fucking beautiful."

Beside him, his brother Paulie—fellow bodyguard and now, it appeared, literary critic—nodded in agreement.

"Yeah, fucking beautiful . . ."

CHAPTER
XLVII

Quayle and Mors headed northwest, taking rooms at the Mill Inn in Dover-Foxcroft. The town lay near the edge of Piscataquis County, about twenty miles southeast of where the remains of Jane Doe had been discovered.

While Mors was resting, Quayle was thinking of Maela Lombardi. He regretted her death, for both practical and personal reasons: practical because her disappearance would eventually attract attention, and it would be best if he and Mors were long gone from this place when it did; and personal because Lombardi had at least been a woman of principle and courage, and Quayle still retained the capacity to admire such qualities.

And for all the risks he and Mors had taken in interrogating Lombardi before killing her and disposing of the body, they had emerged only with confirmation that Karis Lamb had made it as far as Maine, and Lombardi's opinion that the remains found in Piscataquis were hers. But this was lent further credence by the press conference held earlier that day, an adjunct to the ongoing hunt for the killers of the state trooper, Jasper Allen. Before taking questions from the media, a female lieutenant had gone into greater detail than before about the age and approximate build of the woman, both of which matched descriptions of Karis. She had also informed the media that a Star of David carved on a nearby tree might have some connection to the body. Quayle knew from the late Vernay that Karis habitually wore a small Star of David on a chain around her neck. Vernay had found her attachment to this symbol of her mother's faith amusing. Quayle suspected it added to the pleasure Vernay took in Lamb's defilement.

Unbeknownst to Quayle, he was operating on a similar set of assumptions to Charlie Parker: that Karis's child was still alive, and very possibly living in some proximity to the grave. Quayle had sent Mors to scout the site—although she only narrowly avoided apprehension by the police officer assigned to guard it—and her view was that it had been chosen specifically for its remoteness, which suggested local knowledge.

But Quayle possessed an advantage over any other parties, including the police, who might now be looking for Karis Lamb's missing child.

Quayle knew about the book.

That evening, Parker called the Upper West Side apartment shared by Louis and Angel. When

Louis answered, Parker inquired after Angel's health before progressing to the other reason for the call.

"I had a face-to-face conversation with Bobby Ocean a few days ago."

"Uh-huh," said Louis. "And how was that?"

"Like soaking my brain in bile. He stopped just short of presenting me with a bill for his son's truck."

"Does the boy usually let his father do his dirty work?"

"I don't think Billy knew about the visit."

"Why not?"

"Bobby Ocean shares some of his son's moral failings, but the stupidity gene may have skipped a generation. If Billy were to find out who was responsible for blowing up his pride and joy, he might take it into his head to seek some retribution. Bobby's guess is that this wouldn't end well for anyone, but particularly not for his son, and possibly not for him either."

"So he came to you to let off a little steam? Sorry for the inconvenience."

"I've had worse."

"This Billy doesn't sound like an honor roll kid."

"You remember our friend Philip from Providence?"

Philip was the unacknowledged offspring of a liaison between a deceased New England criminal named Caspar Webb and the woman who would eventually inherit, and dismantle, Webb's empire, a figure known only as Mother. Philip had objected strenuously to Mother's disposal of the family franchise, believing himself a worthy heir to his father's fortune, and was now rumored to be taking an extended vacation. If so, it was the kind conducted horizontally, and under a weight of dirt.

"Hard to forget him," said Louis. "But I am trying."

"Well, I think Billy has similar paternal issues, minus the outright criminality, but with prejudice to compensate."

"Maybe I shouldn't have blown up the truck."

"We live and learn."

They talked some more, and Parker told Louis about the body of the woman, and the search for her child.

"If the kid is alive," said Louis, "then someone is probably starting to panic right about now. You think it could be in danger?"

"No."

"You sure about that?"

"The mother died from severe hemorrhaging very soon after giving birth. It's likely that someone buried her with enough care and respect to carve the symbol of her religion on a nearby tree. That doesn't strike me as the act of a person who'd harm a child."

"Just the act of a person who wanted a child badly enough to bury its mother in a shallow grave."

"When you put it that way."

They returned to the subject of the truck. Parker wasn't sure how much Bobby Ocean actually knew about Louis beyond rumor and reputation, but if he expended enough time and effort, he might be able to find out more. It would be better for all concerned if Louis were absent from Portland for a while, although given Louis's current mood, Parker guessed that the city would soon be graced once again by his presence.

"The hospital will get Angel walking in a day or two, encourage him to eat and drink, then send him home," said Louis. "Or that's the plan."

Parker knew that Louis would be engaging nurses to assist Angel during the early stages of his recovery. The internist felt it wasn't strictly necessary, but Louis would have been the first to admit that he wasn't one of nature's caregivers. Parker said that he'd come visit once Angel was settled back in the apartment. They agreed to speak again in a few days.

And Death circled.

CHAPTER
XLVIII

They called themselves the Backers: individuals who had attained positions of considerable wealth, power, and influence, in part through their own energy and acumen, but mostly by aligning themselves with forces older and more arcane than any religion. In doing so they had damned themselves, and were therefore content to see all others damned in turn.

Now five of them—three men and two women—were seated at a table in the Oak Room at the Fairmont Copley Plaza in Boston, the grande dame of the city's hotel bars. In recent years it had been rebranded as the OAK Long Bar + Kitchen, but this quintet, like many of the city's blue bloods, chose to ignore the change. To them, it was the Oak Room, and always would be.

They attracted no particular attention, apart from the solicitous but not overbearing service of their waiter. On this particular evening, the bar was entertaining half a dozen not dissimilar parties of senior patrons, all casually attired—or casually for them, which meant jackets and ties for the gentlemen, and dresses for the women. Their coterie eschewed cocktails for gins and white wine, and declined offers of food since they had a reservation at L'Espalier for eight p.m. Like their meeting, the reservation had been arranged at short notice, but with no great difficulty.

"Well?" said one of the women, once the drinks were served, and they could speak without being overheard. She looked over at the Principal Backer, he who had called them together. "One imagines this is not principally a social gathering."

The Principal Backer raised his glass in a silent toast, and took a sip before replying.

"Quayle is in New England."

The woman who had spoken grimaced, as though the wine were not quite to her taste.

"Where?"

"Maine."

"Why?"

"Have you been following the story of the woman's body found in the northern woods?"

"I think I read something about it. Wasn't she pregnant?"

"Not quite; she gave birth shortly before she died. Quayle thinks he knows who she is. Apparently he's been looking for her for some time."

"So now he can return home," said a thin, dark man with the aspect of a sad, emaciated crow.

"His search, it would appear, is at an end."

The others nodded their agreement. One of the men even laughed.

Bluster, thought the Principal Backer. None was willing to look the others in the face. All feared seeing their own disquietude reflected.

"Unfortunately," he said, "his efforts have not yet concluded. He's now seeking the missing child."

"You've spoken with him?" asked the crow-man.

"Not directly, but he has made contact. He has requested our assistance—'request,' in this case, being something of a euphemism."

Quayle operated largely in seclusion and solitude, a succession of female partners excepted. In times past he had enjoyed a more public profile, but no longer. Nevertheless he was a figure of influence, and one not to be denied.

"What use would a man like Quayle have for a child?" asked the other woman present. The Principal Backer thought he detected what might almost have been concern in her tone. She sat on the boards of a number of charities, including at least two that specialized in seeking cures for pediatric illnesses. Perhaps, he considered, her hypocrisy had become so ingrained that she was no longer even capable of perceiving it as such.

"I don't think he's especially interested in the

child itself," said the Principal Backer. "Although if he did want it, would you really care to know his reasons?"

The woman did not reply. Her silence was sufficient response.

"Then why persist?" asked the man who had laughed, his expression restored to its default smirk. The Principal Backer distrusted those who laughed too easily, perceiving in it a deeper inability to find anything funny at all.

"The mother possessed something Quayle wants. He believes that this object now resides with whomever has the child."

No one needed to ask why this asset was of interest to Quayle. The lawyer had only one purpose to his existence: the reconstruction of the Fractured Atlas, which would reorder the world in its image.

"What kind of assistance does he require from us?" asked the second woman.

"Contacts: police, municipal government, whatever else may strike him."

"And we're obliging?"

"Naturally."

"While ensuring that we're kept apprised of any developments?"

"Where possible."

The Principal Backer waited for their approval to subside. They were coming to the meat of it now.

"Quayle believes he's close," he said, "closer than he has ever yet been."

"But how close?" said the crow-man. "We've heard all this before. My father listened to the same claims coming from Quayle's mouth."

Another bark of laughter: "Your grandfather, too. And mine."

The Principal Backer waited for them to stop. They were of old blood, and old blood grew torpid.

"The last of the missing pages," he said, "if Quayle is to be believed."

The other four absorbed this information.

"And then?" asked the woman of charitable disposition.

"If Quayle is right, the world will become a reflection of the Atlas. The Not-Gods will return, and the Old God will pass into nonbeing. All will be fed to the flames."

No laughter now. These Backers, like those long gone before them, had predicated their existence on the belief that they could pass on the cost of their bargain to future generations. They would be dead before the consequences of their actions were made manifest; or perhaps this pact with an evil that had come into being with the birth of the universe, this covenant agreed centuries earlier, might ultimately be revealed as mere myth, so much sophistry to explain away good fortune. Their success would not come at a price. The Not-Gods did not exist. There was no Buried God lost deep beneath the dirt and rock of this world, waiting to be discovered, just as there was no Old God seeking adoration and remembrance. There was only this life, and then nothingness.

But no: they knew the truth. They had only hoped to be gone before it was revealed.

"So," said the crow-man, "we must collude with Quayle in our own destruction, and the extinction of those we love?"

The crow-man had family: children, a grand-child. So did the others. Only the Principal Backer was without heirs.

"We have always been in a state of collusion," said the Principal Backer. "The abstract now threatens to become concrete. But what did you expect?"

"More time."

"It appears you may be denied it. Why do you think I booked L'Espalier for our meal?"

"I believe," said the crow-man, "that I may have lost my appetite."

The Principal Backer gripped him by the shoulder.

"Then find it again," he said. "This could be our Last Supper."

CHAPTER
XLIX

If the Principal Backer and his associates were ambivalent about the presence of the visitor, Quayle was no less eager to maintain his distance from these colonials. He regarded them as lacking purity: they acted largely out of self-interest, seeking to enrich themselves by subscribing to a doctrine in which they believed only halfheartedly, if they truly believed in it at all.

Only the leader of their little group was worthy of any respect. There were those who suspected the Principal Backer to be black as pitch to the depths of his being, although Quayle had no idea what might have bred in him such hatred for his fellow men that the Principal Backer should be content to see them reduced to ash, and himself along with them. Quayle wondered if the Buried God whispered to the Principal Backer in the night, calling to him in a tongue ancient and unwritten, its words unintelligible but their meaning clear. If so, it might have gone some way toward explaining the Principal Backer's animus toward Quayle, who served the rest of the Obverse Trinity.

But Quayle had other doubts about the Principal Backer. Quayle possessed no evidence at which to point, no indications of irresolution or—whisper it—treachery on the part of the Principal Backer, only his knowledge of men and the depths of their self-interest. The Principal Backer was prosperous, and in good health. He was held in regard. He had authority.

He had no reason to bring all of it to an end.

Quayle, by contrast, was a soul in anguish, and wished only for that suffering to cease. If a way had existed to accomplish this other than through the restoration of the Atlas, Quayle might have embraced it without hesitation, or so he told himself. Quayle was a man convinced that he had lived for centuries, cursed—in an irony only a lawyer could properly appreciate—by a contract he should not have signed. He could recall moments of great import going back to the Reformation and beyond, intimate details of incidents and individuals about which he could not possibly have such knowledge. He was haunted by memories that seemed to belong both to him and to others, a succession of men who bore his name and likeness but could not possibly *be* him.

Once again, as he did whenever he experienced doubt, he feared that these echoes were simply manifestations of mania, while the insight that permitted him to acknowledge his own lunacy represented a clarity that ebbed and flowed according to the patterns of his psychosis.

Lies within lies: like the Backers, he would find no consolation in them.

The Atlas was real.

The Old God was real.

The Buried God was real.

The Not-Gods to come were real.

And Quayle, in all his singularity, was real.

CHAPTER
L

Parker spent part of the following morning in Augusta going through the relevant birth records for Piscataquis County. He managed to assemble a list of registrations from the period in question, but remained reluctant to go knocking on doors to ask about illegal burials and child abductions. Someone would shoot him.

Terri Harkness, his contact at the Maine Town and City Clerks' Association, agreed to inquire about birth certificate filings that might have raised an eyebrow, but she didn't hold out much hope. Clerks took their roles seriously, she said, and nobody wanted a false filing to come back and bite. But she did admit that when it came to home births, they couldn't do much more than take the word of the parent or parents, and she had personal knowledge of two very religious families in which grandparents were raising a grandchild as their own in order to protect a daughter from opprobrium.

"And shouldn't the police be asking these questions anyway?" said Harkness.

"The clerk at the Vital Records Office in

Augusta told me they'd already received a request from the state police for assistance, now that the search of the site is winding down," said Parker, "but resources are likely to be stretched until they find Jasper Allen's killers. My guess is that the police will be in touch with more of your members soon enough, but maybe I can save them some trouble."

"If you do figure out who has the child, you have to know they won't be too pleased to see you."

"If I let the likely pleasure of my company guide my movements," Parker told her, "I'd never leave the house."

Putnam, Newhouse, and Caldicott had proved smarter than anyone might previously have credited, and had so far managed to evade the police. The general view was that Caldicott was the bright one, although it was all relative, given that he was a mid-level Maine drug dealer now being hunted as a possible accessory to the killing of a state trooper.

If Caldicott was clever, Parker thought, he'd have ditched Putnam and Newhouse as quickly as possible and headed north or west. Parker's guess was north—maybe into the County, as everyone in Maine called Aroostook, the largest territory in the state: almost 7,000 square miles, most of it uninhabited woodland. Caldicott knew the terrain; his people came from up Scopan way, close to the Allagash Wilderness. A man could lose himself in there and not be found until someone stumbled on his bones.

But if Caldicott was *really* clever, and also ruthless, he'd have done more than ditch Putnam and Newhouse: he'd have killed them. Right now there was only the word of his girlfriend that he'd supplied the car used in the shooting, and the presence of Putnam and Newhouse at Caldicott's place on the night in question didn't directly link him to Allen's death. While the distinction between being an accessory before or after the fact had largely been erased in law, the reality was that an accessory after the fact faced a lighter sentence. As things stood, Caldicott was only in trouble for knowingly assisting a suspected felon or felons in avoiding arrest or trial, unless the police investigation uncovered evidence linking him to the planning of the drug buy that had ultimately resulted in Allen's murder. There was also the testimony of Caldicott's junkie girlfriend to consider, although it appeared she had now lawyered up in order to counter any possibility of her own indictment as an accessory, and junkies made poor witnesses. Whatever happened, Caldicott was in trouble, but he might be in less trouble if Putnam and Newhouse were to vanish from the face of the earth.

None of which was Parker's problem.

He returned to the matter of the dead woman. What did he know of her? She was probably from out of state, so how did she come to be in Maine? What drew her to the Northeast? She was pregnant, so it was possible that the father of the child was here. Yet somehow she ended up going into labor not in the safety of a hospital but out in the wild, and any witnesses to the birth and her subsequent passing had not seen fit to alert the authorities. Could the father of the child have been responsible for her burial? If so, why hide the body and the fact of the birth, unless he panicked when the woman died, fearing that the law might find a way to blame him for it. What if he was married, and the pregnancy the result of an affair? The lover shows up in his home state, heavy with his child, and he finds somewhere to accommodate her without his wife suspecting. When the lover dies giving birth, he gets rid of her and the baby and returns to his blameless life.

But if that was so, why wasn't the child buried with the mother?

Parker rowed back. One certainty: this was a woman in trouble, because otherwise she would not have ended up in a hole in the woods. She was heavily pregnant, in an unfamiliar locale. To whom would she have turned? Planned Parenthood, perhaps, or one of the women's refuges, yet no such organization in the state had come forward to claim knowledge of her.

Parker experienced a tickling at his memory, a detail from the past that was assuming new relevance in light of the current case. Then it came to him, and he made one final call, this time to Bangor. The person with whom he wished to speak was absent, and would not be back until nightfall. Parker left a message advising that he would travel up to talk to her in person the next day. He knew he could have spoken with her over the phone, but he had learned from long experience that people, even those with no grudge against him, were often more forthcoming when dealt with face-to-face.

And anyway, he had other obligations that night.

CHAPTER
LI

Quayle did not like bars, or not bars like this one: loud, convivial, and filled with staff that might remember a face. Quayle preferred older, darker watering holes, frequented by men and women who did not exchange glances or make conversation with those unknown to them, and only barely acknowledged those they did know; places with names originating from a time when the masses could not read, and inns were identifiable by their signs.

But perhaps in those London hostelries that had been in the same family for generations, a landlord might remark to his son or daughter, as they cleaned glasses or pulled pints, that the customer seated in the corner ("a legal gentleman, if memory serves") enjoyed a similar hereditary link to their beloved establishment, for this man's father used to drink here, and indeed his father before him ("for they bear the same likeness, which speaks of a strong bloodline"), even if the appellation of this august lineage of clientele would not quite come to the innkeeper ("something to do with birds, I'm sure of it"), and it would never cross his mind to ask, because he was certain that this gentleman ("keeps himself to himself, but pleasant enough with it") would not welcome such inquiries, and perhaps the reason he and his forebears had offered their patronage down the years was precisely this discretion on the part of a long line of landlords ("for we know when to look, and when to look away"), and so it should remain.

Therefore Quayle felt unusually conspicuous in a booth at the Great Lost Bear in Portland, even with Mors keeping vigil from the bar, the stools at either side of her curiously unoccupied despite the presence of a large crowd, and with seating at a premium. Quayle waited with a gin before him, although he had barely touched it. He had no desire to be here, and therefore drinking would give him no pleasure. This whole country was encrusting him, like dust falling in the aftermath of an eruption. He wanted to be done with it.

A man made his way through the throng, his body undulating so that, no matter how densely packed the masses, he passed between all without difficulty. He was small and slim, but had learned to make himself less noticeable still. He was dressed in an overcoat that looked older than he, its sleeves hanging below his knuckles, its hem frayed. His eyes were brown and hooded, and his hair very dark and full, its line so close to his eyebrows that he barely possessed a forehead at all. His nose was tiny, and pointed. Combined with the coat, and the swift precision of his movements, these features lent him the aspect of a clever rodent. Quayle caught him peruse Mors and hold the look she gave him, and Quayle thought that the Principal Backer must have described her to the new arrival in forewarning. He held a large glass of soda in one hand, but he struck Quayle as being no more likely to finish it than Quayle was his gin. He took the facing seat in the booth without asking permission, and placed his glass on a coaster. He did not offer a hand in greeting, and Quayle surmised that this, too, the Principal Backer might have mentioned to him: *Mr. Quayle prefers not to shake hands. You should probably be grateful for it, otherwise you might never remove the chill from your fingers, assuming Quayle leaves you with as many of them as before.*

"You're the Englishman."

No names, no preamble. His voice was too high for a grown male, and curiously without accent. He could have been from anywhere, anywhere at all.

"Yes," said Quayle.

"You like this place?"

"No," said Quayle. "Why did you bring me here?"

"Because you're looking for the child." With the tiniest nod of that ratlike head, he indicated

274

a man at the other side of the bar, engaged in conversation with an older, bearded figure. "And so is he."

It was Dave Evans's birthday, and various friends had gathered to wish the owner of the Great Lost Bear well. With Angel and Louis indisposed, and the Fulci brothers acting as temporary bodyguards for the invalid, it was particularly incumbent on Parker to be present. Not that this was in any way a chore, because he owed Dave a lot. Dave had offered Parker a bar manager's job back when times were hard, both personally and financially, and the Bear still functioned as Parker's de facto meeting place and occasional office.

"You hear the Fulcis are looking to open a bar of their own?" he remarked to Dave.

"I thought it was just a rumor, like trickle-down economics."

"No, they sound serious. They have the money, and I hear they've put a marker somewhere on Washington Avenue."

"That's too close to us," said Dave.

Washington Avenue was right at the other side of town from the Bear.

"How far away do you want them to be?" asked Parker.

"Africa. Antarctica. Somewhere else beginning with 'A,' like Alpha Centauri."

Parker did his best to look hurt on the Fulcis' behalf.

"You know, too much of that kind of talk and they'll get to thinking you don't like them. That would be bad."

"How much worse could it be?" said Dave. "They already drink here."

"You still have a roof. And walls."

"Just about."

Over by the men's room, a fist-shaped hole marked the spot where Paulie Fulci had chosen to express his unhappiness at the result of a recent hockey game. Parker hadn't been present on the night in question, but according to regulars, the whole bar shook.

Dave mulled on the Fulcis for a while. His face brightened.

"If they open their own place," he said, "maybe they'll drink there instead."

Parker decided to cut that one off at the pass.

"You're clutching at straws. The Bear is like a second home to them, and you should never drink in your own establishment. Look on the bright side: you haven't had any trouble since they started coming here."

"But we didn't have any trouble *before* they started coming here, either. I think they interfere with my blood pressure. They arrive and I feel the urge to lie down."

"You could always just retire and sell them the Bear."

"It would be like handing my child over to pirates."

"Go on, admit it: you kind of enjoy them."

"I really don't."

"You'd miss them if they were gone."

"I'd welcome the opportunity to find out."

Parker called for another drink, and took in the bar, the other customers, and the two men in a booth by the wall. He had caught both of them peering at him moments earlier, in a manner that was something more than casual—or so it seemed to Parker, and he had learned long ago not to ignore his instincts on such matters. The man in velvet was older, and unknown to him, but the smaller one made his skin crawl, and his face was familiar.

"The guys in the next-to-last booth by the wall," he said to Dave. "One dresses off a frequent-buyer card at Goodwill, the other like he got lost on the way to a séance. Know them?"

Dave didn't even need to look in their direction. This was why Dave was good at what he did, and the Bear ran so smoothly.

"Velvet Goldmine, no. But the smaller one, he's been here in the past. Not often, but enough for me to learn not to like him."

"Any particular reason?"

"His attitude, mostly. Other than that: pure

prejudice. He's usually alone, but always on the periphery of someone else's business. He's the kind of guy who likes watching kids search for lost pets, because he's the one who makes sure the pets were lost to begin with. Why?"

"I got the feeling they're paying me more than passing attention."

"Well, you're a handsome man."

"I won't argue with you on your birthday. The little one—I don't think it's the first time he's given me the bad-luck squint in this place. That may be why he's ringing my bells."

"I get the feeling you're about to make a more formal introduction."

Parker patted Dave on the shoulder.

"Well, this is a friendly place."

Quayle was listening intently to the little man, who had finally admitted to a name: Ivan Giller. Quayle didn't particularly care to find out anything more about him. All he wanted from Giller was what he knew, or could find out, about Karis Lamb and her child.

And now also the private investigator named Parker.

"He was on TV, visiting the burial site," said Giller. "The reporter made a fuss about it. Slow news day, I guess."

"And you've come across him before?"

"Not one-on-one, but our mutual acquaintances

pay me to keep an eye on him, and I pass on anything worth knowing. Not that I have to, most of the time. They learn about the big stuff without my help. If there's trouble, he'll find it. If there isn't trouble, he'll make some, just for a way to pass a few hours."

"Has he made any of this trouble for these acquaintances?"

"It's an ongoing project for him, which is why I'm still here."

"The more pertinent question is why is *he* still here?"

"You mean, why isn't he dead? People have tried."

"Clearly not hard enough."

"You'd be surprised. You—"

A shadow fell across the table, and both men looked up at the face of Charlie Parker.

CHAPTER
LII

Quayle and Giller were not alone that evening in considering the possible implications of Parker's involvement in their affairs.

Holly Weaver was sitting at her kitchen table, drinking a glass of Maker's Mark, light on the ice and heavy on the bourbon. The Maker's was a Christmas gift from her father. Holly rarely drank hard liquor, but once or twice a month she liked to treat herself to a small one, usually over a book or while watching an old movie on TCM. So each Christmas, Owen Weaver presented his daughter with a bottle, and this was usually enough to take her through to the next Christmas.

Not this time, though, Owen thought. This one wouldn't even carry her to Easter, not unless she started watering it.

"I saw him," said Holly. "On the TV. The private detective, the one who hunted down all those bad people."

Owen wanted to ask Holly when last she'd eaten, and if she was managing to sleep at all, because his daughter had begun visibly to waste away since the discovery of the body, and her eyes stared out from reddish blue hollows. Instead, he said:

"We're not bad people."

"It won't make any difference to him."

"He can't know any more than the police do."

"Maybe not yet, but he's not like the police. He's different. Jesus, the stuff on the Internet: if even half of what they say about him is true . . ."

Owen was of the opinion that virtually nothing on the Internet was true, and most of what was true wasn't worth reading. But he also acknowledged that he might just be part of a dying generation, and eventually he, and those like him, would cede their places to men and women who thrived on conspiracy theories, the echo of their own voices, and the opinions of dogmatists and fools.

Owen had Holly's laptop open on the table before him. He was clicking through the searches in her history, taking in a headline here, a report there. He knew Parker's name, and something of Parker's reputation, from his own research, but Holly had discovered much more. Even allowing for falsehoods and exaggeration, this was a man to be reckoned with.

"But who could have hired him?" said Owen. "If he's a private investigator, someone must have paid him to sniff around."

Holly looked at him. She was still frightened, but the tincture of her fear altered.

"What if it's the people Karis was running from?"

"No, it's not."

"How can you be sure?"

"Because I've been reading the same material as you," said Owen, "and I don't think Parker's the kind to accept their money. All those cases—murderers brought to justice, missing women found, children saved from Christ knows what kind of end—they share some sense of morality, of right and wrong."

"They say he's killed people."

"They do," Owen admitted. "But if anyone believes the world is poorer for their absence, they're keeping quiet about it."

Holly knocked back a mouthful of bourbon large enough to empty her glass. Owen hoped that at least it might help her sleep. It wouldn't be good sleep, but in her current state, any rest at all would be a bonus.

"He'll come here," said Holly. "He'll find his way to my door."

"You can't know that."

She was no longer looking at him. She was staring over his shoulder at the window, her gaze penetrating the glass and taking her into the darkness beyond, moving through forest and glade until it alighted at last on a man approaching from the south, his advance inexorable, his intent to deprive her of Daniel.

"You're wrong," she said.

Owen closed the laptop. He'd seen all he needed to see.

"Then we have a choice," he said.

"Tell me."

"We wait for Parker to arrive, and the police with him."

"Or?"

"Some of these stories mention two lawyers here in Maine, one in Portland and the other in Falmouth. Parker's done work for both of them. The woman in Falmouth I don't know, and it doesn't look like she's engaged with Parker lately, but I've heard of the second, Castin. I can talk to him—just over the phone, no names. I'll be careful."

Holly put the glass down. She started to cry.

"No," she said. "It's all the law."

"We need help. We have to tell someone what happened. We should have done it as soon as they found the body."

"They won't believe us."

"We'll make them believe us. It's the truth."

"I can't lose him, Daddy. I can't. I'll die!"

Owen reached across the table to clasp her hands. He closed his eyes. He could feel again the spade in his hands, and the ache in his arms and back as he dug the hole; the form of the woman in her makeshift shroud, and the weight of her in his arms as he laid her in the ground. They had made her a promise, he and Holly, but it was one they should never have kept. Owen saw another path appear, one in which the police were called in the aftermath of the birth, and the child was temporarily taken from them while a process was initiated that ended with Daniel as his daughter's boy, but without the secrets and without the fear.

A fairy tale.

Because there was another possibility: the woman identified; Daniel in foster care; and finally, the appearance of the father, come to claim his son at last.

"Don't let them have my baby."

A dying woman's words, her hand in Owen's, still slick with her blood; Holly beside them, holding the child, this wailing boy; and something in the way Karis Lamb says those words makes Owen want to tell his daughter to smother the child's cries, to silence him with whispers and caresses, with the warmth of her flesh and the scent of her skin, lest the hunters might hear.

Because unspoken yet still acknowledged between his daughter and him is the certainty that Parker and the police are not the only ones to be feared.

"Don't let them *have my baby."*

Them.

He knew it would only be a matter of time before Karis Lamb was identified.

And then they would descend.

CHAPTER
LIII

Despite Giller's efforts to bring Quayle up to speed on Parker, the lawyer was still surprised by his own response to the detective's arrival at their table.

From across the bar, Parker had resembled just another customer: average height, hair graying, his body perhaps refusing as yet to acquiesce entirely to the softness of middle age, or not without a fight. But Parker was different when viewed up close. It wasn't as though any single facet of his character appeared more remarkable in proximity, although Quayle was prepared to make an exception for the eyes, which suggested a degree of insight both unusual and hard earned. Looking into them was like staring at the play of light on the surface of the ocean, the greenish blue of them communicating compassion, sadness, and a potential for violence that, once unleashed, would not easily be subdued. But Quayle thought also that there was about Parker a certain otherworldliness, a sense of one with an acute awareness of the ineffable. Quayle had encountered other such individuals in the past, but they were often ascetics, occasionally fanatics. Parker, from what Quayle knew, was neither. He was simply very, very dangerous.

"Gentlemen," said Parker. "I hope you're enjoying yourselves tonight."

Quayle noticed that he kept his body slightly angled, so he could monitor both them and the crowd at the bar—in particular, Mors. Somehow he had picked up on her presence, even as she kept herself at one remove.

"Very much," said Quayle. "Although it's a little noisy for my liking."

"Not from around here, are you?"

"Just visiting."

"English?"

"Yes."

"Business?"

"Mostly."

"And what kind of business would that be?"

"Are you the welcoming committee?"

"The regular guy is off, and I'm still working on my people skills."

Parker waited for Quayle to answer his earlier question. The three men understood what was unfolding. Neither Quayle nor Giller made any effort to protest at Parker's interruption of their conversation, or to pretend that this was anything other than what it was: an adversarial confrontation brought down upon them by some moment of carelessness on their part, or the detective's responsiveness to threat and predation.

"I'm involved with the legal profession," said Quayle, at last.

"A lawyer?"

"Yes."

"You could have just said that."

"I don't practice very much anymore."

"Yet here you are, on 'business.'"

"Indeed, here I am."

A printed sheet lay by Quayle's right hand: the cryptic crossword puzzle from that day's edition of *The Times* of London. Completing it was one of Quayle's pleasures, and he had been forced to subscribe temporarily to the newspaper using a proxy account, in order to enjoy it while away from home. Quayle's fountain pen lay alongside it, and the index finger of his right hand bore a telltale smudge of ink.

"Puzzle fan?" said Parker.

"Only of this particular crossword."

"Looks like you finished it."

"I always complete it, although some days it takes longer than others."

"I'm sure there's a metaphor in there somewhere, or a lesson for life."

"If I discover it, I'll be sure to pass it on."

"That would be just fine. Do you have a name?"

"Yes."

"Care to share it?"

"No."

Parker nodded once, as though Quayle had just confirmed everything he needed to know about him, before turning his attention to Giller.

"You I think I've seen before."

"I couldn't say."

"I have a good memory for faces. How's your memory for faces?"

Giller shrugged, but didn't answer.

"I ask because it seemed that you were paying some attention to my face this evening. I'm just wondering if on those other occasions when I've seen you here, you might have been doing the same thing?"

"I think you're mistaken."

Parker considered this.

"You could be right," he said, "but I doubt it. And I bet you're not the sharing kind either when it comes to names."

"Smith," said Giller. "My friend across the table is also Smith."

"Well, Smith and Smith," said Parker, "or Smith One and Smith Two as I'll think of you from now on, I'm glad we got the formalities out of the way, broke the ice. Next time, we'll all be more comfortable with one another. I'll keep my eyes open, because I wouldn't want to miss you. Until then, you enjoy the rest of your evening." He backed away from them, pausing only to tap the bar, just to the right of where Pallida Mors was sitting. "You too, miss."

Quayle watched him rejoin the group, but Parker only stayed a few moments longer before leaving through the front door.

"Will he wait?" asked Quayle.

"Possibly," said Giller. "But he can't follow both of us at once, and if we leave now, he won't have time to call for assistance."

"So which one of us will he go after?"

"We'll just have to see."

"And the matter of the child?"

"I'm already working on it. I'll be in touch."

"Sooner would be preferable."

"I'll bear that in mind."

They made their way from the bar, Mors behind them. The owner, the birthday boy himself, gave no sign of noticing their departure, nor did anyone else. Once they were outside, Giller turned left without another word, left again, and was quickly gone from sight. Quayle and Mors headed right, in the direction of their rental car, but as they approached it, Mors took Quayle's arm.

"Let's walk a while."

"What about the car?"

"I'll come back for it later."

"Why?"

"Because he's watching, and the car can be traced. He's sharp."

"Sharp enough to have spotted you."

Mors bristled. "Yes."

Mors checked behind her, but saw no sign of the detective. She looked puzzled, even disappointed.

"Why doesn't he come?" she said.

"Because he knows we're here, and what we look like," said Quayle. "Perhaps he'll use other channels to find out why."

Eventually they neared the ramp for 295, where Mors hailed a passing cab. As they climbed in, neither of them paid any attention to the figure limping along the other side of the street, his progress assisted by a bright red Rollator. Only when the cab had slipped onto the highway did he reach into his pocket and carefully text the company name and license number of the cab to the number he had been given by the man outside the Great Lost Bear.

It was the easiest twenty dollars he'd ever made.

CHAPTER
LIV

Bobby Ocean was also in a bar that night, in his case the Gull's Nest over in South Portland's West End. Bobby had recently used one of his subsidiary corporations to take ownership of the Gull, as it was universally known. Over the preceding eighteen months, related companies had also acquired rental properties in the Brick Hill and Redbank neighborhoods, and along Western Avenue. The city council was planning to revitalize the area by improving roads and building sidewalks, as well as authorizing zoning changes and implementing a public-private proposal for affordable housing. The West End was on its way up, and Bobby Ocean would be in an ideal position to exploit this ascent.

The only blot on the horizon was Bobby's son, who was currently holding court in a corner of the Gull, and had already begun shooting his mouth off about the new proprietors. Billy had petitioned his father to be permitted to manage the Gull, and his mother had added her voice to her son's. How could Billy be expected to become more responsible, she argued, if his

291

father wouldn't trust him with leadership? This seemed to Bobby to be putting the cart before the horse, but his protest fell on deaf ears, just as his wife preferred to ignore all the times Billy had failed to step up in the past. Those jobs, she claimed, just weren't right for their son. They were too restrictive. He was a sociable boy, she said. People liked him.

Maybe she really believed this, but Bobby thought she spoke more in hope than anything else. Their son was not sociable, just easily led. Folks didn't like him: they liked his money, which Billy threw around freely enough to buy himself a circle of regular acquaintances. Some were plain old bottom-feeders, but others were of a more dangerous stripe. Bobby wasn't planning on dying anytime soon, but he still worried about the future of businesses he had so painstakingly built up over the years. Billy was his only child, and the only one Bobby Ocean was ever likely to have. He was also, unfortunately, an asshole.

That fucking truck: if only Billy hadn't bedecked it with Confederate banners, but there was no talking to him. True, he might have inherited his fundamentalist views on race—not to mention women, homosexuals, and the poor— from his old man, but that didn't mean he had to go around advertising them. The truck flags were just part of it: Billy had also involved himself with that Klan nonsense up in Augusta, which was arrant stupidity. Billy had been smiling when he told his father about it, as though expecting to be praised for what he'd done. But Bobby Ocean was a respectable figure in the state, and ensured that his support for far-right causes was discreet and largely anonymous. What effect did his son think it would have on the family name if he were questioned for disseminating hate literature? What the fuck was he thinking?

But Bobby Ocean shouldn't have struck him for it. That was a mistake. The openhanded blow landed on the side of Billy's head almost before his father realized he'd thrown it. And then—goddamn it, goddamn it all—the boy had started weeping.

Jesus Lord.

So maybe he'd have to throw the Gull to Billy. It was a shithole anyway, and eventually Bobby would have to close it for refurbishment, maybe put in a pizza oven once the hipsters began gathering. Billy could do what he wanted with it for a year or two, so long as he didn't run the place into the ground. And if Bobby gave him the Gull, Billy might stop brooding on his truck, and that would be a good thing. There was no proof that Parker and his Negro had been responsible for what occurred, even if Bobby knew they were involved, knew it in his heart. He'd find a way to punish them for what they'd done, given time, but he didn't want his son going up against a man like Parker.

From the heart of a group of laughing men and women, all morons and blowhards, his son raised a glass to his father, and Bobby returned the gesture. After all, he loved his son, and perhaps it was partly his fault that Billy had turned out this way. Still, he couldn't help but feel that some better version of the boy had dripped from his mother's vagina before it could reach the egg.

CHAPTER
LV

The text came as Parker shadowed the man he was now thinking of as Smith One. Parker knew the type: a crony, a consort, a willing servant to the demands of others, regardless of their moral complexion, just as long as they paid promptly— although the Smith Ones of this world preferred that the morality of their employers assumed tones of gray, fading to black.

Which wasn't to suggest Smith One lacked intelligence. He was keeping his head down as he headed along Ashmont, maintaining a steady pace and not looking back, but Parker was sure he was primed for the possibility of pursuit, if not already actively aware of his pursuer. Not that Parker cared. He didn't intend to follow Smith One for very long. What Parker did intend was to grab Smith One at the first opportunity before encouraging him to share any and all information he might possess about his drinking companion, along with details of anyone else that might have paid him to monitor Parker's movements.

Parker closed the gap as Smith One passed Cottage Street. Deering Avenue was the next big intersection, and Parker didn't make Smith One for a Portland local, which meant he was unlikely to have walked to the Bear. Either he was catching a bus on Deering, or he was parked somewhere nearby.

Smith One crossed Cottage before stopping as something to his left caught his attention. He turned slowly, his eyes drawn by a presence as yet concealed from Parker's gaze. For a moment the texture of the night appeared to thicken, the shadows deepen. Parker tasted metal on the air, like the coming of an electrical storm. He could hear cars passing in the distance, but their sound was muffled, and the surrounding houses began to lose their definition. He had the sudden uncomfortable sensation of being immersed in water or lost in a rapidly descending fog without either medium being made manifest. Only Smith One remained fixed and unchanged, so that the two men found themselves trapped in a space warping into immateriality.

A child crouched in the center of the street: pale and malformed, naked and sexless, its leg and elbow joints bent at unnatural angles, its right arm shielding its eyes as though from a light visible only to itself. It extended its left hand toward Parker, and despite the distance between them, he thought he felt its touch on his skin, the nails on its fingers sharp and cold as needles.

Smith One started to run, but Parker could not

tear himself from the child. It possessed a kind of reality, being both present yet insubstantial. It looked as though it might be possible to pass straight through it, but one would deeply regret the experience, like breaching a cloud of chlorine gas.

Slowly, the child began to glow. Parker glimpsed the network of veins and arteries running beneath its skin, and what might have been internal organs—lungs, kidneys, a heart—albeit atrophied and seemingly without function, for the lungs did not swell or contract, and the heart did not beat. The light grew stronger, splitting apart, and Parker heard the roar of an engine, and the clamor of a horn, and he just had time to press himself against the side of a car as a van ripped through the child, its body vanishing at the moment of impact, and passed Parker with barely inches to spare, the driver mouthing obscenities at him as he went.

The child was gone. In its place was a great chunk of dirty ice, possibly displaced from a building or truck by the thaw, and tire-marked by the passage of the van. If it had ever resembled a child, it no longer did so.

Smith One was also gone.

Parker waited for his hearing and vision to return to their normal states, but they did not. He felt nauseous, and it was all he could do to return to his own car, where he remained seated behind the wheel until some semblance of order was restored to his senses. When he was sufficiently recovered, he called the cab company that had picked up Smith Two and his partner. He told the dispatcher he believed he might have left an item in one of its taxis, and was given a cell phone number for the driver. Parker contacted him, but was too tired to make up any more stories. He identified himself as a private investigator and promised a fifty if the driver told Parker the drop-off point for the fare he'd picked up on Forest Avenue about half an hour earlier.

"For fifty bucks," said the driver, "I'd tell you who killed Kennedy."

Parker settled for the location, a single-story strip motel out on Route 1, although he did ask the driver if he'd happened to overhear any conversation in which his customers might have engaged.

"They didn't talk at all," the driver said. "I didn't take them for friendly types, not even toward each other."

"Why do you say that?"

"They were linking arms when they hailed me, but as soon as they got in the cab, they moved to opposite doors."

Parker thanked him, and told him he'd put the cash in an envelope and drop it off at the cab office in the morning. He then drove out to the motel, showed his ID and a twenty, and informed the old guy behind the desk that he was interested in two guests, a man and a woman. Parker described them in as much detail as he could, as well as giving an estimate of the time they had probably returned to their rooms that night. The old guy examined Parker's ID before handing it back, minus the twenty.

"Nope," he said. He was wearing a T-shirt that read *Bowlers Do It With Two Balls,* which Parker decided was barely a single entendre.

"Nope what?"

"Nope, we don't have anyone of that description staying here tonight."

"You're sure?"

"Four rooms taken, two by young couples, two by old. And by old, I mean old. I'm old, but they're *real* old. They're so old they might be dead by now."

"You could have told me all that before you took the twenty."

"You should have held on to the twenty until you got an answer. You been at this PI business for long, son?"

"I'm considering retiring."

"Yeah?"

"Yeah. I might cash out, and use the money to buy a can of gas to burn down this motel."

"I don't care. It isn't my motel. And the way you throw money around, you won't have enough left to pay for matches, never mind gas."

"I don't suppose you saw a cab pick up a couple outside a while back?"

"Saw a cab, but didn't see who got in or out. None of my business."

Parker decided that the night wasn't about to get any better, not at this late stage. Sometimes a man had to learn when to take a write-off.

"You'll understand if I don't thank you for your time. I figure I've paid you enough to skate over the niceties."

"That you have. But if you ever need a place to stay, I'll get you a good deal."

"Someplace else, I hope," said Parker, and left.

Parker's head was still swimming as he neared the turn into his driveway. He used his phone to check the status of the security system. It was second nature to him since the attack that had almost taken his life, but it still irritated him, reminding him of his own vulnerability. The system was green. No one had entered the property since his departure earlier in the evening. Had anyone done so, the phone would have beeped an alarm, and the nearest camera would have sent him a picture of the intruder.

He parked, went inside, and searched the medicine cabinet until he found some pills that claimed to tackle both headaches and nausea: prescription medication left over from the aftermath of the shooting. He wasn't even sure they were still in date, but he swallowed two of them dry before heading to his office and sitting by the window, staring out at the moon on the marshes, the saltwater tributaries trickling like molten silver to the sea.

He thought of Smith One and Smith Two, and the woman with them. Smith One he might be able to trace. Someone had to know of him, and where to find him. But the other two, they were interesting. Maybe he should have stayed with them, and left Smith One for another occasion.

But all this was just a temporary distraction, a means of avoiding the contemplation of what he had witnessed on Cottage. A child, or just a patch of ice in the shape of one, distorted by Parker's tiredness and the tones of the night? But Smith One had seen it, too. What's more, it had scared him. Whomever, or whatever, Smith One was involved with, he'd neglected to examine the small print on the contract.

Parker felt a drowsiness begin to descend. He knew he should go to bed, but he didn't want to leave his chair, didn't want to look away from the marshes. He understood why. He was hoping to catch a glimpse of Jennifer, the gossamer reassurance of her presence. This was her time: night, with her father caught between wakefulness and unconsciousness.

But Jennifer did not appear, and soon Parker slept.

CHAPTER
LVI

Quayle walked alone by the shore of the Piscataquis River, the lights of the inn now distant. Mors was asleep in her own bed, in her own room. If he wanted to be with her later, he would summon her.

The drive back to Dover-Foxcroft had not been a pleasant one. Meeting Giller in Portland had been a mistake because it exposed them to Parker's regard. Quayle could understand why Giller considered it important for them to know about the private detective; could even, at a stretch, accept that Parker had to be encountered in person to understand his strangeness and therefore the potential threat he posed; but Giller should have found another way.

Quayle was smoking, a vice he deeply enjoyed but one that was growing harder to indulge in these intolerant times. He smoked only Chancellor Treasurer cigarettes, silver-tipped and housed in a gunmetal case. They were expensive, but money was not an issue for Quayle. He had more of it than a man could spend in ten lifetimes.

And Quayle would know.

He cared little about this world beyond the square mile or so of London that he thought of as his own—cared little, in truth, for the world beyond his own rooms, for they contained infinities within themselves. He maintained only sporadic contact with those whose concerns impacted his own. Quayle's obsession was the Atlas, and the Atlas alone.

Therefore the fact of Charlie Parker's existence had passed Quayle by until now; but everything he had learned from Giller, confirmed by his own brief encounter with the detective, provoked in him an unease of such intensity as to be almost refreshing. In a life so long-lived, even fear was a welcome distraction from the quotidian.

What troubled Quayle most was the inability of anyone, but particularly the Backers, to deal conclusively with Parker. According to Giller, any number of individuals had tried and failed, with a cadre of concerned citizens in a small Maine town named Prosperous coming closer than most to neutralizing the detective. Yet the Backers possessed pressing reasons to kill Parker, and the resources to accomplish it. Why, then, had they not yet done so? What was lacking?

A possible answer came to Quayle as his cigarette burned down to the butt. He flicked it into the dark, the hiss of its destruction lost in the river's tumult, and turned back toward the inn. A conversation was required. The Principal Backer would be called upon to justify himself.

Reasons: yes, these the Backers had.

Resources: yes.

But the will?

That remained to be seen.

CHAPTER
LVII

Parker drove up to Bangor shortly before noon the following day. The air was bright and clear, and when he stopped for coffee along the way, the conversations of those at the diner counter appeared infused with the kind of hope that he always regarded as unique to northern states. It came with spring, surged with summer, and was entirely spent by the coming of winter.

Because of Dave Evans's birthday celebration, and the less welcome events that followed, Parker had missed most of the coverage of the most recent press conference held by the state police. The conference had been postponed from earlier in the day due to what turned out to be a false sighting of Heb Caldicott up by Crouseville, close to the Canadian border, which meant the news teams had struggled to put together packages in time for their evening broadcasts. As a result, Parker was forced to flip between his phone and the *Portland Press Herald* as he played catch-up.

It was clear that the hunt for Caldicott and his associates had dominated proceedings, with only a few minutes at the end given over to the ongoing mystery of the "Woman in the Woods." A state police lieutenant named Solange Corriveau was now the lead investigator on the Jane Doe case, following a reorganization of MSP resources following Allen's murder. Parker didn't know Corriveau, so she was either new to the force or recently promoted. It stood to reason: the main focus was on the hunt for Allen's killers, so the less pressing investigation was always destined to be handed off to whomever could be spared. On the other hand, the condition in which Jane Doe's body was discovered—buried after recently giving birth, the remains of the placenta interred with her—meant that, by police reasoning, a female officer would present a more appropriate public face.

And in this case, police reasoning might have been correct. Parker went to the Channel 6 website and pulled up the video of the conference, making sure to use earphones to listen in order to avoid bothering the other diners. Corriveau was in her early thirties, and spoke slowly and clearly. She shared with the press almost every detail already known to Parker, and emphasized that law enforcement had a number of aims in the investigation: to identify the woman; to establish the circumstances of her death; and to confirm the whereabouts of her child, because the search of the area around the grave had revealed no trace of the infant.

"Is this a homicide investigation?" asked an unidentified male reporter.

"We have no evidence to suggest it was a homicide," Corriveau replied. "It appears most likely that the woman died as a result of complications in childbirth, but we'd very much like to find out how she ended up in that situation."

She then changed her tone, making it softer, less formal.

"It may be that someone out there believed he or she was doing good by giving this woman a burial, and taking care of her child. Sometimes people do the wrong things for the right reasons, and we understand that. But there may be a mother, a husband, or a partner who cared about this woman, and they have a right to know what happened to her *and* her child. So if you have information that might help us in this, anything at all, we're asking you to come forward so we can start setting some minds at rest. We're not looking to put anyone behind bars, and we'll be as sympathetic as we can, but the longer this goes on, the harder it will become for us to reach a resolution that's best for everyone involved."

With that, the clip ended. Parker was impressed. Corriveau had done well: no threats, but just enough steel at the conclusion. He put his phone and newspaper away, folded his reading glasses, and ordered a second cup of coffee in a to-go cup.

Once outside, he made a call to Gordon Walsh.

"I watched the press conference," he said. "Where'd you find Corriveau?"

"Presque Isle PD."

"She's good."

"Tell that to the boneheads screeching about affirmative action. We'd still have hired her if she was a Martian. Like you say, she's good. Did you call just to compliment us on our progressive hiring policies?"

"I felt like passing the time of day. Whatcha doin'?"

"Seriously."

"I crossed paths with a guy at the Bear last night. Small: five-two, five-three, looks like a rat that's figured out the basics of tailoring. Not local to Portland, but my guess is he's a Mainer, although you couldn't tell from the accent. I think the term is 'studiedly neutral.' He was accompanied by an Englishman claiming to be a lawyer, and a woman who hasn't seen sunlight since Reagan died."

"Any name?"

"He said it was Smith, but I'm not inclined to believe him."

"I'm shocked, but I don't doubt your instinct for dissimulation. Why the interest?"

"I think he may have been keeping tabs on me. Not regularly, just occasionally."

"It's not much to go on."

"I'll talk to Dave Evans. We might get something from the cameras in the bar."

"If you do, send me the images and I'll ask around, but I can't promise anything. You still snooping for Moxie on Jane Doe?"

"I am. In fact, I'm on my way to do some snooping right now."

"If you find out anything, share it with Corriveau."

"Done. You have a number for her?"

Walsh gave him Corriveau's direct line, and her cell phone.

"How's Angel doing?"

"Improving."

"That's good to hear. And the other one?"

"Still no change in his condition."

"That's less good to hear."

"But not unexpected."

"No. And remember: Corriveau."

"Understood, and thanks."

"Doesn't mean we're dating again," said Walsh, and hung up.

The exterior of the Tender House had not changed a great deal since Parker's last visit. Its status as a refuge for frightened and abused women was still unadvertised, and only the electronically operated steel gate, and the fact that its high white picket fence was made of metal instead of wood, suggested the two adjoining clapboard buildings might house anything other than another pleasant condo development.

Parker left his car at the curb, and rang the bell on the gatepost. He kept his head up so the cameras over the main door and on a nearby tree could see his face clearly. His arrival was anticipated, but it was still a good thirty seconds before he was admitted. He knew the reason for the delay: while two cameras were watching him, other eyes were monitoring the street for any signs of suspicious activity, just in case a husband or boyfriend with a grudge decided to seize the opportunity offered by an open gate to enter the property and reclaim his chattel. Cars were parked on the street, but all were empty, and any pedestrians were both distant and seemingly occupied with their own concerns. But Parker was careful to walk quickly into the driveway once the gate opened, and he didn't turn his back on it until the barrier closed safely behind him.

Candy stood waiting for him at the main door. She was wearing her beloved pink bunny slippers, her hair remained slightly unkempt, and her smile had not altered one iota: it signaled unconditional pleasure at Parker's presence. Candy had Down syndrome, and was the daughter of the original founders of the Tender House, both of whom were now deceased. She continued to live and work on the property, and much of its identity was tied up with her. She was a link to its past, but also a symbol of everything it stood for. Candy, in essence, was tenderness.

"Charlie Parker," she said. "What you doing here, my darling?"

She gathered him to her in an enormous hug, and he held her in turn, closing his eyes briefly against the world.

"Are you better now?" she asked.

"Better for seeing you."

"But you got shot."

"Yes."

"You mustn't get shot."

"That's good advice. I'll bear it in mind for the future."

A woman emerged from the depths of the house. She was big and busty, with a manner that projected both strength and compassion. Her hair was grayer than before, and Parker thought she moved with a certain caution, even weariness, that was new to her. This was Molly Bow; if Candy was the heart of the Tender House, then Molly was its brain, its muscle, its sinew.

"I wasn't flirting!" said Candy, as soon as she became aware of Molly's presence.

"Are you sure?" said Molly.

"Give me a break," said Candy. "Charlie Parker's my friend." She turned to Parker for confirmation of this. "Right?"

"Right. And I brought you a gift."

"A gift? For me?"

Parker handed over a bag from Treehouse Toys containing a design-your-own-stationery set, including stickers, stars, and glitter. Candy liked making cards for the women and children in the Tender House. She left them on pillows, and slipped them under doors. Her face lit up when she peered into the bag.

"Thank you," said Candy, and she hugged Parker again. "I must go and make you a card to take home."

"I'd like that a lot."

"A birthday card."

"But it's not my birthday."

"It doesn't matter."

And Parker decided that perhaps it didn't. You accepted birthday cards when and where you could.

"A birthday card it is, then."

Candy headed into the house. Parker walked up to Bow and embraced her, although he noticed that she kept him at one remove.

"How are you, Molly?"

"I'm okay," she replied.

"Just okay?"

"I got beaten up."

"When?"

"About a month ago."

"I didn't know."

"We kept it quiet. The police were informed,

312

but we didn't want to alarm any of the women. How can we expect to make them feel safe if we can't even look after ourselves?"

"Who did it?"

"No idea. He wore a ski mask, so I figure it was some prick whose wife or girlfriend might have passed our way. He caught me as I was coming out of a movie. I should have parked closer to the light. He tried to drag me into the bushes. I think he had a mind to rape me, but he settled for kicking the shit out of me instead."

"How bad?"

"A couple of busted ribs, and a lot of bruises. I managed not to get my nose broken, which is something. I always liked my nose."

"That wasn't what I meant."

"I know. Physically, I'm on the mend. Psychologically, that's another matter. I guess we have that much in common, right? But come on inside. I'll make you a cup of coffee, and you can tell me what brings you to our door."

If the façade of the Tender House was unchanged, its interior had undergone considerable renovation. An extension to the back of the main building now offered two rooms that could be used for meetings or therapy sessions, along with a small medical clinic and a new kitchen.

"We received a bequest," Bow explained. "Enough to put together all this. We also have

313

a nurse who comes in three times a week, and a therapist for two afternoons."

She made coffee for both of them, and left Candy behind the main desk working on Parker's card, with instructions to shout if she needed help. Bow and Parker went into the smaller of the new rooms, leaving the door slightly ajar. They sat opposite each other, a box of tissues on the table between them.

"So why are you here?" Bow asked.

"The woman's body found in Piscataquis."

"I don't know much beyond what I've seen on television and read in the newspapers. They're saying it wasn't a homicide, and she died of complications from childbirth."

"Probably postnatal hemorrhaging due to placental abruption, or that's what's coming from the ME. No sign of any other injuries."

"And you're investigating this?"

"In a way."

"On whose behalf?"

"Moxie Castin's."

"Moxie Castin is a lawyer. So he's employing you on behalf of a client?"

"No, it's all Moxie."

"Why?"

"The Star of David that was carved into a tree by the grave. Moxie's Jewish. Trying to trace Jane Doe's child is his service for the dead."

"Which means you're his service for the dead."

"Yes."

"You seem to spend a lot of time serving the dead."

"I serve the living, too."

"Not so much."

Parker conceded the point.

"Could she have been someone with whom you were in contact?" he asked.

"I don't think so. I went back through our records following the police appeals. We had a couple of pregnant women pass through here during that time, but the ages don't match. Do the police think there's any chance she might be local?"

"It's unlikely. She'd be on file, or someone would have come forward by now. You know how this state is: it's thirty-five thousand square miles of small town."

"You could have told me all this in a phone call, and spared yourself a trip. Why did you need to look in my eyes?"

From outside came the sound of Candy humming as she worked.

"Jane Doe was pregnant," said Parker, "and from outside the state. The fact that she ended up buried in the woods means she was probably in trouble from the start. So what drew her to Maine?"

"Family? A friend?"

"Then why hasn't anyone claimed her?"

"Maybe the father of the child was a Mainer, or living here from away."

"Again, the same question," said Parker. "Why not come forward?"

"Because he killed her."

"Nobody killed her. She died."

"She was left to bleed out. There are all kinds of ways to kill a woman. Some don't even involve laying a hand on her."

"Okay, let's say I accept that. Why let her die and then keep the child? Look at it objectively: What's the point in concealing a postnatal death, and burying the body on woodland—which is risky—all to hide a baby?"

"I can come up with reasons," said Bow, "none of them suggestive of a positive outcome for the child's well-being."

"Once more, all that may be true. But you're starting at the end and working back. I'm still a whole set of steps behind you."

"Where, exactly?"

"At the point where she gets here and looks for help."

"Assuming she did."

"Molly—"

"Fine, fine. So she seeks help—but she didn't come to us."

"And if she'd approached any of the other services or refuges in the state, there'd be a record of it. Someone would remember."

"Right."

"Then who do you turn to if you're really frightened, and really, really at risk, and you don't want to be remembered?"

Molly stared at Parker, but said nothing.

"The Tender House is discreet," Parker persisted, "but the fact that you could be dragged into bushes and beaten, in all likelihood because of your work here, confirms a certain awareness of your presence. Sometimes, discreet isn't enough."

"You're fishing."

"You know me better than that."

"What are you suggesting?"

Parker had been asking around. He'd even spoken to Rachel, his ex. Rachel was a psychologist and had worked with victims of domestic abuse. She'd made some calls, and come back with a piece of information she'd been unable to substantiate but that was, in her view, more than hearsay.

"I've heard rumors."

"About?"

"Safe houses. Women and children in trouble, being passed from place to place. All under the radar, and only the most desperate of cases, the ones barely a step ahead of a violent death. No police involvement, no state or local services. They go in one end of the tunnel and come out the other, far away."

"Fairy tales."

"I don't believe that's the case."

Molly sat back in her chair and folded her arms. Her demeanor didn't augur well for disclosures.

"And if—*if*—all that were true, don't you think these individuals might also want to help solve the mystery of this woman's identity?"

"Not if it meant explaining how they knew."

"You're asking me to betray confidences."

"Molly, there's something very wrong here. I'll do all I can to protect sources, and not endanger anything you or others may have worked hard to establish, but I need to make my way back along the chain. This woman deserves better than an anonymous burial in a pauper's grave, and out there is someone who knows where her child is."

Slowly, Bow unfolded her arms, and Parker thought again about how tired she appeared. It wasn't just the recent assault. Perhaps there was only so long a person could bear witness to the damage men were prepared to inflict on women without falling victim, even temporarily, to despair.

"I'm not supposed to know," she said. "And you make it sound like some kind of formal structure, or secret organization, but it's not like that. There's no one network, no hierarchy. There are only people who want to help, who remain in loose contact with one another, and understand the value of staying low."

"I won't share this with anyone else, not even Moxie."

"Jesus." She breathed deeply. "I'll give you a name, but—"

Parker waited.

"You'll have to tell her I sent you," said Bow, "and then she'll never trust me again. None of them will."

"I'm sorry."

"No, you're not. I like you, I really do, but in so many ways you're just another man. You're convinced of the rightness of your own cause. You know best, and you'll threaten and wheedle and cajole until you get what you want. When you're done, you'll look back at the havoc you've created, and all you'll be able to do is shrug and make your apologies."

Parker didn't reply. He knew some of this was true, and the part that wasn't didn't matter.

"You need to talk to Maela Lombardi," said Bow. "She lives not far from you, over in Cape Elizabeth."

Parker recognized the name.

"She was a schoolteacher."

"Yes."

He tried to picture Lombardi. He thought he might have seen her once, at a community gathering. He asked Bow for contact details, and was given two numbers—home and cell phone—along with an address.

"Are there others like Lombardi in Maine?" he asked.

"Not that I know of."

"And you'd know."

"I would."

"And in the rest of New England?"

"I don't have that information."

"You're certain?"

"Don't push me, Parker."

And when Molly Bow told you not to push, you were advised to stop pushing.

"Thank you," said Parker.

"Don't thank me either. Your gratitude won't make me feel any better."

She stood. Their meeting was over. Parker felt a kind of sadness. He understood that their relationship had shifted irrevocably, and not for the better. She walked him to the door, where Candy was waiting with a birthday card. He accepted it, and received another hug for good measure, before Candy went to her room to take a nap, leaving Parker alone with Bow. Her arms were folded again. It looked like Candy's would be the last hug he received at the Tender House.

"I know," he said to her, as he stood on the step, the street beyond still empty.

"You know what?"

"That you lied to me earlier."

She stared hard at him, and waited for him to continue.

"You can identify who assaulted you. If you're not certain, you're as good as."

She stayed silent for so long that Parker became convinced she was going to let him walk away without any reply at all.

"I have no proof," she said at last.

"He'll do it again. If not to you, then to some other woman."

"I'm not going to give you his name."

"I didn't ask for it."

For the first time, she looked disappointed in him.

"In your way," she said, "you did."

And she closed the door in his face.

CHAPTER
LVIII

Daniel Weaver was no longer answering calls from his toy phone. He had made this decision after seeing the story about the dead lady on one of the news shows Grandpa Owen liked to watch—except Daniel felt that lately his grandpa wasn't much enjoying the news shows, which made Daniel wonder why he continued to monitor them so intently.

But the toy phone kept ringing. It didn't ring while his mom or Grandpa Owen were nearby, or not since the morning of the dental appointment, when his grandpa had remarked on the noise. It was as though the lady who called herself Karis didn't want to draw that kind of attention. It was Daniel with whom she wished to communicate, not anyone else.

And Daniel didn't want to talk to dead people.

Daniel had no proof that Karis and the dead lady were one and the same. He just knew it to be so, the same way you knew the voice coming out of the ventriloquist's dummy was really just that of the man or woman holding it, no matter how still the person's lips stayed. But he wanted Karis to go away. He didn't know why she'd chosen him. He didn't understand why she claimed to have been waiting so long to speak to him. He wasn't important. He was just a boy.

And talking to Karis wasn't like talking to an ordinary adult. It was more like talking to Jordan Ansell, the eldest son of Mr. Floyd Ansell, who owned the laundry in town. Something bad had happened to Jordan Ansell while he was in his mom's tummy, and now one eye was smaller than the other, and he couldn't use his withered left arm to lift stuff. Jordan Ansell was all grown up, but he still lived at home with his parents and got paid to iron laundry. Jordan Ansell would ask a question, and seem to listen to the answer, but the next thing that came out of Jordan Ansell's mouth would be completely unconnected to what was said before, so a conversation that might have started with Jordan Ansell commenting on the weather would quickly jump from rain to stones to dog hair and eventually finish up with shoes, Jordan Ansell having a particular fascination with what folks did or did not wear on their feet. Jordan Ansell didn't really listen to what anyone said. He heard, but he didn't listen.

Karis was like that. Karis would ask a question, and say *yes yes yes* as the answer came, and sound as though she were fascinated by what she was hearing, but her tone never varied, and even Daniel recognized that not everything he said was interesting. Then, once Karis had exhausted her store of *yes yes yes,* she would cut to the chase, like Jordan Ansell focusing on sneakers and cowboy boots, and ask Daniel:

when will you visit me?

when will you come?

The first time she said this, Daniel asked her where she lived, and Karis giggled as though Daniel had accidentally made a joke, but one only she could understand.

in the woods

"Where? In a house?"

not a house

That laugh again. It made Daniel's scalp itch.

"Then where?"

among the trees

"Like a witch?"

maybe a good witch

"How will I find you?"

start walking and i'll find you

"But where?"

north

"Which way is north?"

you wait until the sun starts to go down, and then you keep it to your left

"I can't do that."

why?

"Because the woods are dangerous."

i'll protect you

"Why can't you just come here?"

i like the woods
you'll like them too
i can show you the secret places
and then we'll sleep

Karis kept asking him to go into the woods, and sometimes she'd get mad at Daniel for not understanding why it was so important that he should. She'd begin to talk faster, so fast that Daniel couldn't pick up all the words because they flowed into one another until at last they became just a stream of noise that turned to static before exploding into silence. And when Karis called back again—an hour later, a day later—it would be as if their previous conversation had never occurred, and they would start the dialogue afresh.

when will you visit me?
when will you come?

But that was before Daniel realized who Karis was. Now Daniel was certain that he didn't want to join Karis in her secret places, and he didn't wish to find out where she slept, because when he tried to imagine it he saw worms and bugs, and felt cold, damp earth around him.

He knew he should tell someone—his mom, his grandpa—but Karis had made it clear that he wasn't to do this. She was his friend, not theirs. If he told, they'd be angry with him, and she would be angry with him too. That was when her voice would change, and it made Daniel feel very afraid, because he understood that, deep down, Karis was *always* angry.

Sad, but mostly angry.

But all this had to stop. Daniel was afraid to sleep. He saw the phone in his dreams, and its ringing woke him, even when it wasn't making any sound at all. The stupid smile under the dial gave him the creeps, and the little black eyes that moved in their plastic sockets reminded him of a dying dog he and his grandpa had found by the side of the road a few months back. The dog had been run over by a car. Its skull was all messed up, its fur torn and bloodied, and its eyes were rolling in its head. Grandpa Owen told Daniel to go stand behind a tree while he went to find a big stone.

And the dog hadn't made a sound, not even at the end.

Daniel knew he had to get rid of the phone, but he was afraid to put it in the trash because his mom and grandpa were compulsive sorters, and if they found the phone Daniel would have to explain why he was throwing it away instead of putting it in the box for the charity store. Daniel didn't think that would be a good idea. He didn't want some other kid getting calls from Karis. Neither could he burn the phone, because matches alone wouldn't do the trick, even if he could find a way to get to them.

So Daniel decided to bury it.

• • •

He waited until his mom was at work and his grandpa was napping. Grandpa Owen usually nodded off between four and five in order to recharge his batteries before Rob Caldwell—and later, Lester Holt—came on WCSH. Grandpa Owen said Rob Caldwell looked trustworthy, which was why he liked watching him co-anchor *News Center*. Grandpa Owen said Lester Holt also looked trustworthy, but Rob Caldwell was local, and Grandpa Owen said it was more important to be able to trust the local guy. Daniel wasn't sure why this was, unless Grandpa Owen was planning to leave Rob Caldwell with the keys to his truck, or ask him to look after his wallet.

So while Grandpa Owen snored in an armchair, and Willona was turning down a wedding proposal on *Good Times*, Daniel went to the tree line at the end of the yard shared by the two properties, and dug a hole using a small trowel that he'd removed from the woodshed for this purpose. The ground was harder than Daniel had anticipated, so the hole took a while to dig, and his hands and clothes got messy, but eventually he had a hollow before him that would take the phone. Daniel would have preferred if the hole were deeper—in an ideal world, the hole would have gone halfway to China—but he was afraid Grandpa Owen might wake up and start wondering where he was, so he dropped the phone in the hole and commenced covering it up. He kept his face turned away at first because those plastic eyes were looking up at him like those of some living creature, and they made him feel bad; but eventually he could no longer see them, and finally he could no longer see the phone either. He tramped the dirt down so it was level with the rest of the ground. He thought it still looked a little different, but not so much that anyone would really notice, not unless they searched really hard.

Grandpa Owen was just beginning to stir when Daniel returned to the house, giving him enough time to get to the bathroom and clean the dirt from his hands and under his fingernails. The knees of his jeans were filthy, and he wished he'd had the foresight to bring a piece of cardboard or an old towel on which to kneel, but it was too late now. He stripped off the jeans, stuck them at the bottom of a pile of laundry, and changed into a new pair. They weren't the same color, but Grandpa Owen would never notice the difference.

When all this was done, Daniel went to the kitchen and stared out over the yard to the spot where the phone was now buried. Even if it rang underground, he wouldn't be able to hear it. No one would. He hoped this might make Karis give up. Maybe she'd go back to where she came from, wherever that might be. He'd seen the footage of the body being carried away from the woods on a stretcher. It had looked very small. Daniel wondered if Karis had been little in real life, or if death had just made her so. Perhaps only bones had been left by the time she was found. If so, how was she speaking to him? Skeletons didn't talk, except in cartoons. Daniel had heard his mom and Grandpa Owen say that the dead lady had been taken to a mortuary. When Daniel asked what that was, his mom told him it was a place where dead people were kept before it came time to bury them, although she seemed annoyed that he'd asked, or just annoyed he'd overheard them speaking about the woman to begin with; Daniel wasn't sure which. Did they have phones in mortuaries? Daniel guessed so. Was that how Karis was calling him? Did she creep out of her drawer at night (because that was where they kept the bodies, in drawers, like Grandpa Owen's business files), bare bones clacking on the floor, and hide under a desk so she could call Daniel?

But Karis couldn't be in a drawer, because she claimed to live in the woods, and sometimes Daniel could hear the sound of branches rustling in the background. In the end he decided it was probably best not to think too hard on such matters. Karis was a ghost, that was all, and ghosts weren't like people. They probably had their own ways of doing things. He just wanted Karis to do those things someplace else, and with someone else. Perhaps they just needed to bury her again. It could be that Karis didn't like being locked away in a drawer, although being buried under dirt seemed worse to Daniel, and being burned—like some dead folks were—sounded worse still.

He heard Grandpa Owen calling, asking if he was okay.

"Yes," he said.

Yes, he hoped.

CHAPTER
LIX

Ivan Giller knew nothing of atlases or buried gods. He did not go to church, and believed that death marked the snuffing out of all consciousness. He disliked violence, and consequently did not own a gun, even though he regularly dealt with violent men. He was a buyer and seller, mostly of information. He was a source, and a channel, and was very good at what he did.

Giller's introduction to the lawyer Quayle had been facilitated through a series of trusted cutouts, with the promise of a bonus well above the norm if he could help the Englishman successfully tie up his affairs, and thus—it was made clear—encourage his speedy departure from the continental United States. Giller was aware that the commission ultimately came from the same people who paid him to watch Parker, although he had never met any of them face-to-face, and didn't care to. From what Giller had gleaned of them, a little knowledge certainly qualified as dangerous, and a lot might prove fatal.

Initially it had seemed like a simple assistance job, but now Giller was regretting ever becoming involved in it. First of all, there was the lawyer himself. Giller had met plenty of attorneys in his time, and could count on his thumbs the number he trusted, but Quayle resembled a being created from the distilled essence of all that was disreputable about the legal profession. Giller suspected that when Quayle died, every bone in his body would be revealed as slightly bent.

Next there was Mors, Quayle's shadow, who dressed like a schoolmarm and smelled like a whorehouse mattress. Giller couldn't recall ever encountering a more malformed woman, with her graveyard pallor, her too-shiny skin, her too-small teeth, her fingers like the legs of a spider crab, and a voice that had the same impact upon the ear as an abrading instrument. She made Giller want to hide in a cellar.

Then there was Parker. Giller's days of monitoring him from a discreet distance had come to an end. Parker now knew what Giller looked like and was probably already endeavoring to put a name—other than Smith—to the face. No good could come from having Parker take an interest in the fact of Giller's existence.

Finally, and most pressingly, there was the not insignificant matter of the mutilated child— Giller could conceive of it in no other way— glimpsed the previous evening. He might have managed to convince himself he had imagined it, or conjured it from his subconscious as a prelude to a fever, except he knew Parker had seen it too. Giller understood on some primal level that its presence must somehow be linked to Quayle and Mors, but he wasn't about to invite either of them to clarify the relationship. He was simply aware of having wandered into a situation that presaged no good for anyone, least of all Ivan Giller, and it would be a very good idea for him to extricate himself from it as quickly and efficiently as possible.

With that in mind, Giller made a call to his contact, he who had initially put Giller in touch with Quayle, seeking to void what was, in essence, no more than a gentlemen's agreement, absent the gentlemen. This particular contact was an elderly dealer in rare coins and stamps, although he was said to have secured a comfortable old age by selling very specialized pornography back in the good old days before the Internet drained much of the profit from distributing sexual images on paper and film. The dealer got back to him within the hour, making it clear that Giller's involvement with Quayle could not be undone, and not only Giller's continued good health but the good health of a number of people up the line, including the dealer himself, were dependent on his remaining in Quayle's good graces.

So Giller was screwed, and no mistake. This left only plan B: get Quayle what he wanted, collect the bonus, and consider not answering the phone again for a very long time.

To this end, Giller began calling in a lot of favors.

The Principal Backer was working on the restoration of a Georgian walnut bureau dating from about 1740. It was in miserable condition when he first acquired it, although that was part of the challenge for him, and the pleasure. The feet were beyond salvation, and the handles were incongruous Victorian replacements, but the boxwood inlay and ebony stringing remained intact, and it had somehow retained its original leather writing surface, along with the eighteenth-century lock and key for the desk itself.

He had been laboring over the piece for almost a year now, and had recently sourced appropriate handles from a similar bureau with mortal injuries. His bureau, by contrast, would soon be suitable for resale—through an agent, of course, and without the Principal Backer's own name ever being mentioned in connection with it. He expected it to make about $2,000 at auction, even if this return wouldn't even begin to compensate him for his efforts. Money wasn't the object, though; it was the act of bringing something back almost from the dead.

It was about returning some beauty to the world. This was why he was so careful to conceal his involvement in the restoration. He was surrounded by those who regarded this world as forfeit, and would therefore consider even the most minor of aesthetic improvements to it as indicative of a deeper malaise, one worthy of further investigation.

Beside him, his cell phone began to ring. He wiped the oil from his hands before picking up.

"Yes?"

"It's Quayle," said a woman's voice. Her name was Erin, and she took care of the minutiae of the Backers' affairs.

"What now?"

A pause.

"He wants to meet with you."

The Principal Backer had a certain profile, and a circle of acquaintances, both professional and personal, that knew nothing of his baser vocation, but he remained careful to meet in conclave even with his fellow Backers only once or twice a year, and had never yet encountered Quayle in person. In theory, Quayle did not know the Principal Backer's true identity, but in practice . . .

"I suppose declining the invitation is not an option?" he said.

"It's always an option. Whether it's advisable is another question."

The Principal Backer considered the situation.

Perhaps it was time to call in his marker in return for the assistance Quayle had already received. He would have Erin pass on the necessary details. Quayle wouldn't refuse. He wanted the Atlas too badly.

"Did he nominate a venue?"

"He left the decision to you. What about your club?"

The Principal Backer's Boston club was both exclusive and discreet. It was regularly swept for listening devices of all kinds, and the windows had been treated with signal-defense film to block Wi-Fi transmissions and thwart the use of laser microphones to pick up voice data. It was a safe haven for those concerned about business competitors, the U.S. government, or any number of law enforcement agencies eavesdropping on their affairs, which was why it was able to command membership fees of breathtaking expense.

"Why not? I'll tell them to fumigate it after he leaves."

"That may not be the best frame of mind in which to approach the engagement."

"Thank you for your concern," said the Principal Backer. "Now make the arrangements. And Erin?"

"Yes."

"Keep your distance from him."

"He only has this number."

"Then after you've informed him of the time and place of the meeting—and a small favor I plan to ask of him, the details of which I will forward to you—I want you to change your phone."

This was an unusual level of precaution, even by the standards of the Backers. The phone was new. Erin had only recently circulated its number to the others.

"Would you like me to provide additional protection for you?" she asked.

"There is no protection," said the Principal Backer. "Not from Quayle."

CHAPTER
LX

Parker called Maela Lombardi from his car, but both the cell and home numbers went straight to voice mail. He guessed that Molly Bow would probably have tried to contact Lombardi to let her know that she'd shared Lombardi's details with him, which might be for the best. If Lombardi was involved in sheltering desperate women from violent men, it was possible her view of the male sex could qualify as somewhat jaded. Even in her present mood, Bow would be able to smooth the way.

Parker was traveling against the traffic for most of his journey, and only got snarled up when he reached the outskirts of Portland. He thought about leaving Lombardi until the following morning, as it was now dark and he didn't want to disturb an elderly woman who might be about to settle down with a meal in front of her TV. Then he remembered that this was an elderly woman who was involved in an abuse victims' equivalent of the Underground Railroad, and was therefore probably familiar with being roused from her chair at inconvenient moments. He tried Lombardi's numbers for the fourth time, with the same result, before deciding to call Molly Bow as he crossed the Casco Bay Bridge to South Portland. There was always the chance that Bow had managed to get hold of Lombardi, who was now battening the hatches against him. If so, she was underestimating his persistence.

Bow sounded harried when she came to the phone, but it might have been a hangover from their earlier conversation.

"One quick question," said Parker. "Have you been in touch with Maela Lombardi since we spoke?"

"No. I mean, I tried, but I haven't been able to make contact."

"I haven't either."

"Where are you?"

"South Portland. I'm on my way to Lombardi's now."

"She usually answers her phone. It's rarely off, for obvious reasons."

"If she was planning to leave town, who would she inform?"

A pause.

"I can't give you any more names. I shouldn't have given you Maela's."

"Fine, I understand." And Parker did, although he wished he didn't. "I'll take a look at the house and see what's happening. But if I get back to you, be ready to make some calls. Just don't go alarming anyone yet."

Molly agreed. She didn't have a whole lot of choice, and didn't like not having a whole lot of choice. She was still letting Parker know this when he hung up, but by that point he'd gotten the message.

The Lombardi house on Orchard Road was dark when Parker arrived, and he saw no car in the drive. He rang the doorbell twice, just in case Lombardi was sleeping, before making a circuit of the property. All the doors and windows were locked, and nothing appeared to be disturbed when he shone his pocket flashlight inside.

He was about to call Molly Bow again when a neighbor began hovering in a yard across the street. Parker headed over and showed the woman his ID. She was in her forties, but with the kind of long, prematurely gray hair that suggested either massive self-confidence or the blessed state of not giving a rat's ass. Judging by her clothes, which were expensively casual, Parker opted for the former, but he still felt the hair wasn't doing her any favors. He guessed she might have been described as "handsome," but not by him. Cary Grant was handsome. Lots of men were, but generally speaking Parker believed it was better for women to avoid the label.

The neighbor told him her name was Dakota, which figured, and she'd been living on Orchard for ten years now. She knew Maela Lombardi well; they worked together at various community organizations. Dakota asked if Parker was concerned about Maela, and he answered that he wasn't as yet, but remained anxious to speak with her.

"I haven't seen her for a few days," said Dakota.

"Is that unusual?"

Dakota frowned, and scrunched up her nose. It made her look younger than she was, that damn gray hair apart.

"You know, it kind of is. She'd usually let me know if she was going away, just so I could keep an eye on her place. It's not like we have a lot of burglaries round here, but it pays to be careful."

It turned out that Maela Lombardi had a niece named Janette Howard who lived a couple of blocks away on Arlington Lane, so Parker drove over there, parked outside the house, and rang the bell. The door was answered by a young woman who might have been taken for about fifteen were it not for the three young kids, two boys and a girl, alternately tugging at her arms and calling her "Mommy," while simultaneously peering with varying degrees of interest at the visitor on their doorstep.

"Janette Howard?"

"Yes?"

For the second time in thirty minutes, Parker identified himself and indicated that he was seeking to speak with Maela Lombardi.

"My aunt lives just over on Orchard," said Howard. "She should be home right now."

"She isn't. I was wondering if she'd given any indication that she might be about to leave for somewhere."

"Maela never goes away. She doesn't approve of vacations."

"Would she tell you if she intended to take a trip?"

"Maybe, if she was going to be out of town for a while, but like I said, she's a homebody." She hushed her children, and silence descended for a moment or two. "Should I call the police?"

Parker said it was her decision, but if she wanted to check the house first, he'd be happy to accompany her.

"I don't have anyone to look after the kids. My husband is working nights this week."

Parker could see she was starting to worry now.

"What about the woman who lives across the road—Dakota?" he said. "Would it be okay if she entered the house with me?"

Howard was happy enough to go along with Parker's suggestion, as long as either Dakota or Parker called her as soon as they'd taken a look inside. So Parker returned to Orchard Road, where Dakota was waiting in Lombardi's yard, Janette Howard having called her in the interim to let her know that Parker had permission to enter the house. He wasn't concerned as yet about contaminating a possible crime scene: Lombardi might well have gone away for a day or two, but equally she could have fallen, or been taken ill. Neither was he trespassing on private property, as he had the niece's consent to enter. He pulled on a pair of gloves, just in case, and used Dakota's key to open the front door.

The alarm didn't sound: that was the first unusual thing Dakota noticed.

"Maela always sets the alarm when she leaves," she said. "Shit."

Dakota called Maela's name, but there was no reply. Parker told her to stay by the door while he searched the house, and not to touch anything.

It didn't take long to establish that it was empty. The beds were made, and the kitchen and bathroom were spotless. The bookshelves contained a lot of poetry and alternative lifestyle books, along with some feminist writing and various semi-mystical works—Carlos Castaneda, Robert Pirsig, Kahlil Gibran—but not much fiction. More books of a similar stripe stood piled on a packing chest that functioned as a coffee table in the living-cum-dining room, along with the most recent copy of the *Maine Sunday Telegram*, folded open to a puzzle page. Beside the newspaper were a pen and a pair of bifocals.

Dakota had not moved from her post by the door, but Parker could see her from where she stood, and she him. Her hands were deep in the pockets of her jeans, and she was hunched with unease.

"Does her home always look this tidy?" he asked.

"Maela's that kind of person."

Parker looked at the spectacles again. Given her age, it wasn't a surprise that Lombardi might require bifocals, and it indicated she wore spectacles when she drove.

"I don't suppose you'd know if Maela keeps a spare pair in her car for driving?" he asked.

"I'm sorry, I don't. I guess, now that you mention it, she does wear them to drive, but I couldn't say if she has a pair just for the car."

Parker went back outside and checked the mailbox. It contained some junk mail, but nothing more. He returned to the house and went through it again, this time examining each room more closely. He wasn't any wiser by the end of the process. Finally, he tried the answering machine on the home phone and listened to the voice messages. He heard two from Molly Bow, and a few hang-ups, which were his own earlier attempts to contact Lombardi, but that was all.

Dakota's cell phone rang. She looked at the screen.

"It's her niece," she said.

"You'd better answer it."

"What should I say?"

"Tell her that her aunt's not here, and I'll come by to talk with her as soon as I can."

Dakota did as Parker asked while he stood between the dining table and the kitchen arch, trying to find something, anything, that might give him cause for disquiet, but he didn't know Maela Lombardi and so was unfamiliar with her ways. He could only take Dakota's word that Lombardi maintained a pristine household, and he was wary about raising the alarm over nothing. Dakota claimed that she hadn't seen Lombardi for a few days, but how often did such a period of time go by without one neighbor seeing another? It was hardly shocking. Likewise, the fact that Lombardi hadn't informed her niece she was leaving town might just be because she hadn't gone anywhere in particular. It wasn't against the law for an elderly woman to head out for a while without alerting the army, navy, and National Guard. The alarm hadn't been set, but maybe Lombardi was in a hurry when she left, and forgot to activate it.

And yet there was something off, because he could smell it: an odor, faint but unpleasant. It was strongest over by a big armchair that faced the television. Parker knelt, noticing a faint stain on the fabric of the chair, and another on the floor. He leaned closer. He sniffed. Someone had thrown up here, and recently. He touched a finger to one of the stains. It came back slightly damp.

So: older people were sometimes ill, just like younger ones. It didn't mean much. Except Maela

Lombardi kept a very neat home, and struck Parker as the kind of person who would have cleaned up better than this if she'd puked. It wasn't enough to justify hitting the panic button, but it remained odd.

There appeared to be nothing more he could do. He thanked Dakota for her help, watched while she locked up—noting that she took the time to set the alarm—and returned to Janette Howard's house. He sat at her kitchen table while her kids played computer games, and asked how often she spoke to her aunt.

"Well, not every day," said Howard.

She sounded slightly guilty about this.

"But you get on with her?" said Parker.

"Yes, mostly."

Parker stepped carefully. He didn't want to alienate the young woman.

"I don't mean to pry," he said.

"Maela and I differ on certain issues," said Howard.

"What kind of issues?"

"Uh, she's pretty liberal."

"On?"

"Everything. Gay marriage, abortion. You know, social stuff."

"And you're not."

"Nobody's as liberal as Maela."

"So how often would the two of you speak?"

"I call her once a week, or a little less than that, to make sure she's doing okay."

Parker realized he was back where he'd started: with no idea if Maela Lombardi was actually missing or not.

"Has your aunt been ill lately?"

"Maela?" Howard laughed. "She's healthy as a horse. Why?"

"It smelled like someone might have been sick in the house—not very much, but enough to leave an odor and a couple of stains."

"That's not like Maela, although I'm not sure she'd even admit if she was feeling unwell. She'll probably still be trying to make out everything's fine when they're putting her in a pine box."

Howard realized what she'd said, and looked ashamed.

"God," she said. "Now should I call the police?"

"She's an elderly woman. It can't hurt."

Howard didn't look enthused at the prospect, but then few people ever did.

"Maela has a poor opinion of the police," she said.

"Why?"

"She's countercultural. If I call the cops, then she'd better be missing. If she's just left for the movies and dinner, she's going to be seriously pissed when she gets back."

CHAPTER
LXI

Daniel Weaver crouched by his bedroom door, listening to his mom and Grandpa Owen arguing. Since they often argued, mostly about small stuff, Daniel had grown used to their raised voices as a kind of background noise to his existence. Both his mother and Grandpa Owen lived their lives with the volume turned up. His mother claimed that a lifetime spent in trucks had made Grandpa Owen deaf to reason, so she had no choice but to shout at him. Grandpa Owen liked to respond that at least he had an excuse.

On this occasion, their back-and-forth had a different tone, which was what had drawn Daniel to eavesdrop. He had already learned that if adults were trying to keep their voices down, there might be something worth hearing.

"I did as you told me." It was Grandpa Owen speaking. "I gave you time to think, but this isn't going away. The longer it continues, the less likely we are to get a fair hearing."

"They'll take him from me." Daniel had to strain to pick up his mother's words.

"We'll hire a good attorney."

"With what? Are lawyers accepting coupons now?"

"I got a little left in the bank. And there's the rig."

Silence.

"You can't sell the rig."

"I'm tired. I can't handle the long hauls anymore. There's still money in her—not as much as I'd like, but some."

Dishes being stored away, the jangle of the silverware drawer.

"We should have been honest from the start."

"She made us promise not to."

"She shouldn't have," said Grandpa Owen. "It wasn't fair."

"But look what she gave us in return."

A chair being pulled up, a creaking as weight came to rest upon it. His mother, Daniel thought, becuase Grandpa Owen always groaned when he stood up or sat down.

"What we did was wrong, but not very wrong," said Grandpa Owen. "They'll see that he's better off with us. The state doesn't want to put kids in foster homes, not if they can avoid it. It costs too damn much."

The sound of his mother crying. Daniel wanted to go to her, but that would have revealed his snooping. All he could do was sit and listen. He didn't want anyone to take him from his mom and Grandpa Owen. He'd run away if they tried. If he couldn't run, he'd fight.

"I told you," said Grandpa Owen. "I'll make the call from a public phone. I'll be careful not to stay on the line for too long. I'll test the waters, see what Castin says, and you and I can discuss it before we proceed any further."

"And if we don't like what he has to say?"

Daniel waited for the answer.

"We could leave, I guess. Go someplace far from here."

Grandpa Owen sounded like a man being asked to jump over a stream that looked too wide for him.

"But?"

"If we were to strike camp," said Grandpa Owen, "we might just be giving ourselves away."

"And then they'd find us, wouldn't they? They'd send the detective—Parker. He'd hunt us down. I don't want him coming after us. He scares me."

"So do I make the call?"

This time the silence went on for so long that Daniel was convinced he'd somehow missed his mother's reply, until her voice came, very softly:

"Yes. But not yet."

"Jesus . . ."

Daniel heard a chair being pushed back, and he was back between the sheets by the time his mother appeared at the bedroom door. He pretended to be asleep as she came to sit on the edge of his bed. She didn't touch him, didn't try to wake him, but he could hear her breathing, and smell her perfume, and feel the fierce heat of her love for him. At last she left, and he turned over on his bed as though twisting in his sleep, so he could watch her as the door closed, before she was lost to him.

CHAPTER
LXII

Parker was sitting in his home office, updating Moxie Castin on what amounted to very little progress at all, when the alarm on his phone was activated, and seconds later an unmarked car, its dashboard flasher illuminated to identify the driver as a police officer, pulled up outside his door. Parker had already spoken with Molly Bow, alerting her to the possibility that Maela Lombardi might be missing and asking her permission to refer the police to her should they come calling. That permission had not been forthcoming as yet.

"I shouldn't have told you about Maela to begin with," Molly said. "If the police get involved, I'll be forced to give them even more names."

"You can't be forced to give them anything at all. And let me remind you that you told me you didn't have 'that information.' "

"Then why sic them on me to begin with?"

Parker had to admit there was a kind of logic to the argument, but it was canceled by an equal amount of illogicality. If Lombardi was missing, then Bow had at least helped to set in motion some kind of investigation into her whereabouts, and thus had done the right thing by revealing Lombardi's name to Parker, whatever her concerns about betraying confidences.

But he also had to recognize that a) Lombardi might not be missing at all; and b) if she were missing, her disappearance might not necessarily be linked to the Piscataquis remains. Lombardi's work with imperiled women could easily have left her exposed to acts of vengeance from a host of aggrieved partners, as Bow herself could attest from personal experience. Bow might be sitting on information that could assist the police in finding Lombardi, but she was also putting the squeeze on Parker in an effort to keep her name out of the investigation.

Sometimes, Parker's vocation made his head hurt.

If he retained any doubts about the reason for this police presence, they were dispelled as soon as the car door opened and the plainclothes officer stepped out. Her name was Kes Carroll—Kes being short for Kestrel, which meant she was officially the most exotically named person known to Parker, as well as the tallest woman, topping out at six-two in her stocking feet—and she was the Cape Elizabeth PD's sole detective. Parker had enjoyed occasional professional dealings with her, and always found her to be a straight arrow. Carroll was in her late fifties, and could easily have retired years before, but she appeared to find fulfillment in her work, and who was Parker to question that?

He opened the front door before Carroll had a chance to ring the bell, and invited her inside for coffee. She took a seat at the kitchen table while he found some cups. A pot was already brewing.

"Sorry for the late visit," said Carroll.

"I wasn't doing a whole lot anyway. I take it this is about Maela Lombardi?"

"Her niece called, said she'd spoken with you."

"Did she sound worried?"

"More apologetic."

"She and her aunt aren't particularly close."

"So she told us. Looks like you might have lit a small fire under her, though."

"It could be nothing."

"With you involved?"

Parker poured coffee for both of them, and put milk and sugar on the table.

"So?" asked Carroll as she added milk. "What's the deal?"

"The deal is the Jane Doe from Piscataquis. Moxie Castin hired me to find out what I can about her and the missing child. I can't reveal how I know this, but it's possible—just possible—that Lombardi might have had some contact with Jane Doe."

"Go on."

"I've been trying to figure out why a pregnant

354

woman would head to Maine to begin with, never mind end up buried in a shallow grave with the afterbirth. If she had relatives here, they'd have shown themselves by now."

"Unless they were the ones who put her in the ground—they, or the child's father."

"But why hide a death in childbirth? It's not a crime, unless someone can prove willful neglect."

"You know this state. Once you head out to the willywacks, there's no telling why some folks do the things they do. So what brought you to Lombardi?"

"I've been told she operated an unofficial safe house for women fleeing abusive relationships. What if Jane Doe was running from the father of her child? What if she was desperate? If she didn't want to turn to state services, or Planned Parenthood, or whatever other organizations might be in a position to offer help, where would she go? Even if Lombardi hadn't met her, she might know of someone else who did."

"But wouldn't Lombardi have come forward if she had some knowledge of the case?"

"I'd hoped to ask Lombardi that myself. She might have felt under pressure to protect this network of safe houses, because my under-standing is that Lombardi is just one link in the chain."

"Or?"

"Or Jane Doe made her promise not to tell."

"Why?"

"Because whoever she was running from was so bad that not only was Jane Doe's life at risk, but so was the life of her child, and perhaps the life of anyone who helped her."

"That's a hell of a leap to take."

"I've taken bigger."

Carroll tried her coffee, and gagged.

"This is horrible," she said.

"Organic decaf."

"What's the point of that?"

"Makes me feel virtuous."

"Well, whatever helps." Carroll didn't push the mug away, instead electing to keep it clasped in her hands, welcoming the warmth, if not the taste. Spring might have arrived, but the nights continued to bear winter's mark. "As for Lombardi, I'm reluctant to issue a Silver Alert until more time has gone by."

Silver Alerts sent notifications about missing seniors to highway signs around the state, asking motorists to be on the lookout.

"I did tell the niece that there was nothing to stop her from putting out the word herself on community bulletin boards, Facebook, Twitter, whatever might help," Carroll continued, "and if Lombardi hasn't made contact by morning, I'll look at speeding up procedures. But Howard was adamant that her aunt had shown no signs of dementia. If Lombardi got in her car and drove away, she knew what she was doing, and where she was going."

"Unless she didn't leave willingly."

Parker told Carroll about the stains and the smell.

"You know," she said, "you see a lot of shadows. You ought to ditch decaf, try regular. It might help."

Carroll gave the coffee one more try, if only to be sure it was as unsatisfactory as she thought, before pouring away what was left and depositing the cup in the sink.

"Do you know Solange Corriveau?" she asked.

"Only by reputation."

"I'm going to have to share with her what you just told me."

"I'm speculating. You can see how thin it is."

"Thin or not, she's now the lead on Jane Doe, and she'll take whatever she can get. You should expect to hear from her sometime tomorrow, especially if Lombardi is still missing by morning. She'll want to know more about any possible link between Lombardi and Jane Doe."

"I don't have a problem with that, but my source might."

"Corriveau won't care one way or the other. She drinks her coffee with extra caffeine, and eats her meat raw."

Parker thanked Carroll and walked her to her car.

"How's your daughter?" she asked, as she opened the driver's door. Carroll had met Sam a couple of times when she came to visit, and once gave her a ride with the siren on. Sam was suitably impressed.

"She's good."

"Vermont, right?"

"Right."

"It's a hike."

"It is."

Carroll reached out and gave his arm a gentle squeeze: a strangely tender, intimate gesture.

"You take care," she said.

"You, too."

Parker watched her drive away, and felt a loneliness that made his eyes burn.

CHAPTER
LXIII

Daniel Weaver lay awake for what felt to him like a very long time, musing on all that he'd heard. The earlier conversation, he sensed, was something to do with Karis. Was she the one to whom they'd made the promise? And what kind of promise had they made, if it involved him? The answer prowled as a presence on the edge of his consciousness, but he would not, or could not, allow it into the light.

In time he fell asleep, and dreamed confused dreams, until he was drawn back to wakefulness by the sound of his mother's alarm clock in the next room, except that when he opened his eyes the dark was too deep for it yet to be morning, and the sound was coming not from inside the house, but outside.

He pushed back the comforter. He climbed from his bed. He walked to the window and pulled back the drapes.

There, on the windowsill, smeared with dirt, stood the toy phone.

It was ringing.

· · ·

In her bedroom in Vermont, Sam was roused from sleep by the sound of a telephone. It wasn't familiar to her, not like her mother's cell phone, or her grandparents', or even the landline in the main house that no one seemed to use, but which her grandfather refused to get rid of because, he said, "you never know," whatever that might mean.

The ringing of the phone came from far away, and had an unpleasant, jangling tone. Sam didn't like it. She wished it would stop. She was weary, and it wasn't even close to morning. It appeared to be coming from outside her window, but that couldn't be right, not unless someone was in the garden, and anyone who was had no reason to be.

Quietly, Sam got out of bed and padded to the window. She and her mother lived in converted stables adjacent to Sam's grandparents' property, linked to it by a glass-enclosed walkway that doubled as a conservatory. Sam's room was on the second floor, separated from her mother's by a small bathroom. The bedroom window was a mix of stained and clear panes, recently replaced following an incident involving a bird strike earlier in the year.

Sam opened the window. The garden beyond was dark, and she could see no signs of movement, but still the sound of the phone came, although it was no clearer for being unimpeded by glass. It might have been coming from under water, so distorted was it.

Sam turned to the figure sitting on the window-sill: her half sister, Jennifer, her face glistening behind the strands of hair that overhung it, concealing the worst of the damage inflicted on her by the Traveling Man so many years before.

Jennifer, who walked between worlds.

"Why are you here?" Sam asked.

Jennifer reached out and took Sam's hand. Her touch was cold, but not lifeless. Jennifer's body appeared to exist in a state of soft vibration, as though a small electrical charge were constantly being passed through it. And although Sam had no fear of Jennifer, even loved her in her way, still she did not enjoy physical contact with her. It made her feel dizzy, and caused her head to ache.

But sometimes it was easier for Jennifer to communicate through touch. Jennifer was a creature of emotions and impulses. Jennifer didn't think so much as feel.

Now Sam was made to feel too.

The lake by which Jennifer sat, watching the dead pass, keeping vigil as they were called to the sea; the approach of Jennifer's mother, or some manifestation of her, leading an unknown woman by the hand; an exchange of words, of concerns, with Jennifer by the water; then the departure, the two older women returning to the place whence they came, with a pause only for the familiar exchange between Jennifer and her mother.

how is your father?

alive

and will you continue to stay with him?

yes

if you choose to leave, you have only to say

i won't abandon him

then goodbye

No kisses, no embraces. But then, this was no longer really Jennifer's mother. It retained her form, and some of her memories, but one could not emerge unaltered from the Sea Eternal. To enter it was to be lost, the dissolution gradual but ultimately entire. Each time Jennifer's mother came back, she brought with her less of her old self. In the end, Jennifer knew, her mother would no longer be able to recall her at all, or the man she had once called "beloved," the father Jennifer and Sam shared.

The contact between Sam and Jennifer was briefly broken.

"Who was the woman with her?" Sam asked.

her name is karis

"And what does Karis want?"

for the sad part of her to rest

Jennifer touched her sister again, this time just brushing the back of her hand with an index finger, and Sam understood why the woman named Karis had come to Jennifer for help. In dying, Karis had gone to the sea, but she had left something of herself behind, a vestige entombed in a hole in the ground, surrounded by high trees and the cries of birds. It was a dangerous entity, filled with fear and anger and hurt, but also with a terrible, thwarted love. It had desires. It wanted its offspring close. It sought to take its child and gather him to itself, to hold him amid dirt and roots, and there they would lie together, until in time the child, like this version of his mother, slept in the earth.

our father is trying to put a name to it

Not "her," Sam noted: "it." Whatever remained of Karis was female in appearance alone.

"Does our father know about the child?"

not yet

"You can't let the boy go to it. It will kill him. It won't mean to, but it will."

i know

Only then did Sam notice that she could not hear the ringing of the phone. It had stopped.

And Jennifer was no longer present.

CHAPTER
LXIV

Daniel didn't want to answer the phone. It wasn't just that he feared to hear the voice on the other end of the line. He had buried the toy, and now someone had dug it up and placed it on his windowsill. No, not someone: Karis had dug up the phone, which meant she wasn't just some disembodied voice speaking to him over a plastic receiver. She could sift through dirt. She could walk beyond the woods.

She could hurt him.

But he couldn't leave the phone ringing, because his mother might hear, and then he'd have to lie; or worse, explain to her why the phone was on the windowsill to begin with. Karis had warned him against telling others of their little talks, and while Daniel was starting to wonder if that was more for her benefit than his, he was aware that the injunction contained within it an unspecified threat, one that now assumed a new potency given the reality of Karis's physical presence in the world.

Daniel picked up the phone.

"Hello?"

He thought that Karis's voice sounded clearer than before. It might have been the rage in it, but Daniel also detected a faint echo, just as he did when his mom allowed him to converse with Grandpa Owen over her cell phone when Grandpa Owen was only in the next room. Not one voice, but two: the first real and speaking from nearby, and the second transmitted through the instrument in his hand.

Just like now, because Karis was close.

i'm very upset with you
how could you do what you did?
how could you put the phone in the ground?

"I'm sorry," said Daniel.

sorry doesn't cut it, mister
why did you do it?
tell me

Daniel began to cry.

crying won't help either
crying is for babies, and you're not a baby
why did you bury the phone?

"I was scared."

scared of what?
of me?

Daniel didn't want to say any more. He didn't want to make Karis angrier than she already was.

i'm waiting for an answer

What choice did he have?

"Yes."

But then suddenly Karis wasn't angry any longer.

oh, honey, i'm sorry
you mustn't be scared of me
i'd never do anything to hurt you
i love you
you must understand that
i love you so very—

The phone went dead in Daniel's hand. His attention moved to the yard outside, where a girl was standing on the grass, her head inclined slightly away from him so he could not see her face, her gaze seemingly fixed on the woods at the end of the property. Her hair was blond, and her feet were bare; they gave the illusion of not quite touching the grass beneath. She did not move, but when she spoke, her voice—smaller and softer than Karis's, but with a tonality that was not entirely dissimilar—came from very near, as though she were in Daniel's bedroom instead of twenty feet away on ground still cold with the memory of winter.

go back to bed

Daniel replaced the receiver. It did not occur to him to ask the girl who she was, or where she came from. He could not have said how, but he knew that neither question would have been answered in any case.

"What should I do with the telephone?"

He hiccupped the words some, because he was still crying.

i'll take care of it

"I tried to get rid of it, but it made Karis mad. I don't want to make her mad again."

i will speak with her

"And she won't be mad?"

i will ask her not to be

"I want her to go away. I want her to leave me alone."

i know

"But don't tell her I said that."

i won't

Daniel took a last look at the phone before closing the window and pulling the drapes. Seconds later, he heard a sound from the window-sill as the phone was removed from it.

"Don't make her mad," he prayed. "Don't make her mad, don't make her mad, don't make her mad . . ."

Jennifer stood at the edge of the woods, the two Weaver homes behind her, the trees before her degrading from tangible presences to shaded forms, and thence to darkness.

you must leave him be

No response came, but Jennifer knew that Karis—or what was left of her, the residue that bore her name—was out there, listening. From what materials it had formed itself, Jennifer could not tell: other bones, remains perhaps both animal and human.

you're scaring him

A flicker, gray against the dark, moving low like an animal. Jennifer's eyes followed it.

you'll hurt him

Yes, there it was. Upright now. Watching her.

and i can't let you hurt him

Hating her.

Jennifer placed the telephone on the ground before stepping away. The toy began to blacken as wisps of smoke rose from it. The eyes melted, and the wire connecting the receiver to the body liquefied and dripped to the forest floor. Finally the rest of it smoldered and caught fire, the telephone burning freely now, the flames illuminating Jennifer and the surrounding trees, until at last the toy was reduced to ash that was taken by the wind and scattered over the forest floor until not a trace remained.

But by then, Karis was nowhere to be seen.

3

Thomas: Who shall have it?
Tempter: He who will come.
Thomas: What shall be the month?
Tempter: The last from the first.
Thomas: What shall we give for it?
Tempter: Pretence of priestly power.
Thomas: Why should we give it?
Tempter: For the power and the glory.
—T. S. Eliot, *Murder in the Cathedral*

CHAPTER
LXV

Anyone who still liked to believe that the United States of America was a classless society had only to set foot inside the walls of Boston's Colonial Club to realize the error of the notion. But since anyone who believed the United States of America was a classless society was unlikely to be considered for membership of the Colonial Club, or admitted to its Commonwealth Avenue palazzo through any door other than the service entrance, such illusions were likely to remain intact. It boasted a grand staircase rivaled only by that of the Metropolitan Club in New York, a humidor larger than the Union's, and a wine cellar valued in the seven figures. In a classless society, it could not have existed.

One did not ask to join the Colonial; to do so was a guarantee of lifelong exclusion. If invited to join, one handed over one's bank details without inquiring about the cost of membership. The mention of fees would be enough to cause the sudden and irrevocable withdrawal of the invitation, as well as to suggest that one's finances might not be as watertight as previously imagined. Share prices had been affected by the offer or withdrawal of Colonial membership, or even a failure to renew, and at least two suicides had resulted from rumors arising from such incidents.

In the Old World, blood was the indicator of class: the older the bloodline, the greater the claim to aristocracy. In the New World, money was the indicator, and the older the money, the better the class. At the Colonial, most of the money was very old indeed. The list of rules was considerable, but could be summarized thus:

No Vulgar Displays of Wealth.

And No Poor.

Quayle arrived at the club shortly before noon, and was immediately admitted to a dark lobby, where a functionary behind a desk recorded his name in the visitors' book before rising to open the inner door, where a second functionary was waiting to escort Quayle to one of the smaller private dining rooms. There, the Principal Backer was already seated at the room's only table, built for four but set for two, sipping a dry fino sherry before lunch.

The two men did not shake hands. They were not friends, colleagues, or business associates. They had nothing in common beyond the covenants they had signed, and even these were fulfilled with different gods.

A waiter materialized to take Quayle's drink order. Quayle announced that he would prefer to wait for wine with his meal, but requested a large glass of cold milk in the interim. Both men chose venison for their main course, and afterward were left in unquiet communion.

"How do you find the colonies?" the Principal Backer asked, in a manner that suggested he would have preferred if Quayle had not found them at all.

"Perturbing."

"Have you visited before?"

"I never felt the desire. No man at all intellectual is willing to leave London."

"Dr. Johnson."

"Paraphrased, but yes."

"They say he was a melancholic."

"Among other deficiencies."

"Then perhaps London was not so beneficial to him."

"Perhaps not, but I find its surroundings conducive to health and long life."

"Remarkably long, one might say."

Quayle acknowledged the sally with a small bow of his head. The sommelier appeared, and the wine was poured. Since the main course was to be venison, the Principal Backer had selected a Grand Cru Classé Pauillac from 1996. The wine, having already been tasted and decanted, was opening up nicely. Quayle accepted his glass of milk, and the soup quickly followed. The Principal Backer tested it, found it to his liking, and commenced eating. Quayle, by contrast, left his bowl untouched.

"You haven't asked why I requested this meeting," Quayle said.

"There is only ever one reason for anything you do, or so I'm told: your Atlas."

"Not *my* Atlas. *The* Atlas."

The Principal Backer was not about to argue articles or possessives with Quayle. He wished only for Quayle to be gone from these shores as quickly as possible, and was making no effort to hide it. But Quayle would have understood this even had the Principal Backer made a greater effort to conceal his true feelings.

"You should be more concerned about it," said Quayle.

"Why?"

"The Atlas has changed the world—*is* changing the world—and will ultimately alter it permanently."

"I see no proof of that."

"You're not looking closely enough: war, famine, flood; bigotry, hatred—"

"Has the world not always been so?"

"Never in such supposedly civilized times. I see regression. The Atlas is slowly having its way."

"So you say, but you've been claiming as much for generations—or so you'd have us believe."

"You doubt me?"

"You're a lawyer. I doubt you on principle."

"And beyond my profession?"

The Principal Backer shrugged.

"I hear tales of a man who lives in rooms that haven't been dusted since Queen Victoria died; who claims to have been born before the Reformation; who sits waiting for a book of maps to reconstruct itself because he believes it will transfigure the nature of the world enough to permit the return of the Not-Gods, thus bringing about the end of days and freeing him to die at last. Correct me if I'm in error about any point."

"By your telling, it sounds almost mundane."

"I've heard stranger tales."

"No, you've just managed to convince yourself of such. And this is no tale."

The exchange precipitated another period of silence until a waiter arrived to remove the soup bowls. The Principal Backer studied the lawyer in all his rumpled elegance, and decided that he did not resemble previous descriptions of his appearance. He was leaner; younger, even. If the rumors were true, Quayle's longevity passed unnoticed in London because, at irregular intervals, one reclusive member of the Quayle family would pass away only to be replaced by another—a son, a nephew, a cousin—into whose possession the estate of his predecessor would pass. Thus one became many, and many became one.

On the other hand, he reasoned, Quayle might just be insane.

Two waiters entered with the venison. It was so rare as to be almost gelatinous at the core, but neither diner offered any complaint. They resumed their conversation when the door was safely closed, as though the arrival of the bloody meat had reminded them of their purpose here.

"One might almost believe you would prefer if we did not finish our work," said Quayle.

" 'Our' work?"

"Do we not have the same purpose, you and I?"

"We do not. You serve your own masters."

"Of the same aspect and nature as the Buried God."

"Nevertheless."

Quayle leaned forward. He had consumed a little of the venison, and its juices flecked his chin.

"Explain your position to me," he said. "Please. I'm yearning to understand it—and you."

The Principal Backer regarded Quayle with open hostility, even disgust.

"Your Atlas is a contaminant," he replied. "If what you maintain is true, and it is restored, nothing will survive. The world will turn to fire and ash, and the Not-Gods will watch it burn before turning their attention to war with the Old."

"And in doing so will liberate the Buried God. *Your* god."

"Perhaps."

"You're a fool," said Quayle.

The Principal Backer showed no indication of taking offense. "Am I?"

"You believe you can negotiate with the Buried God. You and your confederates, generation upon generation, have accrued wealth and influence, and now you are reluctant to relinquish your position. Or are you even serious in your search for the Buried God? Perhaps you would prefer to leave it wherever it lies, and postpone indefinitely the settlement of your account."

The Principal Backer allowed his gaze to stray across their surroundings, as though seeking strength and consolation from its dusty portraits of long-deceased members, its nineteenth-century depictions of cityscapes and scenery now so devastated by progress that the artworks bore the same relation to their subjects' present status as a virgin might to a whore.

It was ironic, the Principal Backer mused, that many members of this club, so in thrall to rules and proper behavior when it came to the Colonial, and so protective of its reputation and environment, should have achieved their elevated station in life by conspiring in the despoliation of the world beyond its walls. This was the haunt of men and women who routinely made million-dollar donations to museums and galleries, who regarded themselves—and, indeed, were regarded by others—as benefactors to, and guardians of, the cultural heritage of the nation, yet balked at the prospect of paying a living wage to their workers, or of funding the modest safeguards required to ensure that these same people and their families could enjoy breathable air and drink water untainted by bacteria and poisons. If it were indeed the case that behind every great fortune lay a great crime—and this was as true of the New World as of the Old, if not more so—then the membership records of the Colonial were a testament to criminality on a grand and continuing scale, and the Principal Backer was a greater criminal than any, because he was in league with forces that made the worst excesses of the Colonial's members look like the actions of pickpockets and flimflam men.

Now here was Quayle, reeking of antiquity, heavy with the rot of ages, reminding him that the bill must soon come due. Who could blame the Principal Backer for seeking to defer payment?

"Our lives are short," said the Principal Backer. "Yours are the words of a man who has lived too long."

"In that much, at least, we are in agreement."

The Principal Backer tried a little more of the venison. It was good—the food at the Colonial was always good, although he sometimes found the kitchen heavy-handed with the cream—and he wasn't about to let Quayle's presence interfere with his enjoyment of it, so he continued eating even as his dining companion sat and watched the remainder of his own meal grow cold, with only a sliver of exposed redness to indicate that he had tasted it at all.

"Whatever my reservations about your purpose here," said the Principal Backer, "we have offered you the assistance you sought. We gave you Giller, and he comes highly recommended. We facilitated your"—he searched for the correct word to encapsulate the relationship of Mors to Quayle, and the variety of services she doubtless provided: "cumbucket" seemed too crude, so he settled for a less pejorative term—"*companion's* requirement of a firearm. I should have thought that a personal meeting between us was both unnecessary and, under the circumstances, a considerable risk. So I still don't understand why I am dining with you."

"Tell me about Parker," said Quayle.

The Principal Backer took a moment to dab at his mouth with a napkin and collect his thoughts. To his credit, he had been aware that the possibility of such a question might arise, given Quayle's intrusion on Parker's territory, but he hoped Quayle might be able to obtain what he wanted without ever crossing Parker's path. It was, admittedly, a pipe dream: the mere fact that

Quayle's search had led him to Maine meant Parker must somehow be involved, even if only peripherally. The detective was as implicated as Quayle and the Principal Backer in all that would transpire. The only question was how, and it remained unanswered for the present.

"That you are asking about Parker suggests you already know a great deal. Did Giller tell you of him?"

"Mr. Giller inadvertently enabled an introduction."

"You've met Parker? He's seen you?"

Giller had not informed anyone of this, despite being under strict instructions to relay any and all information relating to Quayle's activities back to those who had organized his employment. Someone would have to remind Giller of his obligations.

"For the first time, you actually sound anxious for my well-being," said Quayle.

"Our experience has been that it is best to keep Parker at one remove."

"Your experience with him is precisely what troubles me."

"How is he connected to your search?"

"It seems he's been hired to find Karis Lamb's child."

"You're certain that the body is Lamb's?"

"Few doubts remain."

"Then I recommend you start paying Giller

double, to encourage him to speed up his efforts on your behalf. You don't want Parker to find the child first."

"Perhaps I should have hired Parker to begin with."

"I'm sure you could always ask him," said the Principal Backer. "I imagine he'd be intrigued to hear your side of the story."

"Your sarcasm rings hollow coming from one who has allowed this threat to persist. Why is Parker not dead?"

"He *was* dead. Apparently he was resuscitated on the operating table—more than once. So his continued presence in the world is not for want of attempts to remove him from it."

"Attempts on your part?"

"Not directly."

"Why not?"

"No single reason, but mostly because he has allies, and to act against him would bring them down on us. Even though we had nothing to do with the attack that almost finished him, the repercussions affected us. As a consequence, I continue to spend valuable time trying to hobble a federal investigation."

Quayle drank his wine. He waited. When no further information appeared to be forthcoming, he prodded.

"And?"

This was deeper than the Principal Backer

wished to delve, but while he detested Quayle, and might have preferred to believe the lawyer was an isolated figure, he knew better: Quayle was the agent of the numinous.

"And," said the Principal Backer, "Parker may be different."

"In what way?"

Having proceeded thus far, the Principal Backer had no option but to continue, even though it pained him.

"There are some among us who believe Parker's nature to be partly divine."

For a time there was silence in the room, until Quayle broke it with laughter.

"Why: because he survived a gun attack?"

"Because he has survived any number of attacks."

"You and your associates are even more unsound than I thought."

The Principal Backer didn't react to the insult. Americans had endured centuries of patronization by the British. One became inured to it after a while.

"You've met Parker," said the Principal Backer. "What was your impression of him?"

"Perceptive. He picked up on my interest in him, although I barely glanced in his direction. He also detected Mors's presence. He's dangerous, I suppose. The evidence would suggest as much. But divine? No."

The Principal Backer didn't try to argue.

"Even if we're mistaken," he said, "it was felt that the risks involved in removing him outweighed the benefits."

"Until now."

The Principal Backer gave up on obtaining any further enjoyment from his meal, and cast aside his knife and fork.

"Let Giller do his work," he said. "He can be relied upon, and he has cash to spend. Parker doesn't pay bribes. Giller does. He'll find the child."

"And if Parker finds it first?"

The Principal Backer showed his teeth, literally and metaphorically.

"You're a visitor to our country, and there are certain rules you are obliged to observe. Do what you have to do. Set your silver drab to work if you must. But I've already informed you: Parker is not to be harmed."

"You didn't answer my question. What if Parker finds the child before Giller?"

"Listen to me, Quayle. I don't care about your missing pages. I don't care about your search. I don't care about your Atlas. I don't care how long you've lived, or imagine you've lived. I have no interest in seeing what may come to pass if, or when, your damned book is restored. I hope even my most distant descendants are long in the ground before that happens.

"We didn't invite you into this country, but you may well need our help in leaving it. Believe me when I say that such aid will be given gladly—although it comes at a price, of which you and Mors have already been made aware. But Parker is a piece of a puzzle, a single, perhaps crucial element in a complex construct, and he will not be harmed until we can be sure of the consequences of this action. Are we clear?"

"Oh, very," Quayle replied. He set aside his napkin, and arranged his silverware on his plate, before carefully inverting his glass of milk, spilling its contents over the dish before him.

"It stops the help from feeding on the same food as their betters," he explained. "Just in case they're tempted to forget their place."

Quayle stood.

"Thank you for your hospitality. You'll forgive me if I don't stay for pudding, but as you've so helpfully pointed out, it ill behooves me to tarry if I'm to find the child before Parker. Mors will take care of your other problem as recompense for your efforts on our behalf. Parker I will leave to you, and I hope he kills you for your cowardice."

The Principal Backer didn't stand, or offer a farewell. As Quayle opened the door, a factotum appeared to escort him from the premises, and the door closed again behind them, leaving the Principal Backer briefly alone with his thoughts, his wine, and the smell of blood and milk.

CHAPTER
LXVI

With no sign of Maela Lombardi, and all calls to her cell phone continuing to go straight to voicemail, Kes Carroll decided that a Silver Alert was warranted. Newspapers and local TV channels were contacted, and a recent photo of Lombardi was distributed, along with her physical description, and the make, model, and license plate number of her car.

Meanwhile, Parker received a call from Lieutenant Solange Corriveau. Parker was cooperative with Corriveau, withholding only Molly Bow's name for the present, although even then he made it clear to Corriveau that he was doing so.

"You want to tell me why?" Corriveau asked.

"Because Lombardi was Jane Doe's contact in Maine, which means Lombardi is the only one who might be able to identify her. I don't see any reason to breach confidentiality when it comes to others involved in sheltering troubled women."

"So why didn't Lombardi come forward when the body was found?"

"Maybe because Jane Doe never made contact, in which case Lombardi had nothing to tell."

"But if that's the case, where's Lombardi?"

Parker didn't need to go through the possibilities with Corriveau, because he knew she would be thinking along the same lines. The first was that Lombardi might have been complicit in what befell Jane Doe—and her child—and decided to run when the investigation began to gather steam. But given Lombardi's commitment to women in danger, this seemed unlikely, if not entirely out of the question.

The second possibility was that Lombardi did indeed know Jane Doe's identity, but was choosing to keep it concealed in order to protect the child. This still didn't explain Lombardi's absence, unless she was now on the road with the child somehow in tow.

The third possibility was that Lombardi's knowledge of Jane Doe meant she was a danger to those who had put her in the ground and caused her child to vanish, which meant that Lombardi might now be dead.

The final possibility was one that Parker would need to discuss with Molly Bow before either he or the police could pursue it further: that someone else was interested in Jane Doe or her child, and had traced her flight along the network.

Which also presaged no good for Maela Lombardi.

Parker promised Corriveau he would stay in touch. It struck him that he was making a lot of similar promises to law enforcement. He might have to start billing the state for calls.

He had barely hung up on Corriveau when his phone rang again. Caller ID gave him a name.

"Molly," he said.

And Molly Bow replied: "I think we should talk."

CHAPTER
LXVII

Moxie Castin had largely put thoughts of Jane Doe to one side. By hiring Parker, he was doing what he could for her and the child—if that child still lived. Moxie was not a good or particularly observant Jew, but he appreciated the subtle distinction between a mitzveh and a mitzvah. Technically, a mitzveh was something done for someone else, a good deed; a mitzvah represented the will of God. By privately funding a search for Jane Doe's child, Moxie figured he was killing two birds with one stone: it was a good deed, and probably also represented God's will.

A considerable number of Moxie's colleagues in Maine's legal community were of the opinion that he was crazy to involve himself with Charlie Parker. Sometimes Moxie was inclined to share this view, but generally he tended to disagree. In its way, Moxie thought, Parker's ongoing presence in his life might also cover a couple of mitzvot.

Plus Parker made Moxie's professional life interesting, and occasionally worthwhile. Right now, by contrast, Moxie was reviewing the file of a woman who claimed to have slipped on artificial snow at a shopping mall, resulting in a fractured ankle, a dislocated shoulder, and sexual assault by a plastic elf. Moxie wasn't entirely sure that a plastic elf could commit sexual assault, being an inanimate object shaped as a mythical being, but it was quite clear from the woman's statement, and the testimony of a number of shocked witnesses, that she had landed intimately and uncomfortably on the outstretched foot of one of Santa's elves. That foot represented at least an extra ten grand in compensation, so Moxie had ordered the elf in question to be wrapped in plastic and held as evidence. It was an open-and-shut case, the only issue to be decided being the extent of damages, but it hardly represented a mitzveh, and was certainly not one of the 613 mitzvot. Moxie didn't have to check to be sure of that.

So when his secretary came on the line, Moxie was grateful for the distraction from the intimate details of the bruising sustained in the elf incident, even before his secretary told him what the caller wanted to talk to him about.

The Woman in the Woods.

Parker met Molly Bow in Augusta, which, while not quite equidistant from Portland and Bangor, represented a similar degree of inconvenience for both of them, Parker being disinclined to drive all the way to Bangor to hear something that Bow should have told him when last they met.

Bow was already waiting when Parker arrived at Fat Cat's on State. She was sipping something that looked healthy and organic, and probably contained soy milk, which always struck Parker as defeating the purpose of going to a coffee shop to begin with. He approached her before heading for the counter, held out his hand, and asked for three bucks.

"For what?"

"For my coffee. I figure I should make you pay for my gas as well, but I'll wait to hear what you have to say before I start calculating."

Bow muttered, but eventually came up with a five from her bag.

"I want change," she said.

Parker ordered an Americano, tipped well, and brought back a quarter.

"Your change," he said.

"You are a frustrating man."

"You have no idea." He sipped his coffee. "So what didn't you tell me yesterday?"

Bow didn't enjoy being forced into an admission, so every word was like a thorn on her tongue.

"That Maela's wasn't the only name I knew."

Parker had suspected as much.

"Someone else in Maine?"

"No, that much was true; Maela is it as far as this state is concerned. The other name is for a woman in Sioux City. She's also been struggling to reach Maela, so she contacted me instead."

"And?"

"She told me that a couple of weeks ago, a fire in Cadillac, Indiana, killed a man named Errol Dobey. He owned a diner, as well as dealing in, and collecting, rare books. He was heavily involved in what we do. His girlfriend, Esther Bachmeier, went missing at about the same time. She was also part of it."

"What do the police think?"

"There's no sign the fire was anything but accidental. Dobey liked to smoke a little pot late at night, and there had been one or two close calls in the past. He lost part of his collection to a fire back in 2008, but it seemed he'd been more careful since then."

"And Bachmeier?"

"She wasn't the sort to go starting fires, either deliberately or accidentally, or so I'm told. She and Dobey were good people. Well, Dobey was, and Esther, I guess, still could be. God, you know what I mean. I shouldn't be speaking of her in the past tense."

"I did the same thing this morning, talking to the state police about Maela Lombardi." He caught Bow's look. "I didn't mention your name, and Solange Corriveau didn't press me on it, but if what you're about to tell me is relevant to the investigation, I'll have to share it with the police."

Bow didn't raise any objections. Parker could see that she was rattled. He waited for her to continue.

"The evening after the fire," said Bow, "someone tried to snatch one of Dobey's waitresses, a girl named Leila Patton, from in front of her home. Patton started screaming and fought back. She managed to gouge her attacker with a key. Patton thinks she might have caught her badly in the face, because there was blood on the key when she was done."

"Caught 'her'?"

"The attacker was a woman. Masked, but definitely a woman."

"So how does this connect to Lombardi?" he asked.

"About five years ago—my Sioux City contact wasn't entirely sure of the dates, because it's not like anyone keeps formal records—Dobey and Bachmeier may have sent a woman on to Maine, via Chicago. She was heavily pregnant."

"Did this woman have a name?"

"Karis."

"Second name?"

"My contact didn't know it, and at least one of those who did is now dead."

Parker was writing everything down in his

notebook. In the good old days, back when he was younger and more vigorous, he might have trusted memory alone, but no longer.

"I need the name and number of the contact."

"No. She told me all she can. I guarantee it. You can set the cops on me if you like, but it won't make any difference."

"I'm sorry, but as I warned, I'll probably have to. I don't imagine it'll involve a whole lot of trouble for you, but continuing to withhold your name will definitely cause problems for me."

"Whatever."

"What about Leila Patton? Anyone have a number for her?"

Again, in the good old days, Parker would just have dialed 411, but half the people he knew now appeared to rely on cell phones alone, and that went double for those under thirty.

"I'll ask."

Parker could always try the Cadillac cops, assuming Patton had reported the attempted abduction, but in the past he'd enjoyed mixed experiences with small-town police departments, given that at least one of them had conspired in attempting to have him killed. Under the circumstances, a certain amount of caution on his part was forgivable.

"You think you could do that now?" he asked.

Bow stepped outside to make the call. Parker watched her as she walked back and forth. He could see she was engaged in a conversation, and not just leaving a message. That was good.

He checked his notes. Karis was an unusual name, and there couldn't be many missing persons who shared it. This assumed, of course, that Karis had been reported missing to begin with. The absence of a deluge of concerned individuals coming forward to offer that name as a possible identifier suggested she might not have been.

Molly Bow returned.

"She's going to call Leila and make sure it's okay to give her number to you. I didn't tell her that you'd probably find Leila anyway. I didn't think it would help."

Bow set her phone down on the table, but muted it so that if a call came through, it would light up without making a racket.

"A woman after my own heart," said Parker.

"I sincerely hope not." She worried at her lower lip. "I saw the Silver Alert for Maela. Do those things work?"

"Sometimes, if a senior has just wandered off."

"But Maela hasn't wandered off, has she?"

"I doubt it."

"It doesn't make any sense to me. Why would someone want to hurt Maela, Dobey, or anyone else because of this body found in the woods? All they could have known was her name."

"If Karis is Jane Doe, she was running from

someone. As she was pregnant, maybe this person was hired by the father of the child, or is the father."

"But to kill someone, just to find out what happened to a baby?"

"You've met men who were willing to kill their partners for trying to take their children away from them."

Bow thought about this.

"I have. I can even understand the kind of rage and narcissism that could give rise to it. But if it is Karis who was buried in the woods, she's long dead. Nothing more can be done to hurt her. So what is this person trying to achieve if Maela and the others have somehow been targeted?"

"To discover where the child is. The rest could be revenge."

"Revenge?"

Parker was thinking aloud now. Bow was only barely present to him.

"For getting involved. For helping to hide Karis. For shielding the child. It's the father. It has to be."

The phone before them lit up. Bow took it in hand and went back outside, but not before Parker gave her his pen and a page torn from his notebook. When she returned, a number was written on the paper.

"Leila Patton will talk to you," she said.

• • •

Parker accompanied Bow to her car, the sun pleasantly warm on their faces. A man might almost have been tempted to venture out without a jacket, if he were prepared to trust in the continued clemency of the weather, and indeed God Himself. Parker wasn't so inclined, on either count.

Across the lot, a woman was putting an infant into the child seat in the back of her car. While she was occupied with this, her other child, a boy of about three, made a break for freedom. Parker was about to call out a warning when the woman saw what was happening, and headed off in pursuit.

That was how easy it was, Parker thought: a moment's inattention.

Jane Doe now had a possible identity: Karis. How did she reach a point where she could have become lost without anyone caring what might have happened to her? Bad luck? Mental illness? Poverty? These were circumstances, not excuses. They could not be used to justify an unmarked grave. It was too late for her now, but perhaps not too late for her child. Moxie Castin understood this, and so did Parker.

He patted the roof of Molly Bow's car as she pulled away, any annoyance with her now departed entirely, because she cared too.

A woman after his own heart.

• • •

Moxie Castin was trying to recall the last time he'd been involved in a telephone conversation as frustrating as the one in which he was currently engaged. The man on the other end of the line was calling from a public phone, but appeared to be under the impression that Moxie enjoyed the same resources as the NSA when it came to establishing the whereabouts of those who communicated with him. The guy would stay on the phone for no longer than three minutes at a time, having decided—probably from watching too many movies—that three minutes plus was required by law enforcement to trace a call. Moxie tried to convince him that this hadn't been the case since the 1980s, although Moxie wasn't tracing calls back then, just as he wasn't trying to trace this call now. But the caller pointed out to Moxie, not unreasonably, that this was just what someone who was trying to trace a call would say, and so another three minutes ended with the sound of a dial tone in Moxie's ear.

From the voice, and his knowledge of telephones and law enforcement, Moxie guessed the caller wasn't young. He was a Mainer, too; that was clear from the accent. But more important, Moxie believed this might well be the man responsible for putting Jane Doe in the ground, which meant the caller also knew the fate of her child.

"We didn't kill her," said the man when he called for the third time.

Moxie wrote "WE" in big letters on his legal pad, alongside the notes he was taking using his own shorthand, of everything that was said.

"Who's 'we'?" Moxie asked.

The caller seemed to realize that he'd made a mistake, but couldn't take it back now. Moxie glanced at the clock. Ninety seconds down, ninety seconds to go.

"Doesn't matter."

"Okay."

"She was in trouble when we found her. She'd started giving birth alone in the woods, but she was bleeding a lot when we came across her. My— Well, one of us knew some first aid, but it wasn't enough to save her, not by a long shot."

"What was her name?" Moxie asked.

A pause, then: "Karis. That was her first name, and it's all I'm giving you, for now."

"What about the child?"

"The child was alive. He still is."

Moxie added "male" to his pad.

"She asked us to look after him," the man continued. "She wanted us to keep him safe."

"Why didn't you call the police, or social services?"

"She made us promise not to, right before she died. She said the boy would be in danger from the father if we did."

Moxie decided to make the big play.

"How do I know you're telling the truth about this? No offense meant, but in cases like this we get a lot of odd people making outlandish claims."

"Why would I call you just to lie?"

The man sounded genuinely puzzled. Under less taxing circumstances, Moxie might have shared the sad truth that a great many individuals called him just to lie, mostly in order to avoid going to jail. The law wasn't a great business to be in if one valued truth, or even justice. It was all Moxie could do to keep from drowning in cynicism.

"Well," said Moxie, "folk make claims because they want to feel important, or they're lonely."

"I know I'm not important, and I'm not lonely."

"Sometimes they're just plain crazy."

"I'm not crazy either."

"You don't sound crazy," Moxie admitted, "but while what you're telling me may or may not be true, I have no way of knowing either way without—"

"I carved a Star of David on a tree near where I buried her."

"That's been on the news."

"I carved it on a spruce, facing north. I started adding a date, then thought better of it, so the bark below the star is damaged."

This could easily be checked, so why would the caller lie about it?

"Right," said Moxie. "Now I believe you. Why did you carve the star?"

"Because she wore a Star of David on a chain round her neck. I thought it was the right thing to do."

"Do you still have the chain?"

"Time's up," said the caller, and the phone went dead for the third time.

Moxie used the interruption to call out to his secretary.

"Get Parker on the line, then put the next call on speaker at your end so he can listen in on his cell phone. I want him to hear this."

But the phone did not ring again.

CHAPTER
LXVIII

The Principal Backer did not leave the Colonial Club immediately after the conclusion of his lunch. Instead he took his time, and read the newspapers, before making some calls. As in so many other matters, the Colonial had strict rules governing the use of cell phones and other such devices in its environs. This was one of the benefits of membership as far as the Principal Backer was concerned, the world outside the club's walls being increasingly inimical to silence, or even good manners, when it came to electronic communications.

The Principal Backer supposed a significant backlash against the ubiquity of cell phones would occur in time, and it was one that he was in the process of accelerating through investments. He was the main investor in a proposed chain of boutique coffee shops that would forbid the making or receiving of cell phone calls, and would require headphones to be worn by those who insisted on watching movies or videos on their screens. The idea had come to him following a trip to Russia, where he was involved in a meeting at a Moscow restaurant that maintained just such a ban and insisted that all phones be deposited with the hostess at the door. In the event of a call being received by a customer, a messenger was dispatched to the table to inquire if the guest wished to take it, in which case he or she was invited to step into a booth in order to ensure that no one else was disturbed by the ensuing conversation. The Principal Backer was optimistic that his modest risk would pay off both financially and in terms of providing him with another refuge from the discourteous.

Now, in one of only two rooms in the Colonial in which it was permissible to use a phone—discreetly, and at minimal volume—the Principal Backer convened a conference call to give two of his closest associates a précis of his conversation with Quayle.

"Can we be sure he won't target Parker?" asked the first, her voice echoing slightly over her Bluetooth speaker.

"I made myself as clear as possible on that score."

"Which is no guarantee of good behavior."

"The difficulty is that Parker's path has crossed Quayle's. A confrontation between them may be unavoidable."

"Then let's hope Quayle finds what he's looking for, and leaves before that occurs."

"It seems," the second Backer noted, "that we

are going to considerable inconvenience and expense to facilitate Quayle, and all we seem likely to get in return is aggravation."

"I have made Quayle aware of the price for our assistance," said the Principal Backer.

"Which is?" asked the woman, this being news to her.

"We have engaged," said the Principal Backer, "the services of his tame murderess."

From her vehicle, Mors watched the limousine pull up on Commonwealth Avenue. Moments later, the Principal Backer appeared at the door of the club, his coat over one arm, and walked slowly down the steps to where a driver waited by one of the car's rear doors.

"What do you want me to do about him?" she asked.

"Nothing," said Quayle, from the back seat. "For now. And we'll expedite his request for our help, unless you have any objections?"

"None, but I can tell that you're concerned. Has he lost faith?"

"I think he's frightened."

"Of what?"

"Of all that is to come."

Mors turned her head slightly so that she could see Quayle's reflection in the rearview mirror.

"When you die," she said, "I will die too. I don't want to stay here alone."

"I'm touched," said Quayle, but he did not look at her as he spoke.

"Don't be cruel," she said, "not to me."

And Quayle thought that in another life, he might almost have cared for her.

CHAPTER
LXIX

Parker was sitting in Moxie Castin's office. The lawyer had recorded each of the conversations with the man who claimed to have buried Jane Doe, and had now played them twice for Parker.

"Mainer, and probably local to Piscataquis," said Parker, confirming Castin's own belief. "But we figured that from the location of the grave."

"And it sounds like he has the child, or knows where the boy is."

"He has him. He wouldn't be calling otherwise."

"Which means he's worried," said Moxie. "Do you think it might lead to harm?"

"If our guy is telling the truth, it was the mother's last request that he should take care of her son. Why hurt the child now? If he were going to do that, he wouldn't have bothered calling you. I'm not even sure why he called you to begin with."

"It's hardly secret knowledge that you're looking into this, and you've been on TV in connection with the case. You've worked for me in the past, so it wouldn't take much to realize that I might be involved, or could serve as a conduit. My guess is he wants to cut a deal, and it might go easier for him if he makes the first approach instead of waiting for the cops—or you—to come knocking on his door."

"I wonder if he's married," said Parker.

"Sounds like it. He did say 'we,' so he is, or was, in some kind of relationship."

"Hard to give up a child you've raised since birth."

"Maybe he's hoping it won't come to that."

"What are the chances?"

"Slim."

"Even with you on their side?"

"Even then."

"That's not what he'll want to hear if he calls back."

"That's why I won't tell him," said Castin. "And he will call back. You can be sure of it."

The sun was setting, and Parker was tired. He'd left a message for Leila Patton after saying goodbye to Molly Bow, but so far she hadn't returned the call. He hoped Patton wasn't reconsidering. He didn't want to have to travel to Indiana to chase her down, and that was assuming she had anything useful to offer. But he'd traveled greater distances on thinner pretexts, and sometimes it paid off.

"How are we going to handle the police?" he asked.

"We need to draw in our mystery caller, and that requires trust," said Moxie. "I'm not going to feed him to the cops until I hear his side of the story."

"At least he confirmed the name Molly Bow's contact came up with."

"Karis," said Moxie, testing the sound of it. "I don't think I've ever known a woman called Karis."

"I think you've known enough women for one lifetime."

"My problem was I married most of them. I got alimony like the national debt."

"Tragic," said Parker. "We should make the call to Corriveau about the Karis lead."

"You want to do it?"

"No, I think you should. If you offer all the assistance you can up front, it might stand to us when you eventually convince our guy to come in with the boy. I know I'll be hearing from Corriveau anyway, once she's spoken to you."

Moxie folded his hands over his belly. His suit, shirt, and tie were silk, and all were certainly expensive, yet they looked terrible on him. Parker had known Moxie Castin for years, and he still wasn't sure whether the lawyer deliberately selected garments that were incompatible with his build, or the cut of any clothing began to deteriorate immediately upon contact with him. It was, Parker surmised, one of life's great mysteries.

"And you're worried about Maela Lombardi," said Moxie.

"More than I was before Molly Bow told me about what happened in Cadillac, Indiana."

Parker had the sense—not unfamiliar to him in the course of investigations—of being surrounded by a series of disparate pieces, some, none, or all of which might be linked. The challenge was to resist imposing a pattern where no pattern existed, because to do so was to follow a path that could take one further from the truth. Parker had learned instead to examine each piece of a puzzle in isolation, while also remaining cognizant of the places where the tabs and slots might join in the hope of ultimately creating a picture as yet unknown. In any given situation, this task was made more difficult by the fact that every piece was open to multiple interpretations. Each was a signifier, but could also be the thing signified. Practical investigation as semiology: perhaps, Parker mused, he might write a textbook on it, if he lived long enough, and was really bored.

"Do you want to go there?" asked Moxie.

"To Indiana?"

"Yes."

"Have you ever been to Indiana?"

"Nope. I don't think I even know anyone who's been to Indiana. You'll be the first."

"I haven't said I'll go yet."

"I didn't ask if you were going; I asked if you wanted to go. That's two different questions."

"I don't remember taking the stand, Your Honor."

"Old habits."

Parker really didn't want to go to Indiana, but Leila Patton was incommunicado and he was worried that she might eventually run. The trip to Indiana could entail just a night or two away, if all worked out well. There were also direct flights from Boston to Cincinnati, marginally the nearest airport to Cadillac, which would save him a transfer. But it was still Indiana. He had nothing against the state; he just didn't want to be there.

"You do seem impatient to be rid of me," said Parker.

"Not at all. But if Lombardi's disappearance is connected to the death of this man Dobey, and the disappearance of Bachmeier, then someone is working his or—given the Patton incident—her way toward the missing boy."

"Which means our caller doesn't just have the police and us to worry about."

"Could be he already knows," said Moxie, "which is why he's reaching out."

"All the more reason for you to reel him in as quickly as possible."

"I'll do my best. In the meantime, go home and get some rest. You look weary. I don't like seeing you weary. You might force me to become distressed. I'll let you know what Corriveau says."

Parker was already at the door when Moxie shouted, "Just one more thing," like some better-fed version of Columbo.

"Any more from Bobby Ocean or his idiot son?" he asked.

"Nothing."

"Good." Moxie returned to his papers. "That fucking kid is trouble."

CHAPTER
LXX

The streetlights caught the mottled paintwork on the replacement truck that circumstances had forced Billy Ocean to drive. Every time Billy got behind the wheel of this used piece of shit, he was reminded of his departed Chevy. Since he was required to drive the second-hand truck in order to work, thereby justifying the salary his father paid him, he was constantly forced to recall what had been lost.

Bobby Ocean owned properties scattered over Portland, South Portland, Westbrook, Gorham, and Auburn. His son's main task was to manage these properties, which Billy did with as little good grace as possible. He ignored at least one call in three to his business phone, since there were only so many complaints about damp, noise, plumbing, smells, trash, rats, and roaches to which a man could listen without wanting to break some heads. There was always some problem to be dealt with—or not dealt with, as the case might be.

Billy's dereliction of duty might have been more of a problem if his father was aware of it, if only because Bobby Ocean didn't want any trouble with the city inspectors. But as the management company didn't bear the family name, and most of the tenants were poor, or immigrants with only minimal English (the Stonehursts being happy to screw over non-natives for having the temerity to infest the United States to begin with), or mentally deficient, Billy was able to ride roughshod over them without having to worry about anyone making a complaint to a higher authority. The tenants had only the management company as their point of contact, and aside from a single secretary, Billy *was* the management company.

It helped that the rents were low, and the occupants lived in fear of finding themselves out on the street if they kicked up a fuss. They'd end up on the street eventually, Billy knew. Gentrification had caused rents in the city to rise 40 percent in five years, and a number of influential people, Bobby Ocean among them, were involved in stifling talk of stabilization. Ultimately even the apartments owned by the Oceans would become unaffordable to many. At that point, it might be worth putting some money into the units and finding tenants a couple of levels above the current intake, maybe ones who could carry on a conversation in English, or whose mouths didn't hang open when they weren't speaking.

But until that happened, Billy was reasonably content to manipulate a system that was purpose-built for the exploitation of the poor. His father paid little attention as long as the money kept coming in, and he wasn't bothered by small shit. This left Billy free to levy cash fines for the smallest of infractions; regard security deposits as non-refundable, using anything from a stain on the carpet to a busted shelf as justification for retention; and turn his correspondence-school lawyer loose for contractual breaches, real or perceived, mainly in the form of regular threats of legal action over insufficient notice to vacate, because even if such notice had been given, it was hard to prove. These people hadn't the resources to file a notice with their own lawyers or accountants because they were barely putting food on the table, albeit food that looked alien to Billy, and smelled like garbage. So it was that Billy was garnishing the wages and bank accounts of half a dozen individuals who had done nothing worse than sign a lease agreement with a venal company.

Billy hoped to leave all this behind someday. He hated dealing with busted toilets and overflowing garbage. Managing the Gull could be the first step to bigger and better things. His father was entrusting him with a new business, and it was up to Billy to run with it, thereby proving himself worthy of still greater responsibility down the line.

At the thought of his father, Billy found himself touching his left cheek, just where the slap had landed. It wasn't tender anymore, but it still hurt deep inside. All because of some leaflets left under car wipers; all because Billy chose to take a stand.

Billy wondered if the Negro responsible for blowing up his truck might not be among his own current or former tenants. He had a couple of Somalis in a place in Gorham, some of whom undeniably had an attitude, but he wasn't sure they even knew what the Confederate flag looked like—or if they did, what it signified. Then again, they might just have spotted his truck and decided to seek some payback for the dump in which they were living. But Billy decided that, on balance, this seemed unlikely.

Of course, it was also possible that someone had learned of his extracurricular activities, the kind that involved sticking racist pamphlets under doormats and windshield wipers in the dead of night. Billy didn't know much about the Klan beyond bedsheets and burning crosses, and cared even less to find out, but he understood the value of the brand.

Which brought him back to the flags.

Which brought him back, as ever, to the Negro in the bar.

Billy Ocean wasn't about to let this go.

It was a matter of principle.

414

CHAPTER
LXXI

Angel was sleeping. A day had passed since his return to the Upper West Side apartment he shared with Louis, in the building they jointly owned, because all that was Louis's was also Angel's. This, Louis reflected, was probably not an unfamiliar situation for Angel: as a professional thief for much of his life, Angel was comfortable with fluid concepts of ownership, and associated transfers of the same.

In the ground-floor apartment, Louis knew, Mrs. Bondarchuk would be watching TV surrounded by yappy Pomeranians, a watchdog among watchdogs. Mrs. Bondarchuk was the sitting tenant when Louis first bought the building, and he had seen no reason to alter that arrangement. Mrs. Bondarchuk paid a rent so small that even she was embarrassed by it, and provided a range of hearty stews and baked goods to make up for any perceived shortfall. She also maintained unceasing vigil over the building, its neighbors, its environs, and anyone who might pause on the street for longer than was necessary to tie a shoelace, take a phone call, or hail a cab. Her TV was positioned so that only a glance to her left was required to ensure all was well. She also chose to collude in the fiction that the two gentlemen occupying the upper floors were merely tenants like herself; and although her upbringing was Eastern European, Catholic, and deeply conservative, she was pleasantly scandalized by their sexuality. It made her feel exotic by association.

Louis took a damp cloth and wiped the sweat from Angel's face. Angel did not react, but continued to breathe shallowly in his narcosis-induced sleep. Only the rise and fall of his chest disturbed the stillness of his form.

He will appear like this when he is dead, Louis thought. *He is forcing me to look on him this way.*

Behind Louis, the nurse appeared.

I do not want him to leave me. I will break.

"I can take over, if you like," she said.

The team of three nurses that would alternately care for Angel, each overlapping with another for an hour each day, had been carefully sourced. Their agency was noted for its discretion, its staff having ministered to the needs of princes, dictators, and criminals. The criminals, according to the head of the agency, were always the most polite.

"Thank you," said Louis. He returned the cloth to its bowl, adjusted the blanket over Angel's chest, and smoothed away the wrinkles in the material.

"You have the number. Call me for anything."

Louis knew that he should remain with Angel, but he could not. He was running away once again. He was a coward.

"I will," said the nurse, "but he'll be fine."

She took the chair, and Louis closed the door softly behind him. When he woke, Angel would understand the reason for his partner's absence. These periods of escape were the only means by which Louis could discharge the fear that built up within him, and so allow him to be strong for this man he loved.

The building housed three apartments, of which only two were ever occupied. The one on the second floor was variously used as a workshop, an office, and a place of retreat when either Angel or Louis—mostly the former, but occasionally the latter—was getting on his partner's nerves. At the moment, it was home to the Fulci brothers, whose guardianship of Angel had now extended—*very* temporarily, Louis prayed—to the early period of his recuperation, thus facilitating Louis's truancy. Mrs. Bondarchuk, for all her vigilance, did not own a gun.

On the other hand, Mrs. Bondarchuk was not crazy.

Then again, she did seem curiously fond of the Fulcis, and Paulie in particular, who was currently watching TV with her. Tony, meanwhile, was sitting in their living quarters, the door open while he worked on a massive kit of the USS *Constitution*. According to his brother, Tony's therapist had recommended the building of model ships as a calming measure. Tony had calculated that the bigger the kit, the greater the therapeutic value, and so the U.S.S. *Constitution* would measure three feet in length when completed.

No, scratch that: *if* completed. This was, it seemed, the twelfth kit upon which Tony had embarked. The previous eleven had been destroyed in fits of rage at varying stages of construction. Tony's therapist, Louis believed, was clutching at fucking straws.

Louis put on his suit jacket and picked up his overcoat. The car was waiting for him outside. When not driving himself, Louis employed the services of an Uzbek chauffeur named Alex. Louis did not trust many people, but Alex was one of them.

He said goodbye to the Fulcis, and to Mrs. Bondarchuk. He instinctively checked the street before opening the outer door of the building, although he knew that Alex would have done the same, or else he would not have been standing patiently by the car, his face a vision of Central Asian calm.

"Good evening, Alex."

"Good evening, sir."

"Is the family well?"

"Very well, sir, thank you for asking."

Always the same conversation. Louis sometimes questioned if Alex would even admit if any member of his family was unwell. Perhaps, under Alex's careful stewardship, it had ceased to be a possibility.

Louis had only a small leather satchel to carry with him on the flight to Portland. It contained a pen and a book. He had moved on to Montaigne's *Essays*. Louis felt that he might have enjoyed meeting Montaigne, whom he found not just wise, but sensible.

The car pulled away from the curb. Louis opened the *Essays*, but instead of reading anew, he returned to a page he had marked earlier in the week, as he listened from outside the hospital room while a young nurse helped Angel shift position to prevent bedsores. From the introduction to the volume, Louis had learned that Montaigne was close to a poet named Étienne de La Boétie, whose death plunged Montaigne into grief. Of their friendship, Montaigne wrote: "If you press me to say why I loved him, I can say no more than because he was he, and I was I."

Louis touched his fingers to the page.

Yes, he thought. *Yes.*

CHAPTER
LXXII

Billy Ocean pulled into the parking lot behind the three-unit rental in Auburn. The building was temporarily empty due to an ongoing damp problem that technically rendered it unsuitable for human habitation, although Billy knew people who'd pay good money to live in it, even at risk to their health. It smelled some, and only a fool would have chanced putting any significant weight on a couple of the boards, but it was better than sleeping under the stars.

Billy was holding off on getting the necessary work done because his usual handyman—who worked cheap but billed high, enabling Billy and him to split the difference—was languishing in the Cumberland County Jail for failing to pay child support. He was unlikely to be breathing free air anytime soon either, since he owed $15,000 for his kids, who lived with their mother in New Jersey. Under federal law, it was a crime for a person to maintain a residence in a different state from his children if that person owed more than $5,000 in child support, which meant Billy's handyman was looking at two years in prison and a fine of up to $250,000. Even with a sympathetic report from the federal probation office, he still wasn't going to be in a position to deal with Billy's damp problem before parts of the building started caving in. This left Billy with the problem of locating a sufficiently crooked contractor to replace him, and good men were hard to find.

Billy opened the lockbox in the bed of the truck and removed a plastic bag of groceries, a case of Silver Bullets, and a bottle of Johnny Drum Black. He put the bourbon in the pocket of his overcoat to save himself another trip, and headed for the building. As he stomped to the back door, a drape twitched in one of the windows on the second floor.

Each of the units contained its own kitchen, but Billy had taken the precaution of having the gas cut off until the maintenance work could be completed. The power was still on, though, so his guest could cook with the microwave, and watch DVDs on a crappy TV. None of this lessened the bitching, as though everything that had occurred was Billy's fault—which it wasn't, but Billy was in the shit now, right up to his chin, with no choice but to keep paddling. He couldn't see how the whole business might possibly end well. He could only hope that when the end came, it happened far from Auburn, and far from him.

Billy took the stairs carefully, sticking to the side closest to the wall, and avoiding the fourth and fifth steps entirely. He'd already put his left foot through the lower one on a previous visit, resulting in a mildly sprained ankle and a jagged hole in the wood like a toothed mouth, and only a warning *crack* from the fifth step had saved him from further injury. This time he reached the second floor without harm, and kicked the door in place of knocking, his hands being otherwise occupied. Eventually, after a certain amount of shuffling and swearing, the door opened to reveal the form of the most wanted man in the state of Maine.

"Well," said Heb Caldicott, "you took your fucking time."

Parker headed home to shower after he was done with Moxie Castin, but didn't bother making dinner. He knew that Louis was on his way back to Portland, and they'd arranged to meet for a late burger at Nosh on Congress. In the meantime, Parker spoke with Kes Carroll, who confirmed that the Silver Alert had generated a few calls, but none of the sightings appeared to be of Lombardi. Parker didn't know if Moxie had yet managed to tell Solange Corriveau of the Karis lead, or of the events in Indiana, but he saw no reason why he shouldn't share what he knew with Carroll. The information didn't make Carroll any happier, but it did help focus her mind. It also increased the likelihood of Lombardi's disappearance being taken off Carroll's hands and absorbed into the Jane Doe investigation—or the Karis investigation, as Parker had now begun to think of it—assuming Corriveau accepted the possibility of a connection.

Parker then tried Leila Patton again. This time the call didn't go immediately to voice mail, but the number rang and rang until eventually it was ended automatically. Patton, it seemed, had turned off her messaging service. With nothing better to do, Parker put the phone on speaker and kept hitting redial while he boiled some water for instant coffee and ate a couple of Fig Newtons to stave off the hunger pangs.

Finally, on the fourth attempt, the phone was answered by a female voice.

"Hello?"

"Leila?"

"Yes."

"My name is Charlie Parker. I'm—"

"I don't want to talk to you. I have nothing to say. Just leave me alone."

Clearly Patton had reconsidered her decision to cooperate. Parker knew he only had seconds.

"Errol Dobey," he said. "Esther Bachmeier."

He could hear the sound of Patton's breathing. At least she hadn't hung up. "Don't you care about what might have happened to them?"

Still no reply.

"Leila?"

She began to cry, and the call was terminated. When Parker tried the number again, he received only a message asking him to try later. He took his coffee to his office, turned on his computer, and booked a round-trip ticket to Cincinnati.

Heb Caldicott wasn't looking well, which was hardly surprising under the circumstances. He'd taken one stab wound to his left side, another to his left arm, and his chest bore a slash mark that was about a foot long and a quarter of an inch deep, all thanks to Dale Putnam, who'd shown a certain amount of spirit in his final moments on this earth.

Caldicott had decided to kill Putnam and Gary Newhouse as soon as they admitted shooting the state trooper. He wished he'd disposed of them before agreeing to give them shelter under his roof, and maybe he shouldn't have suggested that his bitch girlfriend might like to fuck one or both of them in order to give him some time to think, but it was easy to be wise after the fact.

Still, he'd quickly settled on a plan to get rid of them. He picked a van from the lot, concealed Putnam and Newhouse in the back under blankets and junk, handed them a bottle of Old Grand-Dad to help keep out the chill and ensure they stayed nice and relaxed, and drove south, keeping off the highway and below the speed limit. The van still bore the name and contact details of a decorating company that had closed down a year earlier, which made it less interesting to cops than an unmarked vehicle. As it happened, he wasn't stopped once along the way, although he passed a couple of police cruisers with lights blazing, and reached his destination without incident.

That destination was Pintail Pond, although it was many years since a pintail or any other bird had troubled its surface, Pintail Pond being as toxic a body of water as existed in the state of Maine, thanks in no small part to Heb Caldicott's habit of dumping various forms of automotive filth, fluids, and containers in its depths, including carcinogenic used motor oil, empty bottles of engine coolant and refrigerant, and redundant batteries. His intention was to add the bodies of Putnam and Newhouse to this mix, and let nature take its course.

Beside the pond was a hut that had long fallen into disrepair, but still possessed four walls and most of a roof. It was to this structure that Caldicott directed a reluctant Putnam and Newhouse, who were a little drunk, if not as drunk as Caldicott might have wished. Again in retrospect, Caldicott regretted not killing Putnam first, but Newhouse had been closest to Caldicott as the two men entered the hut ahead of him, so it seemed natural to put a bullet through the back of Newhouse's skull before moving on to Putnam.

Unfortunately, it quickly emerged that Putnam

had a suspicious side. Caldicott had earlier managed to relieve him of his gun on the perfectly reasonable grounds that it was unwise to carry a weapon recently used to shoot a state trooper, and Newhouse had never been much for carrying a firearm. But Putnam had retained a knife, an implement of which Caldicott was unaware until Putnam decided to use it on him while Newhouse's body was still twitching on the floor. Putnam managed to inflict a lot of damage on Caldicott before Caldicott got two shots into him, it being a lot harder to hit a moving target at close range than people liked to think, especially a moving target intent on gutting someone with a blade.

It said a lot for Heb Caldicott's physical and psychological resilience that although slashed, skewered, and bleeding, he was still able to drag Newhouse and Putnam to the edge of Pintail Pond and rope a weight to each of the bodies, even though he'd finally been forced to lie on the ground and push them into the water using the soles of his shoes. Putnam had made a kind of gasping sound before he went under. Caldicott didn't know if this was just gas emerging from the corpse, or if Putnam might not have been dead when he started sinking, but he knew which one he was hoping for, and it wasn't the first option.

Then cold, exhausted, and in no small amount

of pain, Caldicott managed to call his good friend Billy Ocean—his partner in prejudice, and co-conspirator in the rejuvenation of what passed for the Klan in Maine—to request that said Billy should come and get him. There were others whom Caldicott might have called, but they were all smarter than Billy. This meant that once they discovered the extent of the mess Caldicott had gotten himself in, they'd be likely to let him die, or even hasten his end before leaving his body somewhere it would quickly be found, thereby bringing an end to any police interest in the matter. But Billy was Heb's boy, and had come through for him, which was why Caldicott was now residing in one of the less salubrious Ocean rentals while he tried to figure out how to avoid going to prison for the rest of his life.

The wound in his side was the problem. The puncture to his arm was barely worth mentioning, and a combination of antiseptics and drugstore sutures seemed to be taking care of the gash to his chest, but Caldicott had felt the blade twist inside him as it entered under his ribs, either intentionally on the part of Putnam or because of Caldicott's own reaction to being penetrated by steel. Billy had cleaned the wound out as best he could, and even applied some stitches, but it was starting to stink, and now walking, or even standing for very long, was agony for Caldicott.

As soon as the door was closed, Caldicott tore

into a bag of potato chips, washing them down with mouthfuls of Johnny Drum. Billy started unpacking the rest of the groceries.

"Who are you," said Caldicott, "my mother?"

Billy didn't dislike Heb Caldicott—he wouldn't have been in this situation if he did—but neither did he regard being Caldicott's mother as an admission to be shouted from any rooftops. This opinion, though, he kept to himself.

"Just trying to keep things tidy," said Billy.

"Have you looked around here lately?"

Okay, so the apartment wasn't exactly pristine, but it wasn't Billy's fault that Caldicott had strewn it with cigarette butts, beer cans, and food wrappers. The smoking was a particular source of concern. If the building burned down with Caldicott inside, questions would be asked to which Billy would not be able to provide satisfactory answers.

"You want me to book you into a hotel?"

"Don't be smart. And it smells like a latrine."

Once again, this was largely Caldicott's doing. Billy had left him with some bleach for the bathroom, but he didn't appear inclined to use it, or even to open a window for a while to let some air into the place.

"I'm just saying. It's the best I can do."

"Yeah, well . . ."

It was as close to an apology as Billy was likely to receive.

Billy finished with the groceries, put the beers in the refrigerator, and sat across from Caldicott. He reached into the inner pocket of his jacket and produced two boxes of Vicodin and a pack of antibiotics. The Vicodin had cost him, but he'd found the antibiotics in his mother's medicine cabinet. Billy was no doctor, but he guessed an infection was an infection, and the wound in Caldicott's side was clearly septic. Apart from the smell, and the pain, Caldicott was running a fever. His clothes were damp with sweat.

Caldicott waved the packages.

"You did good," he said, before popping two of the Vicodin and sending them on their way with a little more Johnny. The antibiotics he swallowed dry.

"I think I might have found someone to take a look at that wound," said Billy.

In the movies, men like Heb Caldicott knew tame doctors to whom they could turn, or waved guns in the faces of veterinarians to bully them into offering treatment. But Caldicott didn't know any doctors who might be willing to risk jail to help him, and Billy couldn't see himself allowing someone to point a gun at Dr. Nyhan, who looked after his mother's Bichon Frise, Toby, and was a very nice woman.

"No need," said Caldicott. "Now that I have the antibiotics, I'll be back on my feet in a couple of days."

Billy wondered if Caldicott actually believed this. Maybe the Vicodin was working faster than expected.

"We still ought to get it seen to so you can start thinking about moving on," Billy insisted. "I can't keep coming over with supplies. Someone will notice."

"You got every right to come here. It's your place, isn't it? Far as I can tell, the only reason you stand out on this street is because you're white."

This was true. The particular area of Auburn in which the apartment building was situated reminded Billy of Kennedy Park in Portland, which was a mix of Somalis, Ethiopians, and Southeast Asians, and was where Maine news shows went when they wanted a guarantee of ethnic diversity for the cameras.

"This guy, he was thrown out of medical school, but he got through the first three years. He's—"

"Billy," said Caldicott, "let it go."

It made Billy sad, this hint of resignation. He didn't want Caldicott to give up. It wasn't just sentimentality on Billy's part: he really wanted him gone from the building, just in case Billy's old man took it into his head to check on it himself, in which case all hopes Billy entertained of managing the Gull, or any other bar, would vanish like the morning dew. But he also knew from experience that there was no point in arguing with Caldicott, who was of a naturally stubborn and recalcitrant disposition.

"Okay," said Billy.

He ate some potato chips before taking a Coors from the refrigerator. It wasn't cold, but it didn't matter.

"I think a Negro blew up my truck," said Billy, by way of conversation.

"Shit. How'd you find out?"

"Someone who works for my old man."

"Which one?"

"Dean Harper. He got fired because he told me."

Billy was feeling sorry for Dean. He also worried about bumping into Dean when he was on a drunk, because he was certain Dean would beat the shit out of him.

"I meant which colored?"

"I got no idea."

"You aiming to find out?"

"Yes."

"How?"

"I don't know that either."

"If I was feeling more myself, I'd offer to help. Even if we didn't get the right colored, we could just pull another from the street, make him pay for the sins of his brother. They all look the same anyhow."

Caldicott laughed, and Billy laughed along with

him, even though he didn't think they all looked the same. He didn't like them, but he didn't think they all looked the same.

Billy turned on the TV, and together they watched a cop movie until Caldicott began to drift into a haze. He wasn't sure if Caldicott noticed him leave. Billy looked up at the apartment windows. The blackout drapes concealed the glow of the TV, and the light fixtures had no bulbs in them. For the present, the only indications of habitation were the grocery drops.

Billy wondered what might happen if he stopped visiting, like ceasing to feed a bird in a cage. Perhaps Heb Caldicott would just die. Or he might try to leave, painfully working his way down the steps until he got to the fifth from the bottom, which with luck would collapse under his weight and, combined with the already damaged fourth step, send Caldicott to his doom in the basement. Then again, he might make it to the street, which would leave Billy screwed.

Billy got in his truck and started the engine, but he didn't drive away, not for a good five minutes. He stared out at the night and thought that maybe things were not going to get any better for him.

Not ever.

CHAPTER
LXXIII

Nosh was quiet when Parker arrived, the bar settling comfortably into the lull between dinner and the arrival of the night owls who would drift in after music shows or late shifts in restaurants. He found a table with sufficient light by which to read, and flipped through the latest edition of *The Portland Phoenix*. Al Diamon, one of the state's leading political commentators, and certainly the crankiest, was getting worked up over the quality of the prospective candidates for governor. Whatever their failings, at least the present incumbent—voted "America's Craziest" by *Politico* magazine back in 2014, before he'd even begun his second term, one that would include a claim that out-of-state drug dealers were coming to Maine to sell heroin and "impregnate white girls"; challenging a Democratic lawmaker to a duel; and allegedly cutting in line to deprive a sexual assault victim of a therapy dog, which he subsequently named Veto—would have to recede into political anonymity, and Mainers could stop blaming one another for electing him. Except, of course, for the ones who *had* voted for him, although it was hard to figure out who they might be, seeing as how they now tended to keep quiet about what they'd done, probably out of a sense of embarrassment.

As for Al Diamon, Parker thought that it must take a lot of energy to be so exercised all the time, even if Diamon managed to be amused—and amusing—along with it. Like the Duc de Saint-Simon in the court of the Sun King, it was probably not a question of whether Al Diamon was annoyed on any given day, but simply with whom Al Diamon happened to be annoyed.

Parker flicked through the listings for upcoming performances at the various music venues around town before deciding he was too old for most of them because he didn't recognize any of the acts. He'd long ago figured that you knew you were aging when you couldn't hum any tune on the Billboard Hot 100. A woman seated alone at the bar smiled at him, and he smiled back before returning to the *Phoenix*. Perhaps that was another sign you were getting old: when you'd rather read the paper than take the time to talk to a strange woman in a bar. But he was also waiting for Louis, whose interest in conversing with strangers of either sex was negligible.

As if to silence any further debate on the matter, the man himself appeared. The woman smiled at Louis, too, making Parker feel a little less special. Louis ordered a dirty martini. Parker had barely touched his wine.

"Angel?" Parker asked, once Louis was settled.

"Sleeping a lot. The infection set him back some, but the doctors say he's a whole lot stronger than he looks."

"We could have told them that."

"But good to have a professional opinion."

They ordered burgers, and fries to share. Parker felt his arteries hardening pleasantly in anticipation.

"Does that mean you're worrying less about him?" Parker asked.

"No. I'm just worrying in a different way."

"Ah. How long are you planning to stay up here?"

"A couple of days. Just, you know. . ."

Parker let it go. They spoke of other things, including Louis's growing affection for this coastal city.

"It's the sea," said Louis. "Once you get used to looking out on it from your window, you start to miss it when you can't."

Parker understood. It was why, no matter how often he considered selling the Scarborough house and moving to Portland itself, he always ended up remaining where he was, even after the sanctity of his home, and his own sense of security, had been undermined by the attempt on his life. It was the marshes, and the tidal channels running through them, and the smell of salt on the air. It was the light on the water, and the distant sound of the sea, like a whispering at the edge of the world.

And it was the knowledge that he and his dead daughter were connected by water. He had sat with her by a lake that fed into a sea, caught between living and dying. He had held her hand, and watched with her as a car pulled up on the road above, the shades of Parker's departed mother and father within, inviting him to go with them, to take the Long Ride.

But he did not join them. Instead he returned— to pain, memories, the living. But still the sea called to him, just as it called to Jennifer. He remembered a child's nursery rhyme, one he would read to Jennifer when she was barely more than a baby, as he knelt by her bedside and lulled her to sleep: "If all the seas were one sea, what a *great* sea that would be . . ." His sea and Jennifer's were one, although each viewed it from a different shore. But when the time came they would enter it together, and all pain would cease.

The food arrived. The woman at the bar was still smiling, but now only to herself. Louis ordered a second martini while Parker shared with him the events of recent days, choosing to omit only what he had seen as he tried to follow Smith One from the Great Lost Bear. It was not that he feared Louis might doubt him—Louis, by now, had few illusions about the nature of Parker's world—but because it was a component he himself did not yet understand.

"Any particular reason to believe the two Smiths might be linked to the discovery of the body in the woods?" asked Louis.

"I can't think of any other cause for circling me. I have nothing more interesting on the books right now, unless the Smiths are fans of insurance fraud."

"You're interesting."

"You say the sweetest things, but you're not my type."

"You know, if I could take back those last two words . . ."

"I'll allow—even encourage—you to rephrase."

"*You* draw attention. Your history draws attention."

"So they came just to see the lion at the circus?"

"Well, when you put it like that, maybe not." Louis chewed a bacon-dusted French fry. "Damn, these fries are good. They'll kill you, but they're good."

A man joined the woman at the bar. He kissed her on the lips before taking the stool beside her.

"She smiled at me as I came in," said Louis.

"She also smiled at me."

"Which is disappointing. Maybe she's just real welcoming."

"It's a welcoming environment."

"Not that welcoming," said Louis. "Back to the spectators from the Bear."

"Gone to ground."

"Permanently?"

"I didn't get that feeling."

"Concerned?"

"Marginally."

"And no hits on Smith One?"

"None. I asked Dave Evans, but Smith One kept his face hidden from the Bear's cameras. I think he knew where they were."

The server arrived to clear their table. Parker ordered coffee.

"I still don't get coffee with wine," said Louis.

"In a world of hurt, you choose odd battles to fight."

"I'm not fighting, I'm just saying. When do you leave for Indiana?"

"Tomorrow afternoon."

"You think this Leila Patton will still be around when you get there?"

"If she's a regular person," said Parker. "Regular people find it hard to run at short notice. And Portland probably seems a long way from Cadillac. She might be worried about more calls, but not about me turning up on her doorstep."

"You want some company? I've never been to Indiana."

"I thought you'd been most places."

"Most places, except Indiana."

"Funny, I've been hearing that a lot."

Parker's coffee came. He chose to ignore the pained expression on Louis's face.

"Under ordinary circumstances," Parker continued, "I'd accept the offer, but instead I have a favor to ask. Moxie Castin is trying to get the man who buried Karis to come in, and if anyone can persuade him to show, it's Moxie. But if someone is looking for Karis's child, for whatever reason, this guy and the boy could be at risk."

"You can let Moxie know I'm around if he needs me."

"Thank you."

"What about the country's northernmost Confederate?"

"Billy? According to Moxie, he's got himself new wheels."

"Same taste in decoration?"

"Not yet."

"Nice to think previous events might represent a positive learning experience for him."

"Nice, but unlikely."

Louis picked up the check. Parker thanked him.

"Don't thank me, thank Moxie. I'm going to bill him for my expenses."

"Moxie," said Parker, "is going to be *so* pleased to see you."

CHAPTER
LXXIV

Since it seemed unwise to stay overlong in Dover-Foxcroft, Giller had sourced for Quayle a base from which to work: a vacation cabin in Piscataquis near Abbot, from a snowbird owner down in Hilton Head, South Carolina, who wouldn't ask questions so long as he was earning a little walking-around money. It made sense for Quayle to remain close to where Karis Lamb's body had been discovered. Quayle continued to believe that if her infant had survived, it was somewhere in the region.

Quayle was in the cabin alone, because Mors was temporarily elsewhere, fulfilling their obligation to the Backers. She would return the following day, once the task was completed. Giller, meanwhile, believed he might be closing in on the child. His tone had betrayed a certain excitement when last he and Quayle spoke on the phone. A possible lead, Giller said, but a cash payment would be required. How much? Five thousand dollars. Mors had delivered the money to Giller on her way south, her very appearance a warning that results were expected in return for the outlay.

How close was Parker to finding Karis Lamb's child? If Parker was continuing to search, he was following different paths from Giller, because Giller assured Quayle that those to whom he had spoken had yet to be contacted by the private detective.

But Giller also provided an interesting tidbit about Parker. He and a black man named Louis, who acted as Parker's shadow and gunman when required, were suspected of committing an arson attack on a truck in Portland. There was no proof of their involvement, and so action was unlikely, even had the will to arrest either man existed in the Portland PD, which Giller claimed was open to debate. Meanwhile the owner of the truck— one William Stonehurst, otherwise known as Billy Ocean—was very keen to establish the identity of those responsible. According to Giller, Billy Ocean was a jingoist and a borderline simpleton. Either of these character flaws provided some scope for manipulation, but both combined represented usefulness on a grand scale. Quayle did not wish to antagonize the Backers by acting openly against Parker, but that did not preclude working through a third party. When Mors returned from Boston, she and Quayle would have a conversation with Mr. Ocean.

And from a corner of the cabin, where no light intruded, the Pale Child regarded Quayle with unblinking eyes, and kept its secrets close to its hollow heart.

CHAPTER
LXXV

Ivan Giller was discovering the difficulty, if not inadvisability, of attempting to serve two masters.

Technically he had been engaged to assist the Englishman Quayle in tracking down a child now in the care of a family unrelated to the birth mother. But the middleman had also advised Giller that important people were very interested in the status of his inquiries, and any discoveries should be communicated to them before being shared with Quayle.

Which was fine, and not unusual in Giller's line of work, particularly where his regular paymasters were concerned. But matters had grown complicated when Giller was taken aside by the woman named Mors, who instructed him to keep his mouth shut when it came to the child, and to deal only with her and Quayle. It was, Giller thought, as though she and Quayle were fully aware of the instructions he had been given; or perhaps they simply operated on an assumption of duplicity in all dealings, which struck Giller as very wise, all things considered. On the other hand, it did nothing to alleviate his concern for his own well-being once Mors and Quayle departed these shores, leaving him alone to face the displeasure of those others who had been cut out of the loop by Giller's reticence.

The resulting dance gave Giller migraines, and—along with the slowly fading memory of the malformed child glimpsed in Portland—came between him and his sleep. With no other option, he'd come clean with Quayle about the conditions of his employment. As a result, Quayle was now permitting Giller to feed carefully filtered information back to the middleman. A reckoning might still take place once Quayle's business was completed, but Giller could point to all he had shared while pleading ignorance about the rest.

But Giller was making progress in his search for the child. Partial information obtained from adoption agencies had enabled him to winnow away some families, and local contacts eliminated a few more, leaving him with a core of about twenty children, based on a late winter or early spring burial of the mother's body. Now, amid light yet unrelenting rainfall, he was driving to Brunswick to meet with a woman who might be able to narrow the search still further, perhaps even to a single child.

The lead's name was Connie White. A couple of years prior, White had been fired from her clerk's job in Piscataquis for leaking information on bids for county contracts and soliciting bribes from contractors. Consequently, she was now filled with enough piss, bile, and vinegar to fuel ten lifetimes of resentment. Although White never dealt directly with the registration of births, which was why Giller hadn't bothered to contact her before, one of his sources claimed White knew as much as anyone about the workings of the county. If she could screw someone over, and make a little money along the way, Connie White would be open for business.

White lived in a double-wide trailer in a small field surrounded by trees, with a stream running along its western perimeter. The whole setting might have been pretty, even bucolic, but only without the trailer, which was shitty looking and brought the whole pastoral vibe down. A big brown mongrel dog was chained to a post set into the ground not far from the door. The dog began barking and straining at the chain as soon as Giller pulled up, which in turn caused the post to wobble alarmingly in the ground. Beside the mongrel was a kennel daubed in bright red paint with the words THIS DOG WILL KILL YOU.

Giller decided to stay in his vehicle until someone arrived to deal with the dog.

The trailer door opened, and a woman stepped out. She wasn't what Giller had been expecting, although he was prepared to accept he had prejudged Connie White on the basis of the trailer, the dog, and the stories of piss, bile, and vinegar. She was slim and blond; probably in her late forties but looking good for it. Her jeans were blue and close-fitting, tucked into tiny yellow high tops, and she wore a blue Red Sox hoodie over a white T-shirt. She raised one hand in greeting and used the other to hush the dog by clamping its muzzle.

Giller stepped from the car, still keeping a close eye on the dog.

"I'm Giller," he said.

"Come on up. Don't worry about Steeler here. He's a sweetheart, as long as I tell him to be."

Giller didn't find this particularly reassuring, and made a mental note not to cross Connie White. The dog growled at him through White's hand as he neared the trailer, showing sharp teeth and pink gums. At least, Giller reasoned, it would probably be a clean bite.

White waited for him to enter the trailer before releasing the dog and following Giller inside. The exterior of the trailer belied the interior, which was as neat and clean as the woman who lived in it, although it boasted too much knit work for Giller's liking. A large plastic bag filled with balls of yarn sat in one corner, and the table before him bore wool, needles, and the beginnings of what might have been a throw.

White saw him looking.

"I make some money from it," she said. "Not much, but enough. Speaking of."

Up close, Giller could see the steeliness to her: the tightness around her mouth, the eyes without warmth. A little flesh on her bones might have helped matters, but not by much. Connie White was all sharp edges: a man could cut himself on her if he wasn't careful.

Giller produced an envelope, the smaller of the two he was carrying, and displayed its contents: $500. He was prepared to go up to $2,500, if her information was good, but no more than that. The rest he intended to keep, possibly for additional expenses, but mostly because he might need it if everything went south and he were forced to disappear.

"That's not what we agreed," said White.

Giller took a seat. He was on familiar ground here. He had spent many years negotiating, and was skilled in the art.

"We didn't agree to anything," he replied. "You told me how much you wanted, and I said I looked forward to speaking with you."

He slid the envelope across the table, and waited for her to pick it up. He didn't have to wait long.

"Take it as a down payment, a token of goodwill," said Giller. "You get to keep it one way or another."

Just as quickly as it had been grasped, the envelope was gone, vanished into a front pocket of White's jeans. She didn't exactly soften—

Giller didn't believe she was capable of it—but a new light entered her eyes, even if only the glow of avarice.

"You want coffee?" she asked.

"Sure."

This, too, was part of the negotiating process: take whatever hospitality was offered, as long as it didn't look like it was going to cost you in the end.

White filled two small cups from a pot on the stove. Giller declined cream and sugar.

"Have you lived here long?" he asked.

"About six months. My brother owns the land. That's his house you passed back on the main road. I lost my home after I lost my job. I tried to hold on to it as long as I could, but, you know, fucking banks."

Giller knew. The judge had given White probation on the corruption charges, but in this glorious Internet age her name was now dirt. She'd be lucky to get a job hawking hot dogs outside ballparks, and bankers habitually looked unsympathetically on convicted criminals, unless the criminal in question was one of their own.

"You keep the place nice," he said. "Uncluttered."

"That's because I've had to sell most of my possessions to make ends meet. I can't clutter it with what I don't have. Are we done with the pleasantries?"

Giller figured they were.

"Tell me what you know," he said.

White sat back, her arms folded. Jesus. Giller relented, and showed her the second envelope, containing a further $1,000. The final $1,000 he'd hand over later if the information turned out to be good.

"There's a guy, Gregg Mullis, lives over in Medford," said White. "He was married to a woman named Holly Weaver, but they split up about six or seven years back. She's up by Guilford now. Has a kid, a boy, aged five or so, name of Daniel. No father's name on the birth certificate, only the mother's."

Giller gave no indication that the name was familiar to him, but Daniel Weaver was on his list of twenty children.

"After his marriage broke up, Mullis went out for a while with a friend of a friend of mine. He wanted kids, my friend's friend didn't—or not with him—and he moved on. It happens. He wasn't a bad guy, she said, just not her pony for the long road."

She paused, waiting. Giller counted out five fifties, and handed them over. They went the way of the first five hundred, except into a different pocket, and White resumed.

"Mullis was sore, though. He and his ex-wife tried to have kids, but nothing ever took. Mullis was afraid it might be his fault, but they both got tested and it turned out it was his wife who was infertile. They talked about adopting, but Mullis didn't want someone else's child. He wanted his own. Funny how some men are."

Giller agreed that it was funny.

"And then, a couple of years later, his wife registers the birth of a son," White concluded. "So how does that happen?"

"Maybe she got treatment."

"Or maybe the kid is Jesus."

"Is that it?"

"Isn't it enough?"

"I don't know, and I won't until I speak with Mullis."

"I have an address for him, and a copy of the birth certificate. I'm sure you could find both yourself, but what's your time worth?"

"Another two fifty. If Daniel Weaver is the child I'm looking for, I'll give you the remaining thousand." Giller thought he might even throw in the extra five hundred, if White's information brought his dealings with Quayle to a successful conclusion.

"You'll give me another two."

"And why is that?"

"Because it isn't your money. I know who you are. You work for people, so you don't care one way or another about this child beyond finding it for whoever is paying you. I got no idea how much you're skimming off the top, but I won't be short-changed, or not by so much that it hurts. You're not just paying for information: you're buying my goodwill, and my silence, because I'll bet your employer means no good for the boy, unless you're going to tell me he's the lost son of a billionaire and you're just trying to make sure he receives his inheritance, in which case I'll want a whole lot more than three grand."

It was quite a speech, the substance of it uncontestable. Connie White was almost admirable in the purity of her corruption.

"I don't know why they want to find the boy—if Daniel Weaver is even he," said Giller. "They're not the kind of people one asks."

The warning was clear.

"I'll bear that in mind," said White.

"Be sure you do." He paid her the final two fifty, before reconsidering and throwing in another fifty on top.

"What's that for?" White asked.

"The coffee," he said.

White folded the bills, and recited Gregg Mullis's address from memory while pulling a photocopy of a birth certificate from a sheaf of bills and invoices beside the microwave. Giller wrote down the address in a notebook barely bigger than the palm of his hand, placed the birth certificate in his pocket, and stood to leave.

"You can stay awhile, if you like," said White, resting the palm of her right hand against Giller's chest. The money had clearly set her juices flowing. Idly, Giller wondered why she wasn't married. She was attractive enough to snare some fool, so long as he didn't look too closely into her eyes and glimpse what remained of her soul.

"Thank you," he said, "but I have to leave."

She didn't take the rejection personally. The cash warming her pockets presumably eased the pain.

"Another time," she said. "Maybe when you bring me the rest of my money."

"Maybe."

But he didn't think so. If Daniel Weaver turned out to be the missing child, he'd have to share the source of the lead with Quayle and Mors. The abduction of a minor—and this, he felt certain, was their ultimate intention—was not the kind of act that passed unnoticed. When it occurred, it was possible that Connie White might perceive a financial benefit in coming forward with what she knew, which would not suit Quayle or Mors at all. It wouldn't suit Giller either. He hoped White spent the money quickly.

But the consideration of White's possible fate also caused him to contemplate his own. If Quayle and Mors might be prepared to act in order to silence White, where did that leave him? It was another reason to hold on to as much of the cash as he could, and also keep a bag packed, just in case.

White opened the door and stepped out in front of Giller to secure the dog. He'd have to warn Mors about it. He didn't think Quayle would be the one to come calling when the time came.

"Be seeing you," said White, as the dog recommenced its snarling, but Giller didn't reply. He walked to his car in silence, as the rain fell and washed his footprints away.

CHAPTER
LXXVI

Garrison Pryor was having a bad day, but then he'd been having bad days ever since some concerned Maine citizens had taken it into their heads to contract out the killing of the private detective named Charlie Parker. The result was not only the annihilation of those citizens, the destruction of half their town, and the continued survival of Parker, but also the unleashing of a greater storm of retribution by Parker's allies—or more accurately, the use of the attack, by elements within the Federal Bureau of Investigation, as an excuse to squeeze the Backers.

Pryor Investments, one of the Backers' main instruments in the search for the Buried God, immediately found itself targeted by the FBI's Economic Crimes Unit—and if Pryor Investments was being targeted, that meant Garrison Pryor himself was being targeted. As a consequence, Pryor was currently under indictment for a range of crimes including falsification of financial information, late trading, securities fraud, wire fraud, and conspiracy. At least some of the charges were spurious at best, but calling "bullshit" wouldn't stand up as a defense in federal court. The scandal had forced Pryor to step aside temporarily as chairman of his own company, although he ensured that the board issued a statement expressing its confidence in him before he did so. Admittedly, he had to draft the statement himself, and force it on the board by pointing out to its members that his problems were their problems, and their support was not only requested but also demanded.

Yet to Pryor's relief, and the surprise of his lawyers, the FBI had made him stew for a couple of months, requesting the pleasure of his company for repeated interviews but otherwise permitting him to remain at liberty on minimal bail, and so far showed no signs of moving to arraignment. His passport had been confiscated, and he was under orders from the court not to leave the Commonwealth of Massachusetts without notice, but these were the sole restrictions to his liberty. True, truckloads of documents had been removed from the company's offices, and its computers seized, but a great many federal agents would have to spend thousands of man hours working their way through the records before they found evidence of even modest improprieties, and then only infractions common to the financial services industry and therefore unworthy of anything harsher than a slap on the wrist, and a fine that could be paid from petty cash. This caused Pryor to wonder if the whole affair might not simply have been a fishing expedition on the part of the feds, based on the mistaken belief that Pryor would buckle and try to cut a deal by naming names in an effort to avoid trial.

But in recent weeks disturbing rumors had begun to filter down to Pryor through his lawyers, whispers that Pryor was supplying information on his co-conspirators to the FBI, and pointing agents toward named individuals about whom the feds should be concerned. Pryor denied everything, but arrests followed, which seemed to give the lie to his protestations. The board, under instruction from its own lawyers, immediately cut off all contact with him, and his access to the company's systems and records was suspended. More worryingly, the Backers isolated him entirely, and this ostracism was mirrored by the actions of the larger financial community. Suddenly Garrison Pryor was a man without friends. He could no longer even secure reservations at his favorite restaurants, and memberships to three clubs had been revoked.

He knew what the feds were doing, of course. Similar strategies were regularly pursued in business. Stories were carefully seeded about the inefficacy of a certain product, the declining health of a long-serving company president, safety issues with a pioneering new drug, all to affect share prices or hamper the competition.

The substance of the assertions was irrelevant. Once out in the world, they took on the appearance of truth. No amount of denial could entirely undo the damage caused.

Now Pryor found himself compelled to rebut allegations of complicity where there was none, and by doing so reinforced the effect of the lie; and pressured into attempting to disprove something that could not be disproved because no empirical evidence of its reality had ever been offered to begin with. Even his latest girlfriend had ceased taking his calls. The only people who did sound happy to hear from him were his lawyers, because he was paying them by the hour for conversation. Sometimes the price was worth it just for some civil discourse.

Pryor had money. The lawyers' fees were eating into his funds, but he was in no danger of penury, not by some distance. But what good was money when a man couldn't eat where he wished, travel when he desired, socialize with those whom he once called friends? What good was money without influence? His life was in limbo. He was doing nothing with his days, yet had to take pills to help him sleep. Despite his awareness of the strategies being used to pressure him, he could not deny their effectiveness. Why should he protect those who had lost faith in him so quickly? Why not simply make an approach to the feds and offer to tell them what he knew of the Backers in return for a new life far from here?

Because I would be exchanging one form of restriction for another. I would never be able to sit with my back to a door. I could never close my eyes at night without armed men to guard me. I would always be fearful, and they would find me in the end.

Pryor entered his apartment building. The doorman was absent, but the mailroom behind the reception desk was open, and music played softly from inside. Pryor was content not to have to exchange pleasantries with the man, even in his current state of isolation. The feds had searched his apartment thoroughly as part of the investigation, and his name had been in the papers, so the doormen knew of his troubles, just like everyone else on the block. They looked at him differently now, and their greetings were offered reluctantly, when they came at all.

He took the elevator to the sixth floor. No one joined him, which was a further mercy. He shifted his bag of groceries as he reached for his key. The contents didn't amount to much, nutritionally speaking, but he took his consolations where he could. He still retained membership to his health club, but he was too well known there to be able to concentrate on exercise, and so had put on ten pounds since the start of the investigation. His suits no longer fit as comfortably as before, but this was a minor inconvenience since he no longer had any reason to wear them.

How had the FBI targeted those whom it was investigating and arresting? This was the question that troubled Pryor as the feds continued to spread their net. Despite what the Backers believed, the names had not come from him. It was possible someone else was leaking information, but the targets were so random—politicians, clergy, police, government employees, business executives—that the source could only be an individual with knowledge of the Backers' entire network. And the targets were deeply embedded. Some had been compromised, or had allied themselves willingly to the cause, decades before. None was a recent convert.

An old list of conspirators, then. *The* old list. It was believed to have been lost or destroyed, but what if this was untrue? What if someone had found it and shared its contents with the FBI? Yet if that were the case, surely the feds would have moved against everyone on it? Why this picking and choosing of unconnected individuals, other than as part of an ongoing effort to turn the screws on Pryor himself? Could someone be feeding selected names from the list to the FBI while retaining possession of the actual document? Who might that be?

The answer came to him as he opened the door. Why had he not considered it before? Because he had been too absorbed in his own problems, too mired in self-pity. Now, at last, he was beginning to think clearly.

Parker. It had to be. He had the contacts, and the will.

Pryor closed the door behind him, placing the groceries on the kitchen table before moving into the dining room. It was still early afternoon. He would call his lawyers and ask for a meeting to be arranged, that evening if possible, with a representative of Grainger & Mellon, who acted for the Backers in all legal matters. He would present his suspicions to them. He didn't even have to establish a pattern. The pattern was that there was no pattern.

He stopped. A peculiar smell came to him: perfume, and whatever the perfume was imperfectly disguising. He turned as a shadow moved against the wall to his left, and a pain entered his neck and spread quickly through the rest of his body. Within seconds he was on the floor, and oblivion followed.

CHAPTER
LXXVII

In the nineteenth century, a seam of fine-grained schist—a seam of layered metamorphic rock that can easily be split into plates—was discovered in the vicinity of Cape Elizabeth, Maine. A schistose structure is generally unsuited to construction materials, but in the case of the Cape Elizabeth schist the rock broke readily into jointed blocks ideal for building. This led to its use around Portland, although the Cape Elizabeth stone later became identifiable through severe staining caused by the oxidation of the pyrite in the blocks.

Two quarries were opened in Cape Elizabeth to access the schist, one larger than the other. The smaller and shallower of the two—known as the Grundy Quarry after its former owner, the Grundy Granite Company—was now the access point for a nature trail popular with residents and tourists during the summer months, but relatively unused in the off-season. With the change in weather, and the return of migrant birds, birders and hikers would soon be tramping its pathways once again, and local volunteers were already preparing to cut back some of the vegetation and pick up the trash.

But for now the Grundy Quarry was still a useful spot for teenage drinking, pot smoking, and necking (if teenagers still necked, which they probably didn't, necking being a too-quaint term for the kind of activities that would have caused Austin Grundy, a staunch Baptist, to spin in his grave had he known of the uses to which the environs of his quarry were being put by the youth of today).

Four male representatives of that same demo-graphic were currently availing themselves of the Grundy Quarry in order to drink and smoke, if not to neck, each of the quartet being resolutely heterosexual, even if two of them had not yet managed to explore this inclination to any practical effect. Although it was raining, three wooden shelters stood around the quarry's circumference, each with a bench table, making them perfectly suited to the illicit consumption of beer, while the damp weather meant that the chances of being disturbed by adults, particularly cops, were slim to none.

The water at the base of the quarry was relatively shallow but very murky. Nobody in recent memory had tried to swim in it, and during the summer its surface bore a permanent haze of insects. But a combination of rain and snowmelt had served to raise the water level, and it was into this pool that Josh Lindley—at seventeen the youngest, brightest, and shyest of the group—was now gazing from high above.

Josh was feeling philosophical, although that might just have been an effect of the alcohol. He had a High Life—the Champagne of Beers—in hand, although Josh figured that if champagne tasted like High Life, he couldn't see what all the fuss was about. On the other hand, High Life tasted better than some of the stuff they'd been forced by necessity to imbibe at their little gatherings. He still recalled the two-day hangover he'd endured after Troy Egan secured for them six 40-ounce bottles of Olde English 800, N.W.A. playing through the speaker of Troy's phone as they toasted the late Eazy-E, who had favored OE800 back in the day. Only later, when he was once again able to hold down solid food, did Josh discover that OE800 was regarded by some experts as possibly the worst beer in the world, although it hadn't tasted so bad to him at the time. It was beer, and how bad could beer be?

Pretty bad, as it turned out.

The sound of a huge splash broke his contemplation: Troy Egan and his cousin, Devin, hoisting another gray block over the quarry edge. Someone had dumped a bunch of them behind one of the shelters. Assholes sometimes did that because the area around the quarry was so easy to access from the road. Folk could drive up to it and toss their old recliners, refrigerators, or ovens into the water, although most just left their crap on the grass for the town to haul away.

"Thar she blows!" Troy shouted, and Devin laughed, even though Josh was sure that Devin Egan had no idea what the phrase meant, and was only laughing because Troy was laughing. Over at a shelter, the fourth member of their little band, Scott Vetesse, was trying to find the right dance playlist on Spotify.

"Come on, guys," said Scott. "Enough."

"One more," said Troy. "This one will be like a depth charge exploding. It's a monster."

And it was. No way were Troy and Devin going to be able to lift that block between them.

"Josh," Troy called. "Get over here. You too, Betty."

Josh wandered over to join them, as did Scott, even though he was pissed at being called Betty, rhymes with Vetty. Josh had to admit that the block was likely to make a hell of an impact. He drained the last of his beer and put the bottle on the ground. Although he could not have known it, this was the final High Life he would ever consume. From that day forth, even looking at the label would bring back unpleasant memories.

Together the four boys managed to maneuver the block to the rim of the quarry, where it teetered, waiting for the final push.

"Bombs away!" said Troy, and Devin laughed

463

again, and down the block went, striking the rock face as it went, dislodging a chunk of stone before bouncing out to strike where the quarry was deepest. An enormous eruption of water followed, just like a depth charge, as Troy had promised. Devin whooped, and the others joined in, but their cries faded away until only Devin's voice could still be heard, before he, too, grew quiet.

The rear of a car had emerged from the water, forced up from the uneven quarry bed by the impact of the block on the hood. The trunk popped open, revealing the body of a woman tied up inside.

Josh Lindley didn't move, didn't speak, didn't puke. He didn't even want to keep staring, but he did because he couldn't look away, no matter how hard he tried. And then he realized that he *had* turned away, but he was still seeing the body in the trunk, and he knew that he would keep seeing it no matter what, and this was one of the burdens he would bear into adulthood, into old age, into the grave.

He took out his cell phone and dialed 911.

Over by the shelter, Troy Egan was already disposing of the beer.

CHAPTER
LXXVIII

Garrison Pryor opened his eyes. He was lying naked in his bathtub, his hands restrained behind his back, his legs and mouth bound with tape. A woman was sitting on the toilet seat next to him. Pale skin, gray eyes, near-white hair beneath a light blue plastic skullcap: less a living being than a washed-out image of one, like a picture fading from the world.

Pryor's head felt too heavy. He forced himself to lift it, and it banged sharply against the faucet behind him. The effort exhausted what little energy he had left, so he stayed as he was, with the faucet digging uncomfortably into his skull. His extremities hurt, and it was all he could do not to throw up against the gag for fear that he might choke if he did.

He watched the woman, and the woman watched him. The more he looked, the worse she appeared, as though the profound ugliness within her could not conceal itself from close regard. Her hands were folded before her, making her seem almost prim in her posture. Pryor could see no weapon, and experienced the first stirrings of hope. Perhaps this was just a warning, the Backers reminding him of his obligations to them. They had to be responsible for this woman's presence in his apartment, because no one else would dare to risk such an incursion. If he could only induce her to take the tape from his mouth, he could tell her what he had deduced about the list, about Parker. He would ask her to make a call, and this would all be over. He tried to speak, using his eyes to indicate the gag. He just wanted the chance to explain.

The woman raised her hands from her lap, revealing a slim leather pouch. She opened it on the marble countertop to her right, exposing a series of blades, hooks, and pliers that gleamed in the artificial light. Next to them was a square of plastic, which she unfolded into a poncho before slipping it over her head. She stood, allowing the material to settle as far as her knees, protecting her clothing. Finally, she donned a pair of gloves.

Only then did she speak.

"Just so you know, they stipulated that it should be painful." She selected a long-bladed scalpel from the pouch. "I'm afraid we're going to make a mess."

CHAPTER
LXXIX

Parker took the call from Moxie Castin while waiting to board for Cincinnati. He regretted not taking an earlier flight from Logan, because this one was a zoo, but he'd been unable to reschedule a morning meeting regarding witnesses in an assault case due to go to trial in a couple of days.

"Bad news," said Moxie. "They found Maela Lombardi's body."

Parker stepped out of line and walked over to an empty gate so he could speak without being overheard.

"Where?"

"The bottom of the Grundy Quarry. There's no positive ID yet, but it looks like someone rolled Lombardi's car into the water with her locked in the trunk."

Parker watched the line grow shorter as the plane filled. Moxie was paying for a first-class ticket, so he wasn't concerned about finding space for his hand baggage. The question was whether he should board the flight at all, but it didn't take him long to come up with an answer. There was nothing he could offer the police that might help with the Lombardi investigation. What he could do was travel to Indiana as planned to find out what Leila Patton knew, or suspected, about the death of Errol Dobey and the disappearance of his girlfriend, Esther Bachmeier. Karis linked Dobey, Bachmeier, and Lombardi; and Leila Patton, who had worked for Dobey, was frightened. Parker wanted to ask her why that might be.

"No word from our caller?" he said.

"None."

"When he does get in touch, use Lombardi. You need to frighten him into coming forward. That way, we can protect him, Karis's son, and anyone else who knows the truth about what happened. Keep Louis close until I get back. Find him a chair in a quiet corner."

The line for his flight was gone, and Parker heard his name being called.

"I have to go."

CHAPTER
LXXX

Holly Weaver and her father were half-watching the evening news, which was broadcasting live from the road outside the Grundy Quarry, police and forensic vehicles congregating in the background just as they had for the discovery of Karis.

"Christ," said Holly, but the word held no real sense of shock, and suggested only a general disgust at the willingness of human beings to inflict suffering on one another. The news was also little more than a distraction for Owen Weaver, who was sitting in an adjacent armchair, drinking a beer. The body at the quarry was someone else's problem. They had their own to deal with.

His daughter continued to procrastinate about meeting in person with the lawyer Castin. He couldn't blame her. Sitting down with Castin would set in motion a train of events that might well conclude with her losing Daniel, temporarily if not permanently, and one or both of the adults ending up in jail. But Holly was also angry with her father. He'd shared with her exactly what he'd said to the lawyer, and her response had been that he'd told Castin too much. He'd revealed Karis's name, and the sex of her child, and that wasn't what they'd agreed. Owen had to admit he might have become a bit confused when talking with Castin, and maybe he should have guarded his tongue more, but like most sensible people he'd spent a lifetime trying to avoid lawyers. Dealing with one of them directly, even over the phone, had given him a bad case of the jitters.

Holly turned away from the television.

"I've changed my mind," she said.

"You can't change it, not now."

"I can, and I have. If we come forward, they'll take Daniel away. If we stay quiet, there's still a good chance that no one will ever find out the truth. It'll all die down soon because the police have bigger worries, like finding the men who killed that trooper, and now the body dumped at the quarry. How much longer are they going to spend looking for a child?"

"But Castin knows."

"What does he know? A name, and that Karis gave birth to a boy. That's all."

"If I don't call back, he'll go to the police."

"Let him."

"What about the private investigator?"

"What can he do: force the parents of every five-year-old boy in the state to take a DNA test? If he shows up, I'll give him the name of every man I ever slept with. Hell, I'll even make up a few more to bring it into double figures, and he can take a guess at which one I decided not to add to the birth certificate."

Her father winced. Like every man with a daughter, there was a small part of him that wished to embrace the concept of a virgin birth.

"Holly—"

"Daniel's mine. It's my decision. I've made it, so we're done talking."

She stomped to the kitchen, where he heard her crashing about, pulling out pots for dinner. He wasn't about to try and argue with her further, not for the present. He'd endured conversations like this with her late mother, after whom Holly took in so many ways, and a man learned when to retreat. And it might even have been that Holly was right: the advantages of confessing were only marginal, and perhaps it would all blow over, the whole business ultimately being consigned to a file in a basement somewhere in Augusta.

The doorbell rang. Daniel was on a play date with one of his buddies, and was due to be dropped home right about now, but when Owen opened the door Sheila Barham was standing on the doorstep. The Barhams owned the property to the east of the Weavers', and both families enjoyed good relations, although the Barhams were closer in age to Owen than Holly, and their kids had long since left home to make kids of their own. Daniel sometimes stayed with the

Barhams if Holly had to work late and Owen was away, although Daniel complained about the kind of TV the Barhams watched—mostly old game shows and religious programming—and the fact that every meal came with broccoli.

Owen invited Sheila to step inside, and Holly greeted her from the kitchen.

"Everything okay?" Owen asked.

"Kinda sorta," said Sheila. "Look, it may be nothing, but I saw someone snooping around your place earlier today."

"What kind of someone?" Owen asked.

"Well, it was a woman. I saw her from the kitchen. She looked dirty, and I don't think she was wearing any shoes. I guess it might have been some homeless person. She seemed to be trying the windows, probably hoping to climb through and steal something. I called Henry and told him to send her on her way, because who knows how long the police might have taken to get here."

Henry Barham was a big man, and a Vietnam veteran. Owen wouldn't have fucked with Henry Barham for a bucketful of silver dollars.

Holly joined them.

"What happened?"

"Sheila says a woman might have tried to break into the house earlier."

"She was gone by the time Henry got here," Sheila continued. "He didn't think she'd managed to get inside, but we have a key so he checked, just in case. He did the same for your place, Owen. I hope you don't mind."

Owen had gone to the bank that afternoon, which was the only reason he hadn't been around.

"No," said Owen, "not at all."

"We're grateful to you both for your care," said Holly.

"We thought we'd leave it up to you if you wanted to report it to the police. We're always around anyway. You know Henry: he don't like to leave the house much, except to go to church."

"I don't think we'll bother the police with it," said Holly, carefully avoiding her father's eye. "We'll make sure the alarms are set, and the doors and windows are locked. Don't mention it to Daniel, though. I wouldn't want to worry him."

Sheila agreed that keeping it between themselves would probably be for the best. They thanked her again, and she went on her way.

"Odd, huh?" said Holly.

"No police?" said Owen. "You sure?"

"You want me to get it tattooed on my forehead? We're not talking to the police, not about anything."

"I think I can remember that." Owen took his coat from the rack, and a flashlight from the drawer beneath. "Maybe I'll take a look outside, just for the fresh air."

He made circuits of the two houses. The only signs of any attempted intrusion were by Daniel's window, where the flashlight picked up muddy streaks on the wood and glass, the kind dirty fingers might have left in an effort to open it. Owen used the sleeve of his coat to wipe them away.

Like Holly said, no point in frightening the boy.

CHAPTER
LXXXI

The call came through to Billy Ocean's cell phone as he was cleaning up trash from outside the twelve-unit Sunlight Haven apartments in South Portland. The complex was the highest earner in the Stonehurst residential property portfolio, with a mature sheltered garden to the rear and bright, high-ceilinged rooms. It rented to Caucasians only, didn't matter what kind of bank references any nonwhites might be able to conjure up. A top-floor unit was currently vacant, and Billy had a viewing scheduled in an hour, but someone had thrown a couple of garbage bags over by the Dumpsters and they'd burst on landing, scattering crap all over the yard. Now Billy was chasing after windblown food wrappers, and picking up pieces of rotten fruit, and thinking that life really did seem determined to shit in his shoes.

He looked at the screen of his phone, but the number was withheld. He hated it when people did that, and usually let those calls go to voice mail. On this occasion he picked up, just in case it was the couple coming to view the apartment today, and they'd had to borrow a phone.

The voice on the other end of the line sounded as though it should be announcing that dinner was served on one of those dull British *Masterpiece* shows that his mother loved to watch.

"Am I speaking to Mr. Stonehurst?" the voice asked.

"You are."

"Mr. William Stonehurst?"

Billy couldn't remember the last time anyone other than his mother had called him William, and she used his full name only when she was pissed at him.

"Yeah. Who is this?"

"My name is Quayle. I believe I may know who was responsible for setting fire to your truck."

CHAPTER
LXXXII

Daniel Weaver woke to the sound of scratching at his window. The drapes were closed, and the house was otherwise quiet. His mom had gone to bed shortly after Daniel returned from his play date, and Grandpa Owen was already back at his own place by then, so Daniel didn't get to see him at all. Daniel thought his mom seemed more relaxed than she had in a while. She sat Daniel down when he got home, and asked him to tell her all about his day, and after that she just held him for a while, and Daniel had liked that. He'd liked it a lot.

The scratching came again. Daniel sat up.

He told himself that it was just an animal: a raccoon, or the Barhams' cat, Solomon, which sometimes wandered over looking for food.

The noise stopped, and he relaxed. He knew it. Stupid—

The scratching was replaced by a soft *tap-tap-tap* on the glass, and the voice of the woman named Karis called his name.

daniel

Daniel started to tremble.

daniel

His stomach tightened, and he tasted something bad at the back of his throat.

open the window

He let out a little moan, and immediately covered his mouth. But it was too late.

i can hear you

"No," he whispered.

don't make mommy mad

And Daniel started screaming.

CHAPTER
LXXXIII

Parker's Delta flight got into Cincinnati at eight p.m. He could have spent the night at an airport hotel and headed to Cadillac in the morning, but airport hotels depressed him—everybody staying in an airport hotel wanted to be someplace else, so they were essentially existential dilemmas with poor bar service—so he picked up a rental car and headed west.

Cadillac, according to the Internet, boasted a grand total of two motels: a family-owned, cabin-style place that looked like the set of a horror movie, with Internet reviews to match; and a Holiday Inn. Parker opted for the Holiday Inn. He arrived shortly before midnight and went straight to bed without closing the drapes, so he was woken by sunlight. He put on a casual black jacket over a white shirt and dark jeans, set off nicely by a pair of black OluKai Mauna Kea boots he'd been saving. He wanted to project a certain degree of formality when he found Leila Patton: not intimidating, just intimidating enough.

He skipped breakfast at the hotel in favor of the Sunnyside Dine-In on the town's main street. He scored a booth by the window, where he ate toast, drank coffee, read *The Indianapolis Star*, and watched a tall, willowy brunette with LEILA stitched on the left breast of her shirt working the seats at the counter.

Leila Patton hadn't been difficult to find: there was only one Patton family on the Cadillac property register, and her Social Security number had recently been added to the payroll record of the Sunnyside. Parker had no intention of confronting Patton while she was at work. It had just been his good fortune to find her present when he went for breakfast. As a licensed private investigator, he had also obtained details of her vehicle from the state DMV, so he was aware that she drove the 2005 VW New Beetle parked in the employee section of the diner's lot. While making conversation, he asked his waitress, Tamira, how long shifts lasted on the floor. Based on her answer, he figured that Patton was likely to be working until two p.m. Even if she left early, he had her home address, but it would be better if he first approached her in a public place. She could easily close the door in his face if he called to her house, and she would be entirely within her rights to notify the police if he hung around.

Cadillac was busy in the way certain small towns could be, especially those that weren't large enough to have attracted significant malls. God only knew what the Holiday Inn people were thinking when they opened their Cadillac outpost. Parker had only counted ten cars in the parking lot that morning, and at least a couple of those must have belonged to staff.

Parker paid the check, left the diner, and drove to the outskirts of town until he came to Dobey's. The building was locked up, and a chain denied access to the parking lot. The letterboard sign outside read BUSINESS CLOSED, and beneath it, ERROL DOBEY RIP. WE'LL MISS YOU.

Parker had read the newspaper accounts of the fire, but the remains of the trailers in which Errol Dobey had lived, and in which he had stored what one report described as "among the finest private book collections in southern Indiana," were gone. Parker stepped over the chain and walked around the property. Only blackened grass and scorched concrete marked the site of the fire that had taken Dobey's life, although Parker spotted signs of minor damage to the rear of the restaurant. Four bouquets of flowers—two wilted, two fresh— lay in the dirt by the service door. He looked for cards or messages among them, but found none.

Parker next paid a visit to the Cadillac PD, but not before making a call to Solange Corriveau.

"Have you spoken to Moxie Castin?" he asked.

"I have, although certain of my colleagues expressed surprise, even skepticism, at his helpfulness—and yours."

"Let me guess: Walsh."

"I'm not going to name names."

"But I'm right, aren't I?"

"Of course you are. That apart, what can I do for you?"

"Have you ever been to Indiana?"

"No."

"Ever wanted to go to Indiana?"

"Not particularly."

"Then I may be saving you a trip, because I'm in Indiana."

Parker heard the sound of paper rustling.

"Cadillac, Indiana?" said Corriveau.

"Got it in one."

"Errol Dobey."

"And Esther Bachmeier, both of whom may have passed our Jane Doe—"

"Karis, according to the man who got in touch with Castin."

"—up the line to Maela Lombardi."

"The *late* Maela Lombardi," Corriveau corrected. "Dental records gave us a positive ID. Saved us asking the niece to view a body that had been in the water for a while."

"Cause of death?"

"Not drowning. I spoke to the ME this morning. Lombardi was already dead when she went into the water, but that's as much as I know for now. We have a recent puncture wound to one arm, though, so we could be relying on toxicology. Now you: Do you have something to tell me, or are you looking for a favor?"

"A favor, but you'll benefit. I'm about to pay a visit to the Cadillac PD. If they want confirmation that I'm on the level, can I refer them to you?"

"Uh . . ."

"You shouldn't listen to Walsh. He's sore about a lot of stuff."

"Still 'uh.' "

"Maybe you really do want to visit Indiana after all, but I have to tell you, the round-trip ticket was expensive, and there's not a whole lot to see once you get here, unless you're a big NASCAR fan. Come on, Corriveau: if I'm not saving you a trip, I'm saving you some groundwork."

"Okay, fine. But you share everything you find out, and you don't piss anyone off."

"Uh . . ."

"Yeah, funny."

Parker thanked her and hung up.

The Cadillac PD was organized along almost identical lines to the Cape Elizabeth PD: fourteen members, of whom five were patrol officers, and one detective. The front desk was staffed from eight a.m. to five p.m. every day, with lobby telephones directly wired to regional dispatch accessible outside those hours. It employed four reserve police officers, and four reserve weekend clerks, with vacancies currently existing for one of each. Parker knew all this because a large sign informed him of it, and he had half an hour to familiarize himself with its details while he waited for the chief to return from whatever it was the chief was doing—which, as it turned out, was enjoying a late breakfast at the Sunnyside Dine-In, and not the first such breakfast he'd had, judging by the strain his belly was placing on the buttons of his uniform shirt. His name was Dwight Hillick, and he proved cautiously interested once Parker explained to him why he was in town.

"Trunk of a car, you say?"

"That's right."

Hillick tapped his pen on his desk.

"We haven't had a request from Maine for information or assistance."

"You will."

"So why shouldn't I wait for them to call instead of talking to you?"

"Because I'm here, and they're there. Solange Corriveau at the MSP will vouch for me."

Hillick put down his pen.

"I don't need a reference," he said. "I know who you are. I looked you up on the Google machine. You planning on shooting anyone?"

"What day is it?"

"I do believe it's Thursday."

"No, I'm not planning on shooting anyone."

Hillick silently regarded Parker for a good ten seconds.

"Well, all right then," he said. "Let's get started."

CHAPTER
LXXXIV

In Ivan Giller's opinion—based, admittedly, on limited exposure to the subject—Gregg Mullis was not Connie White's kind of guy. He lived in a dump, worked in a slaughterhouse, and his demeanor was that of someone who woke each morning anticipating only the many ways that life would find to fuck him before he could go back to bed again. He had at least managed to impregnate a woman at last—a boy, according to the expectant mother in question—but Giller believed Mullis could only have done so by keeping his eyes closed. Mullis's girlfriend might have been described as homely, but only if someone had never actually seen homely, let alone pretty. Also, judging by the ashtrays scattered around their home, the smell from her clothing, and the cigarette dangling from her right hand, her kid, if he survived until birth, would grow up to be the Marlboro Man.

Giller had performed due diligence checks on Mullis before approaching him, and now knew the name of his ex-wife, her home address, the nature of the two jobs she held down, and the school attended by her son—or "son," as Giller had already begun to think of Daniel Weaver. But Giller needed confirmation from Mullis of the truth of the story told to him by Connie White: that Holly Weaver could not have conceived the boy she was calling her own. This was why Giller was now seated at a thrift-store table in a kitchen smelling of grease and boiled vegetables, in a house that would have benefited from a serious clean, or better still, an all-consuming fire.

Mullis was slouched opposite Giller, holding the business card Giller had handed to him at the door. The card identified Giller as one Marcus Light, an employee of the Office of Child and Family Services, a division of the state's Department of Health and Human Services. Giller possessed an array of such cards: some he manufactured himself, while others—as in this case—he retained when they were presented to him, or he had an opportunity to steal them. Mullis and his girlfriend had not even asked to see some corroborating form of ID. The card had been sufficient to enable Giller to gain entry to their home—well, the card, and Giller's assurances that they were not in any kind of trouble, and might even stand to benefit if they would answer a few questions for him.

Giller never ceased to be amazed by just how gullible people could be.

Mullis was five eight, and thin but not scrawny,

as though assembled from scraps of wire. He'd probably been considered good-looking once, before disappointment began whittling away at him.

"You said something about benefits," said Mullis's girlfriend, whose name was Tanya. In case there was any doubt about the matter, she had it tattooed on the back of her left hand, contained in the outline of a heart. On the back of her right hand, a similar heart surrounded the name of her partner.

"*Benefit*," Giller corrected her. "I'm authorized to offer a financial reward to anyone who assists in fraud investigations."

"What kind of fraud?" Mullis asked.

"In this case, supplying false information for the purpose of registering a birth."

Tanya glanced at Mullis.

"Someone we know?" she asked, and grinned, but Mullis wasn't biting.

"Shut up," he said.

"Fuck you, telling me to shut up."

But she shut up.

Giller cleared his throat. "Mr. Mullis, the fact that I'm here means we're already aware of the nature of the fraud committed. I also have to warn you that just as I'm in a position to offer a reward for any cooperation received, so too am I obliged to regard the withholding of information as a crime. This is a very serious matter. Falsification of a birth certificate is a felony, and brings with it legal penalties. Not just a fine, either: depending on the nature and severity of the offense, we could be talking about five years in prison—more, if the welfare of a child is deemed to be at risk."

Mullis put the card on the table and gently pushed it toward Giller.

"I don't know about any fraud," he said.

Giller saw it all now. Any rage or bitterness Mullis might have felt toward his ex-wife had dissipated with the conception of his own boy. He'd loved her once, and he wasn't about to collude in the possible removal of Daniel from her home, or help put her behind bars.

"Your ex-wife registered the birth of a son five years ago."

"So what?"

"Your ex-wife is infertile."

"The hell she is."

"Please don't do this, Mr. Mullis," said Giller, and he meant it.

"Gregg," said Tanya, "let's talk in private."

"I don't need to talk."

Her voice softened.

"Gregg." She placed a hand on his shoulder. "A minute."

And just as Giller had perceived a vestige of old love in Mullis, and a basic decency not entirely excised by the years, so also did he recognize genuine affection and concern in the face of his girlfriend. It made Giller feel bad for them, and sorry that his search had brought him to their home.

The couple left the room, closing the door behind them, but the walls were thin, and Giller could pick up some of what was passing between them.

"They already know . . . It's not your business . . . think about our baby . . . jail."

He made the call while they argued. They had already told him everything he needed to know. What would follow was out of his hands.

CHAPTER
LXXXV

Quayle sat in a rental car across from the Weavers' property. Thanks to Giller's hard work, Quayle already had in his possession a great deal of information about Holly Weaver's life, including the school attended by the boy she was calling her son, but he had no idea what the boy in question looked like. He did know the time Saber Hill Elementary got out, though, and thirty minutes earlier had found himself a spot in a disused lot from which he could watch the road leading to the two Weaver houses.

At one p.m., a blue Chrysler that wouldn't have been worth the price of the gas needed to get it to the dump, driven by a white-haired man in a black coat who was still trying and failing to secure his safety belt as he drove, pulled out and made the turn south. This would be Holly Weaver's father, Owen. Quayle knew all about him as well: widowed once, divorced once; owned a big rig; not much money to speak of, and none likely to materialize at this late stage in his life.

Quayle stayed behind the Chrysler until it

reached the school. He took a space farther along, from which he saw the white-haired man cross the street and join the conclave of parents milling by the gate. Quayle heard the school bell ring, and moments later the first of the children began to emerge, among them a boy with dark hair who moved slower than the rest, as though the bag on his back weighed more than it should, but who still managed the faintest of smiles for his grandfather.

Quayle released his breath, his whole body sagging with relief, like a man long burdened with illness welcoming at last the possibility of an end to his pain. Hand in hand, Owen Weaver and the boy walked to the car, Quayle's eyes fixed on them throughout.

Funny, Quayle thought, how some boys take after their mothers.

He needed no further confirmation from Giller. He had found Karis Lamb's child.

CHAPTER
LXXXVI

The cell phone number went straight to voicemail the first time Giller tried to call, but he had time for a second, more successful attempt before the shouting from outside the kitchen reached a crescendo, followed by silence. He heard footsteps approaching from the hall and put the phone away. Mullis opened the kitchen door. Tanya stood behind him, crying.

"Go on, get out," said Mullis. "We've got nothing more to say to you."

"I'm really sorry you've chosen this path."

"I told you," said Mullis. "Get out of my house."

The doorbell rang—not once but continuously, the caller keeping a finger on the button. Behind the frosted glass, the figure of a woman was visible.

"Who the fuck is that?" Mullis asked.

Tanya moved toward the door.

"Don't answer it," said Mullis.

"It won't do any good," said Giller, loudly enough to be heard over the clamor.

Mullis turned back to Giller. "What did you say?"

"I said that it won't do any good. You can't keep her out."

"You mean this bitch is with you?"

Tanya's hands had clasped instinctively over the swell of her belly, as though that might be enough to protect her baby.

"You'd best just let her in," said Giller.

His eyes were warm. He felt a tear drop to his cheek. He was crying for Mullis, for Tanya, for their unborn child.

For himself.

"Let her in, and we can be done with it."

CHAPTER
LXXXVII

Louis sat in Moxie Castin's reception area, absorbed in his reading, his long legs extended before him. He was currently alternating between Montaigne, *The Sun Also Rises*, and the *New York Times*: an essay, a chapter of the novel, followed by a couple of articles. When he wasn't reading, he was contemplating what he'd just read.

Moxie watched him from the doorway of his office.

"You know what one of my clients asked earlier?"

"No," said Louis. He was back to Montaigne, and did not look up from the book as he spoke.

"She wanted to know what crime you'd committed."

"I hope you thought carefully before you answered."

"I left it to her imagination."

"Probably for the best."

Louis turned another page, but still did not look up.

"That tie," he said.

Moxie fingered the item of clothing in question.

"What about it?"

"Just 'that tie.' "

"It's an expensive tie."

"You sure about that?"

"You want me to show you the receipt?"

"Doesn't go with the suit."

"I like contrasts."

"Good, because it's hard to imagine any suit it would go with."

"It's got character."

"Except a clown suit."

"It's Italian."

"Then maybe an Italian clown suit."

Moxie walked to the mirror by the secretary's desk and examined his reflection. His secretary, he noticed, was keeping her head down and saying nothing. He made a mental note to remind her of the necessity of supporting the man who paid her salary.

"You got me doubting myself now," he said.

"Good," said Louis.

Moxie buttoned his jacket, frowned, and unbuttoned it again.

"I guess it might be a little loud for this suit," he conceded.

"Loud for Times Square."

"Okay, okay, you convinced me. I'll change it. I'll change it, and I'll never wear it again. I'll send it to Goodwill."

"Send it to clown school."

"Enough with the clowns."

Moxie skulked into his office, rummaged in his closet, and returned moments later with a more subdued tie, which he knotted in front of the mirror before turning to face Louis.

"Better?"

Louis flicked a glance over the top of his book.

"Better," he said. "Now about the suit . . ."

From behind his back, Moxie heard what sounded like his secretary choking.

"If you're laughing when I turn around," he said, "you're fired."

CHAPTER
LXXXVIII

Dwight Hillick might have looked like he could have done with skipping a couple of meals, but he was nobody's fool. He took Parker step-by-step through every detail of the fire at the diner, the discovery of Errol Dobey's body, and the disappearance of Esther Bachmeier, all without stumbling, hesitating, or referring to a single file or note.

"So the blaze is being treated as accidental?" said Parker.

"Dobey's body was badly burned, but there was no sign of injuries other than those consistent with a fire, and no trace of accelerants, paper apart."

"And Dobey liked to smoke weed."

"Certainly did. He wouldn't be the first man to have died from dropping a lit joint. We're still waiting on the results of toxicology tests, but we won't have those for another month. On the other hand, there's the matter of Esther's disappearance, which raises a couple of flags."

"Is she a suspect?"

"Officially, we'd sure like to talk to her. Unofficially, I don't believe so."

"What about the women and girls who stayed with Dobey in the past?"

"What about them?"

"Any reason to suspect a grudge? Boyfriend, husband?"

"We haven't ruled it out. We had the Indiana State Fire Marshal down here, and a private arson investigator was engaged to perform an origin and cause. That's still ongoing, but like I said, no sign of accelerants, or not yet. But with all that paper, a match would have been enough."

"Back to the women who passed through: You were aware that Dobey and Bachmeier were running an unofficial shelter?"

"I was."

"Any suggestion of impropriety on Dobey's part?"

"None."

"It never crossed your mind?"

"You didn't know Dobey. I did. I'm not pissed at you for asking. I'd do the same if I were in your shoes, but he wasn't like that."

Parker threw a few more questions at Hillick, just to clarify and confirm. When Parker was done, Hillick made a call to the department's detective, a former Indianapolis PD officer named Shears, asking him to drop by, even though Shears was off-duty that day. Shears arrived shortly after, and together the three men drove first to Dobey's Diner, where they went over everything a second time, with Shears adding what he could to Hillick's account, before they proceeded to the Bachmeier house. Shears led Parker through each of its rooms, which had been examined by detectives and forensics experts from the Indiana State Police, the ISP having jurisdiction over homicides outside major urban areas. There were no signs of disturbance, but equally no indications that Bachmeier was planning to leave for any length of time. A half-finished pint of Ben & Jerry's had even been found melted by the sink, a spoon still inside.

Parker went outside and stood in the sun while Hillick and Shears locked up. He'd expected Indiana to be flat, Lord knows why, but the area around Cadillac was hilly and forested. It was a pretty setting for a town, but he still wouldn't have wanted to live there.

"And Leila Patton?" he said when the lawmen rejoined him.

Hillick adjusted his bulk.

"Yeah, that's a strange one. Leila says she was attacked after she came back from the diner. The staff and a lot of the townsfolk went there to gather after what happened—you know, to console each other, lay flowers, say some prayers—and Leila had just returned home. She couldn't tell us much about what occurred, other than being certain it was a woman that tried to abduct her. The woman was wearing a ski mask, and as soon as it became clear that she wasn't going to be able to take Leila, she turned tail. Leila thought she heard a car pull away, but she didn't see it."

"I hear Leila might have cut her attacker."

"That's right. Keyed her."

"You think it's connected to whatever else may have happened?"

"I'm keeping an open mind. This is a small town. So much occurs under the surface, like in most small towns, but to have a fatal fire, a disappearance, and an attempted abduction all in the space of fewer than twenty-four hours is off-the-scale unusual. So yeah, a link is possible, but I can't see what it might be. Well, I can: it's got to have something to do with Dobey's girls, but it's not like Dobey and Esther kept a record of the ones who passed through; or if they did, we haven't found it yet. Could be any papers went up with everything else in that blaze."

"Leila was working on the night of the fire, right?"

"Yes, she was."

"And she saw nothing unusual?"

"She says not, other than some guy reading poetry. I don't think that's a crime, although I guess it might depend on the poetry."

Parker looked at Hillick. Hillick looked at Parker. Parker looked at Shears.

"Don't ask me," said Shears. "I'm not a critic. I just work here."

"Leila thought that Dobey didn't like the look of the poetry guy," said Hillick, "and was acting a bit antsy after, but Dobey claimed he didn't know him, and Leila believed him. She gave us a description, but it sounded like Ralph Waldo Emerson. And not liking the look of someone wasn't unusual for Dobey. He had his peculiarities."

"He didn't like men who wore sandals with socks," said Shears.

"No," said Hillick, "he did not."

They all considered this, decided it was pretty reasonable, and moved on.

"So Leila Patton is assaulted outside her home, apparently as part of an attempted abduction," said Parker. "She manages to get inside her house and lock the door before calling the police. End of story."

"That's it," said Hillick.

"So why try to abduct her to begin with?"

"You're the PI with the reputation," said Hillick.

"Because," said Parker, "whoever this woman was—assuming it *was* a woman—she believed Patton knew something, or had seen something, that might aid the investigation. But according to you, Patton didn't have anything useful to offer."

"Which doesn't mean she doesn't have

anything to tell," said Shears. "Leila Patton is a bright young woman. She's smarter than I am."

He waited for Hillick to deny this. Hillick didn't.

"Nice," said Shears.

"So the attack could have been a warning?" said Hillick.

"If the fates of Dobey, Bachmeier, and Lombardi have a common root," said Parker, "then we're looking at conclusive actions, not warnings."

Hillick jammed his hands in his trouser pockets and looked around for something to kick. When nothing suitable presented itself, he opted for swearing loudly. Behind him was Esther Bachmeier's garage, and in the garage stood Bachmeier's Nissan. Wherever she was, she hadn't driven there herself. Either way, none of the three men currently standing in her yard believed she was coming back.

"I'm fond of Leila," said Hillick, once he'd purged himself some. "She's a good girl. And Shears is right: she's smart."

"So she could be holding out on you?" Parker asked.

"I guess, but I don't see why she wouldn't want to help us figure out what's going on."

"Perhaps she's scared."

"Yeah, but she's also tough. Her mom's been lingering for a long time. It would be a mercy if she was taken to the Lord, but I've never heard Leila complain, not once. What I'm trying to say is that if Leila Patton had information that could point toward proof of intent to do harm to Dobey or Esther, I'd expect her to tell us."

"So what's she hiding?" asked Parker.

"Well, maybe that's what you're here to find out."

CHAPTER
LXXXIX

Giller sat at the kitchen table, staring toward the front door. Gregg Mullis was lying half in the hall, half in the living room, so Giller could only see his feet, one of which was still twitching. Tanya was slumped against the wall, her legs outstretched before her. The bullet had taken her in the chest, killing her instantly.

Pallida Mors was standing over the woman's body, as though puzzled by the alteration wrought upon it by mortality, a pale ghost with a new house to haunt. Her hair was entirely concealed by the blue plastic skullcap, rendering her appearance stranger still. A pistol, deformed by a suppressor, hung at her side, exhaling a final wisp of smoke. Giller had never heard a suppressed shot fired before. He was surprised at how loud it sounded; not like a little cough, but an angry bark.

As Giller watched, Mors knelt and placed the palm of her left hand on Tanya's womb. She kept it there as she turned to Giller.

"I can feel it kicking," she said.

Giller said nothing. He had wandered into hell,

504

and now one of its demons was speaking to him in a language he did not wish to understand. He put his hands over his ears and closed his eyes, but could still hear what Mors said next.

"It's stopped now."

Footsteps drew nearer, and with them the stink of Mors, potent even amid the gun smoke, the blood, and the smell of dying. She was its quintessence, the crux of it made manifest. It was in her name. She was Death itself. And Giller understood that every moment of his being, from the fusion of seed and egg in a distant congress, through pain and joy and love and loss, to the final clarity of this last poor province, a realm of splintered wood and stinking food, had been leading to just this instant, and so he was defined by what he had caused to be committed here, and the little good he had done in life would be swept away like ash from the final conflagration of his existence.

"Look at me," said Mors.

Giller opened his eyes, and was named by the gun.

CHAPTER
XC

Parker, Hillick, and Shears decided between them that it would be better if Parker spoke with Leila Patton alone. Hillick was of the opinion that any effort to intimidate the young woman was likely to fail, and the depth of the failure would be commensurate with the degree of intimidation involved: in other words, Patton would be three times as stubborn if faced with all of them.

Parker was standing by his rental when Patton finally emerged at the end of her waitressing shift, still wearing the clothes in which she'd worked. He was parked far enough away so as not to risk alarming her, but close enough that she couldn't get to her car and drive off before he could speak with her.

"Miss Patton?"

She stopped by her vehicle, and he noticed that she immediately slipped a key between the middle and ring fingers of her right hand before clenching a fist. Clearly she wasn't about to be taken by surprise again. She squinted at Parker, the sun behind him.

"You were in the diner earlier," she said. "Who are you, and what do you want?"

Parker stopped just out of striking range.

"My name is Charlie Parker. We spoke on the telephone, but didn't get very far. I thought I'd try a conversation in person."

She didn't relax, but she shifted the key in her hand in order to open her car door.

"I told you: I have nothing to say."

"People are dying, Leila, and not just here. I think whoever killed Dobey and Esther murdered a woman in Maine and dumped her body at a quarry. I think they're going to keep on killing until they get what they want."

Patton stopped, the key in the lock, and turned to face him.

"Esther's missing, not dead. Dobey died in a fire."

"I don't think you believe that for one moment, just as you don't believe Dobey killed himself through carelessness with a joint."

"I don't know what I believe."

He had her now. He could hear it in her voice.

"But you cared about both of them."

"Yes."

"Then I'd like to talk to you about them for a few minutes. You may know more than you think."

"I have to get back to my mom. She's sick."

Parker just listened. Anything he said wouldn't

have helped. He waited, and watched the fight go out of Leila Patton. She silently took in the parking lot, the diner, and the town of Cadillac itself, as though wondering how, or if, she might ever escape them all.

"If it's true," she said at last, "about these people, whoever they are, then you're going to stop them?"

"Yes."

"Isn't that what the police are supposed to do?"

"Sometimes I do it better."

She sized Parker up, and still appeared to find him wanting. He didn't take it personally.

"Alone?" she asked.

"I have help, if I need it."

"And have you needed it in the past?"

"Occasionally."

"I suppose I could have googled you," she said, "but I've grown to hate that kind of thing. It's creepy."

"Agreed."

"If I had searched, would I have liked what I found?"

She was facing him now, and he felt certain she had something to tell. He could see it in her eyes.

"I hope so. Not all of it, maybe, but most. Even I don't care for all I've done."

When she spoke again, her voice was so soft that the breeze almost scattered her words before Parker could catch them.

"I'm afraid she'll come back."

"Who?"

"The woman who tried to hurt me."

"Did she say she would?"

"She didn't say anything at all."

"And yet?"

Patton's nose wrinkled, like a small mammal sniffing for the presence of a larger carnivore.

"She smelled bad—not like she didn't bathe enough, but bad from the inside. You probably don't know what I mean. I'm not explaining it very well."

Parker stepped closer.

"You wake in the night," he said, "and you can still smell it, as though she's there in the room with you. When you're low, or scared, you taste it in your food. You catch traces of it from spoiled milk, from open drains, from roadkill."

"Yes," she said. "That's it. Does it go away?"

"No, not if you've been touched by it. It stays."

"So what do you do?"

"You hope for the removal of its source from the world, and live with the memory." He smiled at her. "How about this: if you give me some of your time, *I'll* talk. I'll tell you about myself, and how I know these things. When I'm done, if you don't trust me, I'll leave, and I won't trouble you again. I'll catch a flight back east, and find another way to stop what's happening. I won't involve you in it, but . . ."

He didn't finish.

"But I'm already involved, right?" said Patton. "That's what you were going to say."

"Yes."

"And that woman will come back, won't she?"

"It's possible. Either you're a loose end, in which case she'll return because she has to, or she enjoys what she does, and she'll return because she wants to. For those like her, the ones corrupted deep down, it's usually more the second than the first."

"You could have said that earlier. You could have used the threat to make me change my mind."

"I'm not here to threaten you, and I didn't have to change your mind. You already knew the right thing to do. You just needed someone to confirm it for you. And you're not doing this for yourself. I don't think that's the kind of person you are. You'll do it because it'll save others, but there's nothing wrong with saving yourself along the way."

"That's quite a speech."

"I get a lot of practice."

"I guess you must." She opened her car door. "Follow me."

CHAPTER
XCI

Owen Weaver sat with his grandson on the living-room couch, watching a cartoon custom-tooled to sell toys to kids, and thus wring maximum profit from minimal entertainment.

Daniel had endured a bad night, waking up screaming from a nightmare, which was unusual for him. It meant Holly also had a bad night, since Daniel then insisted on sleeping in her bed, although he didn't actually sleep much at all. On any other day Holly might have kept him home, but Owen had an internist's appointment that morning, for which he'd been waiting weeks, and the Barhams were at a funeral in Bangor, so there was no one to take care of the boy. As a result Daniel—subdued, and heavy lidded—had been forced to spend an unhappy day at Saber Hill.

Daniel's eyes were now fixed on the screen, but Owen could tell he was taking in little of what he was seeing. He'd tried to cajole Daniel into lying down and catching up on the shut-eye he'd missed, but he insisted on staying where he was, and every time his eyes started to close he shifted position, as though to keep himself awake.

"Hey," said Owen.

Daniel looked up.

"You don't need to be scared about falling asleep. I'm here, and I'm not going anywhere. I'll stay on this couch until morning if you want me to, except when I got to go pee-pee, because we don't want to be sitting on no pee-pee couch, do we?"

Daniel didn't crack a smile. Usually even the mention of someone else's toilet habits was enough to make him bust a gut. Daniel's brow furrowed, and he asked his grandfather a question.

"Why don't I look like Mom?"

Owen assembled his features into his best poker face.

"What do you mean by that?"

"What I said. Why don't I look like Mom? Her hair is real light, and mine is dark."

But it was more than that, Owen knew. The boy didn't yet have the vocabulary to express the complexity of his feelings.

"Because the two of you are just different, is all," said Owen. "Could be you have more of your father in your appearance."

"But you said you'd never met my dad."

"I'm guessing. That's how these things some-times are. Me, I always looked more like my father than my mother. If I'd taken after my mother, I'd have been prettier."

Again, no smile.

"Why doesn't Mom ever talk about my dad?"

Where was this coming from?

"It makes her sad."

"Why?"

"It just does."

"Because he died?"

"Yes. Because he died."

Daniel's gaze shifted to the window, and the woods beyond.

"Can someone have two mommies?"

Good Lord.

"Eh, I guess. Your friend Dina at school, she has two moms. Her daddy remarried, and Dina goes to stay with him and his new wife twice a month. Dina gets on okay with her stepmom, right?"

Daniel nodded.

"So she's a second mom, in a way. Is that what you mean?"

This time, Daniel shook his head.

"What if your mom dies?" he asked. "What if your mom dies and you go to live with another mom?"

Owen experienced a sense of constriction in his chest. If his left arm had gone numb and he'd keeled over from a heart attack, it wouldn't have surprised him.

"What about it?"

"Is the dead mom still your mom?"

Owen was in alien territory now, lost in the boonies. There was no right answer here. He could only be honest.

"Yes," he said. "She'd still be your mom."

Daniel's chin trembled, and Owen gathered the boy to him and held him close as he started to sob.

"But which one is real?" Daniel cried. "Which one is *real?*"

CHAPTER
XCII

Days, even weeks, might have gone by before the remains of Garrison Pryor were discovered had the heat alarm in his kitchen not malfunctioned, causing it to beep incessantly, disturbing Pryor's neighbors on either side and necessitating a visit from the super. Now a cadre of detectives and federal agents were staring down at what was left of Pryor's body, along with the various pieces that had been excised from it and placed in the bathroom sink.

"Someone really didn't like him," said one of the agents.

"There wasn't much of him to like," came the reply.

"There's less now."

They heard movement behind them, and turned to see SAC Edgar Ross of the New York field office standing in the doorway. While Boston was involved in the Pryor investigation, the main impetus was coming from D.C. and New York, and from Ross in particular. He didn't look as though he appreciated the agents' humor, but he left it to his expression to communicate his displeasure. Finally, after an awkward minute of contemplation, he departed.

"How the fuck did he get up here so fast?" said the first agent.

His colleague shrugged. "They say he has a place over in Cambridge."

"On a federal salary?"

"You don't know? Ross comes from money. He's not hurting. Shit, he's even a member of one of those fancy clubs . . ."

CHAPTER
XCIII

Connie White deposited into her bank account half the money given to her by Giller, and spent some on wool at the local craft shop and the remainder at Marshalls. Ordinarily she'd have saved a little, just in case, but she'd registered the look on Giller's face when she told him about Holly Weaver's boy: the Weaver name meant something to him, which guaranteed he'd be back with more money. White had no concerns that Giller might try to screw her over. He might not have been averse to negotiation— no businessman was—but she knew from asking around that Giller kept his word once a deal was made. To do otherwise wouldn't have been good for his reputation as an honest broker.

White pulled up outside her trailer, expecting to see Steeler emerge from his kennel, but there was no sign of the dog. Steeler was familiar with the sound of her car, and could sometimes be as lazy as sin, but he always made an appearance to greet her. She could see his chain snaking into the kennel. It was odd, but she wasn't alarmed.

"Steeler?"

A bark came in response, not from the kennel but from inside the trailer. Maybe Eddy, her brother, had dropped by and allowed Steeler to go in with him—she'd been asking Eddy for weeks to take a look at the seal around the oven—although he wasn't supposed to let Steeler enter the trailer because the dog was crazy for yarn and liked nothing better than to tear apart a ball of it with tooth and claw. But Eddy was fond of Steeler, and the dog knew it.

"Shit, Eddy," she said, as she opened the door and stepped inside, "I've told you before about—"

An unfamiliar woman was sitting at the table, Steeler beside her, his front legs on her lap, his tail wagging. Steeler loved his mistress, and liked her brother a lot, but that had always appeared to be the limit of his affection for human beings.

Until now.

The woman was wearing a blue plastic skullcap, the hair beneath smeared tight against it. She had the skin of a drowning victim and the eyes of a doll. Then White was no longer looking at the intruder, or at Steeler, but at the gun that appeared from behind the dog's back, the threat made more real by the suppressor on the muzzle. White had seen enough movies to know that nobody put a suppressor on a gun that wasn't going to be used.

"You have a nice dog," said the woman.

White tried to run, and Mors shot her in the back.

CHAPTER
XCIV

Leila Patton lived on a street of identical single-story houses in a development that probably dated from the seventies. Most of the homes were in good condition, although the Pattons' bore indicators of neglect suggestive of a dearth of time, money, or both. Parker pulled into the drive and got out of his car. He waited, as requested, for Patton to go inside first and make sure her mom was okay. Ten minutes went by, during which nothing stirred on the road beyond a single black cat with a dead bird in its teeth, before Parker heard the sound of a couple of windows opening at the front of the house, and Patton waved at him to enter.

Although he did not comment on it, Parker could tell why she had opened the windows as soon as he reached the door. The house smelled of long-term illness, of the slow failure of the body and the steps taken to ease it. Parker heard the sound of a television from somewhere at the back of the house. A woman coughed, then was quiet.

Patton was waiting for him in the living room.

It was tidy in the way of rooms that are rarely used. Perhaps it was his knowledge of the family's circumstances that colored his perceptions, but Parker thought it felt like a space awaiting mourners. The only incongruous detail was the piano in one corner. Parker didn't know much about pianos, but the instrument was clean and free of dust, and the surrounding carpet bore the marks of repeated repositioning of the piano stool, which suggested it wasn't just a decorative feature.

"Do you want something to drink?" Patton asked. "I was going to make green tea."

"Sounds good."

She left him alone again. He went to the fireplace and examined the framed photographs on the mantel. A younger Leila featured in many of them, often alongside a heavyset man who had started going bald early, tried to disguise it, and finally surrendered to the inevitable before he vanished entirely from the gallery, as though fate, not content with taking his hair, had decided to appropriate the rest of him as well; and a short, dark-haired woman who started out thin and kept getting thinner until there were no more pictures of her at all, freezing her at a stage before her illness became her most pronounced feature. Judging by how old her daughter looked in the most recent photo, Parker guessed that the final pictures of Patton's mother might have been taken four or five years earlier, perhaps even about the time Karis passed through Cadillac on her way to a death in the Maine woods.

"She doesn't like to look at them."

Patton had entered the room behind him, carrying a tray with a pot of Chinese design, two small matching cups, and a plate of cookies that were clearly home-baked. She put the tray down on a low table before joining him at the fireplace.

"My mom, I mean. She doesn't like to be reminded of how she used to be, but I do."

Parker didn't say that he was sorry. After so many years of looking after her mother, Leila Patton had probably heard every platitude in existence.

"How long can you keep caring for her at home?" he asked.

"A few more months." She spoke matter-of-factly, but wouldn't look directly at him. "After that she'll need full-time attention, until the end."

"Is there somewhere nearby?"

"Not really, or nowhere I'd want her to be. We'll have to sell the house to cover the expenses, but I wasn't planning on staying here anyway."

"Where will you go?"

"Eventually? Somewhere with a view. But first, Bloomington: the Jacobs School of Music, if they'll still have me. I was offered a scholarship a while back, but I couldn't accept it because of how sick my mom was. It's being held for me. Or it was. I'm almost afraid to ask now."

"Is Jacobs good?"

She laughed.

"Good? Jacobs is the best in the country, even better than Berklee or Juilliard, although the Curtis in Philadelphia runs pretty close."

"Let me guess," said Parker. "Piano."

"I can see why you're a detective. What gave it away, I wonder?"

"The flattening to your fingertips," said Parker.

Patton instinctively looked at her hands.

"But mainly that big piano in the corner."

"Witty," said Patton. "Just like the detectives in books."

She poured the tea, and they ate a cookie each. Patton sat on the couch, and Parker took an armchair while he tried to explain to her why she should trust him. She listened, and when she asked questions he did his best to answer them honestly. When he didn't want to answer, he let her know. He had no desire to lie to her.

To all this he consented because he believed the young woman before him had something she wished to share, and perhaps of which she needed to unburden herself. And even if what he learned did not aid him in his investigation, and he succeeded only in relieving her of its weight, this would be sufficient, because sometimes the service asked of us is just to listen. Only later did Parker understand that in this room colored by dying, he had laid himself bare before a stranger, and by doing so had decreased the measure of his own pain.

Parker finished talking. Leila—for she was Leila to him now, and Leila she would always remain—touched Parker's hand, and in establishing that connection, she spoke.

"Lamb," she said. "That was Karis's second name, but she told me to keep it secret."

Leila got up and left the room again. When she returned, she was holding a shoe box, which she placed on the coffee table.

"Karis," she said, "told me to keep lots of things secret."

CHAPTER
XCV

Quayle was waiting for Mors when she returned, the killings of recent hours lending a temporary warmth to her pallor, as though in depriving others of life she had absorbed a little of their vigor to compensate for the paucity of her own.

Quayle knew her requirements by now. He had laid out a sheet of plastic just inside the door on which Mors stood to shed her clothing, until she was naked before him. Only then did she step from the plastic and carefully gather up the ends of the sheet, knotting them together to form a neat package. Later she would soak the contents in bleach before dumping them. Burning would have been preferable, but they were concerned about the smoke drawing attention to the cabin.

Mors showered before dressing in fresh clothes. Quayle, lost in thought, had still not moved from his chair by the time she was finished. Mors did not disturb him, but curled up on a couch and fell instantly asleep.

Quayle was very close to what he had been seeking for so long, but the temptation to bring it to an end with alacrity had to be tempered with caution. He did not wish to be the quarry in a manhunt when all this was done, or not before he had safely left this place to return to England.

How soon before the bodies of Mullis, White, and the rest were found? Not long, he supposed. He had no fear that Mors might have been seen in the immediate vicinity of either the house or the trailer—she was too good for that—but one could not account for every possibility, and there was always the small chance that someone might recall an unfamiliar vehicle glimpsed on the road. It would be best if Mors abandoned her car. Giller had sourced two for them, guaranteed clean, and one would suffice for what remained to be done.

Since Holly Weaver worked long hours, and the boy was at school, their home stood empty for most of the day. Owen Weaver was a problem, since his own property was so close to his daughter's, but he had to go out sometime. If he didn't, they would deal with him; nevertheless, it would be better if they could find what they wanted, take it, and vanish without leaving any more bodies behind. The greater the carnage, the greater the likelihood of being caught, and they had already ended enough lives. There had been no choice when it came to the others, but Quayle could see no reason to inflict harm on the Weavers, or none beyond a vague desire for retribution, and that would be assuaged as soon as he had what he wanted.

And then there was Parker to consider, because he was also searching for Karis Lamb's son. With Giller gone, there was no way of finding out how close Parker might be, but Quayle had made provisions for his distraction. They might require one more body, although thankfully Mors's enthusiasm for killing appeared quite inexhaustible.

She really was, Quayle thought, the most remarkable woman.

4

We all know that books burn—yet we have the greater knowledge that books cannot be killed by fire. People die, but books never die. . . . In this war, we know, books are weapons.
> —Franklin Delano Roosevelt
> (1882–1945)

CHAPTER
XCVI

The shoe box remained on the coffee table, but Leila made no move to display its contents. In Parker's opinion, she possessed an admirable sense of theater.

"I liked Karis," said Leila. "In another life, we might have been friends. But we didn't have time for that. She was here, and then she was gone."

"Weren't you concerned when she left and you received no further communication from her?" Parker asked.

"No. She warned me that it was how it would be—how it *had* to be. Because of the man she was running from, and what she'd done to him."

"Who was he, this man?"

"Karis called him Vernay. I don't know his first name, and Karis told me not to go searching for more information about him, not even on the Internet. Dobey knew more, but not much, and what he had, he didn't share with me."

"And did you go looking into Vernay?"

"Of course, but not until later: months, maybe a year, after Karis left. Inquisitiveness, you know?"

"And?"

"There were more Vernays than I'd expected, but I knew the one I wanted was a book collector, so I started browsing forums and blogs. I was careful. I set up a new e-mail account to log on, and used only a Tor browser to make myself hard to trace. One evening, I opened my e-mail and there was a new message in my in-box, from a no-reply address. It read, "Why are you searching for Vernay?" It came with a photograph attached: a picture of a child, a girl no more than three or four years old. Naked. Dead. I deleted the account, and stopped looking. I think Vernay disappeared, though. There was chatter about it on some of the forums before all references to him ceased, and all the old postings were expunged, like everyone had been told to keep quiet."

"You didn't share this with anyone else?"

"No. I'd made a mistake. I didn't want to compound my error by bringing these people to our door."

Parker thought Leila Patton was quite something.

"What did Karis tell you about her time with Vernay?" he asked.

"Not a lot. He started out gentle, she said. That's what Karis couldn't understand. She felt stupid, but she wouldn't be the first woman to have been fooled by a man. By the time she found out what he was really like—the pornography, how he enjoyed watching children being hurt—it was too late. She was pregnant, and he wouldn't let her out of his sight. She was certain he'd kill her once the baby was born. He never threatened her that way, but she knew. It was the child he wanted.

"And he had this weird taste in books: occult stuff—not novels or stories, but old volumes. Grimoires, they're called. He told Karis he knew more about them than anyone else in the country, perhaps even the world. He would receive mail from all over, addressed only to 'M. Vernay,' and men would come and visit him because he was such an expert, but they weren't the type to help a pregnant woman. They were the kind that shared Vernay's interests, and not just in mysticism: they would view films together on a screen in Vernay's library, and exchange electronic files containing images of torture. They liked pain. By that point, Vernay didn't care what Karis did or didn't know about his tastes. He was done pretending.

"Then, in her final trimester, she detected a change in him. He was excited. He started selling parts of his collection, trying to bring in money. Karis thought negotiations might be taking place in the background, because there were phone calls and arguments. Finally Vernay locked her in the basement and left her there. Karis had food and water, some books and magazines, and a little bathroom for her needs. She was trapped for two days and two nights, and when Vernay returned, he had another book. That was why he had shut her up in the basement: so he could go buy a book, a collection of fairy tales."

"Fairy tales?" said Parker.

"*Grimm's Fairy Tales*, printed in London in 1908 by Constable, with illustrations by Arthur Rackham. The original Rackham edition is very valuable. Some copies go for a thousand dollars or more on the Internet. There's also a signed edition, and that goes for more than ten thousand."

"And was this one signed?"

"No."

"Wait: he locked Karis Lamb in a basement for two days, just to possess a book of fairy tales worth a thousand dollars?"

"A guy in England was killed for his first edition of *The Wind in the Willows*," said Leila. "It was worth nearly seventy thousand dollars."

"There's a big difference between a thousand and seventy thousand."

"Especially," said Leila, "for a book that doesn't exist."

Parker felt as though he'd fallen down a rabbit hole.

"I don't understand."

"There is no 1908 *Grimm's Fairy Tales* illustrated by Arthur Rackham. The edition illustrated by Rackham wasn't published until the following year."

"So the book was a forgery?"

"No—or so Vernay told Karis. He wanted an audience, and she was the only one he had. He wanted someone to know what he'd found."

"So what exactly did Vernay buy?"

Leila pushed the shoe box toward Parker.

"Why don't you take a look for yourself?"

CHAPTER
XCVII

Holly Weaver received the call from her father as she was waiting at the drive-thru ATM. Her bank account was about to dip into three figures, but at least she was due to get paid on Friday, and with luck she'd score some decent tips over the weekend, especially if she could get a couple of tables to spring for wine.

"Hi, Dad."

"I'm thinking of taking Danny to a movie, see if it might buck his mood up."

"Sure. Did he nap?"

"He dozed on the couch for a while, but he's still not himself."

"It's just tiredness."

"Yeah."

She heard the doubt.

"Did something else happen?"

Owen thought about telling her of the conversation he'd had with Daniel, the one about dead mothers, but decided to keep it to himself for now. It would only distress his daughter.

"He's just an odd one sometimes."

"I think he picked it up from his grandfather," said Holly.

"Yeah? Then his back talk is all you."

"Enjoy the movie, Dad. Easy on the popcorn, and keep the sodas small."

Daniel sat at his bedroom window. Daylight was fading into dusk, and a haze hung over the woods, but he thought he could still discern the figure of a woman amid the trees. If he opened the window, he might even have been able to hear her call his name.

But he had no intention of opening the window.

"Is she telling the truth?" said Daniel.

He spoke to the girl in the corner, the one who kept her head low and seemed to bring shadows with her in order to conceal her face. Daniel should have been frightened of her, just as he was frightened of the woman: because the girl, too, was dead, except she didn't make him feel scared, just drowsy and relaxed, like the cough medicine his mom sometimes gave him when his chest got tight. He could see the girl's reflection in the glass, but when he looked over his shoulder, she wasn't there.

what did she tell you?

"That I should do what Mommy said, that I should listen to her."

she's not your mommy

"She says she is."

sometimes when people die, they leave a piece of themselves behind

"What kind of piece?"

a sad piece, but it's not really them, only their pain

"She comes to my window."

she's lonely

"She wants me to go with her."

you mustn't do that

"She might make me."

she can't make you

you have to want it

do you want it?

"No. I just want her to go away."

she will

"When?"

soon

"How do you know?"

because she is about to be named, and she will rest after she is named

"Who will name her?"

The girl didn't answer at first. Then:

perhaps my father will name her

Daniel looked from the girl's reflection to the waiting woman.

"Can you ask him to hurry?"

CHAPTER
XCVIII

Parker picked up the shoe box. It had clearly remained untouched for a long time, because Leila Patton's fingerprints had disturbed the dust on it. He lifted the lid. The book lay amid wads of newspaper, the boards worn at the corners, and slightly stained.

"What did Vernay tell Karis?" Parker asked.

"He said the book itself wasn't important, just the pages in it. He said they had altered the volume, and changed the date, because that's what they did. They were part of an atlas, he said, one that was old and enduring. He claimed the pages could rewrite."

"Rewrite books?"

"Rewrite *worlds*. Be careful how you touch it."

"Is it delicate?"

"No, but it can make you feel sick. Let me find some gloves for you."

She returned with a pair of leather gloves. They were too small for Parker's hands, but he managed to get his fingers partway into them. He removed the book from the box, and examined the exterior before proceeding to the contents.

A bookplate was fixed to the inside front cover, featuring the letter "D" repeated twice, and the word "London" beneath. The addition of the location was odd, and more indicative of a store or lending library than a private collection.

Parker moved on to the first of the places where the pages were different. A larger single sheet, much older than the rest of the book, had at some point been folded twice and sewn into the binding between two other sections. The visible sides were blank, and made not from paper but what appeared to be some form of vellum, uncut at the top edges. He moved to the second insertion, and discovered the same.

Very gently, Parker lifted one of the pages in an effort to see what was written on the interior of the folds. They were also unmarked. Why, Parker wondered, would someone go to the trouble of inserting blank pages into a volume? Unless, of course, they weren't really blank at all. He tried to recall the ways in which invisible ink could be applied: lemon juice, wine, vinegar, sugar solution, bodily fluids, their message to be revealed later by the application of heat or chemicals.

"Empty," he said.

"Not always."

"What do you mean?"

"Sometimes, if I leave the book open for long enough, I see patterns."

"What kind of patterns?"

"It'll sound crazy."

"Not to me."

Leila took a deep breath.

"Okay, not patterns, but the ghosts of them. Sometimes they're like maps, and other times they're closer to architects' drawings, but really detailed."

That fit with Parker's thesis: an ink of some kind, activated by heat or light.

"Drawings of what?"

"Of the book's surroundings. Of the room it's in. This room, for example."

"Wait, they *change?*"

"I told you it would sound crazy."

"Sounding crazy isn't the same thing as being crazy."

"It's close enough."

"I guess it is."

Parker turned to the copyright page of the book. There, as Leila had said, was the date: 1908. A printer's error? Wasn't that the kind of detail that made a book more valuable?

"Look at the text," said Leila.

Parker did as she asked, and noticed that some words, and even the individual letters within them, were so jumbled as to render the stories unintelligible, as though a catastrophic error had been made during the setting process.

"If you look at them again tomorrow, they could be different," said Leila.

"Different how?"

"The letters may have rearranged themselves again. Look long enough, and you'll begin seeing messages. I thought it was kind of cool at first—freaky, but cool—until . . ."

"Until?"

"Until they formed the words 'Look Away, Cunt' on page fourteen. I stopped opening the book after that."

She bit at a thumbnail.

"And then there are the illustrations."

CHAPTER
XCIX

Billy Ocean hadn't been in Hogie's in a long time, not since he was old enough to drink legally. Hogie's was one of those bars where the lights were always low, the music always loud, and people tended to mind their own business unless forced to do otherwise, which was rarely the case. It lay between Harmony and Corinna in southern Somerset County, and attracted little passing trade due to the unprepossessing nature of its exterior, which was matched by the unprepossessing nature of its interior, and its restrooms in particular, which were notoriously insalubrious. But a Bud Light in Hogie's was a buck-fifty all day, and the food wasn't so bad if you didn't let it linger in your mouth.

Billy found Quayle sitting at a table away from the bar, a glass of clear liquor before him. Billy identified him by his dress sense. It was possible that someone else had previously worn a velvet vest and knitted silk tie in Hogie's, but if so, it was far enough in the past for the trauma to have faded from the bar's collective memory. Quayle didn't look like he belonged in Hogie's, but neither did he appear particularly troubled by his surroundings. Some people had a way of colonizing spaces, adapting them to form sanctuaries for themselves. Quayle was such a man.

Billy took a seat at the table, and a waitress came by for his order. He noticed that she barely registered Quayle's presence, and even when she did, her gaze slid from him like water from an oiled boot. Whatever vibes he was giving off, they weren't good.

"So you're British?" said Billy.

"I think of myself as English first, British second. It's a way of keeping the Scots and Welsh at a distance, never mind the Irish."

Billy was confused, but didn't care enough one way or the other to seek further clarification.

"What are you doing over here?"

"I'm holidaying."

"You're on vacation?"

"If you prefer."

Again, Billy didn't really give a fuck.

"So," Billy said, once his beer had arrived, "who blew up my truck?"

"A man named Charlie Parker. He's a private investigator."

Billy consumed this information with a mouthful of beer.

"I know who he is. And you figure this how?"

"Because it's common knowledge, or relatively so. The police are aware of it, and I believe your father is, too. But the police won't do anything about it because they have no proof, and there also appears to be a don't-touch rule when it comes to Parker. As for your father, well, I can't say. Perhaps he's concerned you might be tempted to do something foolish, and put yourself at risk as a consequence."

"Why did Parker pick on me?"

"Pick on." *What an interesting choice of words*, Quayle thought. They told him all he needed to know about the man sitting opposite.

"He keeps company with a colored man named Louis. My understanding is that this Louis found certain aspects of your truck's décor objectionable, and Parker assisted him in registering what was, all things considered, a forceful protest."

Billy stood.

"I need to make a call," he said.

He went outside and called Dean Harper, his father's former aide. They hadn't spoken since Harper's firing, but Billy was less fearful of Harper when he didn't have to face him in person.

"What do you want?" Harper asked, when Billy identified himself.

"To get you your job back."

"Least you can fucking do, seeing as how you lost it for me."

"My old man misses you." This was true. Billy's father regretted letting Harper go, but he didn't like backtracking on a decision. He thought it made him seem weak. For Harper, though, he might be persuaded to make an exception. "It won't take much to talk him around."

"And you're doing this out of the goodness of your heart?"

"It's by way of an apology. I only want a word in return."

"What word would that be?"

"Yes or no."

"And the question?"

"My truck: Was Charlie Parker the name you heard?"

No reply, or not the one he wanted.

"Jesus, Billy," said Harper, "you got to let this go."

"You want that job back, or don't you?"

"Sure I do."

"Then answer the question."

"Yes. The answer is yes. But Billy—"

Billy didn't wait to hear the rest. He killed the connection and went back inside to rejoin Quayle.

"Seeking confirmation?" said Quayle as Billy sat down.

"Maybe."

"It's always advisable to secure a second opinion. And what did you learn?"

"That you might be telling the truth."

"That I *am* telling the truth."

"Okay, yeah, so you are. What do you want in return: money?"

"No, I just want to help you retaliate."

"Why would you do that?"

"Because Parker is in my way, and I'd like to see him distracted."

"Getting in the way of your 'vacation'?"

"That's right. I'm also prepared to compensate you for your time. You can put the money toward a new truck, perhaps one with a more subdued sense of ornamentation."

Billy grinned. "Seems to me that you might be up to no good here. Are you a bad man?"

Quayle smiled back, and the lights of the bar gleamed like dying stars in the void of his eyes. "Trust me when I say that you have no conception."

Billy's smile faded.

"What kind of retaliation did you have in mind?" he asked.

"Parker took something from you that you valued. I suggest you do the same to him. A little bird told me that he owns a vintage Mustang. He's very fond of it. Why not burn it?"

Billy knew the car. He'd seen it around town. Burning it seemed like a very good idea. It wasn't worth as much as his truck, but Billy was prepared to make allowances for sentimental value.

"I have a friend outside," said Quayle. "She's quite an expert at destruction. Why don't I introduce you to her? After all, no time like the present . . ."

CHAPTER

C

Leila Patton powered up her laptop.

"Look," she said. "These are some of Rackham's original illustrations for the 1909 edition."

They were not what Parker had anticipated. He was, he supposed, more familiar with the pictures that featured in young children's collections of fairy tales, with their bright primary colors, their knights on horseback and wolves in bonnets. Rackham's work bore no relation to that tradition beyond the thematic. Here the colors were muted, the characters sensual, and an ambience of the ethereal, the sinister, infused all, particularly the depictions of forests and trees, their trunks like hides, their branches the limbs of grasping, emaciated creatures.

"Impressive, right?" said Leila.

"They're beautiful. Unsettling, but beautiful."

"You haven't even started being unsettled yet."

She pulled up a Rackham illustration from the tale of "Snow-White and Rose-Red," in which the two young women of the title stood beside a great fallen tree with twisted, exposed roots, facing a dwarf trapped by the weight of the trunk. The rendering of the scene reminded Parker of Karis Lamb's gravesite.

"Okay," said Leila, "you should be able to find the equivalent illustration in the book."

Parker flipped through it until he found the correct plate.

"I've got it."

"Now compare it to the one on the screen."

He did. They appeared similar, apart from a slight blemish to the background of the plate in the book, where Rackham had faded the forest into darkness.

"They look alike."

"Hold on."

Leila went to a closet beside the piano and removed a magnifying glass from one of the drawers. Parker suddenly felt very old. Apparently he now needed a magnifying glass to identify what a twentysomething could see with the naked eye. His despair obviously showed on his face, because Leila told him not to feel too bad.

"I had trouble spotting some of them at the start. And they alter. Like I said, it's been a while since I opened the book."

Parker took the glass and held it over the blemish. Staring back at him from the depths of the forest was the mutilated child glimpsed back in Portland. Its face was half hidden, and only a suggestion of its body was visible in the murk, but it was the same figure.

"I've checked so many versions of the plate on the Internet," said Leila. "That . . . *thing* is not in any of the others, only this one."

Parker looked at the illustration again. It seemed that more of the child was visible now— he could see its head more clearly, and part of its right leg—except its position had altered, and it was now closer to the fallen tree before it.

Leila was watching him.

"You can say it," she said.

"It gives the impression of movement."

"That's a very noncommittal way of putting it."

"It could be that I find the alternative unappealing."

Leila took the glass from him and used it to peer at the plate, although she remained careful not to touch the book itself. Parker studied the figure once more before turning the page and hiding it from view.

"And you never discussed this with anyone else?" he said. "You never felt the urge to seek help?"

"With what, the illustrations in a book? I don't think you can dial 911 for a literary emergency." She was smiling, but Parker could tell she was close to tears. The secrets she'd kept hidden were slowly being revealed, and the effect was like lancing a boil. "And I've been scared for so long.

I was afraid I was going insane, and that was bad, but then I realized I wasn't, which was worse. I wish I'd never agreed to keep the book."

"Why did you?"

"Because Karis said that if Vernay managed to track her down, she didn't want him to get everything. I think she hoped the book might be a way of bargaining, if worse came to worst. You know: it would be returned to Vernay if he let Karis and the baby go.

"And because I thought it was just a book, an ordinary book. It didn't matter what some childfucker believed. It was a collection of fairy tales with a couple of extra pages sewn in, and they were blank. If having it stolen screwed up his life, then good.

"But to be safe, Karis also asked Dobey to find her a decoy copy. She didn't put it that way, and she didn't tell him why she wanted it. She just needed him to track down a similar edition, and quickly, so he did. I remember it was couriered overnight. Dobey cut some deal for it, but it was still expensive. Karis paid, though. She insisted on it."

"And she brought the decoy with her when she left Cadillac?"

"Yes, although Dobey thought she took both versions. He would never have agreed to my holding on to the original, and I don't think he'd have wanted to hold on to it himself either. But

549

then, he knew more about Vernay than I did."

Parker was turning the pages of the book before him while Leila spoke.

"Does every plate contain an extra element?"

"Most of them."

"Show me."

Leila did. She had to take a break to help her mother to the bathroom, and afterward to prepare a fresh pot of tea, but by the end Parker was under no illusions about the strangeness of the book. Hidden among Rackham's illustrations were hybrid beings reminiscent of the nightmares tempting St. Anthony in the works of Grünewald and Rosa; of the tormenters in Signorelli's *Damned Cast into Hell*; of the haunters in Bosch's *Garden of Earthly Delights*.

And as the intruders in the plates took form beneath the magnifier, Parker began to feel this might be no coincidence, and that these earlier artists had stumbled upon elemental images buried deep in the human consciousness, a shared memory of that which might seek to hunt us in the final darkness, a glimpse of all that observed humanity from behind the glass, waiting to devour.

But the beasts that moved through the pages of the book in Parker's hands were more imminent than any visions captured by artists. They were not simulacra, but neither were they real; rather, they represented the potential usurpation of one reality, its slow infection by another. Parker was very glad Leila Patton had given him gloves with which to hold the book; he also believed she was wise to have hidden it away, and not to have looked at it too often. To expose oneself to it was to risk contamination—and ultimately, perhaps, one's own corruption.

But the book held one more surprise for Parker, and an unwelcome one. The illustration accompanying "The White Snake" showed a servant in conversation with a fish, a forest of white birch as the backdrop. From among the trees, a blurred face of yellow and black stared out at them.

"Uh, that's new," said Leila. "What's wrong with its face?"

Parker positioned the magnifying glass, but already he had a premonition of the answer. It was a head formed entirely of insects.

"Wasps," said Parker.

And the God of Wasps appeared to blink.

In the garden of her grandparents' home, Sam spoke to Jennifer.

"What is Daddy searching for?"

the child

"No, there's more."

what do you see?

"Stories. Something old in the shape of a man, but empty inside. A child, but not a child."

Jennifer raised a hand and flicked it at the air, as though to brush away the unwanted attention of an insect.

"And wasps."

The book was closed once again, the figures within now concealed, and those without protected from their gaze.

"What is the God of Wasps?" Leila asked.

"Some call it the One Who Waits Behind the Glass," Parker replied. "To others, it's the Buried God. Are you religious?"

"I don't go to church much, but I guess I believe in something greater than myself."

"Then the Buried God is its opposite."

"The devil?"

"The Not-God. Or *a* Not-God. Worryingly, there may be more than one."

"How do you know all this?"

"I hear whispers."

Parker placed the book back in the shoe box.

"Do you want me to take this away?" he asked.

"I think so. I've kept my promise to Karis for long enough." She worried at her bottom lip. "I hate that her life ended the way it did, with her all alone in a forest."

"She wasn't alone," said Parker. "Someone was with her at the end, someone who cared enough to bury her and take care of her child."

"And you think she gave birth to a son?"

"That's what we believe."

"It might be better if he wasn't found."

"I'm not sure that's an option any longer, not with what's been happening. The boy is at risk of becoming collateral damage in the hunt for this book. We just have to hope we find him before someone else does—like Vernay."

"It's not Vernay who's looking for the child, or the book."

"How can you be sure?" asked Parker.

"Vernay's dead."

"Because of what you read on the forums?"

"That, and because of something Karis said. She told me she hoped they'd kill Vernay for losing the book. If no one came asking after her, she said, then I could take it that Vernay was dead. And no one did."

"Until recently."

"I guess."

"You kept her secrets well."

"I didn't have a lot of choice, but now Dobey is dead because of it. What will you do with the book?"

"I don't know yet. One thing's for sure: I won't be keeping it in the house."

"That seems wise. Is there anything more you want to know?"

"Tell me," Parker said, "about the night Dobey died."

CHAPTER
CI

Pallida Mors passed through the silent rooms of Holly Weaver's home, absorbing the details of a domesticity that would always be denied her. She considered burning the house to the ground. She thought about waiting for Holly, her father, and the boy, and killing each of them: the old man first, followed by the child, so that Holly could watch them bleed out before her.

She pushed the images aside. Quayle had instructed her only to find the book and leave. Once it was in their possession, they could put this country behind them forever.

Mors entered Daniel Weaver's room and went straight to the bookshelf. There, on the second row, was a worn copy of *Grimm's Fairy Tales*, illustrated by Arthur Rackham, Constable, 1909. It didn't bear the bookplate inside the front cover, but it had the blank pages, and Mors could see no sign of any other copy. But the year was wrong, and someone had added a handwritten and carefully illustrated story.

She heard the sound of approaching vehicles, and headlights appeared in the window: the

Weavers were returning. Without rushing, Mors took the book, walked through the kitchen to the open back door, and left the house, depressing the button on the handle so the door locked again behind her. She had been careful not to make a mess, so it was unlikely the Weavers would spot any signs of intrusion.

Her car was parked nearby. Mors could see the shape of it through the woods, and the quickest way to get to it was through them, yet she hesitated. She couldn't have said why, but the woods disturbed her, and she had learned over the years not to ignore her intuition. In the darkness, the naked trees took on skeletal forms: twisted men, a hunched woman. So Mors stayed at the boundary, away from the depths, and so by circuitous route returned safely to the car before making the first of two calls.

"I found a copy," she told Quayle, "but it may not be the correct one. The year of publication is 1909, and the bookplate is missing, but it has the additional pages."

"There was no other?"

"None that I saw. Could they have sold the original?"

"If they had, I would have heard. It might have become damaged over the years, and the pages could have been transposed into another edition. Only the insertions are important. I'll know once I've had a chance to examine them."

"And if it's not the one you want?"

"Then," said Quayle, "we shall have to ask the Weavers where it is."

The second call made by Mors was to Billy, because it was time to put him into play. She and Quayle had convinced Billy that it would be better if he didn't use his own truck, just in case the vehicle was seen and remembered. Meanwhile, Mors would also be able to help Billy bypass the security around Parker's house.

"How do you know he has security?" Billy asked.

"Because of who he is," said Mors.

Which made sense, when Billy thought about it.

Mors collected Billy from the parking lot of the Tilted Kilt out by the Maine Mall. Billy was carrying a backpack, and Mors could smell gasoline as he placed the bag on the floor of the car.

"I trust you brought a lighter," she said.

"A book of matches, too," he replied.

Mors headed east, Billy doing his best to breathe through his mouth while she drove, because the woman smelled rancid. The gasoline cut the stink some, but not enough. They took Route 1 to Scarborough, and passed Parker's home. Seeing no lights or signs of activity, they made a U-turn and came around a second time, pulling into the next side road after the driveway and killing the lights. Billy grabbed the bag, climbed out, and waited for Mors to join him.

"Did you bring a mask?" Mors asked. "There'll be cameras."

"Shit."

Mors produced a cheap ski mask from her pocket and handed it to Billy before slipping one over her own head.

"Stay in my footsteps," she said.

"You afraid of mines?"

"Just do as I say."

So Billy followed Mors over a ditch and through some trees. She produced an iPhone and turned on the camera, scanning the ground before her as they walked. About a minute later, she stopped suddenly and raised her hand.

"What is it?" Billy asked.

A bright white light partially obscured the screen of the phone.

"Infrared beams," said Mors. "Break them, and it sets off an alarm. Probably takes a picture as well, either here or farther along."

The beams were set at different heights—one a foot from the ground, the second three feet higher—so a small animal wouldn't break both simultaneously. With Mors guiding him, Billy eased his way between them, before taking the phone and doing the same for her. They evaded one more set of IR beams before reaching the perimeter of the house, where Billy was again stopped from proceeding by the sight of Mors's raised right hand. She pointed out the security camera on the wall above the front door.

"Kind of obvious," said Billy.

"That's because the rest aren't."

The Mustang wasn't garaged, but stood to the right of the house under an all-weather cover. Maybe Parker was already hoping to make more use of it with the coming of spring. Mors pulled off the cover.

"Do it," she said.

But now that Billy was here, with Parker's car before him and payback in his hands, his will to act began to leach. Events had gone too far. If Billy did this, Parker would come looking for him, because he would know that only one person could be responsible. And the more Billy thought about it, the more he believed he had contributed in part to his own misfortune. It had been Heb Caldicott's idea to add the flags to the truck in order to piss off the Negroes and the snowflakes, all the bleeding hearts dragging this country down into the dirt, making it a laughingstock. Heb said nothing would happen. Heb said the liberals would just roll over and take it, because that was what these people did. If you told them to go fuck themselves, they would. They'd be too frightened to do otherwise, Heb assured him, because they were always frightened. But Heb hadn't reckoned on Parker and his kind, who didn't seem frightened at all.

"It's a real nice car," said Billy, and it was. Setting fire to it wasn't going to make his world any better, or bring his truck back, or stop him from being everybody's punch bag. It was just going to make him another fool adding to the ugliness of the world.

"Do you want to try and find your way through those woods alone?" said Mors. "Do you believe you'll get back to the car without triggering an alarm, and do you imagine I'll still be waiting for you when you do? Burn it, Billy."

Billy didn't want to face the woods by himself. He didn't want to set off some hidden alarm and have the cops come for him, leaving his father to bail him out, to tell Billy that he'd made an idiot of himself once more, and idiots of his family along with it. Worse: What if Parker returned, him and the Negro?

"Fuck it," said Billy.

He told himself that it was the gasoline making his eyes water as he poured the contents of the can over the car, as he doused a rag and set the match to it, as he tossed the material on the hood, as the flames caught, as the tarp turned to ash, as the fire swept across the body, as the glass cracked and the paintwork bubbled and the tires melted and the tank ignited, as black smoke and sparks rose into the night.

As the car burned, and his future along with it.

CHAPTER
CII

"British?" said Parker.

Leila Patton was recalling the customers that had passed through Dobey's on the night its owner died. They were mostly locals, but a couple of strangers too. That was sometimes the way of it. Cadillac might have been off the beaten track, but a lot of folk preferred the ditch to the highway. It was like Neil Young said: you meet more interesting people there.

"Yes, British," said Leila. "English, actually. He was very specific on that. It was almost funny. We do get tourists through here. I mean, they're often lost, but we do get them."

"Describe him to me."

"I told Chief Hillick all this, but he didn't pay it much mind."

"Try telling me."

"Jeez, well, he was about six feet tall. Nicely dressed: velvet and tweed, and a scarf—not wool, more like a silk cravat. He reminded me of that actor, the guy who played the twins in that weird old gynecologist movie."

Parker knew the one.

"He had, uh, brown eyes," Leila continued, "and he wore red, round-framed spectacles. I remember because he was reading a book of poetry while he ate. We don't get many people reading poetry in Cadillac, whether they're eating or not."

"Brown eyes? You're sure?"

"Yes. I don't usually notice things like that, but the spectacles were pretty unusual. They drew the eye."

It was the Englishman, Smith Two: it had to be, even allowing for the difference in eye color. The man at the Bear had blue eyes, but the change could easily have been achieved with colored contacts, just as the red spectacles had probably been chosen deliberately. Take away the lenses, throw away the glasses, comb the hair in a different way, and even sharp-eyed Leila Patton might have struggled to identify him as the individual who had wandered into Dobey's on a quiet, early spring evening, there to read poetry while—

That was the question. Why show himself? Why take that chance?

"Was there a woman with him?" Parker asked.

"No, he was alone."

"What about at another table? Very pale. Platinum hair. Eyes like bleach in water."

"Yuk. No, I don't recall anyone like that."

Could the woman have been searching Dobey's

trailers for the book while the Englishman monitored the diner, just in case Dobey decided to call it a night and leave the staff to close up? Or did this visitor with his fine clothes and poetry simply wish to take a good look at he who had helped to thwart him; he who had offered aid and shelter to Karis Lamb, with no expectation of return; he who would, in the end, pay for this kindness with his life? Parker was leaning toward the latter. It was the same impulse that had drawn the Englishman to the Great Lost Bear. He was curious, but arrogant with it. Whatever his profession, he had been following it for too long. It had made him incautious, complacent.

"He's the one," said Parker.

"What do you mean?"

"He killed Dobey, and probably Esther. The woman who tried to abduct you travels with him."

"How do you know?"

"Because I've met them. They're in Maine now, looking for this book, killing their way toward it."

"So they tried to abduct me because I'd seen this man at the diner?"

"Did you serve him?"

"No, Corbie did."

"And who else was working that night?"

"Carlos, the chef."

"But no one has tried to hurt them?"

"No, I'd have heard."

"Who was Dobey's favorite? Who among the staff did he like the most?"

"I don't know. He was Dobey. He was the same with everyone."

"Are you sure?"

"He was kind to us all. It was his way."

"Leila . . ."

She relented.

"Okay, so it was me. *I* got on best with him. I could play music. I read books. I watched old movies. I looked after my mom. Dobey liked me. He trusted me. Sometimes, after we closed up, I'd have a beer with him, and Dobey would smoke a joint, and we'd just sit and talk. What does that have to do with anything?"

"Would all this have been clear to a stranger?"

"I don't know."

But Parker knew the answer was yes, or certainly clear to a stranger like the Englishman.

"They probably threatened to hurt Esther if Dobey didn't help them," Parker said. "My guess is they threatened to hurt you, too."

"So?"

"So: they're people of their word. You could say they have principles, even if they're the kind that give principles a bad name."

Leila stared at her hands. What she said next increased Parker's respect for her even more, and left him more determined than ever that the

Englishman, and the woman with him, would never set eyes on Leila Patton again.

"That means Esther really is dead."

Because the danger to herself didn't concern her, or not as much as the fate of Esther Bachmeier.

"Yes, I think she is. Dobey didn't convince them. They wanted to be sure."

Tears from Leila, although they were the kind that didn't alter one's expression, as though the emotions of which they were the outward manifestation ran so deep that the tears themselves were an irrelevance.

"Everyone loved Esther," she said, "or everyone worth knowing. The people who didn't care for her were just dicks." She looked through the window toward the foothills, now lost to the dark. "I wonder where they left her. She deserves a proper burial. She deserves to be remembered."

"I'll try to find her," said Parker.

"How will you do that?"

"I'll make them tell me."

Leila gave this some thought.

"I've never really wished for someone to suffer before," she said. "I've seen too much of what my mom has gone through to want anyone else to experience that kind of pain."

"But?"

"But for the ones who killed Esther and Dobey, I'm inclined to make an exception."

"I'll see what I can do," said Parker. "And I know this won't help, but I'll say it anyway: whatever Dobey told them wouldn't have saved him or Esther. These people weren't just hunting for Karis or the book. They were erasing all those who might have come into contact with either, and probably inflicting some hurt along the way for putting them to so much trouble."

He glanced at his watch. He might yet make the last Delta flight to Boston, but he'd be cutting it tight. At worst, he could fly out first thing in the morning. It would mean having to overcome his dislike of airport hotels, but if he kept his attention fixed on the desk, the elevator, and his room, in that order, he might be able to manage.

"I guess you have to go," said Leila.

"I should."

"I'm glad I spoke to you."

"Likewise."

He picked up the box containing the book.

"No one will ever know you had this," he said.

"If what you say is true, it won't stop them from coming back."

"No: *I'll* stop them from coming back."

Leila Patton kissed him softly on the cheek in farewell.

"I believe you will."

CHAPTER
CIII

Billy could smell gas on his hands as they drove toward South Portland. It was making his head spin. He wanted nothing more than to shower and change his clothes, not only to rid himself of the taint of the fuel but also as a prelude to removing the images of burning from his mind. When he closed his eyes, it was not Parker's Mustang he saw in flames, but his own form.

He and Mors had been able to glimpse something of the conflagration in the rearview mirror before the trees finally concealed it. Billy noticed that the wind had picked up, and was blowing west. He wished the evening was still; it was one thing to set fire to a man's car, another to burn his house down. He didn't hate Parker that much. In fact, Billy realized, he didn't hate Parker at all. He simply wanted to understand why Parker had seen fit to aid in the torching of Billy's truck. Billy could just have asked him. They might even have come to some kind of understanding.

Billy was really sorry for burning the Mustang.

"Maybe we should call the fire department," he suggested.

"Do you have an unregistered cell phone?" said Mors.

"No."

"Then perhaps you'd prefer to just hand yourself over to the police and confess what you've done, because if you make that call, it will be traced."

Billy didn't want to confess. He'd learn to live with his iniquity.

"And I don't think you can go home either, or drive your own truck," said Mors.

"Why not?"

"Because you know as well as I that you'll be the prime suspect for what's just happened, and you'll struggle to provide an alibi."

"I don't care about that," said Billy. "There'll be no proof, and cops need evidence."

"I'm not talking about the police: I'm talking about Parker. Do you think he'll need proof?"

No, Billy thought, *he sure as hell won't.*

"I'll head away from here," he said. "I'll leave the state for a few days."

"That could be viewed as the behavior of a guilty man," said Mors. "The fire will be reported. Parker will be asked for the names of those he might have crossed recently. He can point to you and claim that your family appeared intent on linking him, incorrectly, to an act of criminal damage. Then the police will start looking for you, and whatever vehicle you were last seen driving."

Billy's unhappiness was growing, and with it his confusion. He wanted Mors to stop talking and give him time to think. There were holes in her argument, but he needed to be alone and undisturbed to find them. Billy wasn't good at reasoning under pressure.

"Do you have a place near town you can go, somewhere quiet, even just for a couple of nights?" Mors asked. "It may be that Parker will take the smart view, and decide this has all spiraled out of control. An accommodation might be reached between him and your father, on your behalf. Mr. Quayle and I have no interest in seeing this situation deteriorate further. We only want Parker to be diverted. As long as you don't mention our involvement, you'll never hear from us again." She gave Billy a look that spoke volumes. "And that, I don't need to tell you, would be for the best."

Billy got the message, but he was still prepared to ignore its contents. If Parker chose to seek his head in retribution, it might be that Billy could buy himself out of trouble with what he knew of Quayle and Mors. But for the present, Mors was right: the best decision Billy could make would be to lie low for a couple of days and see what transpired. At some point he'd have to admit to his old man what he'd done. It might even be wise; his father retained a number of high-powered lawyers, and once they became involved, Parker would have to back off and seek a compromise.

"What about my money?" he asked.

"In the glove compartment."

Billy opened it, and found a thick envelope filled with fifty-dollar bills.

"A thousand dollars," said Mors. "Not bad for a night's work."

Billy started to feel a little better about the world.

"I manage a building in Auburn," he said. "It's vacant. I can stay there for a while, if we stop off first for some food and beer."

"Well," said Mors, "that sounds like a plan."

Parker made the last flight to Boston with only minutes to spare, and managed to get a call through to Bob Johnston in Portland before the doors closed. Johnston owned a rare book dealership that operated out of a brownstone in Munjoy Hill, but he also had a sideline in the restoration and rebinding of old volumes. Johnston was a little antisocial, like a lot of book people who operated in the more specialized areas of the market, but given the nature of the object Parker wanted Johnston to examine, this was probably for the best. Parker told Johnston to expect him after eleven p.m., and Johnston said that Parker could take his time because he never went to bed before one a.m. anyway.

Parker put the shoe box under the seat in front of him, but did not open it. He had no pressing desire to look at its contents for a while.

Billy and Mors stopped at a convenience store to pick up chips, cold cuts, bread, milk, and beer. If Mors thought that this seemed like a lot of food for one person, she didn't comment. They drove to the Auburn property, where Billy instructed Mors to park in the back lot so he wouldn't be observed entering the building. He was pleased to see that the windows on the upper floor remained dark, without even the telltale glow of the TV. Maybe Heb Caldicott was asleep, or dead. Either would be fine with Billy, the latter being infinitely preferable.

Billy got out of the car, Mors following behind with the second bag of groceries. Billy fiddled with the lock, and the door opened.

"I can take it from here," he said.

He turned, and Mors shot him in the face.

CHAPTER
CIV

Holly Weaver was woken by the sound of her cell phone. She'd gone to her bedroom intending only to put her feet up and watch television for a while, maybe even read a book, but a combination of tiredness and the softness of her mattress had quickly set her dozing.

It wasn't the easiest of rests. She was experiencing a sense of violation. She was certain she'd double-locked the back door before leaving home that day, for the simple reason that she always did, yet when she checked it later only one lock was in place. Her father assured her that he hadn't gone near it when he was with Daniel. She had also picked up a peculiar smell in the house, as though someone had trailed dead animal matter through its rooms.

But Holly wondered if she would ever be at peace again, because she couldn't remember a time when she hadn't been restive, not since Karis Lamb had breathed her last. Now her phone was ringing, when what she needed more than anything was some undisturbed sleep. She glanced at the number, and saw Dido Mullis's name on the caller display. Dido was her former sister-in-law, and she remained on Holly's contact list partly because she was the only member of her ex-husband's family for whom Holly retained any affection, but mostly because Holly was hopeless at deleting old numbers.

"Dido," she said. "Long time."

"I thought you should know," said Dido, snuffling and hiccupping her way through the words. "Gregg was found shot at his home today, him and his girlfriend. They're dead."

Parker arrived at Logan and switched on his phone as soon as he reached the terminal. He picked up a message from Moxie Castin, asking him to call back as soon as he could.

"Moxie," he said. "What's happening?"

"I have good news and bad news. You'll probably want to hear the bad news first."

"Go on."

"Someone set fire to your Mustang."

Parker stopped walking, causing the man behind to begin swearing until he saw Parker's face and decided that silence might be the better option.

"And the good news?"

"I think we have a pretty good idea who was responsible."

Owen and Holly were sitting in Holly's kitchen. The bottle of Maker's stood on the table between them, and each of them had a glass of bourbon in hand. As predicted, the events of recent times had taken their toll on the bottle, and only half an inch of liquor remained at the bottom.

"Why do you think it has something to do with Daniel?" Owen asked, although he couldn't believe he had been cast in the role of skeptic. He was posing the question for the sake of it, and little more.

"Gregg was a jerk, but even I didn't want to kill him, and I had more cause than most. Back when Dido and I were still in regular contact, she told me that Gregg was real pissed when he heard about Daniel. His exact words, if I remember right, were that you couldn't grow weeds in my womb."

Owen let the bourbon wet his lips and tongue, trying to make it last.

"I never liked him," he said.

"You only told me that a thousand times. You even told me on my wedding day, both before *and* after I'd married him."

"I was trying to save you from yourself."

She took his hand in hers.

"I know, but I was in love with him."

"Almost as much as he was in love with himself."

Holly had to admit this was true. Gregg Mullis had lived life as though the world were made of mirrors.

"And he did have a big mouth," she said. "I think he might have shot it off about me and my womb, and someone recalled it."

"So why not come here instead of going to Gregg?"

"I don't know: To find out for sure? And it could be that they've been here already, checking the place out."

"The kitchen door?"

"Yes, and more than that: the house doesn't smell right, doesn't feel right."

"So now we talk to Castin?"

"First thing in the morning," said Holly. "The only thing worse than Daniel being taken from me would be to have him get hurt."

Owen stood.

"I think you and Daniel should go find a motel room for the night," said Owen. "Pay cash, and don't take your car. I'll call a cab, and follow behind for a while to make sure no one is watching."

Holly didn't argue, except to ask, "What about you?"

Owen shrugged.

"I got a tire iron. Always had a hankering to use it on more than a tire."

Parker called Louis when he was about twenty minutes out of Portland and arranged to meet him at Bob Johnston's place. He was tempted to head straight home, but he needed Johnston to take a look at the book, and it wasn't as though he was going to be able to do much about the Mustang anyway. Nevertheless, he still wanted to find Billy Ocean very badly indeed, despite Moxie Castin's warnings against doing anything rash, which had sounded hollow even to Moxie.

Louis was already parked by the time Parker reached Congress Street. Parker pulled up behind and waited for Louis to join him. Once Louis was in the passenger seat, Parker shared with him everything he had learned from Leila Patton, including her fears about the book.

"It's in the box?" asked Louis.

"You want to see it?"

"Nope."

They crossed the street and rang Bob Johnston's bell. He buzzed them in, and they climbed two floors of book-lined stairs, past rooms filled with shelves and boxes, and the workshop in which Johnston did his binding and printing, until they reached the top of the building. More books here, along with a small kitchen, bedroom, and living area, all of which served as Johnston's home. His business didn't have an actual store, although customers could visit by appointment. Few chose to do so, or not a second time, Johnston being of the opinion that if the only good author was a dead one, the only good customer was a distant one. He was a lanky being of cardigans and slippers, with red hair running to gray, and a face that appeared to be collapsing from the brow down in a series of V-shaped furrows of annoyance. Parker had bought some books from him in the past, mostly as gifts. Johnston had been recommended to him by Carlson & Turner, the antiquarian bookseller farther down Congress, although they'd sent Parker on his way with the air of generals dispatching a soldier on a mission from which he was unlikely to return unscathed.

Johnston gave Louis a nod of greeting, took the shoe box from Parker's hands, and carried it to a desk on which sat old invoices, a lamp, a magnifier, and a one-eyed stuffed cat.

"I'd suggest using gloves," said Parker.

"Why?" asked Johnston.

"The person who gave it to me said touching it made her sick."

"It's just a book of fairy tales."

"No, it's not."

Johnston offered a sigh that spoke volumes about his tolerance, or lack thereof, for the world's nincompoops, and rummaged in his drawer until he found a pair of white cloth gloves.

"If he does jazz hands," said Louis, "we'll have words."

Johnston scowled at him, or at least his permascowl deepened.

"And what is it *you* do, exactly?" he asked.

"I shoot people," said Louis.

Parker had noticed in the past that Louis occasionally amused himself by experimenting with honesty as the best policy.

"Uh-huh," said Johnston, pulling on the gloves. "Do you take commissions?"

"Contracts," Louis corrected.

"Whatever."

"Not so much."

"Pity. I have a list."

"Is it long?"

"Gets longer by the day. You got a card?"

"Yes."

"Can I have one?"

"No."

Johnston sighed again. Parker guessed that he spent a lot of time sighing.

"I suppose I'll just have to kill them myself," said Johnston, "but I was good for the money."

Gloves now arranged to his satisfaction, Johnston opened the box and removed the book. He examined the spine and boards, checked the copyright page, and progressed to the illustrations, pausing at the additional blank sheets.

"Odd," he said.

He took in the typesetting, with its disarranged words.

"Odder," he said.

Finally, he turned on his desktop computer and checked the listing for the book on various websites.

"Oddest," he concluded. "Looks like it was faked. The year's wrong."

"It's 1908," said Parker. "One year too early."

"You know something about it?"

"Not much more than the date, and that the inserts may have something to do with an atlas."

"What kind of atlas?"

"Maybe you can find out."

Johnston adjusted the angle of the book, perhaps to see if the alteration in perspective might reveal a previously hidden detail.

"Errors to copyright pages happen, although no authority has previously noted the existence of one for this edition. It might have been a test printing, but if so, it's unrecorded. Curious, I'll give you that." For the first time, he was perusing the book with real interest. "What were you hoping to find out about it?"

"Where it came from," said Parker. "What the bookplate at the front might mean. Why those additional pages were inserted. What they're made from. Whether they're really blank. Anything you can tell me. There is a 'but,' though."

"Go on."

"You can't tell anyone you have it."

"May I ask why?"

"Because it's breeding corpses."

"Ah." Johnston poked the book, as though to goad it into showing its teeth. "Well, that's a good reason to be discreet. I might have to take it apart to get a better look at those blanks."

"Can you put it back together again after?"

Johnston looked offended, and gestured at their surroundings.

"Mr. Parker, what exactly is it you think I do here?"

It didn't take long for Mors to get Billy Ocean's body inside and close the door behind her. She made only a cursory effort to hide his remains, dumping him in the shadows at the end of the hall along with the bags of food. The body wouldn't be visible until morning, and then only if someone were actively searching for it. She didn't want Billy's remains to be discovered before she and Quayle were ready. Mors considered checking the place, but it felt empty and smelled foul, and the stairs up to the second floor already had a hole in them where someone had put a foot through the rotten wood. It wouldn't be a smart move to incapacitate herself on the same premises to which she had so recently contributed a corpse. She left the same way she came in, and didn't detect any signs of interest in her vehicle from the surrounding residences as she pulled onto the street and drove away.

Mors paid no attention to the building itself.

Had she done so, she might have seen a flash of light from the upstairs window and a figure silhouetted against it.

CHAPTER
CV

Holly woke Daniel. He made a show of rubbing his eyes, but she wasn't sure he'd really been asleep.

"I want you to pack a bag," she said. "We're going to stay at a motel for a couple of nights."

Daniel didn't ask why, and didn't protest, but climbed out of bed like an automaton. Holly saw the dark rings under his eyes, and knew they weren't only from his recent troubled night. It bothered her that she hadn't noticed them before, so tied up was she with her own concerns.

She took Daniel in her arms and held him close. "Honey," she said, "what's wrong?"

But whatever answer she might have anticipated was not the one she received.

"Mom, the fairy-tale book is gone."

CHAPTER
CVI

Parker stood before the burned-out remains of his Mustang. The night air reeked of hot metal and melted plastic, of gas and charred rubber. A deputy chief from the Scarborough Fire Department had explained to Parker how fortunate he was that they'd reached the car before the wind carried the flames to the house. Even so, the eastern wall of his home was scorched black, and a couple of windows had broken in the heat, leading to some water damage from the hoses. A glazier was already at work on the panes. Parker was now giving a statement to a Scarborough PD patrolman, but could only inform him that he had no idea how the fire had begun, as he was midair between Cincinnati and Boston when it occurred. Neither were the security cameras a help, as whoever was responsible had come through the woods without breaking the beams, and stayed out of range of the cameras on the front and back of the house.

"We're guessing arson," said the patrolman, whose name was Cotter. He didn't look old enough to drink. "Can you think of anyone who might have a grudge against you?"

But Parker was barely listening. He'd really liked the car. If it was a midlife crisis on wheels, nobody could claim he hadn't earned the right to one.

It was Louis who replied to Cotter's question.

"You do know who he is, right?"

Louis and Parker had debated whether it might be wiser under the circumstances for Louis not to accompany him back to the house, before eventually deciding, oh, to hell with it.

"Yeah, I know," said Cotter.

"And what he does for a living?"

"Yes."

"So how many pages of that notebook would you like to fill with grudges?"

Cotter got the message and put the notebook away.

"If you think of anything solid, give me a call."

He handed his card to Parker, who thanked him for his time. Cotter then wandered off to shoot the breeze with the deputy chief.

"Guess maybe I shouldn't have set fire to Billy Ocean's truck," said Louis.

"You could probably just have stolen his flags," said Parker.

"But it wouldn't have had the same impact."

"No."

"We going to look for him?"

"Not now. It's late, and I'm tired."

Parker's phone rang. It was Moxie Castin again.

He considered ignoring it, but instead handed the phone to Louis.

"Moxie. You mind seeing what he wants?"

Louis answered the phone.

"What you want?" Louis listened. "Uh-huh, uh-huh." He covered the mouthpiece with his hand. "Says you're to do nothing about this until you speak to him at his office in the morning. Says you don't want to end up in jail over a car."

"Give me the phone."

Louis handed it over.

"Moxie, I want the names of Billy's known acquaintances, and a list of all the properties he manages for his father, available to me by noon tomorrow."

Louis heard Moxie's voice coming from the phone. Moxie Castin, he thought, didn't distinguish between indoor and outdoor voices.

"Yes," said Parker in reply, "I realize finding out that kind of information is what I do for a living, but I'm angry, and sore, and I really liked that car. Just make it happen, Moxie."

He hung up. The remaining fire truck pulled away from the house, followed by Cotter's Scarborough PD cruiser.

"You want company?" Louis asked.

"You have anything better to do?"

"Not until we go looking for Billy Ocean."

"Then sure," said Parker, "company would be appreciated."

• • •

Bob Johnston worked his way slowly through the book, carefully checking each page, at first bemused, then increasingly disturbed, by the apparently random arrangements of letters and words. He noticed that the complications appeared more concentrated on the pages closest to the vellum inserts, although they persisted throughout.

But it was the illustrations that were most fascinating. Parker had brought to his attention the differences between the plates in the book and their equivalents on the Internet, but Johnston regarded the Internet as the devil's work, even though it made his profession easier by reducing the necessity of contact with actual human beings, who had a tendency to try to remove volumes from shelves by the headcap or the delicate spine, and couldn't understand why his titles cost more than the ones at their local used bookstore, or, God forbid, on Amazon. So instead of making comparisons between page and screen, Johnston found in his own collection a later edition of Grimm containing Rackham's illustrations, and the two books now rested side by side on his desk, carefully illuminated and positioned so he could move the magnifier easily over each.

Johnston had to admit that he'd never encountered any book quite like this one before. It was clear that the lithographic plates of the illustrations had been altered at some point, thus allowing the printing of the alternate versions with their additional figures, but he struggled to find any record of their creation. It seemed a great deal of trouble to take just to put together a one-off with botched lettering, especially given the exquisite detailing to the panels. In fact, Johnston thought, the closer he examined them, the clearer the additions became, so that his explorations took on a certain rhythm; a primary perusal, followed by a break to rest his eyes, followed by a closer study, which invariably yielded a different, odder result:

Horns glimpsed here, a second set of eyes there; a torso, a tail.

The additions were not Rackham's work; of this much Johnston was certain. They were almost medieval in execution, but with none of the flatness that he associated with the period. Some were almost familiar to him: in the background of the depiction of Rumpelstiltskin was a creature that Johnston might initially have mistaken for a bull, were it not for the brightness of the animal's coloration. Now the richness of its blues was becoming more noticeable under the light, and the oddness of its form more apparent. The beast definitely had a bull's head with sharp yellow horns, but its skin was scaled, and it walked upright on its hind legs.

The illustration nagged at Johnston. Like many

dealers in antiquarian books, he had accumulated a certain knowledge of diverse matters, most of it deeper than he revealed but shallower than he might have wished. Just as someone with even a casual interest in great art will be able to identify the *Mona Lisa*, or Michelangelo's *David*, so was Johnston able to recognize masterpieces across a variety of ages, styles, and media. He had seen the blue bull—no, blue *demon,* because that was what it most assuredly was—somewhere before, but in a less alien context than a folk tale. He stared at the figure again through the magnifier, the shadows surrounding it continuing to fall away so that it, rather than the more traditional aspects of Rackham's genius, became the focal point of the plate. Back to the infernal Internet, back to searches, and there it was: the Parish Church of St. Mary the Virgin in Fairford, England.

A church had existed in Fairford since the eleventh century, but the present incarnation, built in the Perpendicular style, dated from the late fifteenth century. What distinguished St. Mary's, apart from its great age, was a complete set of late-medieval stained-glass windows created between 1500 and 1517 by glaziers from the Netherlands, almost certainly under the supervision of Henry VIII's own glazier, Bernard Flower. The most famous of these was the Great West Window, or more particularly the lower part of it, since the upper half had been damaged during a storm in 1703 and was now largely a nineteenth-century replacement. The window depicted the Last Judgment, with the elect being escorted to heaven on the left, and the damned being consigned to hell on the right. Seven panels in total, of which the most interesting to Johnston was the third from the right. There, in the bottom right-hand corner, stood the same blue demon, a twin-pronged fork in its hands, and one of the damned on its shoulders. Behind it lurked a similar creation, this time in red, scourging another poor soul with a spiked mace.

Johnston proceeded to the tale of the Frog Prince, and Rackham's drawing of the princess carrying the titular royal up a flight of ornate wooden stairs. Hanging on the wall to the right of the princess was a tapestry with hints of scarlet. In the original illustration, a figure was barely discernible on the material, but in the alternative version contained in the disordered book, the scarlet was more vivid, the horned shape clearer. Even the spiked mace in its hands could be identified.

So, Johnston wondered, why had someone taken such care to add elements of late medieval stained-glass art to a series of unconnected twentieth-century plates? And why also stitch additional blank folios into the binding? The answer, perhaps, might be found in those vellum insertions themselves.

Johnston placed the book back in its box and carried it down to his workshop, where he could begin the process of disassembling it. So engrossed was he in his new project that he did not register how deep the darkness had become; how muffled his footsteps, as though lost in fog; how silent the night beyond.

He was lost in the book.

And lost, perhaps, to the book.

Parker poured Louis a glass of wine, but stuck to coffee himself. He replayed the events in Cadillac, returning again and again to the Englishman, sitting calmly in Dobey's with his book of poetry, waiting for his chance to interrogate, and kill, the diner's owner.

"You're sure it was the same guy?" Louis asked.

"Unless he has a brother with eyes of a different color, in which case they're in it together."

"Doesn't sound likely."

"No, it doesn't."

"So what are you planning to do?"

"Flush him out. I've seen him up close. I know what he looks like. First thing in the morning, I go to Corriveau and give her a full description, suggesting that this man may be a person of interest in the murder of Maela Lombardi, as well as a suspect in a possible arson attack leading to a fatality; a disappearance; and an attempted abduction, all in Cadillac, Indiana, and all linked to the discovery of a body now believed to be that of one Karis Lamb. We get his likeness out on TV, in newspapers, on the Internet. We make it hard for him to hide, and see how he reacts."

"And the woman with him?"

"Probably the same one who tried to take Leila Patton. I'll give Corriveau a description of her as well."

"But you're not going to tell Corriveau about the book?"

"No, or not yet."

"Why not?"

"Curiosity. Let's see what Bob Johnston comes up with first."

"Curiosity, hell," said Louis. "You want to keep it to yourself in case you can use it as bait."

"Maybe."

"No maybe about it. You are an untrustworthy motherfucker."

"Harsh."

"Okay, I take back 'motherfucker.'"

"Appreciated. You speak to Angel?"

"Yeah. He's disassociated, needy. Same as always, except he now has more scars."

"Seriously."

"He sounded better than before. I was planning on going back tomorrow, but I might stick around here, see what happens with your book and the visitor from overseas. Nothing I can do for Angel that one of the nurses can't do better."

Parker set aside his coffee cup. It was time to sleep. But he had one more question for Louis.

"You ever think about what it is you're running from?"

"You mean with Angel?"

"Yes."

Louis finished his wine.

"Not death," said Louis. "I never paid much mind to death."

"Then what?"

"The aftermath. Grief, if you want to give it a name; even the possibility of it. I don't want to grieve for him."

"Which is why he's going to live."

"Exactly, because I'd never forgive him otherwise."

Parker stood.

"I won't tell you that you should go back to New York," he said. "You make your own choices. And, if I'm being honest, I'm glad you're here. I get the sense that the Englishman and the woman with him are as bad as people come."

"You don't think he'll run when we start pasting his picture around town? You know, bide his time before coming back when we're not expecting it?"

"No. He's too close to getting the book."

"Which he doesn't know you have."

"Yes."

"Which means, somewhere down the way, you're going to have to find a way to let him know you have it."

"Yes."

"Which will be risky."

"Yes."

"Which means I may get to hurt someone."

"Almost certainly."

"You know," said Louis, "things are looking up already."

CHAPTER
CVII

Parker called Solange Corriveau shortly before eight a.m. While Corriveau was working out of MCU-North in Bangor, she agreed to meet with Parker at state police headquarters in Augusta, where he would be asked to give a formal description of the Englishman and his acolyte. She informed Parker that Walsh would certainly join them, since MCU-South was investigating the killing of Maela Lombardi. Thanks to Parker's trip to Indiana, the MSP now had a full name for Jane Doe, a link to Lombardi, and a potential suspect in the form of the unnamed Englishman, all in return for zero expenditure. Parker hoped that he might even receive a letter of appreciation from the governor, which he could then stick to the sole of his shoe.

"I need to be back in Portland by noon," Parker said.

"This wouldn't be connected to what happened to your car last night?" Corriveau asked.

"News travels fast."

"Not as fast as the Stonehurst boy, if he has any sense."

Parker stayed quiet. He wasn't about to be drawn into admitting anything that might restrict his room for maneuver when it came to dealing with Billy.

"Come on," said Corriveau. "I hear he might have taken it into his head that you were somehow involved with what happened to his truck."

Despite the distance between them, Parker had the uncomfortable feeling of being interrogated.

"I might have heard something about that," said Parker. "I can't imagine where he got such a notion."

"Well, just be sure to take a deep breath before you go knocking hard on any doors. Your help with the woman in the woods isn't unappreciated, but it will only buy you so many favors. Turning a blind eye to some feud with the Stonehursts isn't one of them. I'll see you in Augusta in two hours."

She hung up, leaving Parker to listen to Louis, who had spent the night in the guest room, complain about the quality of coffee in the house and question Parker's ability to purchase an acceptable form of bread. When Louis was finished bitching, and had resigned himself to whatever he could scavenge, he said, "So what's the plan?"

"I go to Augusta. You head over to Moxie."

"You want me to start tracking down Billy?"

"No, I just want you to do what you've been doing for the past couple of days."

"Which is nothing."

"Which is wait."

"Why?"

"Because by this afternoon Solange Corriveau should be ready to put the description of the Englishman out there. If she's lucky, she may even get a hit on Karis Lamb, because she's getting nothing from federal databases. She'll also make a final appeal to whoever put Karis in the ground, warning them that they may be in danger. Finally, she's agreed to thank Moxie and me for our assistance, and trail the Indiana connection."

"You're putting blood in the water."

"Best way to draw sharks."

"And Billy?"

"We let him go."

Louis paused in the act of drinking his substandard coffee.

"For real?"

"You did blow up his truck."

"Because he was ignorant."

"And he paid for it. Look, I could find him, and beat the shit out of him, but I'm not going to feel any better about myself afterward, and it's not going to change Billy, or his father, or anyone else like them."

"You saying you're trying to be the better man? Doesn't work, not with their kind."

"No, I'm saying that if this continues, someone will get badly hurt, or even killed. Likely it won't be either of us, but the consequences will be messy."

"You're making me feel more guilty about your car."

"Good."

"Not so guilty that I'm going to buy you a new one, but still bad."

"That level of self-examination on your part is compensation enough," said Parker. "Plus, I have insurance."

Mostly for reasons of surveillance, Parker owned three cars—now reduced to two after the destruction of the Mustang—and used the less offensive of the remaining pair to get to Augusta, the Taurus being both crappy and forever tarnished by association with a burning truck. The final vehicle was a 2002 Audi A4 in dark gray that made him feel like the kind of accountant who worked out of a strip mall, and not a good strip mall either.

Corriveau and Walsh were already waiting for Parker by the time he got to Augusta. With them were Kes Carroll from the Cape Elizabeth PD, and Sharon Macy, who seemed to progress one rung higher up the law enforcement ladder each time Parker met her. Although Macy remained officially—for now—an officer of the Portland

PD attached to its Criminal Investigations Division, she was also heavily involved in the state's Violent Crimes Task Forces, and had the ear of the AG. In other words, everyone had to be nice to Macy. She and Parker had dated a couple of times, but their timing was off. He could at least be grateful that he hadn't behaved too badly toward her, and had picked up the checks.

"Sorry to hear about your car," she said, as she escorted him to the meeting room.

"I'm getting so many messages of condolence, I may hold a wake."

"The word is that Billy Ocean should consider leaving for somewhere safer, like Syria."

"The word, as usual, is inaccurate."

Macy raised an eyebrow. "That doesn't sound like you."

"If Billy did it," said Parker, "he's a fool. If he didn't do it, he's still a fool. I have no proof that he did it. I only have opinions on Billy's foolishness, which hardly makes me unique."

"Maybe you're mellowing as you get older. Then again, it's not as if you could become any less mellow."

"Hush now, or I'll start to regret paying for those dinners."

He stepped back just in time to avoid a punch on the arm.

"Jerk," she said.

"Sticks and stones. Meanwhile, it seems you're being kept busy."

The news bulletins were filled with four Maine murders in twenty-four hours, including the shooting dead of a heavily pregnant woman as part of a triple homicide, to add to the killing of Maela Lombardi. The state could usually count on twenty homicides a year, give or take, at least half of which would be domestic killings. This meant that the last week alone accounted for a quarter of the annual total, and the year was not yet three months old.

"The triple is strange as hell," said Macy. "We've got a positive ID on Gregg Mullis and Tanya Wade, but the victim at the kitchen table was initially a mystery. No driver's license, but he had a wallet filled with business cards, and we found one on the table belonging to Marcus Light, an employee of the Office of Child and Family Services. Light lives in Millinocket, but is currently at a wedding in San Diego, and has no idea why his business card should be center stage at a murder scene."

"Misrepresentation?" said Parker.

"That could be it. Fortunately, one of the vehicles at the scene was registered to an Ivan Giller. Single, apparently unemployed, living in a nice condo in Bangor."

"Too nice for a guy without a job?"

"Too nice for a lot of guys *with* a job. He was a

fixer. Business deals, politics: if there was a price on information, he could find a way to buy or sell it."

"Any connection between those three and the Brunswick victim?"

"Connie White? Well, we're going to be waiting a couple of days for the forensics analysis on the bullets, but it looks like they were all killed with .380 ACPs, with a cleanup after; no shell casings. So yeah, it could be the same shooter, which means we need to find out how Mullis or Wade tracks to Connie White. Mullis has an ex-wife in Guilford, and his girlfriend has an ex-husband down in Florida. We'll start with them and work outward. White got fired from her job for taking kickbacks and selling information on state tenders, so there may be something there. Oh, one more weird detail: Connie White's killer spared her dog, and that mutt is a piece of work, with an extra shot of mean. According to White's brother, it tolerated his sister and him, but no one else, but we think the shooter may have put out extra food and water for it, just in case it was stuck in the trailer for a while."

"What about the brother?"

"In work during the time-of-death window, with witnesses to say he never left."

"So you're looking for a sentimentalist who's good with animals."

"Great. Let me write that down, in case I forget.

Is 'Doolittle' spelled with one 'o' or two?"

"Two," said Parker, as they reached the meeting room. "Or just keep an eye out for a guy with a two-headed llama."

Once inside, Parker took a seat, accepted an offer of coffee, and walked the assembled detectives through a carefully edited version of his time in Cadillac. He then spent time working with a trained officer to produce facial composite pictures of the Englishman and the woman from the Great Lost Bear. It was after one p.m. by the time he was done, so his self-imposed deadline of noon had fallen by the wayside. Macy and Walsh had departed by then, and Corriveau dropped by just to okay the pictures for release, thank Parker for his efforts, and advise him, once again, to stay away from Billy Ocean.

As it turned out, Parker had one final piece of the puzzle to offer, because Corriveau was holding in her hand the driver's license photo of Ivan Giller, the second male found dead at the home of Gregg Mullis. Parker hadn't bothered to give the police a description of Smith One at the Bear because he'd already discussed him with Gordon Walsh, and anyway, Corriveau was more interested in the Englishman and his female shadow. Now Parker could put a name to Smith One.

"Your Ivan Giller was with the Englishman at the Bear," said Parker. "I tried to follow him from the bar, but . . . I lost him."

"If the Englishman you saw is the same one

that passed through Cadillac," said Corriveau, "we now have a connection between Karis Lamb and Mullis, Wade, Lombardi, Giller, and maybe Connie White, too. All this for a missing child?"

Parker was almost tempted to tell Corriveau about the book, but the moment passed. The longer he kept it hidden, the more trouble he'd be in when—or if—he was finally forced to reveal the fact of its existence. He could not have said why he was keeping the truth about the book from Corriveau, beyond its potential usefulness as bait. It made sense to share it with her, and yet every instinct told him to hold back on mentioning it. Instead he said:

"People have been killed for poorer reasons than a child."

"Doesn't make it any less disturbing."

Parker could only agree. He said goodbye, and felt his phone buzzing in his pocket as he left the building. Moxie Castin's name appeared on the display.

"Where are you?" Moxie asked.

"About to leave Augusta."

"You need to get down here right away. I think I have Karis Lamb's son in my office."

Parker paused in the parking lot.

"What?"

"Just start driving."

"Call Louis."

"He's already sitting in the lobby."

"I'm on my way."

Bob Johnston had worked into the small hours on the book, and went to bed only after he successfully managed to separate the vellum inserts from the main body, with the cover set aside. He had not slept well, though. The figures added to the Rackham plates intruded on his dreams, and twice he was woken by sounds from inside the house, including a persistent tapping that seemed to come from somewhere deep within the staircase to the third floor, as though an animal were trapped in its regions. Finally, sometime after seven a.m., he resigned himself to the impossibility of further rest, and performed his ablutions before trying and failing to consume breakfast. It wasn't that his appetite had deserted him—breakfast was never his favorite meal of the day—but his food tasted odd, spoiled by what he could only describe as a dustiness that rendered even his beloved Kona coffee undrinkable.

Usually such a state of affairs would have sent Johnston straight back to bed, but the book was calling to him. He might have succeeded in detaching the vellum pages from the whole, but he was unable to determine the original animal source of the material, or make any educated estimate of its age. He suspected it was goat parchment, because the grain side of the sheets, from which the hair had been scraped, was brownish gray, and not the yellower color of vellum derived from sheep, but it smelled different from goat, even after all this time, and the texture did not feel quite right to him. The grain had the smoothness of velvet, suggesting that the outer layer had been carefully pared back, and the curling of the parchment was minimal, a further indication of the quality of the material. The magnifier revealed traces of follicles, but they were larger than goat hairs.

Johnston remained baffled by the effort required to insert these seemingly blank pages into another volume. Invisible ink appeared to be the likeliest explanation, but the gentle application of heat using an incandescent lightbulb produced no result, and neither did the careful use of a non-steam iron. Oddly, the vellum did react to human contact, as though some transfer of warmth occurred, resulting in a network of tiny veins being revealed under the desk magnifier. When he placed his hand flat upon one of the pages, Johnston imagined he could almost feel it pulsing.

His fingertips began to itch, leading him to wonder if the vellum might not have been impregnated with an irritant. Belatedly, he returned to wearing gloves before touching the pages, and noted with satisfaction the disappearance of the veins. Yet for a moment, just before they vanished, he thought he detected a pattern to them, and could have sworn he was looking at the outline of his own room.

So fascinated was Johnston by the vellum additions that he had barely glanced at the cover of the book itself. Only now, while sitting back in his chair, was he struck by the thickness of the spine. At first he had taken the addition of a layer of cloth sewn to the inner part as an effort to accommodate the vellum blanks and provide greater structural support. But as he ran a thumb over the cloth, he thought he detected something else beneath.

Johnston moved the magnifier into place, arranged his tools before him, and slowly began to unpick the threads.

Parker was pulling out of his parking space when Corriveau appeared in the lot. She waved at him to stop, but he just slowed and rolled down his window to hear what she had to say.

"I have to go," he called out.

"I need you to come back inside," Corriveau replied, and Parker didn't like her tone.

"What is it?"

"I'll tell you once we're both sitting down at a table again. In the meantime, I have to ask you for your firearm, and the keys to your vehicle. I'd also like you to hand over your phone."

Two big state troopers emerged from the lobby behind her. Each had a hand on his weapon, although the guns remained holstered—for now. Parker looked to his right and saw a state police cruiser pull up to the gate, blocking his exit. In his rearview mirror, he caught three more troopers advancing.

"Am I being placed under arrest?"

"No."

Parker knew his rights. If he was not under arrest, then he had no obligation to cooperate, or even to wait. The fact that he was not under arrest meant the MSP lacked probable cause, but he was clearly suspected of something, and under exigent circumstances the police could seize his car, which was why Corriveau was asking for the keys, and his weapon. The phone was a stretch, but not much of one. Meanwhile, as he considered his options—which included handing over everything, as requested, before calling a cab to take him back to Portland—he could see Corriveau examining his clothing and the interior of the Audi with fresh eyes. If he left, he would only be postponing the inevitable, and perhaps sowing the seeds for worse to come.

Parker killed the engine, and gave Corriveau the keys.

"I'm reaching for my gun," he said. "Don't let anyone shoot me."

He handed her the weapon, and added his phone. He knew the procedure, knew it as he stepped from the car and headed back to the MSP building, a phalanx of uniforms as an escort. If he wasn't yet under arrest, he soon might be.

What he didn't know was why.

Bob Johnston had to peel away only an inch of the spine's lining before his suspicions were confirmed. He continued working at the material with a thread nipper and a micro spatula, his pace never varying, his concentration never faltering, as he delicately separated the cloth from the boards, slowly exposing a single folded sheet of vellum.

CHAPTER
CVIII

Parker sat in an interrogation room, stewing quietly. He had been given water, but told nothing other than that they were awaiting the arrival of detectives from Auburn who were investigating a possible homicide. He asked to be allowed to call a lawyer, but was informed—by Corriveau herself, no less, although her manner toward him had now cooled considerably—that he had not yet been charged with a crime, and so a lawyer was hardly necessary. Parker told Corriveau to save that routine for the rubes, and give him his call. He was brought to a phone, from which he contacted Moxie Castin.

"You almost here?" said Moxie.

"The state police are holding me, or as good as. They're waiting for Auburn CID to arrive."

"What are you supposed to have done?"

"Someone got killed in Auburn. Ask around. Find out what's happening."

"Okay, but I've got a woman and a kid here who are starting to get shaky. Her father was supposed to have joined her by now, but she can't get hold of him on the phone."

Parker thought for a moment.

"Move her and the boy. Have Louis take them to a hotel. Tell her it's for their own safety. It's not a lie, and it'll make her less likely to cut and run."

"I'll do that. In the meantime, I'll call Phil Kane and have him head over to you." Unlike a lot of the bigger law firms in the state, Moxie didn't operate offices outside Portland, but instead maintained informal arrangements with a handful of trusted independent attorneys. Philip Kane was a former Kennebec County prosecutor who had jumped ship to criminal defense back in 2006, and made his name defending drug traffickers. Behind his back, he was known as Co-Kane. He was good at what he did, although hiring him was generally regarded as an instant admission of guilt.

Parker thanked Moxie, and was escorted back to the interrogation room. Fifteen minutes went by before Kane arrived and immediately asked for a moment alone with his client. Once the door was closed, he sat close to Parker and began whispering so softly that Parker had trouble hearing him. Kane, Parker thought, had trust issues when it came to the police.

"Billy Ocean's body turned up in an empty apartment building in Auburn," said Kane. "He was probably killed late last night or early this morning. Single gunshot to the head. Moxie filled me in on this business with his vehicle, and your car. Do you have an alibi for last night?"

"I was at home."

"Alone?"

"No, I was with the guy who blew up Billy Ocean's truck."

"Be serious."

"I am being serious."

"Then that," said Kane, "may not be the best of alibis."

Bob Johnston placed a clean piece of cotton on the surface of his workbench, and opened upon it the fragment of vellum retrieved from the spine of the book. He was surprised at how easily it unfolded. Manuscripts benefit from moderate handling; without it, they grow less supple, but this one remained flexible and in a state of near-perfect preservation. It looked so fresh that Johnston wondered if it was actually of the same age, or even the same vellum. As an experiment, he used a blade to remove from the bottom edge a fragment of about an inch in length, but still barely a sliver in width. He placed the piece in a metal bowl, took it to the sink, and applied a flame. The material began to shrivel and burn, the heat eventually reducing it to a black worm at the bottom of the bowl, but failing to destroy it entirely.

So it burned like vellum. That, at least, was something.

Johnston was about to throw away the column of dark ash when a thin rim of white appeared at one end. He stared at it for a time, not entirely sure of what he was witnessing. A minute went by, then two. Johnston took the bowl back to his desk, sat in his chair, and waited.

It took exactly one hour. He timed it.

One hour for the fragment of burned vellum to reconstitute itself.

The door to the interrogation room opened. Gordon Walsh appeared, Sharon Macy behind him. Both gave Parker the hard eye.

"You," said Walsh, "are a lucky son of a bitch."

According to the dispatcher, the original tip-off had come from a woman. The anonymous caller claimed to have heard what she believed to be a gunshot from the vicinity of a property in Auburn the previous night, and to have seen a vehicle driving away at speed shortly after. She said she hadn't called the police at the time because she didn't want to cause a fuss over what could have been a car backfiring. On reflection, she decided it was better to be safe than sorry. She declined to give her name, and used a pay phone to make the call. She had noted the license plate number of the car, she added, and thought it might have been a man behind the wheel. When the plate was checked, it was found to be one of three vehicles registered to Charlie Parker, a licensed private investigator living in Scarborough, Maine.

The Auburn PD sent out a patrol car to investigate, and the officer responding glimpsed, through the filthy glass at the rear of the property, a body lying in the hallway. He called for backup before entering, and confirmed that the victim was deceased. A driver's license identified him as William Stonehurst. Only when backup arrived did officers commence a full search of the building, although one of them almost ended up in the basement when a stair gave way under his weight. They found evidence of recent habitation in the top-floor apartment, including prescription and non-prescription medication, food, and used bandages, but all the units appeared to be empty.

While the investigators were flooding the rooms, a noise was detected from one of the bedroom closets. It sounded like weeping. The closet was opened, and a crawl space was discovered behind the boards. In it lay Heb Caldicott, almost delirious with pain from the suppurating wound to his side.

"She killed Billy," said Caldicott. "The bitch killed Billy."

Parker wasn't in the mood to play nice with Walsh, Macy, Corriveau, or anyone else representing the forces of law and order in the state of Maine. He'd traveled to Assbend,

Indiana, returning with detailed descriptions of two individuals who qualified as chief suspects in five killings in Maine, and potentially two more in Indiana, and as a reward he'd been kept in an overheated, underfurnished room on suspicion of killing an unarmed man. Under other circumstances, Parker would have damned to hell anyone with a badge, but Corriveau in particular wanted to make amends, and he decided he might be glad of some favors to call in further down the line.

And so, with Philip Kane departed to seek out clients who might actually be guilty of something, Parker briefly consented to batting around ideas on who might be glad to see his existence made uncomfortable for an undefined period. Walsh made a crack about digging out the last census, but no one laughed, and Parker was mildly gratified to see Walsh look embarrassed.

"Odds on it was the Englishman's partner who made the call," said Parker.

"Because you're looking for Karis Lamb's child?" said Corriveau.

"Yes."

"Which means they must think you're close."

"Yes again."

"And are you close?" Macy asked.

"I'll tell you once I get back to Portland."

"How about you tell us now?" said Walsh, recovering some of his mojo, and in the process extirpating whatever modicum of goodwill Parker had succeeded in dredging from the bottom of his heart.

"How about you try doing your own police work?" Parker replied. "And if you ever call me a son of a bitch again, I'll put you down."

He picked up his jacket and headed for the door.

"We're all done here."

Bob Johnston called Parker as he was passing the Freeport exit.

"I'd like you to come over, when you have a chance," said Johnston.

"It could be a couple of hours."

"I'm not going anywhere, and there's something you should see."

CHAPTER
CIX

Moxie Castin had installed Holly Weaver and her son in a room at the Inn at St. John, which stood at the western end of Congress Street, near the former site of the beautiful old Union Station, now a strip mall. Parker had stayed at the inn when he first returned to Maine, and he retained a great deal of affection for the last of the city's railroad hotels. But Castin's reasons for choosing it as a safe house were less to do with sentiment or aesthetics, and more closely related to issues of protection. The Inn didn't have a restaurant or bar, so the only people with an excuse to be inside its walls were staff and guests, and the latter had to pass through the lobby to get to their rooms.

The suite selected for the Weavers was just off that lobby, with exposed brick, wood floors, and a flat-screen TV. Its window looked out on the parking lot at the back, with only a short drop to the ground if it needed to be used as an exit point. When Parker arrived, Daniel Weaver was sitting on the bed watching a movie, his mother beside him. Louis had taken up a post near the window, giving him unimpeded sight of the door and the lot, and a clear shot at anyone approaching through either. He had also ensured that the location services on Holly Weaver's iPhone were disabled before bringing her to the Inn, so her whereabouts couldn't easily be traced through the device.

Parker introduced himself to Holly, and asked if she and her son were okay.

"I'm worried about my father," she said. "He should have called by now."

Parker looked at Louis, who shrugged.

"Moxie asked the local cops to swing by the house," said Louis. "Found a big rig, and Mr. Weaver's car, but no sign of him. The neighbors have a key, and Ms. Weaver here gave them permission to let the cops take a look around. Empty, and no indication of a struggle."

"Do you have any idea where he might have gone?" Parker asked Holly Weaver.

"He's supposed to be here, with us," she replied. "That was what we agreed. And how could he have gone anywhere without a vehicle?"

Daniel Weaver's eyes moved between the TV and the adults in the room. He was a somber-looking child, with very dark hair that accentuated his pallor, and his aspect was so different from the woman with him that they might almost have been born of different species. Parker wondered how much the boy understood of the truth of his parentage, and guessed that Daniel probably suspected more than he actually knew. It never paid to underestimate children.

"I think we need to speak in private," said Parker to the woman.

"Not until you tell me what's being done to find my father."

Parker was familiar with a couple of private investigators up in Piscataquis. One of them, Julia Hancock, was smarter than the average bear, and knew her way around a missing-person case. More to the point, she also had good relations with the Dover-Foxcroft PD, the Piscataquis County sheriff, the Warden Service, and the Maine State Police.

"Give me a minute," said Parker.

He stepped outside, called Moxie, and suggested he engage Hancock to work with the police to trace Owen Weaver. Moxie agreed.

"She doesn't work cheap," Parker warned him.

"Then she's in good company. This case will put me in the poorhouse yet."

"When you die, maybe they'll only have to say ten months of Kaddish for you instead of the full eleven."

"I'm sure that will be some consolation to my bank manager and ex-wives. I'll call Hancock now."

Parker went back inside to inform Weaver of what had been arranged. Only then did she consent to leave the boy. He watched his mother go, but made no complaint and showed no signs of concern. In fact, Parker noticed that Daniel Weaver hadn't spoken once since his arrival.

"You hungry?" Parker asked him, while his mother waited at the door.

Daniel thought about it before nodding.

"You like pizza?"

Another nod.

"Do you talk?"

Daniel smiled, and nodded again, which made Parker warm to him. He felt sorry for what the Weavers were going through, and all that must inevitably follow.

"So what kind of pizza do you want?"

Daniel opened his mouth, but shut it again before a sound could emerge. Instead, he raised his hands in a "Dunno" gesture.

"Well," said Parker, "maybe we'll just get a few different kinds delivered from Pizza Villa across the street. God forbid you might have to break your vow of silence."

Castin had given Parker much of the story while he was driving down from Augusta, but he wanted to hear it again from Holly Weaver. The staff at the Inn allowed him the use of a second room, and in it he and Holly Weaver now sat, a table between them, the empty bed a curiously unwelcome distraction in a space occupied by two strangers.

"Tell me," said Parker.

And she did.

CHAPTER
CX

If it were a folk tale, a story to be shared with a child before bedtime, a boy like Daniel Weaver, this is how it might have begun:

Once upon a time there was a young girl who was spirited away by an ogre. The girl did not know he was an ogre at first, because the ogre was very clever. He disguised himself as a wiser, older man, and treated the girl kindly, more kindly than anyone had ever treated her before.

But as time went on, the spell concealing the ogre's true form began to weaken, and the girl perceived him as he truly was, in all his cruelty and wickedness.

"Kiss me," the ogre would say to the girl. "Kiss me, so that I may know you love me."

And if the girl refused to kiss him, the ogre would tie her down and make her kiss him, and his kisses were so hard that she would bleed for days after.

The ogre had no love for anything but books. They filled every room in his house, the house that the girl could never leave unless the ogre was with her, and in the gardens of which she was not even permitted to wander without his shadow beside her. The ogre collected books of spells, and rites of dark magic, but one volume in particular obsessed him: a collection of fairy tales, beautifully illustrated, into which two additional leaves had been sewn, fragments of a greater work: the Atlas.

The book of fairy tales was believed to have been lost, but the ogre continued to search for it because he knew that nothing is ever really lost until it has been destroyed, and the fragments, like the Atlas of which they were a part, could never be destroyed. It was beyond the capacity of men to remove them from this world, because the Atlas was not the creation of any man.

But the ogre did not desire the fragments for his own collection, and had no intention of keeping them if they were found. There were others who shared his nature—his, and worse. Whoever secured the fragments would gain great credit, and might even evade punishment for all the wickedness of a life long lived. The ogre hoped that this might be true, for he had lived a life of considerable devilry indeed.

And after many years of searching, after decades of promises and lies, of threats and bribes, the book came to him, and he rejoiced. But the girl overheard him, and learned the reason for his exultation, and saw in it the opportunity to revenge herself for all the kisses, and all the blood.

So she stole the book from him, and ran away with it.

But she did not steal only a book from the ogre: she also stole a child, because she was carrying the ogre's baby, an infant she could not let him possess because she knew he would consume it. Yet neither would she let him have the book. It was all that could save the ogre, and she wanted him to be punished for his crimes. Without the fragments, the Atlas would never be complete, and the ogre would be damned.

The girl attempted to remove the fragments, but they held stubbornly to the book's spine. Touching them made her sick, and the longer she touched them, the sicker she became. She began to fear for her unborn child, in case some infection might find its way from the book to her womb.

The girl tried to burn the book, but it would not take fire.

And the girl tried to drown the book, but it would not sink.

And the girl tried to bury the book, but the earth would not yield to it.

By day the girl traveled. By night, she examined the book, and the more she saw of it, the more frightened she became. She understood that if the ogre captured her—as it seemed he surely must, for the baby was heavy inside her, and she was so very tired—he would take both the book and the child, and his triumph would be complete. So the girl found someone to accept the book and guard it, while another, similar volume was substituted, and she moved on with her unborn child. Once the baby was born, and was safe, she would try to find those who might know how to get rid of the original forever.

The girl moved north, ever north. She was given the name of a woman who could help her, and stayed with her for a while, but soon the girl became afraid. What if the ogre had followed her trail? What if he knew of this woman, and those like her? So the girl booked passage that she did not intend to use, leaving false trails so that she might safely follow another path.

A man agreed to transport her across the border in return for most of the little money she had left, and she sat alongside him on his journey through the dark. But there was something of the brute in this man too, and he reached for the girl as they passed through a great wood, reached for her with the claws of a wolf.

"Kiss me," he said. "Kiss me, so that I may know you love me."

But the girl would not kiss him. She fled from the man with claws for fingers, and found herself lost in the woods. Her belly was hurting, so she lay down on the forest floor. The baby was coming, but something was wrong. The pain was too great, and the blood—

Oh, the blood.

She saw the lights of a house through the trees, but could not reach it. She tried to call out, but the wind howled her down. And just as she thought she must surely die out there in the cold, and the baby with her, a man came walking, his daughter by his side. The daughter had a little medical knowledge, and together she and her father brought the baby—a boy—into this life. They saved him, but they could not save his mother.

Before she died, the girl made them promise to tell no one of her or the baby, for the child was at great risk from his father. They should raise the boy as their own, and hold in trust only some small possessions that once belonged to his mother—a Star of David on a chain, a book of stories—until the time came for him to learn the truth.

Then she kissed her son, and closed her eyes, and the best of her departed. She was buried in another region of the forest, far from the house of the man and his daughter, and the daughter raised the boy as her own, because she had long wished for a child but had despaired of ever receiving such a boon.

And she named the boy Daniel.

It was dark by the time Holly Weaver finished recounting her involvement in the tale, to which Parker added what he had learned from Leila

Patton, with conjecture to fill in the blanks, although he did not share all of this with Weaver, and the full truth of the story would not be known until much later. He lit the lamp on the bedside table, and wondered anew at the strangeness of the world.

"How much have you told Daniel?" Parker asked her.

"Nothing—yet."

"Do you think he's guessed something of the truth?"

Holly nodded. "But I'm afraid to talk to him about it," she said. "I'm scared he'll hate me."

Whatever came next, Parker knew, it would be difficult for all of them. Who could say how the boy would respond to the revelation of his birth, and the lies that had been told to protect him?

"You have hard times ahead," he said. "The only consolations I can offer are these: Karis Lamb may have given birth to Daniel, but you're his mother, the only one he's known, and the only one he'll ever know; he's very young, and the young are resilient; and Moxie Castin is the best lawyer in town, and a good man. He may pretend otherwise, and do a fine job of it, but it's the truth. A promise made to a dying woman doesn't absolve you of any crime committed as a consequence, and the law frowns on secret graves. Moxie's on your side, and he'll do his best to convince the police that you did the wrong thing for the right reasons. But people have died because you hid Daniel, and some of those deaths could have been prevented if you'd come forward sooner, when Karis's body was first found. I can understand why you chose not to, but it doesn't change that fact."

"I can't lose Daniel," she said.

"We'll see what we can do to make sure that doesn't happen."

He stood, and Holly Weaver stood with him.

"What now?" she asked.

"You're going to stay here for tonight, and Louis will remain with you. You'll be safe with him. I may take over the watch later, just to give him a break, but you'd be surprised how little rest he needs. Meanwhile, Moxie will consider how best to open discussions with the police. You should probably speak to Daniel tonight, because the Department of Health and Human Services will become involved almost immediately. It's possible, even likely, that your son may be placed in foster care for a time."

Parker used the word "son" deliberately. He knew that Moxie would too, throughout what was about to unfold. Ultimately Moxie's task would be to convince a judge that no one's best interests would be served by separating Daniel Weaver from this woman and her father, or by putting anyone behind bars. Parker knew that Moxie was already lining up a child psychologist and a specialist in family law to assist with the case.

All because of a Star of David carved on a tree.

"And my father?" said Holly.

"I'll check in with Julia Hancock, but my instinct would be to tell the police as soon as possible that we have you and your son in a safe place. We'll advise them that you'll consent to an interview tomorrow in which you'll share with them all you know about Karis Lamb, but we have some concerns for the safety of your father, and would like their immediate help in tracing him."

"He's in trouble," said Holly. "I know it."

"He may be," Parker conceded.

"He's the most reliable man I know. He calls if he's going to be late coming home from the store."

"If someone has taken him, then it's not in their interests to hurt him. They'll want to use him as leverage."

"To get to Daniel?"

Parker saw no sign of deception or artifice in her.

"I don't think they ever wanted Daniel," he said. "They're looking for a book stolen by Karis."

He watched the cogs turn in her mind.

"A book was taken from my son's room last night. It belonged to Karis."

"It's not the one they want," said Parker. "It may have resembled it, but that's all."

"So where is the version they're looking for?"

"Somewhere else," said Parker neutrally. "But if they have your father, it's important that they continue to believe you might know the whereabouts of the original."

"Who will they contact?"

"Possibly you, but more likely Moxie or me. By now your father will have told them what he knows, or they'll have figured it out for themselves. They'll know you're protected."

Holly Weaver held her head in her hands for a long time. Parker had rarely seen a human being look more miserable.

"Can I ask a question?" she said at last.

"Of course."

"Why are you helping us?"

"Moxie's doing it as a service for the dead."

"And you?"

"Moxie's paying me."

"That's not an answer. I've read about you. You don't work just because someone pays you."

"Then call it a service for the living," said Parker. "I'll leave the dead to others."

In the woods behind the Weaver home, a gray figure paced back and forth, back and forth, like an animal driven mad by captivity.

Observed from the shadows by the ghost of a child.

CHAPTER
CXI

Parker left the Inn through a rear security door leading directly to the parking lot. Thin rain, barely more than a mist, was falling on the city, blurring the streetlights and coating the cars with a patina of moisture.

Parker's thoughts turned to Bobby Ocean, who would soon be burying his only child, all because he had bequeathed his prejudices to his son, whose death would serve only to intensify the malice of his progenitor. As for Louis, Parker doubted that Billy's passing would cause him a great deal of distress. Louis's conscience was a nebulous entity, and dwelt largely in slumber. Louis would regard Billy's murder as the inevitable consequence of the man's decision to advertise his ignorance, and to target the weak as an outlet for his own inadequacies. Billy, in Louis's view, should have realized his actions might eventually draw the attention of someone whose tolerance for such incitements was inversely proportional to his capacity for retribution. Violence called to violence, and intemperate words were the kindling of savagery.

And where did that leave Parker? He recognized his own willingness to use the rigor of his moral judgments as justification for his rage. The pain of his grief had dulled, but was always present. He could spare others from similar suffering by acting on their behalf, or achieve a measure of justice for them if the harm had already been done, but he knew one of his reasons for doing so was that it allowed him to feed his own rage without even pricking his conscience in the process.

He wiped the rain from his face as the darkness of the lot conjured up a specter. The Englishman no longer resembled the individual Parker had described to the state police in Augusta. His hair was grayer, his spectacles were new, and the eyes behind them, visible as he drew closer, were brown once more. The stubble on his face was already growing into a beard, and he walked with the slightest of limps to his left foot. Each was a small change in and of itself, but together they virtually guaranteed that no connection would be made between him and the man sought by the police.

"Hello, Mr. Parker," he said. "I think the time has come for us to talk again."

Bob Johnston was progressing from plate to plate through the book of fairy tales, scrutinizing each illustration in turn beneath the lighted magnifier, his confusion growing.

The flaws in the plates were no longer visible. They were all as Rackham had originally intended.

The unworldly figures were entirely gone.

Salvage BBQ was quiet as Parker entered, the Englishman close behind. It felt odd to Parker to be visiting a family-friendly restaurant, with its mostly communal tables, its gaming machines and rolls of paper napkins, in the company of one such as this.

The Englishman had warned Parker to keep his hands away from his weapon and his phone.

"You're being watched," he said. "The old man's life may depend on how well you behave."

Parker had been unable to detect any trace of the woman, but he chose not to doubt the Englishman's word on this occasion.

Salvage operated bar service only, so Parker ordered a soda for himself and a gin for the Englishman. They took a smaller table, and sat so that neither had his back to the door, and each could see at a glance anyone entering. Up close, and away from the darker interior of the Great Lost Bear, the Englishman appeared older. His face was etched with tiny wrinkles, like the skin of some ancient animal, and the tissue surrounding his lensed pupils was closer to yellow than white. He had a sense of weariness about him, as of one who desires only to sleep.

"You look sick," said Parker.

"I'm touched by your solicitude."

"It was just an observation. I don't think you're going to live very long, although that's unrelated to the current state of your health."

The Englishman leaned forward slightly, as though to offer a confidence.

"Whoever or whatever brings my life to an end," he said, "it won't be you or your pet darkie."

"I'll let him know you said that. It'll be a test of his sense of humor." Parker sipped his soda. "What do I call you? And don't say 'Smith.'"

"My name is Quayle, but if you try looking for me when all this is over, I guarantee you won't find me. And you're almost correct in your estimation: I have no intention of living much longer."

"What do you want before you die, Quayle? The boy?"

"I think you know better than that. I heard your name mentioned on the news bulletins. What did you bring back from Indiana?"

"I don't know what you're talking about."

"Then I'm wasting my time, and Owen Weaver will be dead before morning, unless he learns to breathe through dirt."

"How can I be sure you have him?"

Quayle closed his right fist and rotated it before him, like a sidewalk illusionist demonstrating a trick. When he opened the hand again, a gold signet ring lay on the palm.

"It's dated on the inside. You can show it to

his daughter, if you like. She'll confirm that it belongs to her father. But I doubt you'll feel the need to do so. You know I'm telling the truth."

Quayle's tone changed. It was neither hostile nor conciliatory, cajoling nor threatening. It brooked no argument, like a schoolmaster explaining the realities of life to an errant pupil.

"I want the book, Mr. Parker. Give it to me, Owen Weaver lives, and no one will ever see me again. And if you say 'What book?' you'll force me to conclude that you're a cretin."

"I wouldn't want that," said Parker. He saw no point in denial. It would only condemn Owen Weaver, if he wasn't dead already. The book was the only advantage Parker had. "Suppose I do know where the book is?"

"Wonderful," said Quayle. "We're already making progress. Weaver says the only copy of which he is aware is the one we removed from a shelf in his daughter's house. I'm inclined to believe this is true, after what we had to do to him to demonstrate our commitment to its recovery."

Parker breathed in deeply, and overcame the urge to strike Quayle. His effort at restraint was obvious to the other man.

"Broken bones heal," said Quayle. "Even older bones like his."

"We'll want proof of life," said Parker.

"You'll get it. He'll be permitted to call his daughter. Which brings us back to the book. I didn't realize my error until Miss Mors retrieved the copy from the Weaver house. It was a first edition, but not the one I was seeking. It was then a matter of establishing when the exchange occurred. Errol Dobey was a buyer and seller of rare books, and it would have been easy for him to trace a suitable replacement copy. He even went to the trouble of inserting some antique vellum pages, probably from his own collection, or picked up cheaply on the Internet. It was a crude effort at dissimulation, but then neither Dobey nor Karis fully understood what it was they were dealing with.

"And when I learned you'd traveled to Indiana, I knew you wouldn't have returned empty-handed. I've discovered a lot about you during my time here. You should be dead, but the fact that you're not is indicative only of resilience, and a measure of good fortune. You're a remarkable man, but that's all you are, despite what others may believe. As for what you yourself believe, I couldn't possibly speculate."

Parker didn't bite, but quietly filed away the name of the woman: Mors. "The vellum additions," he said. "What are they?" He gave Quayle no clue that he was aware of the larger work of which they were a part.

Quayle's dead eyes took on a new light, like flames igniting in a pair of polluted pools.

"Maps, or parts of them."

"To hidden treasure?"

"Of a sort."

"A lot of people have died because of them."

"You have no idea how many. So where is the book?"

"It's safe, but you're not."

Quayle dismissed the threat with a wave.

"No safer than Owen Weaver, perhaps. You could call the police, but they'll find nothing to connect me to those killings, beyond the presence in Indiana of someone who might have borne a passing resemblance to myself. My background is in law, Mr. Parker. I know whereof I speak. But while all that is going on, Owen Weaver will be dead, and soon after so will his daughter, and Karis Lamb's son, before we move on to everyone who matters or has ever mattered to you or your friends, until no one will be left to speak your names.

"And it won't change what is to come, because eventually the book *will* be traced. I've been hunting it for a very long time, and I've never yet been closer. I can wait a little longer. I'm very patient. You, by contrast, have no room to negotiate. You've already seen what we're prepared to do. Don't add your own child to the list of the dead."

With those words, any doubts Parker had entertained about killing Quayle vanished. Whatever might occur in the hours or days to come, he would eventually find Quayle and Mors, and put an end to their lives.

"So," said Parker, "how do we do this?"

CHAPTER
CXII

Quayle departed first, and didn't appear worried about turning his back on Parker. He stepped outside, a car appeared, and Quayle climbed into the passenger seat. By the time Parker got to the sidewalk, the car had turned down Forest Street at speed and vanished into the night.

Parker first called Louis, and waited for him to get out of earshot of the Weavers before updating him.

"It's like I thought," Parker said. "Quayle doesn't care about the boy. He only wants the book."

"Are you going to give it to him?"

"What choice do I have? It's a simple trade: the book for Owen Weaver."

"And no police."

"No police. He says the woman will kill Weaver if they see blue. And he's only given us an hour to get moving, so there's not enough time to call in outside contractors."

"Which, unless I've miscounted, just leaves the two of us."

"Quayle told me to come alone."

"Doesn't mean you have to."

"Call Moxie. Get him to move the Weavers again, just in case. I'll meet you back at the Inn."

Parker next called Bob Johnston, and told him he was on his way to collect the book.

"It's still in pieces," said Johnston.

"Then stick them together again."

Parker hung up, but didn't return to his car. He crossed the street to the taxi stand by the bus station, hopped in the only cab waiting, and asked the driver to cruise around while gradually making her way toward the East End. He kept an eye on the traffic behind as they pulled out, but could detect no signs of pursuit. He didn't want to lead Quayle straight to the book.

"Worried about being followed?" the driver asked. She was small and white-haired, and her cab smelled of the kind of perfume that stores didn't bother to tag against thieves. Parker had seen her around town over the years. Her license declared her to be Agata Konsek, and she looked old enough to have once driven horse-drawn carriages.

"Not with you at the wheel, I hope."

"Okay. Just so's I know."

Agata Konsek had missed her calling as a spy—or, given her name, maybe she hadn't—because she demonstrated a skill at elusion that was obviously hard learned. She ran red lights, cut down one-way streets, and took shortcuts through alleyways, all while watching the rearview for signs of pursuit, before making a bootlegger's turn after a blind curve and crossing two lanes of 295 at speed. Parker might have been even more impressed if she hadn't caused him to fear for his life. Eventually they reached Bob Johnston's building, where Parker asked Konsek to wait. He could see no lights burning, but Johnston must have been watching for him, because Parker was buzzed in before he pressed the bell. He walked up to the top floor and found Johnston seated at his desk, the book loosely assembled beside him, although the vellum leaves remained separate from it.

"I didn't even bother trying," said Johnston.

"What did you want me to look at?"

"Where would you like to start?"

"Bob, I don't have time for games. Just give me the simple version."

Johnston opened the book at the plate from "The Frog Prince," and handed it to Parker.

"There isn't a simple version," he said. "Unless you can explain the changes."

Parker instantly spotted the alteration. The tapestry on the wall was once again indistinct, the bull-headed creature no longer visible. He flipped through a couple of the others, including "Snow-White and Rose-Red," with the same result. None of the figures that previously appeared to have been added to the plates could now be seen.

"They're all gone," said Johnston. "Every one of them. And that's just the appetizer. This is the entrée." He showed Parker the third sheet of vellum, about six inches in length and an inch wide. "It was concealed in the spine of the book. My guess is it's of the same age and provenance as the other two."

"Have you opened it out?"

"It's blank—kind of."

"Bob . . ."

"Look, I can't be certain. At first I thought I was looking at veins from the original animal, whatever that might be, because blood collects in the skin at death. Also, natural flaws in the parchment can sometimes resemble topography. I began to wonder if I'd just been looking at the pages for too long, but I took a break to rest my eyes, and when I came back they were still there: rivers, islands, coastlines."

He unfolded the sheet, and pulled the magnifier and its light into place.

"See?"

Parker stood over the glass, and saw that Johnston was right. The lines were very faint, but not random. It confirmed the truth of what Quayle had told him: these were pieces of a map.

"If it's a country," said Johnston, "it's none that I know."

Parker stepped back from the desk. "Why would this have been hidden?" he asked.

"Why is anything hidden? Someone didn't want it to be found, but didn't care for it to be lost either. The concealment might have been done in a hurry. The stitching on the spine wasn't perfect, but if the binding had been properly reinforced, I might not have spotted it at all. Maybe the other two pieces are less important than this one, or are incomplete without it. You know: the book is found, the visible sheets are removed, the remnants are discarded, but whoever has only those two pieces is still denied all the information."

Although time was pressing, Parker took a few moments to think. He wondered how much Quayle really knew about the book and its contents. Had Quayle ever seen it? How detailed were the available descriptions? Judging by what Karis Lamb had shared with Leila Patton, the man from whom she stole the book had spent years searching for it, and he wasn't the only one looking. Was Vernay aware that it contained three fragments, or was he under the impression it held only two? And if so, was Quayle also laboring under the same misapprehension?

Suddenly, Parker had an advantage.

"Just what is this thing?" Johnston asked, his gloved hands lightly moving over the cover of the book like a blind man searching for braille, the question more rhetorical than anything else. "Those fragments aren't vellum. It's skin of some kind, but it doesn't burn. Well, it does burn, but it doesn't *stay* burned."

"What do you mean?"

"It reconstitutes itself. I reduced a sliver to ash, and an hour later I had the sliver again." He took off his spectacles and wiped his eyes. "I have to admit I haven't slept much since you brought it to me. It's intruded on my rest. But my interest is piqued. I want to know more."

"You know what they say about curiosity?"

"Do you see any cats in here?"

"Just a stuffed one."

"It died, but I'm alive and well. Curiosity hasn't done me any harm."

"Yet."

"Yet," Johnston agreed. "If it's okay with you, I'd like to keep looking into this."

"I can't leave you with the book—or the insertions. You may never see them again."

"I don't need them. The additions to the illustrations didn't reproduce when I tried to make copies, but I got one of the 'DD' plate inside the cover. I'll start with that."

"Then find out what you can—unobtrusively."

Johnston walked Parker down to the street.

"Can I ask what you're going to do with it?"

"I'm going to trade it for a life."

"Sounds dangerous. You taking your friend Louis with you?"

"Yes."

"Probably a good idea. Tell him I wasn't kidding about that list, if he's looking for work."

"He's semi-retired."

"But if he finds himself getting bored."

Parker was beginning to feel concerned about Bob Johnston, and made a mental note not to cross him at any point.

"I'll let him know."

"Appreciate it."

By the time Parker reached his cab, the door had closed, and all the lights were out once again.

CHAPTER
CXIII

The proof-of-life call came through to Holly Weaver's phone while Parker was with Bob Johnston. It was short, but confirmed Owen Weaver was still breathing, although Holly told Louis that her father sounded as though he were in some discomfort. By then Moxie had sent a driver to move Holly and Daniel to a new location, although Parker instructed Moxie not to tell Louis where they were being taken. If events went south, and it turned out Quayle was lying about his intentions toward the Weavers, Parker didn't want either Louis or himself to be in possession of information that might put mother and child in danger.

Parker knew he might well be making the wrong call by declining to involve the police. Unfortunately, it was the only call he could make. Quayle was deliberately squeezing him, restricting Parker's options. Neither did he doubt for one moment that Quayle and Mors would be willing to dispose of Owen Weaver before disappearing, if only temporarily. They would return for the book eventually, perhaps under new names and guises, and then the killing would commence again.

The parking lot was dark when the cab returned Parker to the Inn. Someone had broken the main outside light in the interim, casting in shadow the section of the lot in which Parker's Audi stood. He opened the door, and noted that the interior bulbs did not activate. He said nothing as he got in the car, nothing as he drove away.

Nothing to the figure lying uncomfortably on the floor in the back, concealed by a dark blanket, gun in hand.

Quayle called Parker's phone while he and Louis were heading toward Piscataquis County, just as Quayle had instructed him to do before leaving Salvage.

"You have the book?" Quayle asked Parker.

"Yes."

"Then take down this zip code."

Parker repeated the zip as he input it into the car's GPS, which immediately began calculating the route, guiding Parker toward Waterville.

"Is someone in the car with you?" said Quayle.

"No, but I'm old and I mishear."

"Don't be clever, not if you want Owen Weaver returned alive."

"If Owen Weaver dies, you'll never see the book again."

Quayle hung up, and Parker headed northwest. Waterville was a little more than an hour from Portland. If Parker guessed right, this would be only the first in a possible series of stops. He was pretty certain that he wasn't currently being tailed, but he'd probably pick up a spotter when he reached Waterville: either Quayle or the woman, depending on who was watching Owen Weaver. That was how Parker would have done it, just as he would have tagged the vehicle in which he was traveling, given time, or installed a listening device; anything to gain an edge. For now Parker had no way of knowing if his car had been tampered with, which was why he was staying silent. He did not want to give away Louis's presence. Quayle might have his suspicions, but if Parker handled everything right, suspicions they would remain.

He found 1st Wave on Sirius, turned the volume down low, and let the sounds of eighties British synth music fill the car.

He ignored the small moan of torment from behind.

Parker was skirting Waterville when the phone rang again.

"Get off the interstate and take the 104 into town," said Quayle, and Parker did as instructed. Quayle stayed on the line, and told Parker to pull over across from the McDonald's on Main. Vehicles were parked on both sides of the road and in the surrounding lots, including three or four outside the McDonald's itself. Parker waited until Quayle gave him an address on Ash Street, farther down off Main. This time, Parker did not repeat the address aloud. Louis, who had been following their progress on his own phone, would have to trust him. Parker watched the road behind, and spotted no signs of pursuit, but at least one of the cars in the McDonald's lot had been occupied, the shape of a driver clear at the wheel. He was prepared to lay good money on someone checking to make sure he was alone. This was confirmed when he received two more calls in quick succession, sending him back on his previous route before proceeding through a series of residential streets, until finally he was left to wait at a dead end on Butler Court.

Parker tensed. He heard Louis shift position, and the rear door clicked as it was opened slightly in case of trouble. The agreed signal was a cough from Parker, but this place didn't feel right for a hand-over, or an attempt to seize the book. When the phone rang again, Parker was not entirely surprised. The delay, he felt, was probably to allow whoever had been monitoring Parker to go on ahead.

"New destination," said Quayle, and something in his voice told Parker that this was it. They were coming to the end. The GPS was giving an hour and fifteen minutes to Piscataquis County as he pulled away from the curb.

And as though speaking to himself, he said: "Here we go."

• • •

Daniel Weaver was asleep, lulled by the motion of the vehicle. His head lay on his mother's lap. The driver had given her a blanket with which to cover him, although the car was warm. Other than to tell them that his name was Karl, inquire about the temperature, and point out the bottles of water in the side compartments of the doors, the driver spoke little to them. He was not uncaring—quite the opposite: Holly regularly caught him glancing at them in the rearview, his eyes soft—but he was careful not to intrude. The car was a Mazda Hatchback; clean, but nothing fancy. Light jazz played on the radio.

Only when they had passed Augusta did Holly ask Karl where he was taking them.

"Bangor," had come the reply. "You'll be safe there."

They were approaching the outskirts of the city when Karl left the highway. He made a couple of turns before pulling up in front of a pair of houses guarded by security gates, which opened at their approach. A woman stood silhouetted in the doorway of one of the buildings. She waited for Karl to help the Weavers from the car, Daniel woozy at being woken from his sleep. It took Holly a moment to notice that the woman had Down syndrome.

"I'm Candy," she said. "Welcome to the Tender House."

CHAPTER
CXIV

Parker was sure he'd made the correct call when the GPS took him along a road marked "Private," the evergreens along its edges encroaching like shards of a greater blackness against the night sky. When the phone rang again, he pulled over to the side of the road, and did not look over his shoulder as the rear door on the right opened and Louis slipped out.

"Why have you stopped?" said Quayle, giving Parker the final confirmation he required. Wherever Quayle was, he could see the Audi.

"The road is dark. I don't want to end up in a ditch."

Parker wondered if Quayle was using an infrared lens to observe the car. If so, Parker could only hope the trees would work in their favor, and that Louis was staying low. He held his breath, and released it only when Quayle began to speak again.

"There's a turnoff to your right, about a quarter of a mile ahead. Take it, and continue driving until you see two houses. You'll spot an oil can in the yard. Don't proceed beyond it. Stop, and wait, but be sure to keep your hands on the wheel. And leave the phone on speaker."

Parker did as he was told. He drove slowly along the road until he came to the turn, which took him uphill. The road was even rougher and narrower than before. If another car appeared from the opposite direction, one of them would have to learn to levitate, but he encountered no other vehicles, and eventually two dwellings came into view. The first looked like a pretty standard Maine camp: a single-story wood cabin that probably contained just a couple of bedrooms, a living area, and a bathroom. The other building was larger and older, consisting of two levels topped by a curiously ornate cupola, although the whole structure had long fallen into disrepair, and anyone taking up residence would have been forced to share with some of the local wildlife.

Parker pulled up at the oil can, but kept the engine running. He didn't think Quayle planned to kill him, or not before the book was safely in his possession, so when Mors emerged from the bushes to his left, a gun in her hand, he tried not to fear actively for his life. Of Quayle, he saw no sign.

"Turn off the ignition," said Quayle's voice from the phone.

Parker did so, and silence reigned for a time. Mors ceased her advance, but kept him under the gun.

"Are you armed?"

"Yes," said Parker.

"Get out of the car and kneel on the ground," Quayle instructed. "Tell Miss Mors what you're carrying, and she will relieve you of its burden."

Parker opened the door, keeping his hands raised once he was out, before easing himself onto the damp gravel. Within seconds, Mors was behind him.

"Where is it?" she said.

"Holster under my left shoulder."

She moved around until she was facing him.

"Reach in and remove it with your left hand, thumb and index finger only."

Awkwardly, Parker took out the gun, and held it before him like a dead fish.

"Gently throw it at my feet."

Parker did as he was told. The gun landed an inch from her right foot.

"Any others?"

"No."

"I'm going to frisk you. If I find more weapons, I'll shoot you."

Parker decided against dying.

"Knife at my left shin, revolver in an ankle holster on my right."

"Lie flat, hands on the back of your head, fingers interlocked."

The ground smelled of spilled gas, and up close Parker could see the glitter of broken glass. He tried to avoid putting his face against it while Mors removed the knife and the revolver before frisking him anyway, just for her own peace of mind.

"You should see a doctor," Parker said, when her face was close to his and he could smell the foulness of her breath. "I think you may have cancer."

Mors didn't reply, but seconds later she used a foot to spread Parker's legs before kicking him hard in the balls. His vision went black, and he curled in upon himself, his eyes closed.

"You mustn't be rude," said Mors.

Parker stayed still for a while, until he was sure he wasn't going to puke. He was just getting to his knees again when Quayle materialized from the old house and stepped down to the yard.

"It's not wise to goad her," he said. "She's led a difficult life."

Parker's pain was slowly receding, but nausea was taking its place. He now wanted to hurt Mors very badly.

Quayle squatted before him.

"The book," he said.

"Owen Weaver," Parker replied.

"That's not how it's going to work. If I don't have the book in my hands within the next thirty seconds, I'll take my chances and tell Miss Mors to kill you."

Parker saw no sense in arguing.

"The book is in the trunk."

"Get it."

Parker managed to rise to his feet. He was unsteady, and it hurt to walk, but at least he was staying upright. Mors and Quayle tracked him to the rear of the car, but from different angles. They were understandably wary of the trunk, just in case Parker had not come alone after all, but they were looking in the wrong place, which was all that mattered.

Parker opened the trunk. The book lay in its shoe box, the front cover facing up.

"Hand it to me," said Quayle.

Parker picked up the book, holding it so that Quayle could see the blank pages loosely inserted.

"Owen Weaver," Parker said again.

"Mr. Weaver?" Quayle shouted. "Let us know you're alive."

"I'm okay," said a voice from inside the house. Parker guessed Weaver was on the second story, because one of the windows to the front was open.

Parker extended the book toward Quayle, who reached for it. When his fingers were within touching distance, Parker relaxed his grip and the sections fell apart, the wind sending them skipping across the dirt.

A number of things then happened simultaneously.

Quayle followed the progress of the pages, already moving to try to catch them. Mors shifted the barrel of her gun and pulled the trigger, firing not at Parker but at the figure of Louis emerging from the trees. Parker, caught between two guns, dove to the ground, jarring his tender balls painfully in the process, and scrambled to where his own weapons lay.

And finally, the first floor of the old house burst into flames.

CHAPTER
CXV

Holly Weaver made her son a mug of hot chocolate in the kitchen of the Tender House, and brewed a cup of tea for herself. It was past Daniel's bedtime, but he showed no signs of wanting to sleep. It was almost, she thought, as though he knew a conversation between them was both necessary and imminent.

The Tender House was quiet. Four of the other bedrooms were occupied, two of them by women and children, and two by women alone. Holly had already exchanged words in passing with a couple of the women, and learned their names, but the kids—both girls of a similar age to her son—were in bed by the time she and Daniel arrived. Daniel might meet them over breakfast in the morning, according to Molly Bow, who introduced herself once Candy had shown Holly and Daniel inside.

Holly had never heard of the Tender House, although she'd encountered her share of victims of domestic violence. It was hard to be a woman in this world and not pick up on rumors, or even glimpse the evidence, but she never imagined she'd end up in a shelter herself. It made her feel ashamed. She wanted to knock on doors and explain that she wasn't here because a husband or boyfriend had beaten her, threatened rape, or abused her child. She was hiding behind these walls because it was possible that a violent man might want to hurt her and her boy. But then she realized that had she made such an admission, the other women might well have nodded their heads in understanding, and pointed out that they were *all* in this place because of the fear of injury or death at the hands of men, and it didn't much matter what mask their assailants might wear, or what their relationship to them might be. No one here was any better or worse than another, and there was no shame in seeking help when faced with male rage.

Now Holly sat Daniel on the double bed that they were to share, in a room filled with just enough color and quirk, and held her son to her as he sipped his hot chocolate, and said:

"I have something to tell you."

CHAPTER
CXVI

Events move fast in a gunfight, particularly when the participants are in close proximity, as Heb Caldicott had learned to his cost. The Gunfight at the O.K. Corral lasted just thirty seconds and left six of the nine participants dead or wounded at the end. So by the time Parker had retrieved his gun, and was ready to fire, Louis was already slumped against a tree, bleeding heavily from one wound to his right shoulder and a second to his groin; Quayle and Mors were disappearing into the woods with most of the book; and the yard was bathed in the glow of fire. Somewhere inside the old house, Owen Weaver was screaming.

It had taken about fifteen seconds for everything to go to hell.

Parker first tended to Louis. The injury to his shoulder looked like a bad graze, but the wound to the groin was serious. Parker took off his jacket, wadded it tightly, and forced Louis to maintain pressure on the injury. Louis moaned, but managed to hold the compress in place.

"I hit her," said Louis, "but she didn't go down."

Parker wanted to head after Quayle and Mors. He wished for nothing less than to watch them bleed, but he would not leave Louis, and Owen Weaver was trapped by the conflagration. Parker thought he heard a car starting over the crackle and roar of flames, but he ignored it. Instead he called 911 and gave the dispatcher directions to the property, even as he was pulling a blanket from the trunk of the Audi and dousing it with the container of water he stored there in case of emergencies. He soaked a rag, tied it around his face as best he could, and headed for the house.

The heat and smoke were already intense, and the fire was feeding on the staircase. It couldn't have progressed so far, or moved so fast, without an accelerant, and Parker knew then that Quayle had never intended for him or Owen Weaver to survive the night. Parker placed the blanket over his head and upper body and tried to stay low, moving as quickly as he could up the stairs as the fire bit at his shoes. The ends of his jeans ignited, and he could feel the skin on his legs start to blister, but he held off until he got to the landing, which was still clear, before reaching down to pat out the flames.

Owen Weaver was lying on his side in a room to the left, still tied to a chair. His feet were bare, the left foot badly swollen, its toes misshapen; the work of Mors, Parker guessed. He figured that Owen Weaver must have fallen while trying to free himself, and it might just have been for the best. The fire had not yet risen to this level, but the smoke had, and the floor offered the possibility of breathable air. Parker knelt beside the semiconscious man, and examined the plastic restraints used to bind him to the arms and legs of the old Carver. Parker's knife lay on the dirt outside, and he couldn't risk using a boot to break the arms and legs of the chair because he might well fracture Weaver's arms and legs in the process.

Parker searched the room and found some old cardboard. He rolled it into a cylinder and held it to the flames that were now spreading to the landing. The staircase and its walls were now entirely ablaze; he and Weaver wouldn't be going out the way they'd come in, if they were lucky enough to escape at all.

The cardboard caught, and Parker returned to Weaver, closing the door behind him. He placed the flame against the ties and watched them melt, burning Weaver's skin in the process but also shocking him back to full consciousness. When he was free, Parker raised him up and helped him to the window.

"I'm going to lower you down," Parker told him, as Weaver kept his injured foot off the floor. "It'll hurt when you land, but being burned alive will hurt a lot more."

Weaver nodded, but his eyes were glazed.

Parker realized that Weaver would be largely a passive participant in what was to come.

The window was painted shut, and Parker had to kick out its panes. He gazed into the night, hoping to see fire engines coming up the road, just as they would in a movie, but he could discover no trace of their approach, although he heard, or imagined, sirens in the distance. Louis was still sprawled against the tree, and lifted a hand to let Parker know he was holding on.

Flames were sprouting from between the floorboards, and the smoke was now so thick that Parker could no longer see the chair to which Owen Weaver had been tied. He made sure the sharp edges of glass on the window were all removed before he maneuvered Weaver into position so that his lower body hung down and his upper half remained over the frame. Holding on to Weaver's forearms, Parker managed to get him out of the window, his feet dangling about twenty feet above the yard.

"I'm letting go," said Parker. "Try to keep your legs bent."

But Weaver was already deadweight, his eyes closed and his chin at his chest. Parker dropped him. Weaver landed awkwardly, but by some miracle he came down on his right side, largely sparing his left foot further injury.

Seconds later, Parker followed him down.

This time, he heard the sirens for real.

CHAPTER
CXVII

Daniel left Holly sleeping in their shared room. The Tender House was quiet as he walked down the stairs. He didn't know where he was going, or what he was looking for. He just knew he needed to be alone for a little while.

He was trying to process what he had been told, even though some small part of him had always suspected it; had felt it as a dislocation, and glimpsed it in the way his mom looked at him sometimes when she thought he would not notice. She was his mother, yet there was also another. She had lied to him, she and Grandpa Owen both, but Daniel was not angry. Confused, yes, and sad, but not angry. He could not have said why, but it was so.

He found the toy room and sat down amid dolls, and board games, and jigsaw puzzles. Before him was a large painting of mountains against a blue sky, the landscape rendered in big bright colors, the kind that existed only in cartoons.

Cartoons, not fairy tales.

Daniel heard a noise from one of the toy boxes.

It was almost as though he had been hoping for it, and his hope had made it happen.

It was the sound of a toy phone ringing.

He rummaged among wood and plastic until he found the source: a plastic phone on wheels, not entirely dissimilar to the one he had owned, the one on which Karis would call him.

But she was no longer just Karis. She was something more.

Daniel put the phone on his lap, lifted the plastic receiver, and held it to his ear.

"Mommy?"

Jennifer watched the gray form kneeling amid the trees, speaking in a voice that sounded like the rustling of dead leaves.

Jennifer had been mistaken. She believed it would be for her father to name the woman, and thus bring her peace, but she was wrong. In these final moments, she was no longer a vestige of Karis Lamb. Karis Lamb was Before, but with the crying of a child she had been transformed. What came After was another.

What came after was Mommy.

And as she listened to the voice of her child acknowledge her at last, the gray being began to slip away, disintegrating into splinters, dirt, and dust, carried off into the darkness until all that was left was the memory of her, held in the heart of a boy.

Daniel hung up the phone. He was tired. He wanted to sleep now.

Candy stood at the door. Daniel did not know how long she had been there.

"Come," said Candy. "I'll bring you back to your mother."

And after only the slightest of hesitations, Daniel took her hand.

CHAPTER
CXVIII

Owen Weaver survived. His lungs were damaged, and he would always walk with a limp, but he would live.

Louis survived. He was concerned that his principal sexual organ might never be the same, but the doctors assured him it would continue to function as well as before, just not for a little while. Parker, nursing a busted ankle, advised Louis to think clean thoughts. Louis told Parker to go fuck himself.

And Angel survived, although he was quieter now, and sometimes he found himself numbering his days.

In the matter of Daniel Weaver there would be pain and recriminations, court cases, and custody hearings. Moxie Castin would do what he could for all involved, and because Moxie was a most accomplished attorney, nobody would serve jail time, and Daniel Weaver would call Holly Weaver, and no other, his mother. The tale of the "Woman in the Woods" would enter the lore of the state, and like all good stories much of the truth of it was destined to remain hidden.

The man named Quayle vanished, and the woman called Mors vanished with him, although she left a trail of blood in her wake, both figuratively and literally.

Louis was right. He had hit her.

For the time being, Parker chose to store in a safe-deposit box the single vellum page he had kept from Quayle, while Bob Johnston worked on establishing its provenance.

And eventually, Parker sat down with SAC Edgar Ross of the FBI, and shared with him most of what he knew about Quayle and the vellum leaves. Parker did so with some reluctance. Ross had once sent a private detective to spy on Sam, Parker's daughter—why, Parker did not know—although Parker had decided to keep his knowledge of the surveillance to himself, for now.

So he did not entirely trust Ross.

But then, Parker had never entirely trusted Ross.

CHAPTER
CXIX

The Principal Backer sat in the library of the Colonial Club, sipping a scotch.

Thinking.

Worrying.

Quayle and Mors were gone. They had not availed themselves of the Backers' assistance in returning to England, choosing instead a route home via Mexico, which suggested a certain lack of trust. And although reports indicated Mors had been injured in the confrontation with Parker, it was also clear that Quayle was in possession of the pieces of his precious fucking Atlas when he left.

The Principal Backer had expended a great deal of time and energy in hampering the search for the Buried God. He had done so with the active collusion of a number of his fellow Backers, each of whom was as eager as he to ensure the continuance of the status quo. They had wealth, power, and influence, all of which they would someday bequeath to the next generation: old blood in new bottles.

But if Quayle was not deranged, and the Atlas

could do as he claimed, then the world was already being reordered, its boundaries redrawn in preparation for the coming of the Not-Gods, and the war on the Old. The Backers would not be spared. No one would.

Not unless Quayle was stopped.

CHAPTER
CXX

The funeral of Billy Stonehurst took place on a clear spring morning amid blossoms, birdsong, and rebirth, when no young man should be laid to rest. A choir sang, and handshakes and sympathy were offered to the grieving parents. Afterward, drinks and a buffet were served at a hall in South Portland, not far from the cemetery. During the reception, Bobby Ocean's wife slapped her husband repeatedly on the face. She subsequently departed, and did not return.

Two weeks later, Bobby Ocean commenced his retirement from business, and initiated the sale of his companies. Two weeks after that, he and his wife announced their separation. By then, Bobby Ocean was already in the process of establishing, in memory of his son, the William Stonehurst Foundation for American Ideas, which would quickly ally itself with the American Freedom Party, American Renaissance, the Council of Conservative Citizens, and the National Policy Institute, among other white-power organizations.

Bobby Ocean had become pure hatred.

● ● ●

Parker ran into Gordon Walsh after a movie at the Nickelodeon. Walsh was with a woman Parker didn't recognize, and he was no longer wearing a wedding ring. Walsh introduced the woman as Jessica, but offered no further details. He and Parker stood outside the theater while Jessica went to the bathroom. It was the first time the two men had spoken properly since Parker's brief confinement in Augusta.

"I wanted to apologize for calling you a son of a bitch," said Walsh. "I mean, you are a son of a bitch occasionally, but I wouldn't like to think it defined you."

"You should market that as a greeting card."

"I have others. I'll just add it to the pile."

"You see that thing about Bobby Ocean?" said Parker.

"The far-right business? Yeah. No surprise, but still."

"Not good."

"No," said Walsh. He sniffed at the night air. "You smell that?"

Jessica appeared beside Walsh.

"Smell what?" said Parker.

Walsh laid his left hand on Parker's shoulder, and used his right to point in the direction of Commercial, and the waterfront, and a parking lot still slightly blackened by fire.

"A hint of smoke," said Walsh. "You shouldn't have let Louis burn that truck."

It took Parker a few moments to respond.

"You're right," he said.

"Yeah?"

"I shouldn't have left it to a black man to call out a racist. I should have done it myself."

CHAPTER
CXXI

The crossword setters for *The Times* of London took great pride in their work, and rarely invited, or tolerated, outside interference in their puzzles. It took a great deal of convincing, the intervention of an agent of the U.S. Federal Bureau of Investigation, and the promise of some small favors to the newspaper's parent company— and, indeed, to the setters themselves—before the insertion of a very particular set of clues into the cryptic crossword of March 30 was permitted. Even then, rumblings of immense discontent accompanied the inclusion of one clue, because its appearance would require an apology to be made to *Times* cruciverbalists the following day, with all blame for the error being ascribed to a mysterious, and forever unnamed, assistant.

London's Jamaica Wine House, a wood-paneled Victorian pub, lies in St. Michael's Alley, a pedestrian laneway between Cornhill and

Lombard Streets, not far from the Thames. On March 30, shortly after midday, a figure dressed in velvet and tweed sat at a quiet table to the rear, drinking coffee and studying, as was his wont, the *Times* crossword. The Jamaica was one of his regular haunts, although he had not been seen in its environs for some time, and he appeared more troubled than usual, and was short with the staff.

He was musing on ten down, which read, *To pursue, fearful or not, the bird thus flown.* A poor but obvious clue, he thought, and well below the usual standards of the setter. It seemed to him that "hunting quail" must be the answer, but the final letter had to be "e," to allow for "locomotive" (*The reason, perhaps, for a murder on the Orient Express*), while the second last must surely be "bombshell" *(Alarming blast of beauty).* But how could the compiler misspell "quail" as "quayle"? There would be complaints about it.

The lawyer Quayle paused. He looked at nine across, another odd clue that had bothered him with the awkwardness of its construction: *Jazzes up, but only once the vehicle is secure.* That had to be "Charlie Parker."

He placed circles around the solutions to the two clues in question, isolating four words.

668

C H A R L I E P A R K E R
U
N
T
I
N
G
Q
U
A
Y
L
E

Quayle looked around him. He was alone and unwatched.

The trouble was, he no longer *felt* alone or unwatched.

He folded the newspaper, and left the Jamaica to lose himself in crowds.

ACKNOWLEDGMENTS

Lieutenant Brian McDonough, formerly of the Maine State Police and now enjoying what I hope will be a very long and happy retirement, kindly answered my questions on procedural matters for this novel. My gratitude also to Stephen McCausland, spokesman for the Maine State Police, for his assistance. Dr. Fergus Brady, my fine physician, clarified medical details for me. Thanks also to Brian Cliff and Mari Rothman for answering some of my odder questions. Any errors and inventions in law or medicine are entirely my own.

As ever, my thanks to my American editor, Emily Bestler, and all at Atria/Emily Bestler Books, including—but certainly not limited to—Judith Curr, Lara Jones, Stephanie Mendoza, and David Brown; my British editor, Sue Fletcher, and all at Hodder & Stoughton, especially Carolyn Mays, Kerry Hood, Swati Gamble, Lucy Hale, Auriol Bishop, and Alasdair Oliver; my agent, Darley Anderson, and his wonderful staff; Ellen Clair Lamb and Kate O'Hearn, for kindness and support; John Dodson and the staff at Trend Digital Media; and David O'Brien, aka Envoy, for composing the fine soundtrack CD that accompanies this novel. Love and gratitude to

Jennie Ridyard, Alistair Ridyard, and particularly on this occasion, Cameron Ridyard, who created the new johnconnollybooks.com website. And very nice it is, too.

John Connolly has compiled six previous soundtracks to accompany his novels, mostly comprising songs with a lyrical or thematic connection to his work. The seventh, THE HONEYCOMB WORLD, is a little different, as it features music specially composed and performed by the group Envoy, and inspired by the Charlie Parker novels. The entire suite of music is made up of twenty tracks, and is available as a free download to readers as a thank you for their support for John's books. To download your copy, go to: www.WomanintheWoodsBook.com.

To find out more information about the use of music in the books, and to access Spotify playlists of the earlier soundtracks, go to www.john connollybooks.com/curiosities.

Center Point Large Print
600 Brooks Road / PO Box 1
Thorndike, ME 04986-0001 USA

(207) 568-3717

US & Canada:
1 800 929-9108
www.centerpointlargeprint.com